BROOKE MARIE

Dreams of Ash and Smoke

Book 1 in the Fates Aligned series

This book was professionally typeset on Reedsy.
Find out more at reedsy.com

To myself for making the leap and finally finishing an original novel.
To the ones who never believed in me.
To the ones who never stopped believing in me.
And a cheers to my first novel, may she be the stepping stone to a legacy.
xoxo

Contents

TW

Please read at your own risk!

This book will contain:

- mentions of sexual assault
- sexual assault
- mentions of domestic violence
- domestic violence
- smut
- fighting
- mentions of kidnapping
- death
- kidnapping
- emotional trauma

Playlist

Outside . breakk.away
Ashes . Celine Dion
To Die For . Sam Smith
I'll See You When The Night Comes . breakk.away
Is It Over Now . Taylor Swift
Shameless . Camilla Cabello
White Flag . Bishop Briggs
Lover.Fighter . Svrcina
Blood In The Wine . AURORA
I Dare You . Bea Miller
Tomorrow We Fight . Tommee Profitt ft. Svrcina
Wide Awake . Katy Perry
The Wolf . The Spencer Lee Band
Raise Your Flag . Hidden Citizens ft Ranya
The Fear . The Score
Bad . Bishop Briggs
Cinderella's Dead . Emeline
Don't Blame Me . Taylor Swift
Enchanted . Taylor Swift

Dictionary

Definitions and Pronunciations:

Seren Fach (*seh-ren vaak*): Little Star
Zorya (*zoor-ee-uh*): The southern kingdom on the continent. Holds the Court of Dawn.
Dimencreas (*dih-men-cree-uhs*): The name of their planet, not to be confused with the term used for the element, earth.
Khyrel (*kye-rell*): The northern kingdom on the continent. Holds the Court of Dusk.
Asterlayna (*ass-tur-lay-nuh*): The capital city of Khyrel.
Marcam (*maar-kham*): A pen-like utensil used for tattoos, runes, and unification rituals for permanent markings.
Verena (*vir-in-uh*)
Dryston (*dris-ton*)
Hadeon (*hey-dee-on*)
Eryx (*air-icks*)
Esmeray (*ez-mer-aye*)
Ruelle (*roo-el*)
Calanthe (*cuh-lan-thee*)
Amaelya (*a-male-ee-uh*)

Prologue

"Do it!" The man's voice bellows at his wife gesturing to their 2-year-old child. "Her pure white hair is a blessing from the Gods and you want me to defile it?" Vaia Nightcrest seethes, her fists clenched so tight that her nails draw blood. She stares daggers at her husband, fueled by a mix of anger and fierce protectiveness toward their precious baby girl. The mere thought of changing anything about her sends chills down Vaia's spine, and she can feel her heart pounding with rage and fear.

"I don't give a damn about the Gods and their so-called gifts. This is a curse, and it will bring nothing but death upon us all!" His voice booms with rage as he turns to face his wife, his eyes ablaze with fury and fear. With a forceful hand, he thrusts the bottle of black ink into her chest. "Do it now, before it's too late." His tone brooks no argument, commanding obedience through sheer force of will.

Vaia recoils from the force of her husband's words, her heart pounding in her chest like a wild drum. His eyes, once filled with love and warmth, now burn with a fearsome intensity that she had never seen before. But she refuses to back down, her love for her daughter and her resolve, stronger than ever, fueling her determination to protect her at all costs.

Taking a deep breath, she looks into her husband's eyes, trying to see the man she had once fallen in love with. He trembles now, his voice hoarse with fear and desperation. She knew that if she didn't do this, he will. And he won't be nearly as gentle as she is.

Slowly, Vaia reaches out and takes the bottle of black ink, her fingers trembling slightly as she clasps it in her hand. She glances down at her daughter.

Tears stream down her face, carving tracks through the dirt and grime that coats her cheeks. With trembling hands, she drags her child to the table and forces her to sit, her eyes locked into a deadly stare with her husband. "You are the reason we are in this hellhole. Khyrel was paradise compared to this nightmare," she hisses, her voice thick with anger and despair. How did their perfect life spiral into this pit of misery? Their daughter had been promised to the prince, an unbreakable bond between their families. But everything changed in an instant, leaving them trapped in a world where they must hide their true selves from those who would condemn them. A world where their daughter's future is nothing but lies and deception. It shatters her heart to see her child forced to live a lie, a prisoner of false love and shattered dreams.

But as Vaia dips her gloved fingers into the black ink, a fierce determination settles over her. She will not let her daughter's fate be decided by fear and manipulation. With a steady hand, she begins to paint intricate patterns on her daughter's pure white hair, every strand a defiance against the darkness that threatened to consume them all. The room falls into a heavy silence, broken only by the sound of the brush against her daughter's hair. Each stroke of ink a whisper of rebellion, a silent cry for freedom in a world that sought to crush them.

The black ink weaves through the strands of their daughter's hair like dark magic, but Vaia infuses every caress with love and protection. She refuses to let their daughter's light be extinguished, even in the face of overwhelming darkness.

The white haired baby with the dark blue streak running through it reaches up, clawing at her mother's tear-stained face with tiny fingers. The toddlers cries fill the room as her mother sobs uncontrollably.

"We have a better deal now. You heard the prophecy, Vaia. She will be safer here. I did this for the two of you. For our family." He tries to reason with her, but she pushes him away violently, her fingers smearing ink over his chest, her eyes full of a wild desperation. In a moment of madness, she snatches their child further from him and holds her close, rocking back and forth in a frantic attempt to protect them both from the danger that looms ahead as she finished her daughters hair.

"You did this for yourself. For the greed that runs through your veins. I hoped you'd be happy with her life. That the greed was momentary when we met. But I was wrong and now we'll both be unhappy." She snaps at him. "I will raise our daughter here, against my will, and I will try to give her a great childhood. But, make no mistake, Arzhel." Her eyes burned from anger, tired of crying over her tarnished marriage. "I will never forgive you if we do not get to see her grow into a beautiful person. I will rip you apart piece by disappointing piece until there is nothing left but unsatisfied greed and hunger for more. I will pray to every God, every Goddess, every celestial being and magical element that you rot and burn in the Underworld and that they show you no mercy." She seethes, her eyes glowing the bright purple she's hidden.

Pure, unbridled terror shines in his eyes as he stumbles backward and scrambles out of the room, leaving her alone to cry. Vaia sobs silently as she stains her baby's soft hair, a stark contrast to the dark blue streak that remains untouched by the black dye that has consumed the rest of her locks. Little did they know, this one small detail would be the catalyst for a catastrophic turn of events that would shatter her entire world.

Chapter 1: Pinkberry Clouds

Verena

1 Week until Dryston's Coronation

Hues of violet, indigo, and cyan fill the dark night sky, as they usually do in my dreams. The movable paint-like structure reminding me of my own indigo eyes as I stand on the balcony. I had only ever seen them far away, an almost microscopic flash of color for the briefest moment as the sun descended from the sky and the moon came out to play.

A hand grasps my shoulder to turn me and I gasp, noting the familiar faint black marking on the hand just before I jolt from my slumber to find myself alone— as I have been for the torturous decade of this haunting dream.

The bright ball of light filters in through the glass windows, allowing me to see the familiar room. The same bed I've had since I was a young girl rests on the concrete floor underneath me, a chaise lounge at the foot of the bed holding a dress I was to wear today. The light-stained, scuffed vanity rests just a few steps to the right of me, outside the doorway to the bathroom holding a toilet, tub, and sink. It wasn't extravagant, but it's nice.

My beloved fae kingdom, Zorya, thrives in the daytime. She is the beautiful country I will rule someday soon alongside the heir to the throne, Dryston Whitewell. His family has been ruling this country for centuries. The former king, Tarius Whitewell– Dryston's father– was murdered a month ago. And after a grieving period for the land and castle, Dryston's coronation will be held one week from now with our wedding and then my own coronation following shortly after.

Prince Dryston and I have been in a courtship since we were of age, but our history dates back to our childhood. We were betrothed as toddlers, and everyone has been eagerly anticipating this moment.

There is a soft knock on the door, and before I can give permission to enter, a maid appears in front of me. I do a double take, surprised by her sudden presence. "His Majesty has requested my services to prepare you for today's celebrations." She says in a meek and timid voice, resembling that of a mouse. Her gaze never meets mine as she speaks.

It's common knowledge that kings often had mistresses, so it came as no surprise to me. Just as I was expected to become queen, he was anticipated to have a few affairs in his lifetime. And knowing Dryston's reputation as a ladies' man, I can tell by the way she avoids eye contact with me that he had already caught her attention.

"No problem, Mya." She had become my ladysmaid a couple years ago after mine had passed away from a poison I assume was meant for me. As the maid busies herself with arranging my hair and adjusting my gown, I can't shake off the unease settling in the pit of my stomach. The weight of expectations and obligations pressing down on me, threatening to suffocate the remnants of the carefree girl I once was.

I steal a glance at the maid, her hands deftly working on my elaborate hairstyle, and can't help but feel a pang of sympathy for her. She was just a pawn in this grand game of alliances and power, caught in the intricate web of court politics.

But as her fingers brush against my skin, a sudden chill ran down my spine, and I realize that there was more to her presence than she let on. Her eyes, though downcast, hold a glint of something not quite servile—a flicker of defiance that hints at hidden depths beneath her demure facade. Even while she helps me get ready for the day, dressing me in a bright yellow-green gown, to match our Aurora Australis, I can't help the thoughts of the opposite.

* * *

The expectations for the upcoming events was palpable as whispers and excitement courses through the kingdom. In just a couple of days, the Royal Brunch will kick off the festivities in honor of Dryston's rule. The grand dining hall had been meticulously prepared, decorated with lavish displays of flowers and draped in rich fabrics. Mouthwatering aromas waft from the kitchen as chefs bustle about, crafting a feast fit for royalty. Everyone could sense that this will be a celebration unlike any other, marking a new era for their kingdom.

The day before the Coronation, a grand celebration known as the Royal Gala will take place. This highly anticipated event promises to be a dazzling display of dancing, music, and elegance. It's sure to be the talk of the century.

The following day marks the long-awaited Coronation, where our beloved prince will finally be crowned as ruler. And after that, there will also be a knighting ceremony where Dryston would carefully select his personal guards from among the bravest and most honorable knights in the realm. The air is thick with anticipation as everyone eagerly awaits these momentous occasions that will shape the future of the kingdom.

The day after will be our wedding and my coronation the day after that.

It will be a long ten days.

"Where are we with the decorations? Did you alert everyone of the colors I asked you to get?" I ask the young lady as we walk through the halls hastily. I eye the surrounding decor, noting the floral arrangements and banners.

She looks at me quickly before turning her face to the floor, her eyes wide. "Uhm, I- Dryston wanted-" My fingers wrap around her arm gently before stopping in our tracks, my eyes wide, grazing around the area to make sure we are alone.

"You will refer to your future king as His Majesty or Prince Dryston. You will not disrespect his title again, do you understand?" While the words are firm, my tone hushed yet urgent.

Even the slightest mention of his name sends a shiver down my spine, knowing if he heard her, he'd be filled with silent rage. I still bear the scars from the time he punished me for calling out to him by name, a reminder of his possessive nature. It seems that all he desires is for me to acknowledge him as the dominant one, to only speak of him with reverence until our marriage was official. Another shiver runs through me at the thought of being bound to this wild and unpredictable man for eternity.

She nods profusely, apologies added in too, before we continue our walk to the throne room.

The royal family was small but powerful, ruled by the mighty King Tarius and his beautiful queen, Rya. Rya, with her regal grace and sickly green eyes, had birthed two children — her firstborn son, strong and determined like his father, and her daughter Lianna, with her mother's delicate features and fiery spirit. Together, they are the shining stars of the kingdom, their legacy destined to endure for generations to come. Although, mostly everyone is scared of Rya. She has a very demanding presence and her relationship with Dryston was excruciatingly nauseating.

Rya mourned her husband's passing with little emotion. However, she took on the temporary responsibility of ruling the country until her eldest was officially crowned. Although the people of Dawn may not like her, the High Fae are well aware of her subtly cunning ways. The court members fear her, knowing she was not truly wicked but rather manipulative and self-centered, with strong greed and narcissistic tendencies.

As we made our entrance, Mya follows etiquette and stays behind me, allowing me to take the lead. My eyes scan the grand hall, taking in the regal figures sitting upon thrones adorned with jewels and gold. The prince sits confidently on his father's throne, his posture exuding power and authority. His queen mother sits gracefully on her own throne beside him, her gaze shifting between her son and me. I curtsy before the prince, feeling a twinge of nervousness as his piercing chartreuse eyes study me intently. He then turns his attention to my companion, Mya, causing a subtle tension to form between them. Or perhaps it's just my own insecurities that made it seem that way. Either way, there was an undeniable sense of unease in the air.

I am not the prettiest female in Zorya, let alone the entire continent, — as I'm constantly reminded of by the future king— but I found I quite like myself and how I look. I stand tall, my stained jet-black hair falling in smooth waves down my back. My bright indigo eyes sparkle with determination and a hint of mischief. The bridge of my nose was slender and delicate, matching the smallness of my ears with their subtle points at the tips. Years of secret training with my guard, Hadeon, had honed my body into a perfect balance of strength and grace. My muscles are lean but defined, hidden beneath the slimness of my frame. I take pride in my appearance, confident in my own beauty, though it seems that Dryston often finds fault with me.

I watch as he navigates the intricate political landscape alongside his mother, his features strikingly similar to hers. He possesses her golden locks of hair and light green eyes. As a member of the fae community, Dryston stands out as one of the tallest and most robust males on this side of the border. His broad shoulders and well-defined muscles spoke of his strength and stature within society.

During our childhood, we spent countless hours playing together. But my mother always had a wary eye on him, her face twists with disapproval. I never understood what it was that she saw in him, but her sudden death left it lingering on my mind. It wasn't until my first punishment from him that I began to see the darkness that my mother saw. Where once he was carefree and easy-going, now there was a coldness in his eyes and a cruelty in his actions. Every time I did something that displeased him, a punishment would swiftly follow, leaving me trembling and fearful of what he might become.

Standing steadfast beside me, my guard dons his distinguished green royal armor. His dark chestnut hair cascades over his broad shoulders, framing his chiseled features and dark hazel eyes.

Hadeon is my trusted personal royal guard. He was hand-picked by Tarius to protect me when I was just twenty years old, after he saved my life from an attempted assassination. Hadeon had recently completed the rigorous training program for royal guards before being assigned to me, and I've been grateful for his presence ever since. Through our constant companionship, we have developed a strong friendship that extends beyond our duties.

Hadeon never spoke of my punishments, but sometimes when I look at him I can't be sure he actually knows. He didn't know us when we were younger.

He was a formidable figure, with a towering height and bulging muscles that Dryston had always resented in comparison to his own stature. Despite this, Hadeon remains unbothered by the prince's jealousy, focusing solely on protecting and serving his charge with unwavering dedication and loyalty.

I thought it was humorous.

The prince's voice cuts through the air like a sharp blade, silencing the entire room. I stand tall under his intense gaze, feeling the weight of his expectations bearing down on me. "Verena," he addresses me with a cold tone, "how are the decorations coming? You know how crucial this coronation is."

My heart races as I curtsy in front of him, trying to stay composed. "Everything is proceeding smoothly, Your Majesty," I reply my eyes darting to Mya for support. But she remains silent, her lips pressing together in a tight line.

His eyes burn into mine with a look that can only be described as contempt. I know that he was overwhelmed and stressed, but that doesn't make his stare any less unsettling. "Keep my mother and I updated on everything," he commands before dismissing the court.

As we all disperse and go about our duties, I can't shake off the unease that settles in my stomach at the prince's harsh demeanor. This coronation is more than just important to him — it seems to be a matter of life and death for our kingdom. And I can't help but fear what consequences will follow if anything goes wrong with the preparations.

* * *

Hadeon follows as he usually does while I carefully made my way to all the castle halls and rooms that guests will be staying in during the coronation, and the events leading up to it, to make sure the decorations are up as they should be. It was a lot of work but I know that he will be happy with it all. All the colors came in and the staff started on everything else.

At the end of the day, I was completely worn out. Hadeon slept across the hall from me and retires to his chambers as soon as I did mine.

I treat myself to a bath, adding the special scent. The soapmaster in the city makes it just for me, calling it Pinkberry Clouds.

After soaking for a moment, I ran some of the scented soap through my hair, washing away any sweat and dirt before washing my body too.

When the water went chilly, I deem it the end and stand up to dry off with a light pink fluffy rag the size of my body and made my way to the bed.

Sometimes, Dryston would visit me uninvited and I'd allow my mind to wander back to the colorful night sky of my dreams to block out his time in my bed and scrub myself raw of his scent after before curling into myself with tears streaming down my face. Sooner or later a new maid or towns person will catch his eye and he seems to be done with me.

Until he grows bored of her.

When it first started, I'd allowed it– welcomed it, even. He told me I should be happy to please him because he will be king and he wanted me comfortable before we have children together.

Now the thought makes me want to hurl.

Chapter 2: The Garden

Verena

3 Days until Coronation

The coronation was getting closer. The court whispers of my queenship constantly, the chatter filling my ears as I walk the halls. I fist my hands in my dress, trying to maintain my breathing so they don't know how nervous I truly was as I walked.

Hadeon stays by my side as we leisurely stroll through the palace garden, a place of beauty that never fails to captivate me. Blossoming flowers of every hue embellish the lush greenery in a breathtaking display of nature's artistry. The air is filled with the sickly sweet scent of roses and peonies, carrying us along like a fragrant breeze. I can't help but pause at each familiar flower bed, admiring the intricate patterns and vibrant colors that dance together in perfect harmony. It is a serene oasis within the bustling palace grounds, and I can' imagine a more peaceful escape from the demands of royal life.

With just the two of us, I twirl my hands nervously and ask Hadeon, "Do you think I have what it takes to be a good queen?"

A deep, rumbling chuckle escapes from Hadeon's lips and I found myself unable to look away. His features are strikingly handsome, with chiseled cheekbones and hazel eyes that seem to gleam in the sunlight. Even though I had always been dedicated to Dryston, I can't deny that Hadeon was undeniably attractive. Without the looming pressure of my engagement hanging over me, I would consider pursuing him without hesitation. "You never fail to ask me that question every week, princess," he remarks, his voice smooth like velvet.

I sigh, "I told you to call me Verena when we are alone, Hadeon."

He came to a halt, and I mirror his actions, facing him as he reaches out and grasps my arm. His voice drops to a hushed tone as he spoke, "We are hardly ever alone, princess. As a protector, it is my duty to see things that you do not."

My brows raise, looking around now in suspicion. "Am I alone when I am in my quarters?" I ask in a whisper, staring at his handsome face.

His eyes peruse my face, before nodding, "I would never allow someone to disrupt your peace, my Queen. You are always safe when I am around, and I am always around. I swore my loyalty to *you*, no matter who hired me to protect you." Chills ran through me, goosebumps tickling my skin. I only nod in response to his ominous statement. He stands straight once more and starts walking. "Yes, you'll make a wonderful queen. One that people will remember for centuries past your rule." I smile, nodding in thanks. He gave me the same answer every time I asked and never once complained about me constantly doing so.

As his words settle into me, I thought about the specifics he spoke; *no matter who hired me to protect you.* What an odd way to phrase that sentiment.

We continue in silence walking through the floral arrangements as I choose some for our coronations and our wedding— just a few days until he is crowned. "What about you? What is your dream? You know I am becoming queen but what do you want?"

He chuckles and I can sense the unsure feeling he has about answering. "I don't have anything."

I scoff, "That is ridiculous. Everyone has a dream." I smell pink flowers, sighing in content at the scent.

"Fine then. Your happiness."

"What? That is *not* a dream!" I laugh, smacking him softly on his muscular chest.

"Yes it is. My dream is to see you happy. Thriving." We stop walking for a moment and face one another. "I dream of everlasting happiness for you. If there is anyone in this world to deserve it, it is you, Verena."

Silence ensues once more and my heart is full of love and appreciation. He truly is my family in this kingdom. "I just worry, you know? I know everyone's expecting me to become queen, they have since I was born. But…" I trail off, not wanting to say what is actually on my mind. The air around me changes and suddenly, I do not feel as if I can say what I think. A bird flies into my walk path from the bushes, making me jump out of reflex. I breath heavy, placing my hand over my heart as if it will help calm myself.

"But?" He asks me in a smooth voice, as if the bird did not faze him. I shake off the bird's presence and look at him, giving him eyes that say *I shouldn't say* and he seems to understand. I've spoken to him before about my dreams of the aurora borealis— dreams I definitely should not be having. "If I may, I think you are more complacent than you should be. You're a smart, skillful, capable fae. Prince Dryston should feel lucky he has you as his queen, even if you are too amenable with him. I know you're not always quiet about your opinions, but I think you could be louder." His eyes bore into mine, almost as if he were daring me to do so.

"Then it is a good thing you do not get paid to think, Hadeon." A jolt of fear shoots down my spine as a deep, familiar voice pierces the air. I grip my dress tightly between my fingers once more, heart racing. His intense gaze remains fixed on Hadeon, sending shivers down my arms and making my palms slick with sweat.

Hadeon takes a step from me and we both bow. "Your Majesty, Hadeon did not mean-" I start and Dryston raises his hand to stop me and out of reflex I obey rolling my lips together, knowing Hadeon was mentally rolling his eyes at me as I look to the ground in submission.

"Hadeon meant what he spoke, but I do not care for the trash coming from his mouth. I know you obey me and you are proud to do so. As a queen should." His eyes sparkle with something I can't place, but I know it made me nervous. "Walk with me." It's not a request but a demand and I link my arm through his awaiting one while Hadeon steps further back before trailing behind us.

"I want to speak to you about your duties. My coronation is in a couple of days and you're doing well with the preparations." My heart wants to sing the praise. "But," He starts back and my heart stops singing and starts screaming, begging him to just see me for all that I am and do for him instead of the mistakes I might make. "I notice the colors are not what I want." My brows furrow.

My heart races as we came to a halt, my mind reeling with anxiety. He releases his grip on my arm and I immediately began rubbing my hands together and picking at my fingers, a nervous habit that had plagued me since childhood. Those vivid shades of color have consumed my life for as long as I could remember, seeping into every aspect of it and fueling my obsession with understanding them.

"I told you red was going to be the main color. I see barely any." I stare into his eyes, waiting for him to tell me it was a joke. No one chose different colors. Tradition has been using green and silver since the beginning of the kingdom. And if he told someone, it wasn't me.

"Dryston, I assure you I have heard no such thing." Confusion marking my face until I recognize my words when he stares at me, eyes darkening in fury. Not only did I just tell him he was mistaken, I called him by his name. My eyes widen and subconsciously took a step back to brace myself for the hit, my hand flying to my stomach to keep my lunch down. I look at him, watching the anger dance behind his light green eyes. My eyes flick to Hadeon, thankful he was here but I also know the punishment would be worse later. "I am so sorry, Your Grace. I meant no disrespect. I know you are busy and there has been much on your plate. I just mean, are you sure you hadn't told someone else and they forgot to mention it to me?"

He scoffs, "I am no idiot, Verena. You are the future queen of this country. You are supposed to be in charge of these tasks. If you can't even take care of minuscule things such as color schemes, how can I trust you to take care of my kingdom? Why do you always have to be so confrontational and opposing? Fix it before the coronation or there will be no crown and no wedding for you." He shook my arm off of him like it disgusts him and struts off but before he can get far, he turns to look at me. "I will see you tonight." He whispers but not low enough for my royal guard to miss it.

Chills wrack my body when he leaves our sight. Hadeon and I are the only two left in the garden when my knees give out, my chest heaving in rapid breaths as I try to regain myself. My body hadn't had time to slap against the rock, though, as Hadeon's arms wrap around my slim waist, hold me up. "What meeting does he mean? I wasn't told of any." His voice was firm. "Answer me, Verena." Softer this time but I know he won't give up.

After regaining the strength to stand on my own, I shove his large muscular frame. "As if you do not know. I arrive sore and wincing to session after session of training before we even begin. I miss out on half the galas we throw or get invited to because I can barely walk let alone dance." My voice breaks at the end making me clench my fists in anger at my weakness.

His eyes darken in anger, and I only hope it's not because of me, "Are you telling me he hurt you?" He steps closer, eyes assessing me as if I was bruised now. "Because *if* you are confirming that he deliberately sets out to harm you, I will take care of the prince." I want to believe him but he took an oath to the throne, to the king. Even this talk is treason enough for Dryston to execute him.

I blink and scoff, "Dryston is our soon-to-be king. He does whatever he pleases— *whomever* he pleases. And I am his betrothed. You should not say things you do not mean." I start to walk away and he follows in silence. I build my internal walls up as I walk, attempting to hold myself together.

* * *

I stand by the grand door at the front of the castle awaiting the carriages pulling up to come to a halt in front of the steps. The palace sits on a hill, overlooking the bustling city. Even from here, I can hear vendors at the market calling out their specials. Cheerful chirping birds fly around, singing their tunes to each other. And the mouthwatering scent of fresh food from our chefs fill the air. As I wait, the feeling of someone dangerous lurking wracks my body, sending chills through me but I try to push the thought from my mind. I am safe here.

The first carriage pulls up, it's luggage following it in another as it breaks me from my reverie.

"Good afternoon, Lord Bishop. It is an honor to host you for our grandeur festivities. I hope you find everything to your liking, Antoine will take you to your chambers and his team will escort your luggage." It was the same speech I gave every guest as they came to the doors. Two hours and one hundred guest arrivals later, I can finally

17

take my leave. The smiles are bright and I never let up on my cheery demeanor to add to the hospitality. I wish they'd arrive at the same time but I know they all travel from different places and it would overwhelm my staff if they did.

Each guest typically has been here before and as future queen, I see to it that all their preferences are met as an assurance of their continued support.

It, on top of all the decorating, has been consuming all of my time and energy. I am exhausted but I know everything will pay off. It has to.

* * *

Metal clangs together before slinging apart as I direct all my weight and force into the blade, forcing him back a few steps.

Anger surges through me, as it did when I train. My blood pushing and pulsing amid my body.

I can feel the heat radiating off my face and know that my cheeks are bright red.

Sweat rolls down my hairline, begging me to wipe it before sliding across my skin in a race to the floor. At this point, I had been training for hours and my lungs feel like they were seizing up. I definitely don't want to train today after all my hard work but my stubborn guard convinced me. He says 'If you can fight tired, you can fight refreshed'.

Hadeon lunges for me again, trying to slice through me. But I'm quick in my smaller size and dart forward, sliding against the ground under his blade as mine scrapes the ground. I push back up on my feet, twisting and aiming for his back.

Our blades clang again when he turns, the force so fast and strong, that they push against each other, and our hands twist, releasing our swords and letting them clang to the ground.

Immediately my hands are up, a small dagger I usually keep in my belt is placed in my right and I don't hesitate to go forward once more.

We go back and forth, getting the better of each other before he trips me and we tumble down as I take him with me. My muscles finally giving out.

Both of us grunt out air as the oxygen is knocked from our lungs by the force. I'm almost wheezing from the energy coursing through my veins.

I stare at his face and when I see the little gleam of liquid seep from his hairline and down his cheek, I gasp and slap him, trying to grab the droplet from his skin. "Sweat! A-HA!" I jump up, holding my now wet finger to his face as he stands and looks at me with confusion in his eyes.

"What?" He asks trying to play off his exhaustion.

I shove my finger in his face, "Sweat! I finally got through enough training to make you sweat." I start laughing and squealing in delight, jumping excitedly up and down. For years, I was never able to fully keep up with him. He'd never even break a sweat from what I could tell. But, today is a great occasion for that alone. He let me have my cheer, holding back a smirk as he caught his breath too.

"You're insane, princess." I laugh at that too before walking over to grab my dagger from the floor as he grabs the swords, feeling better already.

"You're just upset now that I've gotten the better of you." I stick my tongue out.

"I still beat you. I tripped you to pin you." He gives me a pointed look.

"Yeah, but you have perspired from training with me so I feel like I

19

won." He rolls his eyes at me and hands me a rag for the sweat pouring from my skin.

"What's got you so angry?" He changes the subject and I freeze. My body goes rigid and I turn from him in the wooded area we train in.

"I have no knowledge of what you mean," I say, stretching out my tired limbs. His fingers wrap around my arm before I even know he was close. "I've known you long enough to know something is wrong." I know he says that. But how do I know if he knows the real me? Does he truly know me well enough?

"Do you?" I ask, trying to brave the possible answer. My eyes meet his, and I know my indigo ones are practically begging him to say yes. I am exhausted from being quiet. From holding my tongue. From keeping myself locked away. But I know it's what I must do for this kingdom and as its queen it is a price I am willing to pay.

A rustle of leaves breaks us from our stare. He drops my arm and we step apart.

A raven flies out from the trees, toward the river to grab a drink. How very odd. I didn't realize Zorya had so many native ravens. I shake my head, clearing my thoughts as we both continue packing up our things before heading back to the castle.

On the way back to the castle grounds, I realize I never got his answer.

* * *

By the time the sun drops behind the horizon, I'm dressing down for the night and sitting at the vanity desk. My golden jewel-encrusted brush glides through my long black hair as I brush out any knots and tangles.

A knock sounds at the door as I finish up, running my fingers through my silky locks. and I freeze. Only one person visits at night and it's never good.

I walk to open the door, knowing he'd want me to greet him. I try to take steady breaths, slowing my heart rate and trying to stop my shaking hands. I raise my chin, feigning confidence, and open the door. "Your Highness." I curtsy. I open the door wider for him, placing my hands behind my back to hide the tremor before smiling.

"Verena. You look lovely this evening." He steps in, closing the door.

"Thank you." I wasn't sure how he would punish me tonight and I don't like not knowing.

"Do you understand your mistake from the garden?" He rolls up his sleeves. He did it every time he punishes me and I never understood why other than to keep any blood off his shirt. I nod at him. "Words, Verena." He demands in a louder tone, making me jump in my spot.

"Y-yes, Your Highness." He looks at me expectantly and I feel like a child being chastised. "I did not use your title when addressing you and I understand it's disrespectful." He nods back. "I truly am sorry. I have been doing a lot better but today was a complete accident."

"I understand. Thank you for your apology." His hand slices through the air like a razor, catching me off guard. The sharp sting on my cheek is enough to make me flinch, and I know better than to try and dodge his blows. He never strikes me in the face, but this time he makes an exception. My head snaps to the side from the impact, a red-hot heat spreading across my skin. A whimper escapes my lips before I can stop it, and I curse myself for showing any sign of weakness. "Now. I figure I will go lighter today since I noticed the decorations are looking better already and you apologized." He violently yanks my hand away from my cheek and grips my face with an iron grip, forcing me to meet his cold, unyielding gaze. "You know I hate having to discipline you, but it's for your own good," he sneers through gritted teeth before his facial features change like magic, revealing a joyful smirk and playful eyes. "Now, come relieve my stress. I've had a long day." With a wicked glint in his eye, he maneuvers us toward the chaise lounge and forcefully pulls me onto it. I feel myself begin to disconnect from my body as I prepare for what is about to happen — a painful detachment that has become all too familiar under his twisted idea of love.

"Take down my trousers, make up for what you did today." The threat of tears burns behind my eyes, but I swallow hard and force them back as I take a deep, shaking breath. With trembling hands, I unzip his pants and push them down,. My knees buckle beneath me as I lower myself to the ground, ready to perform my task at hand. A single tear escapes from my eye, betraying the mixture of fear, disgust, and resignation that consumes me.

Chapter 3: The Market

Verena

2 Days until Dryston's Coronation

> *The royal family hereby requests your presence*
> *for the Royal Brunch in celebration of*
> *Prince Dryston Whitewell's coronation.*

I stare at myself in the mirror as Mya attempts to hide the mark on my cheek. "Thank you, that's as good as it'll get." When Dryston slapped me, it's the back of his hand and he had worn his family ring. I hadn't felt it last night but there was a small cut on my cheek, barely missing my eye. There was also a small bruise surrounding it.

After putting another excruciatingly ugly dress on and fixing my hair, we leave the room— Hadeon meeting me on the other side of the door. "Good morning." He greets me and I smile at him, not meeting his gaze so he doesn't notice my cheek.

"Good morning, Hadeon." I reply, starting our journey toward the dining hall. The walk was standard, my dress swishing across the marble floors. I hold myself up, as if I were already queen. If any of these guests smell a weakness in the castle, Dryston will have my head.

We make our way to the double doors, and the Herald greets me to everyone already in their seats. Dryston sits at the head while his mother sits at the other side. I take my place next to him while Hadeon, Mya, and other maids or guards stand off to the side of the room.

"Did everyone arrive?" Dryston asks me as everyone converses. I smile at him as if nothing is wrong and our lives are perfect.

"All but one. King Eryx has not arrived but our scout informed me that he is on the way. He should arrive by tomorrow for the gala and your coronation. I still haven't received confirmation that he will be attending our wedding." I watch as he grips the arm rests on his chair, his knuckles white. I involuntarily flinch, my eyes meet movement from the side, Hadeon itching to move closer to me but I top him with a shake my head.

"That damn tyrant. I almost wish he would have declined in total. Him showing up late is disrespectful. We are supposed to be at peace." His speaks in a low volume, anger radiating off him. There's a gleam in his eye at that statement and it drives my curiosity but I know better than to ask during such a busy time.

When all guests arrive from their rooms, we finally get to eat.

Laughter echoes around the table, mingling with the buzz of excitement and the warmth of camaraderie. Everyone is thoroughly enjoying their time together, caught up in the infectious energy of the moment. My gaze is drawn to Dryston, a strikingly handsome High Fae who exudes confidence and a hint of arrogance. His blond hair is impeccably styled, framing his sharp jawline and high cheekbones that are just one part of his undeniable beauty. He embodies the essence of High Fae, from his flawless appearance to the way he

24

carries himself with poise and grace. And then there's his gift — the ability to manipulate metal with ease, a true reflection of his inner self. Each High Fae's gift is uniquely attuned to their essence, bestowed upon them by the Gods and Goddesses themselves. As for me, my own gift has yet to be revealed, waiting patiently to shine forth in its own time.

Growing up, he was never truly a gentle being. He would pull my hair, tease me, and we had this teasing banter that my mother hated. But, he protected me from another kid that tormented me. I haven't seen them since the last time they pushed me down when we were ten but I assumed it's because they knew Dryston will be king and I was his betrothed.

The memory brings up my childhood. My mother and father had passed away when I was coming into adolescence at the age of 13, just before my dreams started up. I've been an orphan for over a decade and it's never easy. I didn't have a great relationship with my father, mostly because he and my mother never got along. But she was my entire world. Where my father made me feel like an object, my mother had treated me like the only thing that was important. She told me she grew up in Khyrel but anytime she'd try to give me more details, my father would silence her. And now, the only thing I have left of her is a small necklace with a tiny aurora borealis in the pendant that I hide in my gowns. I find myself missing her dearly before shaking off the memories.

I stare at Dryston until he catches me, a blush rises to my cheeks from embarrassment as he scolds me with one look and I don't look at him the rest of breakfast.

* * *

Hadeon knocks on my bedroom door this time, signaling the carriage was ready. Today, I want to go into the city and look at vendors for a breath of fresh air after brunch. "Are you both ready?" He asks us as Mya opens the door. I nod, keeping my head at an angle so the bruise was out of sight.

He walks behind us as we make our way to the carriage at the front of the palace. I had to change my gown from less formal and now don an elegant yellow that makes me nauseous.

The ride was smooth, as usual. Dryston always reminds of how dangerous being his betrothed is, even with him, so I rarely get to leave the castle.

"Remember to stay close. The Prince isn't wrong, it is dangerous being the betrothed." Hadeon spoke to me. I roll my eyes, nodding regardless.

When Hadeon saved my life five years ago, I was in the city, wandering around and enjoying meeting vendors and the people of our kingdom. A man was waiting to ambush me next to one of our food vendors but Hadeon intervened just before he could. At the time, there was a lot of talk about a war brewing between countries and Dryston had told me my attackers were from Khyrel, but I could have sworn I had seen them before here in town. Of course I was called crazy for it.

"I know. Thank you," I say to him.

The horses pulling the carriage come to a halt and Hadeon exits first before he holds his hand out to me.

A sharp pain shoots through my ankle as my slipper catches on the step, causing me to stumble and fall. He moves with lightning speed to catch me, his grip tight as he pulls me upright. His eyes scan over my face, darkening with anger when they land on the bruise and cut decorating my skin. Without a word, he stands me up and I shake my head in warning, glancing at Mya. His posture stiffens as he nods curtly, understanding that this is not a matter to be discussed with others before allowing me to lead us forward.

We amble leisurely through the vibrant city streets, taking in the sights and sounds of bustling shops and energetic people. As we pass by storefronts, I exchange friendly greetings with shopkeepers and merchants, their welcoming smiles and warm voices adding to the charm of our visit. My senses are full of the delectable aromas of varied cuisines and freshly baked goods, beckoning me to taste and indulge in their tempting offerings. Though they never charge for their samples, I always insist on paying as a gesture of gratitude and appreciation. This is my favorite part of exploring the city — immersing myself in its rich flavors and unique culture.

These townspeople deserve our attention. They are the only thing holding this kingdom together. Dryston never sees it that way, another reason I want to be queen. He promised me it was because he never had time to think about it and that I'd be in charge of everything regarding our care toward them.

Hadeon never wants to taste a cuisine, but I always get him to cave and try something I know he'll like so I can see the look on his face when he realizes I am right.

Mya looks as if she hates being here, distastefully regarding each vendor. I try to ignore it as I enjoy my time.

We stop at the modiste so I can grab my new dress for tomorrow and have my final fitting for my coronation gown. Then, we stop for a wedding present for Dryston, before we finally settle on a little table outside the eatery with some food we picked up. "I love that everyone here treats me like a normal person. I'm not hoarded around and overwhelmed by people. I hope Prince Dryston can work on the peace pact with the Khyrel. I can't imagine sending anyone to war right now." The topic seems to make Hadeon tense, but Mya doesn't notice his sudden change in demeanor.

27

"I need to speak with you." He stands and motions for me to follow. "Mya wait here and watch the food. We don't need anyone poisoning our future queen."

We step away from the group, out of earshot, and he leans in close to me. The scent of his cologne wafts over me, a mix of sandalwood and citrus. "What happened to your face?" he asks, his voice laces with concern.

"I think you already know," I respond, crossing my arms in irritation.

"I want to hear you say it," he demands, his dark irises staring into mine.

"This mark is my punishment," I admit, my heart sinking at the memory. "I should be grateful that he didn't do worse."

Anger flashes across his face as his hands clench into fists at his sides. I watch as he trembles with rage, knowing that he will do anything to protect me from harm.

"He should be thankful I am not ramming my fists through his face. I cannot allow him to continue doing this, Verena. I am your friend— your guard and I am not doing my duty to you if I allow this."

"He is your king-"

His eyes blaze with a fury that I had never seen before. The once tranquil eyes now seem to darken, reflecting the intensity of his emotions. "He is not my king," he spat, each word dripping with defiance and resentment.

"Not yet, but he will be," My tone softens slightly. "I made a mistake and I got punished. I know my place, and you shall know yours. Leave it." His jaw clenches as he tries to contain his rising anger.

Before he can say anything else, I turn on my heel and strode back to Mya. She quickly averts her gaze, pretending she wasn't trying to eavesdrop on our conversation. I wasn't sure how much she heard and the tension between us only grew thicker. The rest of our time in the city goes by fast, but I am no longer in a wandering mood.

When we arrive back at the palace, I hastily head for the stairs. Today was emotionally exhausting. Since it's the only time I can leave the castle, I usually enjoy leaving the castle but lately something feels as if it's missing. Everything feels darker in the world and I can't do anything to stop it. It feels as if someone is holding a pillow over my face and I can no longer breathe.

Maybe it's the possibility of oncoming war or the fact that my place here in the palace seems less and less significant with each day.

I sigh, laying on the bed without even changing from my day clothes. I hope for a dreamless sleep, but once again the unknown male with the black markings on his hand visits me.

Chapter 4: Freshly Baked Dessert

Verena

The Eve of Dryston's Coronation

> *The royal family hereby requests your presence*
> *for the Royal Gala in celebration of*
> *the Prince Dryston Whitewell's coronation.*

The highly anticipated gala was mere hours away. The past week had been a grueling one, with endless preparations and demands to ensure its success. I long for the event to be over so I can finally rest before taking on my duties as queen. My heels click frantically against the marble floors, creating a staccato rhythm that echoes through the halls, and drawing curious gazes from those around me. I bark out orders to the staff, maintaining a respectful tone despite my haste. It was all hands on deck to make this night a memorable one for all in attendance.

The cooks are profusely preparing a feast large enough for hundreds of people. I will be sure to give them all time off for a bit when it's all over. But the smells? Delicious. Our chef is phenomenal as always. I can easily get lost in the way bread smells and it made the bakeries by far my favorite section of town.

I greet people with a smile as I pass our temporary guests, stressing over the days event.

The king of Khyrel still has yet to arrive and Dryston is getting antsy, which of course makes me nervous. With Mya taking up his nights, leaving me in peace before the building stressful days— one after the next.

"I need to get this garnet color up completely. His Majesty was very specific." I tell Mya, who lately has had a scowl on her face but I genuinely do not care enough to ask. She has never seemingly cared for me, only being here out of some duty chosen by the prince. It grates my nerves and that is probably the reason he made her my ladysmaid.

"Yes, Verena." She huffs and I stop in my tracks, eyeing the surrounding beings before gracefully pulling her to the side.

"What in Sorin's name is the matter with you? Are you not thankful to work in the castle? Are you not thankful to be my ladysmaid? I am so kind to you and you seem to treat me with such disrespect." I lightly snap at her, crossing my arms over my chest as I await her response.

"Nothing, princess. Of course I want to be here." She answers, not looking in my face but I see the look of discontent, the challenge in her eyes, the formal way she carries herself. She was not bred for being staff and now my curiosity consumes me on why she is here.

I calm myself before saying anything more as Hadeon stands to the side, allowing us a private discussion.

"Mya. If you are not happy with your placement, I will speak to the future king about gracing his mother with your presence instead or one of the Ladies of the court. I do not wish to force you into anything you do not care for."

She looks at me now, staring into my eyes, searching for what, I do not know. It feels as if time slips by us as we stand still. One of my brows remains raised, as if challenging her myself. Then, as if it never happened, she blinks the condescending look away and looks at the floor. "No, Princess Verena. I wish to stay with you. My apologies for my behavior, this week has been stressful and as I am sure you know, the future king is not easy to please." There's a smirk that she tries to keep off her face but I see the twitch in her lips as her eyes keep to the floor.

It is not what she says, it's how she says it that triggers something as red as blood in me. The dig, as if she finds me weak for allowing the prince to find solace in other women. I smile brightly, instead of the wanted reaction I am sure she waits for.

"Very well." I smile so big, as if I had the best news, "I do hope we become friends. It is always easier when you have someone in your corner when he decides he no longer wants to waste his time with women who hold no actual purpose in his life." Her lips tilt downward and I turn from her, seeing Hadeon's smirk before continuing on my mission to get tonight and tomorrows list of to-do's done. All my decorating will be finished by the time tomorrow comes and then I can finally rest.

* * *

A red tint dusts my dress. The feel of the silk fabric brushes my soft skin and I revel in the feel of it. I chose the color after Dryston changed his mind about the scheme. It was supposed to be a dark green but my last minute change at the modiste pulled through to the dark garnet hue. Tradition always has the queen or future queen match the theme of the event.

Tonight should flow smoothly.

I excused Mya from helping me get ready tonight, not needing it and honestly not wanting it.

The slash on my cheek was now gone, healed by my fae body.

With steady hands, I trace the charcoal pencil along my lashline, darkening my eyes and adding a sultry edge to my appearance. Next, I carefully brush on the rouge to my cheeks, creating a subtle flush of color. My lips are stained in a deep red, giving them a luscious, inviting look. Finally, I run my fingers through my long black hair, smoothing out any tangles and arranging it into loose waves that cascade down my back.

As I step into the dress, I can't help but feel like a goddess. The deep v-neckline shows off my décolletage while the open back reveals smooth, bare skin. Thin straps crisscross over my back, adding an intricate touch to the otherwise simple design. The fabric clung to my curves in all the right places, accentuating my figure. And then there is the high slit — just enough to reveal a tantalizing glimpse of leg without being too revealing.

I wish I could arrive without shoes on my feet, but Dryston would lose his mind.

I take one last glance in the mirror, satisfied with the way I look. With a confident smile, I head out for the evening's festivities.

I open the door to my chambers to reveal Hadeon dress in his royal guard uniform. The deep jade color brightening his eyes.

His intense gaze fixes on me, causing a rosy tint to bloom on his cheeks. He stumbles over his words, unable to find the right ones to express what he sees. I chuckle softly at his flustered state. "You look stunning," he finally manages to say before gesturing for me to lead the way.

We enter the grand throne room, where all of our royal events take place. The expansive space is furnished with elegant tapestries and sparkling chandeliers, creating an atmosphere fit for a queen.

As I step inside, the herald announces my name and title, causing curious eyes to turn toward me. But most of the attendees already know who I am — the prince's betrothed. Not necessarily a captivating title but I was going to be their queen and that gave me a certain level of respect and understanding.

My eyes sweep over the grand hall, taking in my finished work. The rich hues of red and gold drape gracefully over the beams, casting a warm glow throughout the space. Delicate candles twinkle on every surface, adding to the enchantment of the room. And in the midst of it all stands Dryston's approved decor, complete with a touch of vibrant light green that ties the whole design together.

I spot Dryston conversing with a Lord and make my way toward them, Hadeon following close behind. As I approach, I give a respectful curtsy before addressing Dryston. "Your Majesty," I say, my voice steady, despite the nerves fluttering in my stomach.

His gaze lingers on me for a moment before turning back to the conversation at hand. He doesn't seem as pleased as I had hoped, but he also doesn't look disapproving. At least not yet. Turning to address the Lord, I smile brightly and offer a polite greeting.

"My Lord," I greet him with a bright smile, hoping to mask any signs of anxiety. "It is an honor to have you here to celebrate this wondrous occasion. I trust Lady Jacoby was able to join us as well?" My words are polite and carefully chosen, reflecting the grace and poise expected of me as an event planner for the royal court.

He smiles back, pleased with my attention and appearance. "She did. My lady is off with the others, gossiping, no doubt," He laughs. Dryston motions for me to make my rounds so I take my leave and do just that, greeting familiar and unfamiliar faces.

In the lively and bustling room, I retreat to a quiet corner and savor the smooth burn of bourbon as I observe the revelry around me. The band's melodies fill the space, inviting people to sway and twirl on the dance floor. My senses are overwhelmed by the intoxicating combination of music, tantalizing food scents, vibrant sights, animated chatter, and alluring perfumes. The rich warmth of bourbon coursing through my body soothes and comforts me.

Hadeon, my companion for the evening, is nearby charming a pixie from our court. He periodically glances toward me, making sure I am well in his absence.

It's nice.

Until it isn't.

As darkness creeps into the room, a hush falls over the crowd, with only the lively music of the band continuing to fill the space. Goosebumps prickle along my skin, but it's not from the cold, nor is it the same dreadful chill from Dryston I am use to.

The grand doors swing open, revealing the Herald, his staff hitting the ground with a resounding thud as he announces the arrival of our guest. "May I present King Eryx of Khyrel." The heavy doors slam shut behind him, cutting off any outside noise and amplifying the tension in the room.

As the people around him turn to stare, Dryston's sharp gaze fixes on the approaching king in a show of respect. I follow his lead and make my way toward them, but as Dryston catches my eye from behind the imposing figure of the Dark King, he subtly shakes his head at me. Taking the cue, I shift my path and continue forward with purpose, each step closer to the throne room as it fills with tension and anticipation. The air is thick with a mix of awe and fear, as all eyes are fixed on the meeting between two powerful rulers.

* * *

The first dance of the night consists of the King— or in this case, soon-to-be— and whomever he chooses. Since I am his betrothed, it is naturally me.

Dryston leads me to the middle of the dance floor as the band prepares for the next song. I chose it to be the same song we first danced too, wanting to be a little romantic in my softer heart.

He takes my right hand in his left and places his right hand on my hip, fingers delicately playing with the skin of my bare back. Dryston pulls me closer. "This dress is dangerous, Verena." His voice deepens and sends a rush of tingles down to my stomach mixing with the booze.

"I hoped you'd like it. I had it made with you in mind." A blush creeps along my chest up to my cheeks, the overwhelming need to gain his approval burning my skin from the inside out. "I wasn't sure red would look this nice on me."

"I prefer pink on you, you know that. I forget how beautiful you are until we have events like this and then I get a lovely reminder." He speaks low, his fingers still rubbing small circles on my back as we dance together.

I take note of everyone's reactions; the smiles and whispers about how perfect we are together. But it doesn't flood me with the sensation of pride it use to.

I can't help but stew on his words. He is complimenting me but why does it feel as though he is insulting me? Was it the answer I wanted? Of course not. But he gets busy and we rarely see each other.

But... then why do I feel as though his touch is suddenly making me sick? A wave of nausea hits me as I force it back, smiling through the feeling taking over.

The dance ends and as he bows his head, I curtsy, then we walk our separate ways.

The ladies joining us, who are not married, usually have to accept dances from everyone who asks. But, even as an adolescent, I was never asked by anyone other than Dryston himself since we are engaged to be married. Dryston refuses to let anyone else dance with me—always has. He said it was disrespectful for anyone to dance with me because it meant they thought they had a chance.

I quickly down another glass of bourbon, hoping to drown out my nerves. As I glance up from the beverage table, I am met with a pair of mesmerizing dark brown eyes, penetrating me as they study my every move.

Couples twirl and sway on the dance floor, their laughter and joy filling the air. Meanwhile, Dryston is deep in conversation with his mother and some important Lords. Hadeon continues to charm and flirt with a pixie, leaving me alone with the Dark King.

My gaze remains locked onto his, unable to tear away. Despite my fear, I can't help but admire his tall stature, chiseled physique, and strikingly handsome features.

He is quite literally the most beautiful being I have ever laid eyes on. In that moment, time seems to stand still and I find myself holding my breath in awe of him.

His ebony eyes seem to absorb all light around them. His tousled jet black hair cascades over his forehead, giving him a effortlessly handsome appearance. As I look at him, I can't help but wonder if he just woke up or had the most passionate lovemaking session of his life. The thought sends shivers down my spine and a wave of red-hot envy surges through me.

I find myself subconsciously tracing my fingers over my birthmark, hidden under my dress. The small bird shaped patch on my hip always brings me comfort, but in this moment it seems to be pulsing with an intensity that matches my own racing heartbeat. As I take a deep breath and remind myself to remain calm, the air fills my lungs and replaces the dizzying sensation that had taken over me for a moment.

I open my mouth to speak, to greet him, but he spills words out between us before I can make a sound.

"Dance with me." Unlike when Dryston tells me things, this is not as much a command as it is a request— one brimming with need in his liquor colored eyes.

But, almost as if my brain stops working, I stand frozen. Shadows billow around him and it's then I notice his High Fae gift is shadow manipulation.

He works his way from the other side of the table to mine and gently takes my much smaller hand in his tan muscular one. He's wearing formal clothes, perfect for a ball but seemingly less uptight than everyone else here. His black button up shirt reveals a part of his chest, also muscular and littered with tattoos. I can feel the heat spill from him, adding to the bourbon effects.

The Dark King leads me to the dance floor and people seem to notice immediately before parting the way for us in hushed, confused whispers.

I feel Dryston's eyes burn into me but I can't convince myself to look at him and see the disappointment in them.

The kings left hand stays with my right and he pulls me close, the scent of him consumes me.

The concoction of maple and brown sugar make the air taste like cookies and waffles. I take a deep breath in, hoping he doesn't think I'm smelling him even though I definitely am trying to engrave this scent to memory. It smells like... home. A home— something foreign to me my entire life.

Our eyes meet again and in no time, our feet are moving in precise synchronicity. Like we've danced together a million times before. I hadn't realized he already placed his right hand in a respectful position on my back. Others dance around us, even as their eyes follow our movements.

I've danced with a total of four people in my entire lifetime; my father, my mother, Dryston, and now this male. This Dark King Eryx that looks like heaven and hell— that smells intoxicatingly like freshly baked dessert.

Our movements are fluid and smooth, just as smooth as the dress. My body is hot and I can't help but feel moisture between my thighs, suddenly needing a relief. My chest rises and falls in heavy and hasty succession.

Why am I acting like this? What has come over me?

His fingers twitch on my bare skin and my breath hitches in my throat until the song ends, and our feet stop moving. The bottom of my dress swishes against my skin from the sudden motion.

He lets go of my body before catching my left hand in the same one that graced my back, bringing it to his lips as his darkened eyes stay locked on mine like they had this entire dance. "You are truly breathtaking, Princess Verena." He plants a kiss on the back of my hand, then again just past the first row of knuckles. I let out a shaky breath, freezing on the spot while my blood runs cold when my eyes find his tattooed hand just as it releases mine.

He takes a step back and leaves me alone surrounded by guests. My entire body flushes in a deep blush. My hands are as shaky as my breathing. My heart thunders inside my chest cavity.

It feels as if ice water is poured over me. His hand. The markings.

It is an exact replica of the hand from my dream— the same dream that has haunted me for a decade.

Chapter 5: Long Live the King

Verena

Dryston's Coronation Day

> *Your presence is hereby cordially requested*
> *by the Royal Family*
> *to witness the momentous Crowning of*
> *Prince Dryston Whitewell*

I have been awake for five hours and the staff is barely even up themselves. It is so early.

But, I want to get a workout in. So, here I was in the woods again with Hadeon to train.

We spar back and forth, the same as usual except this time I can handle him... mostly.

"I just don't understand." I speak, throwing my weight into each hit. "Was it to piss Dryston off? To get to me? I am a High Fae. I have *class* and I am about to be this country's queen. That means something to people. And he just demands me to dance with him? Like... like-

ugh!" I say, frustrated at my lack of meaningless words to spew.

Hadeon fights back, as per usual. "You don't seem like you minded." He smirks at me and I squint my eyes back, punching him in the chest. "Ow!" He rubs the sore spot. We stop sparring, breathing heavy. "Not that I think Dryston noticed. I just know you better than he does. You just seemed..." Hadeon pauses, "I don't know." He shuts off, as if he has said too much.

"What?" I ask. He shakes his head, waving me to continue. "No, Hadeon. What? I seemed what?" I demand of him, not taking no as an answer. He's silent for a moment, almost unsure of what to say if anything but the truth. I give him a light push, hoping to pull it from him.

He sighs, holding my hands to his chest. "Content. Peaceful." He tells me, looking into my eyes. "Like everything was falling into place." I jerk my hands from his grasp, not because I hadn't wanted him to touch me, but because I was so confused on what he meant.

"What? I am content here. In my home. In Zorya. This is my life. This is my home." I say softly, knowing I'm trying to convince him as much as convince myself. And it works just as well for him as it does me.

"Whatever you say, princess. You asked, I answered."

"Well, you're wrong. You clearly do not know me as well as you think you do." I grab my things before leaving. "I am done for the day."

Heading back to the castle, I sneak in through the kitchen, as always, and make my way through the staff's tunnels before arriving in my room and taking a hot bath to try and scrub away any negative thoughts of this place.

The warm water soothes my tired muscles and I let out a deep sigh, sinking deeper into the bathtub. As I close my eyes, images of the upcoming coronation swirl in my mind. The thought of Dryston becoming king sends shivers down my spine, not out of excitement, but out of dread. I can't shake the feeling that something sinister is lurking beneath the surface of his charming facade.

This place has been my home for as long as I can remember. The Whitewell family raised me, taught me, and groomed me to be their future queen. But as much as I owe them, I can't help but feel trapped by their expectations and plans for me. Their son, who I am promised to, may be cruel and arrogant, but it's a sacrifice I'm willing to make for the sake of duty and destiny.

A bird lands on my window sill, jerking me from my thoughts. I look over at the jet black bird, a raven. "Why are you so ominous?" I ask it and the bird looks at me before turning it's head.

My brows furrow and I rub my eyes before looking again, but it isn't there. I really need to get more sleep or I am going to lose my mind. I'm already seeing things, apparently.

I had excused Mya for the next few events as well, deciding to change her out but not wanting another maid right now. I'll choose one when I become queen.

As I got dressed for the King's coronation, I carefully put on a floor-length blush pink gown, adorn with intricate silver embroidery. My hair was styled in loose curls cascading down my back, and I apply light makeup to enhance my features. The King had always said he loves seeing me in pink, so I made sure it was perfect for this special occasion.

And when it is time, Hadeon knocks on my door, dressed in his military uniform— just as he was yesterday and will be in for our wedding and my coronation. We walk down the halls together as he escorts me to the throne room.

"I didn't realize you excused Mya from being your maid." He spoke first, I was still steaming from this morning, unsure as to why though.

"I-" I gasp, grabbing Hadeon and shoving us both into an alcove.

The halls are empty, since everyone gets to the throne room early to get good seats. King Eryx had not yet gone, apparently.

"What-" I clamp a hand over his mouth, giving him a look that says 'shut the fuck up'. His brow raises.

I jerk my thumb over my shoulder in the direction of King Eryx around the corner of the little alcove we're in and he slowly glances over before lurching himself back inside. His eyes tell me he saw the king and I feel him smirk against me before I remove my hand from his mouth and peak around the stone wall, seeing no one there. I let out a breath of air, allowing my guard and I to continue our walk to the throne room.

"Why are you hiding from his royal highness?" He asks, smug. I want to punch him.

"I do not know what you are talking about. Do not question me, I am a princess." He laughs out loud, to which I slap him on the chest. By the time we arrive we grow quiet. Making our way to the right. I stand next to Princess Lianna with Hadeon standing behind me next to her guard.

Music starts to play, the doors open, and Dryston walks down the aisle of the throne room; all court members and higher fae constituents stand along the sides like it were a wedding. His mother sits on the Queen's throne until he arrives at the front. She stands as the archbishop crowns the king, handing him his scepter before he vows his loyalty to the kingdom and declares his oath to protect while doing everything in his power to do what's best for the country, regardless of personal agendas.

I know he had been waiting for this day for a long time. And I was so proud of him for reaching this goal.

As the ceremony continues, I can't help but feel a sense of unease wash over me. Dryston looks regal and confident as he accepts his title, but there was something in his eyes that made me shiver. Despite the cheers and applause echoing through the throne room, I can't shake off the heavy feeling on my heart as I finally see him in a new light.

No, I was obviously just seeing things again. This was good. This is exactly what we've waited for our entire lives.

After a long time of preparation and stress, it was finally here. I know how stressed he's been and I know once the coronation is done the punishments will stop.

At least that's what I keep telling myself.

His sister grabs my hand but I'm not sure if it's for me or herself. Either way, I squeeze back.

I look around the room, finding King Eryx near the back as if he slipped in barely on time.

With the crown placed on Dryston's head. He turns to the archbishop. "I solemnly swear to rule Zorya as it's king. And as it's king, my duties are as follows: I will rule as the center of life in Zorya, I will stifle any strife between beings, I shall school those in need of righteousness, I will use my power to cause Law and Justice, in Mercy, and to execute all my judgments. I will uphold all customs and practices of our culture. I will be fair, merciful, and love my people as I hope they love me. The things in which I have here before promised, I will perform and keep. So help me God Sorin." He speaks the oath, loud and clear to everyone here.

My eyes water in excitement. "Now ruling: King Dryston Whitewell of Zorya. Long live the king!" The archbishop calls. Everyone in the room, including myself, repeats.

"Long live the king!" Others chant it, continuing for a moment. A smile is resting on his lips and while I think he'd look my way, I watch him find Mya in the crowd. And for some reason, my heart drops to my stomach. Bile threatens to rise in my throat, sweat breaks upon my brow, and the room gets chillier. And I have no idea why.

He rests the scepter down on its rightful pillow before raising his hand to silence the room.

"Let's feast!" The entirety clears to the dining hall and I release Lianna's hand as we smile at each other and she goes to hug her brother. I follow her up to him and stand patiently aside until his mother and sister are done.

"King Dryston," I greet him and he smiles big, perfect teeth showing as he looks at me brightly.

This. This happiness is what I had hoped for him. "I am so proud of you." I beam and he wraps his arms around me and before I can take a breath, his lips meet mine.

I stand in shock before kissing him back. He hasn't kissed me publicly since we were teens since it was very unbecoming of unwed couples to do so.

After letting go of me, he pulls back and they continue toward the dining hall as well. I stand there, Hadeon off to the side patiently waiting as I take it in.

I feel a pair of eyes boring into me and when I glance toward them, it's the same dark ebony eyes from last night. A seemingly permanent scowl rests on his face. I see Hadeon glance over to where I am looking and I watch as his brows raise in confusion at King Eryx.

As the feast began, I can't shake off the feeling of unease that lingers within me. The grand hall is full of nobles and courtiers celebrating the coronation of King Dryston, but my mind was preoccupied with the enigmatic presence of King Eryx. His intense gaze seems to follow me wherever I went.

I try to push aside my apprehensions and focus on the festivities, engaging in polite conversation with other guests and exchanging celebratory toasts with the newly crowned king. But every so often, I catch a glimpse of King Eryx observing me from across the room, his expression inscrutable yet unsettling.

45

As the night wore on, I found myself drawn toward the balcony in my room, overlooking the palace gardens, seeking a moment of respite from the revelry below. The cool night air brushes against my skin, offering a brief reprieve from the stifling atmosphere inside.

I can't help the feeling of being watched. I try looking around outside, seeing no peering eyes or dangers lurking. It's assumingly just my leftover feelings of the Dark King. Why does he get under my skin? Why do I feel like this?

The need between my legs forces my thighs to rub together until I can't take it any longer. I move to my bed, laying down and lifting the hem of my night gown to fit my hand between my legs, feeling the moisture building from the thoughts of the King of Khyrel.

I gasp at the feel of my hand, maneuvering it in a sensual way, feeling myself out to determine what I want— what I need.

I find myself succumbing to desire and longing that had been building within me. The memory of King Eryx's intense gaze fuels the flames of passion that courses through my veins, igniting a hunger that demands to be sated

With trembling hands and a racing heart, I trace patterns of need across my skin, losing myself in the intoxicating dance of pleasure and yearning. Each touch sent shivers down my spine, each whisper of breath a symphony of forbidden desires. My other hand pinches my peaked nipples, a face flashing in my mind revealing onyx eyes unlike anything I've seen before.

My back arches in ecstasy as my fingers rub my clit. The energy humming inside me builds and builds as I try and fail to remove Eryx's face from my mind. I imagine what it would feel like if he were here, touching me the way I'm touching myself.

Would he be giving, unlike Dryston? Would he force me to come over and over until my body feels like water? The hand playing with my chest moves down and I insert two fingers inside myself, a moan slipping from me before I bite down on my lip to silence myself.

I surrender to the sweet torment of my own making, not yet allowing myself a much needed release.

I feel a cool breeze brush over me, realizing my balcony is still open but I can't be bothered. My eyes squeeze shut at the sensation, as if the whisper of wind is trailing over my body in a tantalizing feel. When I feel the chill of air move down further, touching my center as if on purpose, I can't contain it anymore. White-hot blinding ecstasy burns within me as I finish.

I regain my breathing, happily sedated when I open my eyes. I know I need sleep now, but my vision catches the moving breeze of shadows in my room. Must be the wind, I think to myself before remembering to shut the balcony, I move under the covers for a rest that consumes me.

Chapter 6: I Vow

Verena

King Dryston and Princess Verena's Wedding Day

Your presence is hereby cordially requested by the Queen Regent
to witness the marriage of
His Majesty Dryston Whitewell
to Princess Verena Woodall

My mind keeps racing about the Dark King.

His hand. It could not have been a coincidence... right? The marks. They are the same. I would know, I've been dreaming of them for years. The same exact tattoo. But what does it mean?

It shouldn't matter. I am getting married today. To Dryston— the same man who protected me as children, the same man who keeps me safe in the castle, the same fae being that I have known forever.

We are meant to be, meant to rule side by side as King and Queen of Zorya. To keep peace between our bordering country and have royal babies and live happily ever after— as well as we could. And maybe, just maybe, we'd fall in love. We respect each other, care for one another, and honor each other. And I do love him, as much as you do when you grow up with someone with the same goal as yours.

I shake any unwanted thoughts from my head, trying to not be distracted in the early dawn. No one is yet awake, and I managed to sneak into the war room, wanting to leave Dryston a wedding present knowing he'd be in here today.

My gaze lingers on the massive table, its surface graced with a detailed map of the continent. My eyes trace over the jagged edges and winding rivers, eventually settling on our own country, marked in bold colors. But something else catches my eye — yellow pieces scattered across Khyrel, our soldiers strategically placed in key locations. I thought we were prepping to negotiate a peace treaty, not prepare for battle to wage war. The atmosphere in the room suddenly becomes tense and uneasy as I realize the true nature of his hostility about Eryx. My heart sinks as I wonder how long this conflict has been brewing beneath the surface and what it will mean for our people.

I'd naturally assume it's just scouts enforcing the border but the solider count is more than triple what would be needed for that. Why would he be planning on a war? There aren't any Khyrelian pieces on our land so I know this was all Dryston's doing. That is why he has been so busy. He is planning on surprise attacks to weaken Khyrel.

I take engrave the map to my memory, not wanting to forget a single piece of it. Each Khyrelian spot, and each Zoryan one.

Instead of leaving the gift here, I will leave it with his guard posted outside his room. This feels as if I should not be seeing it.

I stare at my wedding gown once I reach my room and start dressing. It is not exactly what I want but Dryston loves it. It was big, dramatic, and light pink. His favorite color on me. It was also his mothers wedding dress.

I had it altered, of course. But in all it's old fashion glory, it was his mothers. Definitely not what I would've chosen for myself but I do enjoy traditions. It is just as much his wedding as mine, even if he did have most of the say-so on everything. I did not plan this wedding, I simply carried it through.

But, today was the day.

Lianna and some ladysmaids arrive to my room and Hadeon lets them in to help me ready.

We go through the same routine as I'd assume any wedding would. They bathe me, scrubbing me down in my signature scent.

After, they carefully construct my hair while a couple of the girls paint my face.

Charcoal lines my eye lids, rouge dusts my cheeks, and a sparkly powder highlights my cheekbones, jawline, and the tip of my nose.

My hair is all down, once again curled to perfection. The girls work to hide the blue within the black locks and I mentally roll my eyes.

With gentle hands, Lianna helps me slip into my dress. The fabric is a delicate lace, draping over my arms and down to my wrists in elegant sleeves. It cinches tightly at the waist, accentuating my figure before cascading out into a grand ballgown style. Intricate patterns of laced leaves and winding vines adorn the top layer of tulle, adding an enchanting touch to the already stunning gown. I can't help but feel like a princess from the stories my mother would read to me as I twirl in front of the mirror, mesmerized by the intricate details of the dress.

"You look so beautiful. I can't believe you are becoming my sister today! And then Queen tomorrow! This is so exciting!" Lianna exclaims. I know we've enjoyed each others company, but Lianna has been more of a confrere than a friend, which neither of us have ever minded.

"Thank you, Lianna. I'd be honored to be considered your sister, even if we are just in laws."

She smiles before placing a hand on my shoulder and excusing the other ladies. Lianna is beautiful. She looks more like their mother but true beauty graces her. She helps me sit and joins me. "I want you to know," She lowers her voice, "You can come to me for help with anything. I know Dryston can be… a lot. Honestly, I wasn't sure if you would marry him. Since you have connections to the court-" A knock interrupts her and we freeze.

"What? Connections here?" I question, confused, but she goes to stand.

"No, silly. The court of D-" Another knock before she puts her fingers to her lips aimed at me and opens the door as if we weren't just talking.

"Oh good! I was hoping you'd still be in here. Hello sweet girl. How are you?" Rya smiles big. Queen Whitewell is anything but happy with me. I know. She is obsessed with her son and she loves being queen.

"Great! Just chatting with Lianna about the future." I state and note Lianna's thankful look. How so very odd. If I had connections here, why wouldn't I know about them? Unless she was trying to say the Court of Dusk but who in the world would have connections on the opposite side of the continent? And why wouldn't I know? I knew my mother was from Khyrel but I just assumed she was from low-income and not High Fae, that I had become High Fae because of my father based on how they acted.

"It's an exciting day. I can not believe you're marrying my baby boy. Let me fix that hair for you." Even though nothing was wrong with it, she goes in and 'tidies' it up. "You look beautiful in my dress, although not as beautiful as I did. Obviously. It was hand made for me. One of a kind. I can't believe they had to take it out a little." I leave my face stoic, knowing shes trying to get a reaction out of me.

For another few minutes, we sit in silence. And then, Lianna and Rya stand up with me to leave the room and start making our way to the throne room once more this week.

They leave me at the doors. Hadeon is supposed to already be in there and since I don't have a father, I was walking alone.

I was torn between anger and sadness as I realize my parents were not going to be at my wedding. My father, who always claimed to have sacrificed so much for me to make this happen, won't be here to witness it. And my mother, who I know did her best despite their constant fighting, was only here in spirit through the necklace she gave me. Holding back tears, I take a deep breath and hid the necklace under my dress. How can I celebrate this day without them? I hate that they were taken from me.

At least she is here with me in spirit.

I nod to the guards that I am ready and they simultaneously open the double doors to reveal me. The same decorations that fit the coronation, also fit the wedding. Aside from the fact that there are more flowers now than then.

Dryston stands at the altar with the archbishop. His mother and Lianna at the front of the crowd. I take another breath.

All eyes are on me and music starts to play. I go to take my first step when a body steps to my side.

"Hadeon?" I question him, looking up into his hazel eyes. In his military uniform, he is still so handsome.

"You didn't think I'd let you walk alone, did you?" He smirks before putting on a stoic face and walking me down the aisle that was littered with loose flower petals. "Don't worry, I asked for permission." And it seemed true. Dryston doesn't look at him with disdain at this moment.

He looks pleased as we walk. Everyone stares, as they did when a bride walks.

When we make it to the front, he hands me to Dryston and stands on my side of the room.

The archbishop greets everyone, going through his speech on marriage and our duty to the Gods and to each other. My eyes meet Eryx's watchful gaze and after the initial shock disappears, I remember he hadn't reserved his seat for the wedding. What made him change his mind? Something burns inside me before I jerk my eyes back to Dryston.

It feels like it takes forever but while Dryston watches the archbishop, I watch him.

He gave Hadeon permission to walk me down the aisle. He put thought into the fact that I was an orphan who was going to walk alone. This is the man I am marrying. The one who knows everything about me, who treats me as his princess and who will treat me as his wife as I rule beside him. He might not be in love with me. But, he does care for me. And in this world? That's all I can ask for. We're not mates, no. But the chance of finding your mate are slim, a rare commodity.

We will have a grand life together. A great rule and reign. One for the history books.

"Verena Woodall, repeat after me."

And I do.

"I, Verena Woodall, vow to respect you and cherish you. I vow to help you when you are sick, support you in your health and your decision. I vow to stay true to you, to stay loyal to you, and to obey you as my husband. May the Gods bless our union."

Dryston had already said his first, now it was time for the marriage unification ritual.

Dryston is handed a marcam, a utensil used to permanently mark us for the wedded rune so the Gods bless our unification.

He pulls the sleeve up and away from the skin and starts to draw the eloquent silver mark on my forearm. But, as he does, the birthmark on my hip flares into a burn so harsh, a hiss leaves my lips. Dryston can only assume the pain comes from the marcam but that feels like nothing compared to my hip. When he is finished, I do the same to him and hand back the marcam to the archbishop. The burn less evident but very much still there in an ache.

"In the power vested in me by the God Sorin, I hereby announce you husband and wife in the eyes of the Gods. You may kiss your bride." Dryston greedily pulls me to him and slaps a sloppy kiss on my lips in front of everyone.

Cheers erupt and while I should be happy, my hip burns and suddenly I do not feel like celebrating.

* * *

After celebrating with everyone, Dryston and I are in his room, alone.

I stand off to the side of the room, my hands resting in front of me as I hold myself out of comfort.

"Why are you so far away from me?" He asks, waltzing over in a playful mood. It makes me want to fall for it. I love when he's in this mood. It helps me forget the punishments and the anger.

His hands grasp mine, pulling them from my body and pressing my body against his. "We're married now, Verena. We must consummate this but I do love you." He speaks before moving his lips to brush against my throat. He places a gentle kiss there.

Maybe he's right. Maybe now that are married everything will be better, easier. I'll be queen shortly enough, practically am now without the actual power since I haven't been vowed in like you are during the coronation. I know we love each other— we've been friends since childhood. My body relaxes at his lips pressing sweetly to my neck, my jaw, and finally my lips.

He has an almost metallic taste to him but I know it was residual from his High Fae powers. I power through it and kiss him lovingly back.

It will be different this time. It has to be.

I melt into Dryston's embrace, letting myself be consumed by the love and hope that his touch brings. As his lips move against mine, a sense of peace washes over me, momentarily pushing aside the weight of my worries and doubts. The world outside this room fades away, leaving only the two of us entwined in this moment of intimacy and connection.

But as our kiss deepens, a nagging voice at the back of my mind begins to whisper, reminding me of the challenges that lie ahead. The brewing tensions between our kingdoms, the shadows of past betrayals, and the looming responsibilities of ruling a realm on the brink of war—they all threaten to shatter this fragile illusion of happiness.

I push the thought back, enjoying this moment with him. Who knows if it will last?

But reality comes crashing back all too soon. As Dryston's hands move with a familiar urgency, a sense of unease creeps over me. The weight of my unspoken fears presses down on me, suffocating the joy that moments ago felt within reach. I pull away slightly, searching his eyes for any sign of the boy I grew up with, the one who used to chase me through the palace gardens and share in my dreams of a better future for our people.

But all I see now is a man hardened by the expectations placed upon him, by the burdens of his crown and the secrets he must keep. I see a stranger wearing Dryston's face, and it fills me with a sense of apprehension I cannot ignore.

As his hands roam eagerly over my body, I feel a sense of detachment settle over me. This is not how it's supposed to be. But, I see no room for negotiation or compromise, only a fierce determination that sends a shiver down my spine. I lay back as he urges me to follow his lead.

After all, I am going to be queen. I will be his wife, the mother of his children. I will do what I can without expecting anything else in return. This is the life that was chosen for me and I will accept it with grace.

Chapter 7: Castles Crumbling

Verena

*Your presence is hereby cordially requested by the Royal Family
to witness the momentous Crowning of the
Princess Verena Woodall*

Everything I have ever done... ever endured... and sacrificed has been leading up to this moment in time.

The crowning of a new Zoryan Queen. The co-leader of the Court of Dawn.

My coronation.

It sounds as if I thirst for power but in truth? I want this country to thrive and to live in the very best way it can. And I do not believe it to be doing so right now. But, I can help. I can fix it. As queen, I can make Zoryan history and get this country to be one that the other continents teach about. I can make us happy, healthy, and excited to be apart of such a culture.

Dryston never cares for any of that, he cares about power and wealth and sure, the betterment of this country. But, in his terms, better meant bigger or richer.

Where he wants rich in coin, I want rich in cultivation. Together, we will make this country better.

Eryx left this morning before anyone was awake, except me of course. I barely slept and saw him slip into his carriage and take off. None of it should matter but something in me is sad at the fact that he hadn't stayed for my coronation.

My gown came in this morning— delivered by the seamstress herself. She designed it and I gave her the inspiration for it.

I know I could never get away with wanting it purple, my favorite color that matches my eyes. So I went for a dusty rose hue, perfect for this court's theme.

It has a modest neckline and shoulder sleeve but it's still gorgeous, sexy, and queenly all wrapped up into one gown. The length was long, the detailing was gorgeous.

I will wear matching heels and silver jewelry. My hair will stay down so the crown fits easily and I will wear minimal makeup.

Today is a day I have been preparing for practically my entire life. I was ready for it.

I was wondering around the library, thankful for it being so gargantuan and well-lit. It was a beautiful place.

There was nothing really to do today. Hadeon follows me around, Rya was being in a more joyous mood than ever, but Lianna seems distant, almost. It bothers me but she promised everything was fine.

"You weren't in your room last night." Hadeon finally speaks. He hadn't said anything to me all morning except hello when we first saw each other. I look from the books to his tall build, scrunching my eyebrows in confusion before a blush creeps along my skin.

"I… I, uh, spent the evening with my husband." I answer, unsure of how to speak about this. No one has spoken to me about those relations before, except Dryston.

Hadeon grunts and my light smile drops. "What?" I ask him. He crosses his arms, fully facing me now and taking a step closer. We stand a foot from each other and he lowers his voice.

"I thought you'd be back in your room before you slept. Or that he'd visit you in yours." He tries to stay quiet so no one overhears this completely inappropriate conversation.

"Well, it was our wedding night. I just followed him to his. What's wrong with that? Dryston and I are married now. Things change."

"Nothing changes overnight."

I huff, "Well this clearly did." I reply sternly, my voice raises in irritation. "Dryston isn't going to be the same. He's different now, I can feel it. Hadeon, I know you are protective of me but I am fine. Trust me." I, once again, am trying to convince myself more than him.

His gaze softens, his body droops into it's more relaxed frame, "I trust *you*, Verena. I do not trust *him*."

* * *

After speaking with Hadeon, I felt dirty. Off. As if something deep inside of me was screaming... clawing... begging and pleading for a way out. My chest hurt, my hip was starting to ache again. It has been since the wedding.

Last night, Dryston trailed over it and after hissing in pain, he had stopped with worry. It was sweet so I pushed through the pain and let him continue. Although, he's spoken to me before about wanting to get it fixed by the healer. He hated the look of it so I tried to keep it hidden from him when we are together.

The first time he saw it, he bombarded me with questions on it but I told him the truth, it's a birthmark. I don't remember a time when it wasn't there.

I shake off the thought, rubbing the aching mark shaped like a bird. I bathe and dress into my coronation outfit, silence ensues around me, driving me crazy. I open my balcony doors to let in a fresh breeze, birds chirping break the dead air in my room. I take a deep breath. As much as I am prepared for this, I feel as though simultaneously I am not ready for it. I take a step out from my room, looking over the lawn full of guests mingling. The coronation was starting soon and while the festivities after will be in the dining hall, I crave for it to be outside. But, Rya and Dryston assure me inside is the better option.

None of this was my choice. Not technically. I was born into this world and 'sold' to a betrothal for my safety. And because of that betrothal, I was to be the future reigning queen of Zorya.

My entire life has been planned out for me and now, I can't breathe.

I gasp for breath, stepping from the edge of the railing and stumbling into my room as I fight for air to enter my lungs.

My chest rises and falls in quick succession and I whimper out in pain from my heart hurting.

A knock sounds, "Verena?" Hadeon's familiar voice breaks through the door but I can't answer him. "I'm coming in." He calls out, not hearing me.

My knees give out and Hadeon closes my door before rushing over to me. "V, what is wrong?" Words refuse to leave me as I gasp for breath with his arms wrapped around me.

My vision gets blurry as he questions on how to fix this but I have no answers even if I could speak.

Pain shoots through me before fading out almost just as fast. My hand flies to my face, holding my cheek. I jerk my face back to him, his eyes and the way they swim with worry.

"You were not well. Please tell me you can speak now? Your breathing seems to be back to normal." He was right. My heart still beats fast but my breaths are coming and going just as they did my entire life.

"You slapped me."

"I've been privy to a few episodes of these sorts before we met. Breaking the attention from your panicked breaths help you return to normal." I allow him to hold me, regaining my composure.

"I am sorry you had to witness such a scene. I am to be queen in a short time and I can barely handle stress."

"You handle it fine. It is a big accomplishment— becoming queen." He smiles at me, allowing me to stand while he assures I do not fall over.

I scoff, "*Accomplishment.* This was handed to me for my soul, it seems. None of this was my decision. I thought it's what I wanted but maybe I was wrong?" I finally voice my fears to him in a whisper so quiet he almost doesn't hear it. I am trusting him although I refuse to meet his gaze.

"You will make a phenomenal queen. If you desperately wanted this, I'd question otherwise. You're not starving for power. So, to me? I shall say you are pretty well off. But, I'd follow you anywhere— were you to run though." I laugh, finally, relaxing. I know he is joking, we'd be fugitives against the crown. But, I appreciate the gesture all the same.

"Thank you, Hadeon. For everything. You are truly the only family I have." He smiles at me before hugging my smaller frame. "I must finish getting ready and then we can start. Let the king know?" He nods before taking his leave and I gather myself.

Time to show this court and this country who I am.

Standing at the doors, alone again, and this time I know Hadeon can't prevent me from walking by myself. I take another steadying breath and nod to the guards at the doors who look at me like their queen already.

The guards and the staff here have respect for me because I have respect for them. That I am more than sure of. Of course the guards answer to the king over me but some of them have made me question if that is true. I have allies and that makes this easier.

The doors open and I walk in to the music selected. All eyes are on me, some with disdain, others with awe, and a few are neutral like they could not care less about being here.

I make eye contact with no one, staring straight ahead of me at the gorgeous queens crown. I can see Dryston on his throne, his mother standing off to the side with her mother regent crown on next to Lianna. Hadeon stands by my throne. The archbishop stands in front of the thrones on the top of the few steps leading to them.

Stopping just before the steps until the archbishop leads me up, we stand side by side like a wedding altar and face each other. Lianna comes forward, fixing my gown and moving back to her mother. I smile at her sweetly.

Practically the same as Dryston's, the archbishop speaks his monologue before my vows and hands me the scepter.

"I, Verena Woodall, solemnly swear to rule Zorya as it's Queen. And as it's queen, my duties are as follows: I will rule as the center of life in Zorya, I will stifle any strife between beings, I shall school those in need of righteousness, I will use my power to cause Law and Justice, in Mercy, and to execute all my judgments. I will uphold-" My vow is cut short by an all too familiar voice.

"Ladies and gentle-fae of the court. I thank everyone here and appreciate all your support." Dryston stands from his throne and refuses to meet my gaze. "Now that I am king, I cannot allow this to happen. Lady Verena has been groomed to take over as queen her entire life. But she will not be our queen." There it is. The room falls into a deafening silence, the only sound is the pounding of my heart against my ribcage. I see lips moving but no words reach my ears, as if I am trapped underwater. My vision blurs and darkens at the edges, an ominous sign of impending danger. Hadeon steps closer to me with a determination in his eyes. My hands shake uncontrollably, nails digging into my palms until they draw blood. Tears well up behind my eyelids, threatening to spill over and betray my fear. "And as one of my first decisions as King, I place the royal guard Hadeon under arrest for treason. Because of his affair with *Lady* Verena." I audibly gasp and Hadeon stops moving. I watch as royal guards, also shocked, come over to grab Hadeon who doesn't even fight them. I look to Lianna, whose face is ghostly white, shaking her head at me saying she didn't know. And then my eyes find Hadeon. He will know what to do. He goes to reach for me, but Dryston's personal guard grabs him tightly after slamming the hilt of his sword into the mans gut.

"No!" I scream, smacking guards away from my best friend. The room stops talking, the guards stop moving him. I step closer to Dryston, "How *dare* you. Hadeon and I have never been anything but respectable. I understand not liking him but this petty accusation is pathetic. You will not crumble my reputation or name. Or his for that matter. Where is the proof?" I search the crowd frantically, waiting for someone to say something. But the cowards wait and do nothing.

He scoffs, stepping down and walking to me. "I need no proof. I am King. But if you must have it, Mya says she's seen both of you together intimately."

"She's lying. She is just angry I removed her from being my ladysmaid because of how ignorant she is." Again, another scoff.

"Where is *your* proof? You are no one. You were not born into royalty, your parents are dead, and you have no one of statue to take your word as their own." To prove his point, no one stands to defend me. It was like a punch to my heart. He was ripping the organ out and stomping on it. A power surges through me wanting to burst, it's a foreign feeling but it dissipates just as quickly. "You are lucky I am not throwing you in the dungeon with him. You are dismissed, Lady Verena. Unless you do want to be thrown in there and hung for treason with him? You may be my wife but you will not be this country's queen." I look to Hadeon, who shakes his head almost unnoticeably. I turn and leave the room, not wanting to see him carried off or let everyone see my tears. My whole vision is blood red in rage and it takes everything in me not to snap and kill everyone.

Once the doors shut behind me, I run to my room.

What am I supposed to do now?

Everything I've ever been told to want and groomed to be is ripped away from me, my castle crumbling to the ground. The last thing of my parents wishes.

My soon-to-be empire was once a golden age where I was adored and loved. People— the people of Zorya— cherish me.

Or do they? No one said anything. *No one cares.* This overwhelming pain runs through my veins, burning me from the inside. I've been following all the rules, drawing inside all of the lines, staying quiet and never asking for anything since I was a little girl. I've allowed this scum of a male to consistently hurt me and tear me down for this crown I was told I should want and be grateful that I have it. Then why has it always felt like a burden? Sure, I wasn't always easy to manage. I love adventure and I love causing a little trouble but this? And to lie to get his way? Branding me as a treasonous whore was the lowest he could go. No one will have me as their queen now even if he changed his mind.

I slam my door shut, screaming to myself while pulling my hair in frustration.

I wait patiently for twenty-six years and he just says *no*?

I am done.

Done.

I am exhausted from constantly putting on a facade of politeness and allowing others to mistreat me. My frustration simmers beneath my skin, a seething rage that threatens to erupt. I hastily wipe away the tears streaming down my face, untangling my hair from its disheveled state and quickly weaving it into a braid. With determination fueling my movements, I storm toward the closet and violently strip off the suffocating dress before donning practical pants and a tunic. I then wrap myself in my trusty fighting leathers, hidden away for moments like this.

A flash of black on my forearm, catches my eye and I freeze entirely. With the wedded rune: spouses can track each other, feel each other's life, and feel each other's death.

Knives now line me along with a sword— my eyes stick to them, the gifts from Hadeon for my first time pinning him. Even if I'm still convinced he let me win. I will need to cut the skin off but Dryston would immediately know because the connection will feel as if I died.

In fact, the leathers were also a gift. As if he knew something like this would happen.

He said he'd follow me anywhere, let's see if he was telling the truth.

I will get him out of the prison and we will leave the kingdom.

Dryston is bold. And stupid.

I know he thinks so little of me that he would never assume I'd run.

Well, that will be his first of many mistakes after today.

Today is the start of the future I will make for myself. And I know just where to go so he never finds me.

Chapter 8: Secret Passage

Verena

As the last hint of daylight fades, I know the time has come to make my move. With a trembling hand, I hastily tie off the blood flow to my arm with a ragged strip of cloth, biting down hard on the leather strap between my teeth to suppress a scream. My limb goes numb from the tourniquet, and I take a deep breath before pressing my dagger into the skin, steeling myself against the searing pain that follows.

Agony consumes me, my screams silent by the tight leather gag that threatens to choke me. With trembling hands, I carve off the intricate rune on my arm, each slice cutting deeper and drawing out more blood. As the black dots dance in my vision and tears stream down my face, I feel a sense of satisfaction knowing that this will finally sever our connection. The sharp blade makes it easier, but the excruciating pain was nothing compared to the overwhelming relief and empowerment coursing through my body.

When I finally peel off the last bit, I throw it to the ground with the blood leaking from me. Grabbing bandages, I wrap my arm until my fae healing can do its job. Tears finally spill down my face from the pain.

Taking more breaths and calming my racing heart, I finish grabbing what I need.

I crack my door open and hope to just slip out but a voice stops me. "Where do you think you're going?"

I froze, recognizing it. "I am the wife to the King. Am I not allowed to walk the court?" I ask him. I turn to face the man, one of the royal guards. I know him. I know all of them and their names. Along with the other help in this castle. Meanwhile, Dryston can barely remember his own personal guard's name.

He takes in my attire, eyebrows raised. "What happened to your arm? Where did you get fighting leathers? And a sword? Can you even use it?"

"Allyric, please let me go." At his name, he looks back into my eyes. "I know it's surprising hearing me call you that. The king can barely remember my name, let alone all his guards. But guards and maids and everyone else who works here talk and you all know I know your names. Hundreds of them. I made it my job to know. I know of your family and where you're from and I care about your lives. He does not. But I am not going to hurt him. Not today. I am going to grab Hadeon and leave this castle before we are both executed for a treason we did not commit." I can see the gears turning in his brain, completely unsure of what to do. "Please. He does not deserve to die. And I do not deserve to be trapped here." My voice was soft. But, for Hadeon, I was prepared to fight this guard. Was I prepared to end his life? No. But I will do what I needed.

"You'll have to knock me out. If I let you go, I'll die. You have to make it look like this was not voluntary. You know how to hit with the hilt of your blade?" He asks me, making a breath release from my body in relief. I nod and he stands like he was before I came out before adjusting his body and allowing me to knock him unconscious.

67

I whisper a prayer to our healer goddess, Althea, to make sure he heals quickly after.

I rush down the halls, hiding in the shadows along the walls to make a clean getaway.

It was relatively easy so far. Most of everyone in this court was in bed by the time nightfall hit and asleep well before midnight like it was now. It had been hours since the coronation and I'm hoping Hadeon is fine.

A scuffle and voice sounds from around the corner and I froze, not seeing anywhere to hide. They round the hall. Two guards freeze at the sight of me. I can be mistaken for someone else since I wasn't dressed in a way anyone had seen before but recognition flares in their eyes. And for some reason, I know this time won't be as easy as it was with Allyric.

"Gentlemen, thank the gods I've found you. Someone knocked out Allyric who was stationed at my door!" I raise my voice and force tears to well in my eyes. "Please help." Males love being heroes. They look at each other before the older one spoke.

"Jordan, go check on him. I'll ask Princ- *Lady* Verena some questions." The title halts my fake tears and my expression harden after the younger one left us.

"So, I am no longer a princess to anyone else either?" He looks at me cautiously at my voice change.

"When you commit treason by sleeping with your guard, that's usually what happens. Although you got lucky with your fate. You get to spend your days as the king's whore wife." He sneers as I walk closer. "Where do you think you're going dressed like that?"

"I do not have to explain myself to you."

My hand instinctively reaches for my dagger as he makes a move for his sword. We both know one wrong move and this could be the end. But I can't risk using my weapon, it will make too much noise.

So I lunge forward, catching him off guard, before he can draw his sword. With a swift slice, I cut through his wrist, causing him to let out a strangled cry of pain and shock. Blood spurts from the wound, coating us both in red as I hold my weapon steady. "Get that to the medic," I command, my voice low and deadly. "You might just survive if you go now." He hesitates, torn between his desire for revenge and the need for medical attention. But eventually, he turns and runs toward the infirmary, leaving a trail of blood in his wake.

I cannot keep getting this lucky. There's no way.

I rush even more now since there were two people aware of my whereabouts. The way to the dungeon was further than I wished for. I hurry down three flights of stairs and many halls before coming across the dungeon stairway. Luckily, no one else had been around to see me. After living here for your entire life, you know this sort of information. I know there would be barely anyone out.

I pull the heavy door open, running to the bottom of the steps and rounding the corner. A few men are in the cells, some sleeping, some mumbling to themselves, and a couple are whistling at me while making kissing noises. I roll my eyes. Typical.

Hadeon's cell was at the end and while I am not surprised it was, I am surprised he has a guard assigned to his door. Lucky, again, for me he was asleep. Hadeon, however, was not.

As soon as our eyes meet, I am gripped by a sudden shock. His face is marred with bruises and splatters of blood, stark against his once flawless skin. Deep purples and dark blues form a grotesque canvas over his features, streaked with angry red gashes. The sight takes my breath away and for a moment, I am too stunned to react.

My hand covers my mouth, choking back the emotion before I steel myself and continue quietly forward. He sits up, eyeing me and not saying a word. I spot the key from the guard and expertly retrieve it to unlock the cell.

Just as the bell starts to ring.

I can barely slip the key into the lock before the guard wakes and stands, wrapping his arm around my throat. "He knew you'd come for your lover." I roll my eyes again, trying to steady my breathing as Hadeon taught me. I watch the man in the cell, beaten so badly I wasn't sure if I'd have to carry him out of there. He can't help me right now. Not with the look of worry in his eyes as he watches me.

The guard's hands press hard against my body, the cold metal of his blade digging into my side while he tightens his grip on me, cutting off my air supply. I struggle against his hold, widening my stance and drawing in a deep breath before unleashing all my force into a brutal elbow strike to his solar plexus. He grunts in pain and his grip weakens, giving me the opportunity to stomp on his foot with all my might. As he recoils from the pain, I use all my strength to break free, driving another powerful elbow strike into his nose. Blood spurts from his nostrils as he releases me completely. With no time to waste, I draw my sword and point it directly at him, my eyes blazing with unbridled fury. "I am leaving with Hadeon," I growl, the sword trembling in my hand. "Whether I have to kill you or not." A menacing grin spreads across my face as I prepare for whatever comes next.

"Then you'll have to kill me." The man states. I shrug, feigning nonchalance at the idea of murder. But my heart is racing faster than the horses we race.

"Your choice," I growl before lunging toward him, my blade flashing in the dim light. He blocks my attack with ease, his muscles bulging as he swings his own blade in retaliation. But I am relentless, slamming my weapon against his again and again, fueled by a fierce determination to stay one step ahead.

Despite his towering stature, I refuse to back down. Instead, I use every ounce of strength and agility to land a deep slice across his forearm. As he howls in pain and falters, I see an opening and go for the kill. But at the last second, I pull back, unwilling to cross that final line.

With adrenaline still coursing through my veins, I bring down the hilt of my sword with brutal force onto his temple, knocking him unconscious. Another enemy defeated.

"You should've killed him." Hadeon coughs out. I gather my wits before walking over to him pushing open the cell door.

"I couldn't."

"I know. You did well. What's your plan?" I stop moving from the question.

I look down the hall, making sure it's clear before wrapping my arm around him after sheathing my weapon. "Escape. I didn't exactly have a lot of time to plan this. I couldn't let you sit there till morning. You'd be dead by then." He grunts as we move. "How bad is it?" I ask, nerves wrecking my body.

"I'm fine."

"Liar." He lets out a strained chuckle as we make our way down the hall, turning the opposite way of the door. "Where are we going? The exit is that way." I try to turn him but the strength he has even like this is more than I have.

"There's a secret passage." My brows furrow. How in the afterworld does he know that?

"I'm not even going to ask right now but I expect to be told how and why exactly you know this."

He says nothing but we stop in front of the bare wall and I look at him incredulously as he places his palm against the bricks and it moves. "What the fuck?" It reveals a tunnel, dark and wet. I can smell the rats and moist walls and hold back a gag.

"What, fuck, what about your rune? Your wedded rune, he'll find us." He voices, scratchy vocal chords rubbing together. Then, he eyes my bandage and stares back into my face.

"Let's go." I state, not answering him but I think he knows based on the look he gives. "Do you even know where you're going?" I ask him, following him as he starts.

* * *

As the moon rose high in the darkened sky, we press on toward our destination, our weary feet carrying us closer to the end. The gates loom ahead, bathed in silver light that filters through the ornate iron bars. Despite our exhaustion, we can still hear the distant sound of bells tolling and occasional echoes of noises coming from the tunnel. As we drew nearer to the gate, I caught glimpses of the city beyond, its buildings towering against the night sky. The scent of hay and horse manure waft toward us, signaling that we were deep within the city walls. In the distance, I can make out the hazy outlines of guards and their steeds hurrying about their duties. Our hearts race with anticipation as we approach the gates, knowing that our journey was finally reaching its end.

I look at Hadeon, noting the milky color in his eyes. "Hello? Hadeon." I try to get his attention but he's not looking at me.

Whatever. Ever since I've known him, he's done this. It happens randomly and he's zoned as if he is not here except in body. I've learned to embrace it. The only time I asked about it, he says it's a way to communicate to his family, I assumed it was because they were dead or some weird enchantment I hadn't heard of but it wasn't brought up after.

I give him some space and peek around the gate, searching for a fragile spot. The gate was rusted over and looks weak. I go to push it open, but his voice stops me. "Wait." I turn to him, still with the off look before he blinks and it's gone. "Okay, I know where to go."

He helps me push the gate open, with ease, and suddenly I feel wetness coating my bandage that rests against his. "You're bleeding," I tell him. He tries to brush it off but I grab it, showing him I know it hurts. "Stop moving real quick." I take the bottom portion of my tunic and rip it across to get the most out without revealing all my skin. I wrap the makeshift bandage around his forearm before tying it off tightly. "The last thing I need is for you to lose more blood and pass out. I don't know if I'll make it to our destination without you or with you if I need to carry you." I speak the truth. Hadeon stares into my eyes with an incredulous look.

"You are stronger than you give yourself credit for. Your entire life is proof of that. And I haven't been training you for nothing." Then his eyes flash. "And where, pray tell, are you planning our destination to be?" I pull my bottom lip into my mouth, lightly chewing on it with nerves. He's waiting for an answer but I don't think he suspects where I want to go.

"I do not know about you, but I plan to make it to Khyrel. I wish to seek out the king. I believe he and I now have a common enemy. But, if you do not wish to join me, I understand."

Something else flashes through his face, and I want to believe it is relief but I'm not sure. Why would he be relieved? I thought he'd talk me out of it. I squint my eyes at him as he turns away.

"Let us go."

* * *

After a long and treacherous journey, we finally emerge from the bustling city and enter the lush forests that act as a buffer between the grand capital of Zorya and its smaller surrounding towns. As we move deeper into the trees, our chances of being noticed decrease, but I can't shake off the feeling that the guards are still on high alert. However, one positive sign was the absence of any alarm bells ringing in the distance. The air around us was cool and crisp, carrying with it the scent of pine and damp earth. The only sounds are the gentle rustling of leaves and the occasional chirping of birds, a welcome change from the constant noise of the city.

My hands stop shaking from adrenaline and I've calmed my heart a bit.

"We need to stop, take a breath." Hadeon finally spoke, seemingly having a harder time breathing. "Are you hurt anywhere?" He asks, trying to look me over.

"I don't feel any pain. The adrenaline's worn off by now so I would feel something if there was anything wrong." I assure, looking at him. "Aside from my arm but it's fine." I look down at it, noting the blood that seeped through the bandage.

The silence was deafening. Even the creatures remain asleep when the sun went down. The wind howls as it usually did this time of year but in the short moments of true silence, I heard it. A stream. "Stay here, I'm going to fill up on water." I shake the empty drinking skins but before I can leave him, he grabs my bicep.

"Not alone." I roll my eyes again tonight before motioning him with me. The stream wasn't far from us and I know it was safe. I fill up the skins and seal them before ripping a piece of my sleeve to wet it, walking over to Hadeon.

"Let me clean up your face, please." He looks like he wants to refuse, but doesn't. He surprises me by allowing me to swipe across his face gently. There were cuts and bruises littering him but I did my best to clean him up before we start our venture again. His fae abilities are already healing him.

74

I can tell he wants to ask me something but the cloudy look in his eyes return. Maybe it's from the injuries. He could've hit his head at some point. I wait, wanting him to speak first but still nothing. After what seems to be an hour, his eyes are still cloudy as we continue our trek.

Finally, I watch as he tunes in, looking at me.

"What are you doing?" I ask him. He looks confused.

"Nothing," I want to push more on the subject. Was he talking to his family? Did they know of his plans to leave the country?

I speak, "We are far enough away now to rest. You get some sleep, I'll take the first watch." I can tell he wants to argue but I held my hand up before he can speak, "I am not nearly as tired or as injured as you. Get some sleep." I demand. We try to get comfortable in the sand bed by the creek, avoiding sharp rocks and twigs.

I sit there, counting our rations and my weapons. I didn't notice before but Hadeon had grabbed the sword from the guard as we were leaving so at least he also had a weapon.

Only when my eyes start drifting do I blink it away and shove him— hours later— to wake him so I can rest too before our day's worth of journey.

Sleep takes me and I slip into another dream of the aurora borealis. This time it's closer and my heart feels warm; like it's supposed to be closer so I can feel more at peace. Blonde hair bellows around me in the wind, the dark blue strands sticking out. I watch as the lights dance across my vision again and again before suddenly it gets darker and a hand appears, reaching out toward me.

Black marks trickle along the muscular skin and chills run up my spine. "I'm coming for you." The voice whispers, barely audible, and again, I jolt awake, my necklace scalding my skin.

Chapter 9: The Dark King

Verena

The gentle timbre of Hadeon's voice pulls me from my dream, coaxing me back into the waking world. As I stir, he shook me with more urgency until I swat his hand away in annoyance. Before I can ask what was wrong, he presses a finger to his lips and motions toward the trees where the murmur of voices can be heard. His hand found its way over my mouth as if to silence any potential protest, and I follow his gaze with trepidation. The shadows dance and twist among the foliage, hinting at unseen figures lurking within. Every rustle of leaves sent a shiver down my spine and I realize we are not alone in this peaceful glade.

The sun was coming out now and we both gather anything resting on the forest floor before rushing off further North.

"They made it far," I speak when we are out of earshot, hopefully making it further than they are. "How much farther do we have until we get to the border?" I ask him.

"Another two days at least. We'll have to find resources soon. Did you pack any food?" I nod to his question before grabbing some rations from my pack with water from a skin.

The farthest I had ever been on foot was maybe an hour from the castle and my mother punished me for it since it's dangerous. But, it didn't make it the last.

Thinking back to the day Hadeon saved me as I wandered around the city alone, no matter how hard I concentrate, I can't remember why I was out there. But it was the first day I truly knew the danger my title held. I was trying to find something, as if I was in a trance, and before I could find it, I was attacked.

My first meeting with Hadeon is a treasured memory to me; he was young and one of the most handsome fae I had ever met, yes, but there was something about him. I wasn't sure if he felt it too but I know I could sense something familiar about him, something that always made me feel at ease and at home. Having him with me for the past five years has been a blessing. He truly was my only friend, aside from Dryston's sister.

Five years had passed since everything changed in my mind. I found myself speaking up more, but with each word came a punishment from Dryston. Yet, I refused to let his manipulation control me completely. I was starting to find my own voice and identity, even though it went against everything I had been taught.

And now that I'm finally free? Well, that part hasn't hit yet, I'm still trying not to die in the woods during the manhunt that has us now running toward our supposed enemy lines.

"Do you know of the king?" I ask out loud, his head jerks toward me in surprise.

After coughing from the piece of food in his throat, he answers, "More than most." His tone said to not ask further but I needed to know.

"And? What about him? We are going into enemy lines, Hadeon. I need to know if I'm on a suicide mission or not." A large sigh escapes him and he shakes his head, as if unsure of what to say.

"King Eryx, or the Dark King as some call him, is rumored to hate women. He doesn't even take lovers, so they say. But once, Eryx saw a woman in trouble at a little pub in some small town. And even though everyone thinks he hates females, he beat the fae male who was antagonizing her so far into the ground his own family couldn't recognize him. His face was smashed in." I shiver at the thought, "Not that they wanted to since their son was a rapist." The faraway look in his eyes was familiar to me.

"Eryx? You speak of him like you truly know him." I say with raised brows. His eyes meet mine before he shakes his head like he was dismissing his own thoughts. He lets out a light scoff as if I were delusional. I speak again. "Wasn't he betrothed once before? And she died right? Did he kill her?" I ask, the questions spilling from my lips.

"That's what the rumors say…" He trails off and I realize he doesn't want to talk anymore about it. But I wasn't done this time. I need to know for my own safety.

As we trek on, I continue. "Have you ever seen him aside from the gala? I heard he was hideous but I've also heard he's so beautiful that human women die at his feet from the beauty."

"What do you think of him? You did dance with the king at the gala." I scoff at the change in conversation. I don't want to talk about me. He continues, "He seemed quite entranced with you."

"I do not know what you are talking about." He gives me a pointed look at my feigned ignorance.

"Verena, please do not take this any specific way but you are one of the prettiest beings I've ever seen. That alone will have given him curiosity. But, your energy and your charisma are exquisite. You're smart and kind. Not to mention you have never fit in with the Court of Dawn or anyone in Zorya. I am your only friend, no offense."

"A little taken." I cut in, giving him a smile.

"*But*, it is simply because you do not belong there and they do not deserve you."

How could he possibly know where I belong? Hadeon grew up in a small Zoryan town. Why would he say these things about his own home? A small part of me wants to second-guess my friendship with him, maybe he isn't who he says he is.

Growing up in this country, I always felt like an outsider. But Hadeon was the one person who understood me, who shared my feelings of displacement. Our friendship was a refuge from the judgmental eyes and whispers of others. Yet, as I look at him now, I can't shake off the feeling that he's been keeping secrets from me. Why is he so distant from everyone else? And why did he risk everything to save me that day? Is there more to our relationship than just friendship? Despite my trust in him, doubts begin to creep into my mind.

"I definitely do not believe the king to be ugly." A blush creeps up my cheeks as I speak honestly. Hadeon looks at me, brow raised as if to question me. "I don't know. It's not like I've seen many Khyrelians. He was different, his energy darker in a good way." My eyes stay distant as I think back to a couple of days ago. "The urge to dance with him was so strong. I had never felt anything like it. And when we danced?" For a moment, I didn't feel as if I were in the woods with Hadeon escaping our fate in the Zoryan Court of Dawn, I was back in the throne room, spinning around with the most gorgeous male I had ever witnessed. The same male who complimented me as if he were compelled to do so and-

"And when you danced?" He asked, a playful twinkle in his eye as he gave me a knowing look. I shove him.

"Shut up," I laugh and brush it off, "I don't know. It was weird. He was weird, right?" I say, changing my tune and closing off again.

Hadeon laughs lowly, "Yeah. He was weird." He smirks to himself but we say nothing else.

Every fiber of my being was unsettled by this situation. It left me with a sense of unease that I can't shake. As I mull over my decision to leave the Court of Dawn, one question plagues me: had I made a grave mistake?

We keep trekking through the woods, changing up our paces and foot steps every so often to keep hunters off our trail. I wasn't daft enough to believe Dryston wouldn't send hunters after his prized possession.

The rustling of leaves and snapping of twigs beneath our feet are the only sounds that broke the silence between us. The tension in the air was thick, weighted down by unspoken truths and lingering doubts. I stole a glance at Hadeon, his eyes fix ahead with a determined focus, his jaw set in a firm line. Despite the gravity of our situation, a small flicker of admiration sparks within me as I watch him lead us through the dense forest with unwavering confidence.

As we travel deeper into the woods, my mind wanders back to our conversation about King Eryx. The enigmatic ruler had always been shroud in mystery, his reputation precedes him wherever his name was spoken. The conflicting tales surrounding him paint a complex picture that left me more intrigued than ever.

Lost in my thoughts, I almost don't notice when Hadeon suddenly stops in his tracks, causing me to bump into him. His hand shot out to steady me, and he places a finger to his lips, signaling for me to be silent. I follow his gaze and feel my heart drop to the pit of my stomach at the sight before us.

Through the thick foliage, we can see a group of armed men clad in the colors of the Zoryan Court of Dawn. They move with purpose, their eyes scanning the surroundings as they search for any sign of us. My breath catches in my throat as I realized we are dangerously close to being caught.

Hadeon's expression hardens as he turns to me, his eyes conveying a silent urgency that fuel my determination. Without a word, he gestures for us to change course, leading us deeper into the undergrowth to evade our pursuers.

As we navigate through the dense forest, every rustle of leaves and snap of twigs reverberate through the tense silence that envelope us. I can feel the weight of our predicament pressing down on me, a constant reminder of the perilous game we are entangled in.

The sound of footsteps drawing closer behind us spur us to quicken our pace, our hearts pounding in unison with the echoing drumbeats of fear. We dart through the trees, our breaths coming out in frantic gasps as we struggle to maintain our advantage. The intensity of the chase only heighten as the branches claw at our skin and the roots threaten to trip us with every step.

A sudden clearing ahead offered a brief respite, a small pocket of safety in the vast expanse of the forest. Hadeon grabs my hand without hesitation, his touch grounding me in the midst of chaos. Without a word, we sprint toward the open space, our muscles burning with exertion as we push ourselves to the limit.

As we burst into the clearing, a sense of relief wash over me briefly before being replaced by a sinking realization. Before us stands not a sanctuary but a trap, a circle of Zoryan hunters waiting with weapons drawn and grim determination etched on their faces. I turn to Hadeon, panic rising in my chest as I search his eyes for a plan, for a way out of this dire situation. But instead of fear or despair, I saw a steely resolve glinting in his gaze, a spark of defiance that spurs me to stand taller beside him.

As the hunters close in around us, their leader steps forward with a menacing sneer curling his lips. "Well, well, well, what do we have here?" He taunts, relishing in our cornered state. "It seems the little traitors thought they could escape the wrath of the Court."

I feel a surge of anger boiling within me at his words, at the injustice of being hunted like prey for a crime we didn't commit. But before I can retort, Hadeon steps forward, his voice cutting through the tension like a blade.

"You would believe that, Dorian, " I say, recognizing his face from the castle. "But Dryston is not the man you think he is. He is not the king you believe him to be."

"Traitors will say anything to defy the king. You both should be hung. But I'll take great pleasure in bringing you back dead instead of alive." He pulls his sword from its sheath, aiming for us.

Hadeon, sensing the danger, quickly moves from behind me and positions his body in front of mine, taking the brunt of the hunter's attack. The sword swings down, and I brace myself for the impact, but Hadeon's reflexes are too quick. He deflects the blade with his own sword, the force of the collision echoing through the clearing. A momentary lapse of surprise flickers across Dorian's face before he charges at us again, renewed in his determination to capture us or end our lives.

"Escape while you can!" Hadeon shouts at me, pushing me toward the edge of the clearing. I know he is forcing me away from danger, but I can't leave him behind. With a cry of defiance, I run back toward him. The hunters close in on us again, their weapons ready. But this time, I am ready too.

"Not a chance!" I tell him, before joining the fray of the fight. I use the training he's given me and put it to good use to help get us out of this alive.

The clashing of our swords against theirs fills the air, a deafening symphony of steel and determination. Sparks fly as blades collide, the scent of blood and sweat permeating the clearing. Amidst the chaos, Hadeon and I form a united front against our pursuers, our bond strengthened by our shared purpose.

Each strike was calculated, each parry a testament to our training and skill. We dance around the hunters, our moves fluid and precise, the rhythm of our blades harmonizing with the pounding of the hunters' feet on the hard earth.

In the midst of the fray, I caught a glimpse of Dorian, his eyes burning with a mixture of rage and hatred. He had not expected this resistance, and the surprise was evident in his struggle. But we will not relent. We press on, our resolve greater than our exhaustion.

As the last few hunters fall, I want to smile in victory, but do not have time before seeing Hadeon's eye widen at the sight behind me but I move out of the way, ducking and rolling to the side before I can be impaled by a sword. I swipe my sword out in defense, slicing across his legs and when he drops, I stab my blade through his chest, apologetic tears in my eyes before I blink them away.

It is either us or them. I have to keep that in mind.

Chapter 10: Where There's a Will, There's a Way

Verena

After two more days of travels, we had barely slept. But we are lucky enough to not run into more trouble.

The thick scent of sweat and dirt clung to both of us, despite our efforts to rinse off in a nearby stream the day before. My feet throb with stabbing pains as we trudge forward.

But I had a plan, a desperate plea to make to the king. I just don't know if what I can offer him in return will be enough. The weight of this uncertainty rest heavy on my shoulders.

Hadeon attempts to lift our spirits with jokes, but they fell flat against our exhaustion. With sheer determination, we press on toward the northern border. Our fighting leathers are relatively common in this area. The small village we were coming into a popular place for hunters and assassins.

My body buzzes with an unknown tingle. It started the further we got from the castle and now it hums strong within me. The foreign feeling hadn't hurt yet but it made me nervous.

As I push open the heavy wooden door to the local tavern, a

cacophony of scents hits me all at once. The rich aroma of freshly cooked food fills my senses, making my stomach growl in response. We had run out of rations yesterday and our water supply was nearly depleted. We are also dangerously close to the border, only an hour away, so we need to keep moving. But the promise of warm food and a chance to rest our weary bodies was too enticing to pass up.

"We can't stay here for long," my companion whispers in my ear, his breath tickling my skin. "We'll just eat and drink and leave once we've rested enough." I nod in agreement, taking in the dimly lit interior of the tavern. Despite its rough exterior, there is a sense of coziness and warmth emanating from within. Tables are filled with boisterous patrons, their laughter mixing with the clinking of glasses and the strumming of a lute in the corner. As we make our way to an empty table, I can't help but feel a sense of relief wash over me. For a moment, we can forget about the dangers that lie ahead and simply enjoy this brief respite in the comfort of good food and company.

"How long will it take to get to the castle?" I ask him, staring into his side profile as he scans the place. He pauses, almost seemingly unsure of how to answer me. Maybe he doesn't know? He was fresh out of guard training when he met me. He hasn't exactly had time in Khyrel— unless his hometown is here somewhere along the border.

Finally, after a brief minute, he answers, "That won't matter right now. Let's focus on not drawing attention to ourselves. The sooner we get over the border, the better off we are."

The conversation seems to fizzle out, leaving a lingering sense of unease between us. I can't quite put my finger on it, but something feels off about him. We made our way to the bar, the soft glow of lanterns illuminating our path. The scent of hearty mead, freshly baked bread, and pungent cheese fill the air as we place our order. Hunger gnaws at our stomachs, reminding us that our journey was far from over. But for now, we can savor this small moment of warmth and comfort before setting off once again into the cold night.

Some people stare, but anyone who knows what's good for them tends to keep to themselves. This town is notorious for travelers to stop and rest or get food and drink.

No one stays long except the small number of locals who run it, and everyone else either passing through on business or personal fun. But business is the usual route. Beings don't typically pass through from Khyrel and Zorya on personal matters unless they're moving and they rarely do that from what I know.

"I'll be back. Talk to no one and do not move."

I am rendered speechless as he abruptly exits the establishment, leaving me to my own devices. Taking a deep sigh, I thank the woman who has brought me my food, hoping that it will settle the nervousness in my stomach. Slowly, I begin to eat, careful not to upset my delicate digestive system.

As I gaze around the dimly-lit room, I can feel his teachings coming back to me. Every sight and sound is carefully noted and etches into my memory. The assorted ascents mixing together. My eyes scan the room, taking note of every being present and their movements, just as he had taught me to do in situations like this.

There are many different races here tonight— I assume it's always like this— but from low fae, humans, and some sprites, to elves, vampires, and werewolves. I always enjoy seeing mixed races within the city and court. But you had some people, much like Dryston, who think high fae are the more important beings.

"Do you think she made it this far?" A voice spoke, loud enough for me to hear, on their way inside the building. I peek at them as they walk closer to me, taking the table next to mine. The one who spoke has to be a pixie, with the way her wings appear.

"Who?" Their companion ask, their skin green and their eyes bright blue, which tells me they are a selkie. I studied species in the castle.

There wasn't much else to do other than study and study some more. I know more about our history, our species of beings, our fauna and flora, and our geography than the average creature.

"The princess." The pixie whispers. My eyes widen before trying to keep my focus on my food. "I heard she ran away after the king embarrassed her in front of everyone by preventing her coronation. Poor thing. I've never heard bad things about her before."

The selkie scoffs, "There's no way she made it this far if she did escape. I think he killed her and told everyone otherwise so he'd look like the better being. Which is complete poppycock. King Dryston is just like his father." I hold back a snicker.

The pixie gasps, "Don't say that. That's enough for him to charge you for treason. I hope he didn't kill her, she didn't deserve it." Where was Hadeon? He needs to eat so we can leave before-

"You!" The room falls silent as the stranger's accusatory finger points directly at me. My heart races with fear and I can feel everyone's eyes on me, waiting for an explanation. "Why does your hair look like that?" His voice is full of disdain and my mind races to come up with a plausible excuse.

In a desperate attempt to deflect attention, I stammer out a lie. "I wanted to mimic the princess's hair, so I used berries to dye it. But… it turned out darker than I anticipated." The words taste bitter and false on my tongue as I struggle to maintain composure under the intensity of his gaze.

"Then you won't mind standing before the king so he can confirm whether or not you're the princess?" The pixie and selkie next to me audibly gasp and the man— probably a bounty hunter— smirks at me.

"Absolutely, no problem." I slowly stand, hoping to get him outside so I can fight him. If I start inside, more than he will likely try to attack me. "But I doubt the princess had time to grab an outfit like this and weapons like mine before running away from the dreadful king." More gasps and this time I smirk. Why did that feel so good to say?

"That's enough out of you." His voice was booming.

Seriously, where was Hadeon? My skin buzzes in anticipation and the foreign energy tingling through me turns harsher, more erratic.

When the man grabs the back of my neck, something triggers inside me and I snap. I grab his wrist with one hand as I spin around while throwing my weight into my other arm against his elbow, bending it in the wrong direction it's supposed to go. A crack reverberates around the pub, as does his cry, leaving everyone else silent. "Do not touch me."

Rage boils within me, threatening to engulf me in its fiery grip. My eyes feel like they are ablaze with the intensity of my anger.

Suddenly, Hadeon bursts through the door, his eyes darting around before locking onto me and widening in shock. He opens his mouth as if to speak, but hesitates, unsure of what to say.

"Let's go," he finally says, breaking the tense silence. But just as I start to move toward him, more men rise up from their seats, ready for a fight.

"I don't care if you're the princess or not. You'll pay for that." One says before they all come at me.

I draw my sword out, ready for a fight as Hadeon marches forward.

A swarm of men rush toward me, their faces contort with malice. I narrow my eyes and ready my sword, swiping it across one's abdomen with swift precision. But my element of surprise is short-lived as two more attackers close in on me. With a quick maneuver, I retrieve the dagger from my belt and hold it tightly in my free hand, bracing myself for their blows. The chaos around us has cleared out, leaving only the sounds of clashing metal and grunts of pain as we fight for our lives against a relentless onslaught of enemies.

A blade slices across my cheek, drawing a thin line of fire and I curse before driving my dagger into the side of the man too close to me. The hilt of his blade smashes against my head, sending a shockwave of pain through my skull, but I push through it with sheer willpower. Suddenly, everything goes black as a sharp blow to the back of my head knocks me off balance. My body continues to move on instinct, thrashing around as I swing my blades wildly in all directions. But then a heavy weight crashes down on top of me, cutting off my breath and crushing me to the ground. My vision flickers back for a brief moment, just long enough for me to see Hadeon sprawled out on the ground, lifeless, while a hunter stands above him preparing for the final blow with a bloodied weapon in hand.

With every ounce of strength I have left, I thrust my knee upwards, pushing against the weight of the male pinning me down. Finally, I manage to create enough space to slip my knee up and forcefully shove him back. My feet connect with his chest, propelling him even further away from me. But as he stumbles backwards, his fist snags my mother's necklace, tearing it from my throat in one violent motion. The alien energy surges through my veins, intensifying until my eyesight turns a deep indigo. In a burst of power, the matching hue blasts out from within me, knocking out everyone else in the vicinity with its sheer force.

* * *

Licks flicker across my face and I jump up, holding my throbbing head in my hands and looking around me. Bodies lay all over the floor, wood splintered with it from broken tables and chairs.

Glass and food and liquids from beverages follow.

I feel terrible about this happening. But, I'm not sure what even happened. What was the light from me? It couldn't have been me, right? Who else could do that? The buzzing from my body had stopped. can it be coincidence?

I slowly stand, walking over to Hadeon and slapping his face to try and wake him. He groans in pain, letting me know he's alive. I release a breath of relief before assessing the damage. I need to fix him up enough to move him across the border, then we'll rest and heal. My side feels sticky and I glance down, seeing blood slip from a wound. I take off my small pack of medicine, grab the healing tonic for me, and pour some over any bad wounds. It'll stop any bleeding while it heals. I use the rest on Hadeon's wounds before wrapping cloth around the more superficial ones on both of us. I re-braid my hair back since it had fallen out during the fight. Exhaustion pumps through me and the moon is still high which is perfect for our travels but it doesn't look like it'll be out much longer. I dump some coins on the counter, enough to fix this place up. I feel guilty for destroying it.

I take deep breaths, trying to keep myself awake. I push Hadeon's feet together, setting them up with his knees bent. Then, I grab his hands and face my back to him and with the force of pulling him toward me, I throw myself back too, getting him to rest on me and walking out of the building with him on my back.

He groans at first, "I am getting us across that border, Hade." I mumble enough for him to hear if he can. But, I need to talk as little as possible since I'm out of breath from carrying this muscular 250-pound man. "If we stay here, we have a higher chance of dying." I readjust him as he groans in response and from then on, I'm silent. We have a couple of hours of walking and I refuse to slow down.

I try to focus on the trees, naming each plant in my head to distract me from everything else.

He better not die on me or I will kill him.

A black oaken tree, on my left, is one of our holy landmarks. It's said to be the tree of Nyxie; the goddess of night and death. There are a couple of them close to the border, it's how you know you're getting close. It's said to have a few white oaken trees just on the other side, letting Khyrel know when they're getting close to our border. Those trees are from Sorin, the god of day and life.

Nyxie and Sorin were lovers in their time; both so vastly different but alike in some ways. The trees were a gift for one another. I never thought I'd see them in my lifetime but I don't have time to stop and gaze upon them. I had to keep Hadeon alive— keep myself alive.

As I trudge forward, my feet heavy with exhaustion, I sense that I am roughly halfway to the border. Suddenly, a warm sensation trickles down my back, making me stop in my tracks. My initial thought is sweat, but as it continues to flow down, I realize it is something else entirely. It is thick and sticky, leaving a trail of moistness along my skin. I shudder as it drips separately down my side and leg, the unfamiliar feeling causing a sense of unease to bloom within me. What can this be? An injury? Something from the forest? "Fuck!" I wanna yell but my throat is hoarse now, without any water, so it's barely a whisper.

I try to let Hadeon down gently, but after walking with him on my back for half an hour, he more so drops to the ground and I groan from the release of weight before apologizing mentally to him. His lack of groans makes me nervous but I don't have time to think about it right now.

I look over Hadeon first, checking for a pulse and finding it weak. I curse again, ripping the bottom of his shirt and using it to wrap around his bleeding side before laying my head down on his chest. Tears slip down, mixing with the dirt and blood on my face.

I want to cry. I want to stop and lay down and cry.

Why am I even doing this? Why did I leave the comfortability of the castle?

His shallow breathing moves my head.

"I can't do this…" I cry, my voice is raw. "I can't do this Hadeon." Tears continue to flow. What was I thinking? There is no way I can possibly do this.

A ravens cry comes from above and I jerk my head up, searching around us for something making the noise. Nothing.

I quickly dry my tears, trying to calm my heart.

Another chime happens and this time it is not a bird. Now in view, a glowing dark blue light spirals around the wind before coming to a sudden halt next to me.

It flickers at me, almost as if it is trying to communicate.

"What are you?" I ask in a whisper, trying to think back on all the books I've read. I know of many, if not all, the lores from both kingdoms, and I search my brain for one.

It hops around me before meeting my gaze and turning its head North, where the Court of Dusk reigns. It hops three times North and I can only assume it's trying to keep me going. I stand, trying to keep my breathing even.

Then, more blue lights appear, trailing North, one after the other. I freeze.

The Will O' The Wisps.

I've only ever read the stories about them. The ghostly blue orbs are said to be the work of elemental spirits, and were thought to lure travelers astray down dangerous paths, where many don't come back from.

I can't stop my brain from yelling at me, telling me not to follow them. But, there's something familiar and I want to trust them. They're going in the very direction I was already going. It can't be that bad. I don't have a better fate if I stay.

I have to continue.

I look at Hadeon and take a deep breath before making sure he's breathing still, even if it is shallow, and place his body just as before, back on top of mine.

Another half hour and I should be over the border.

Please, Gods, help me through this.

The lights float through the air as I trail after them, trying to focus on the ground in front of me and not the duration of time I have left.

I should work on what I'm going to say to the king and get my mind off of the pain.

'Hello, Your Grace, please allow me (an enemy to your country), and my guard who is half dead (also an enemy to your country) to reside in your dark and gloomy castle where bones rest as lamps and the bedding is made of thorns.'

Absolutely not.

I do not know for certain what their castle is like at all, but it's from rumors I have heard.

'Please help me get revenge on your enemy by allowing me the courtesy of using your army for war.'

I cannot insult him. The predicament I have, though, is the fact that I do not know him. I do not know if he is truly evil or maybe misunderstood. He could have started all the crazy rumors himself, truly, if he wanted to. But I don't see what good it will do unless it's to keep everyone away— which sounds dark and gloomy, right?

Hadeon had not told me much, and while he had made it seem as if he did not know much, I know him. And I know he's keeping something from me. I'll get it out of him whether he likes it or not. If we even live through this.

The wisps eventually fade out and stop leading the way, so it's safe to assume I'm either about to die or get very lucky and find what I am looking.

I look down, seeing the blood ever-so-slowly seep from my wound when I note the dark tint.

Why must this happen to me? Have I not been a great person? Humble? Kind? Generous?

I spent over two decades becoming the perfect woman— the perfect wife. The perfect Queen. And it all ends with this? Poisoned by a blade from the meaty hands of a mediocre bounty hunter?

I keep trudging along the path, trying to keep from dropping Hadeon again but the big meaty brute is getting heavier with each minute that passes and I'm not sure how much longer I can hold on.

My feet start getting heavy next, my arms after that. I'm staring at the ground, keeping track of my movements.

I can't do this much longer. My head rises to look up again so I don't hit a tree.

I-

My words flee my mind.

In front of me are trees— multicolored trees in a straight line going further than what I can see in opposite directions from East to West. *The Border.*

My body cries in relief. I know logically I have longer to go. But, there is a certain danger on this side of the continent. It's a guessing game for the North side and I am taking my chances.

I stumble forward, walking the last few steps to the entry tree, the only orange one from what I can tell within my eyesight. No one else is around, thankfully.

Each tree is a different color, signifying the Gods and Goddesses, before starting over when it hits the last one.

Purple trees for the Goddess Althea of healing; blue for the Goddess Terra of earth, water, and sky; black trees for Nyxie, the goddess of night and death; white for the God Sorin of day and life; red for the Goddess Gyda of war, wisdom, and fire; the God Kallias has a pink color for love and beauty; Conan, the God of animals is green; and finally in the lineup is yellow for Lumi, the Goddess of storms—

before starting with white once more. I see an orange tree where I am but in the books, they state there is only one orange every so often but not many. Maybe 5 in existence. Orange is not for a God or Goddess but for the keeper of the trees.

I thank them, every single god and goddess in existence.

This. This is what I have suffered the last few days for.

"We made it," I whisper to Hadeon as I reach the edge of the trees.

A glimpse through, the narrow opening within the orange tree tells me I made it.

I slowly step through, careful not to trip or drop him.

"We made it, Hade," I repeat, knowing he likely isn't awake. After passing through the threshold, I smile. I smile truly for the first time in a long time. I gently set him down once more, taking a breath.

But, now, my vision gets spotty. "Oh no." My voice trembles out, barely audible. I quickly look around, assessing my surroundings when I spot the large group of beings in front of us. I stop, placing my hands on my knees to lean forward for a fuller breath. Then, a man steps forward— no. Not a man. A fae, a King rightfully. His build is similar to, if not slightly larger than, Hadeon's. He's close enough for me to see his familiar eyes.

Dark eyes that look onyx stare back at me. His face showing nothing as his eyes trail over every inch of Hadeon and myself— while I, barely stable, take a step in front of him protectively.

When his eyes twitch and narrow, I know it. I'm going to die and the King Eryx of Khyrel is going to be the one to do it.

But, I cannot fight them.

Thankfully, my vision goes black and I fall to the soft mossy forest floor, unconscious.

Chapter 11: Waiting

Eryx

As I stumble into my room, the first thing I notice is the imposing four post bed at its center. The black sheets and pillows match the dark wood frame while swirls of purple and gold add a touch of opulence. Against the back wall, a door leads to my personal bathing chambers, a luxurious space with matching dark walls accented by splashes of gold and hints of vibrant purple that remind me of my younger days. On the opposite wall, a large wardrobe full of a king's array of clothes stands next to a grand desk and chair, fit for royalty. This room exudes wealth and extravagance in every detail, a true reflection of my status.

As I make my way toward the bath, my mind already weary from the day's events, a sudden sense of alertness strikes through me. My hands instinctively flare out, casting shadows around me as I turn to face the balcony. In the distance, a woman stands with her back to me, her gaze fixed upon the shimmering aurora borealis dancing across the night sky. Her pale hair billows in the wind, almost blending in with the wispy green and pink lights above. Drawn by a strange pull, I walk toward the open doors and step onto the balcony, feeling a gentle breeze brush against my skin and playfully tousle strands of my hair. The air is crisp and cool, carrying a hint of floral scents from the garden below. In this moment, everything else melts away and all that exists is the beauty before me.

"This is possibly the dumbest thing you could do."

The sound of my voice echoes through the empty room, but she acts as if she can't hear me. I take a hesitant step forward, crossing over the threshold of the doorway and onto the cold, cemented balcony that overlooks the city. "Hello? Are you deaf?" I ask, my hand reaching out to grab her shoulder and turn her toward me.

Just as my fingers brush against her skin, she gasps and whirls around. But before I can catch a glimpse of her face, my eyes fly open and I'm awake. The memory of the dream fades away, leaving nothing but a lingering sense of longing and unanswered questions.

I rest on my throne, heart beating from my chest as I'm now staring at the empty room before me. It feels cold but not from temperature. The sky is dark outside, allowing the cast of moonlight and colored streaks from our aurora borealis to dance across the floors of any room with an open wall. Of course, my predecessors had to make it their entire personality, making the throne room an entire open concept. It's practically a giant balcony.

When I was younger, I was very fond of it. The magical feeling it gave, letting me believe I could be anyone or anything.

What a lie.

The dream wasn't a surprise. It's been recurring for years and I've learned to stop questioning it.

Hands snake up form behind me, a dangerous task in itself. But I know them, much to my dismay.

"Not tonight, Alyra." I tell her, already feeling disgusted by her touch. Her manicured hand continues and I snatch it, twisting her in front of me. "Not. Tonight." I know my eyes darken with fury and she sees it, "Let me remind you that disobeying your king is an act of treason." She jerks her hand from mine and scoffs, even with the fear radiating off her.

"You can't do anything to me, Your Grace, respectfully. My father is one of your higher lords on the council and I am his only daughter."

I stand, stalking closer to her, in all her smirking glory. "You mistake me for someone who gives care toward your fathers influence. Let me assure you, I do not, *disrespectfully*." I speak with arrogance dripping off the last word and her face drops before she huffs and stomps away like a child as I roll my eyes.

I stare ahead, awaiting my adopted brother to respond to me telepathically. As my second in command and my army General, he has a telepathy connection with me through magic, something we've used while he's been away on a solo mission.

"You know, this is why everyone believes you to be unhappy." My sister walks into the room, admiring the sky with her careless mannerisms, the dress she wears trailing hastily behind her. Some of the stress fades as she enters.

My sister, Esmeray, is the middle child. Our entire lives all she has ever done is support me; aside from the bullying and just being annoying to top it off. She knew how high our fathers expectations were for me but, she was never afraid to stand up to him. I held our fathers title in my hands my entire childhood. It follows me everywhere and so did his constant attention.

Our youngest sister, Ruelle, was the sweetest creation ever made. Our father catered to her every whim and wish. Not that we can blame him. But with his attention mostly on Ruelle and I, Esmeray would get into all kinds of trouble. Whether it be boys or fighting or even just making a mess in the kitchen or all over the castle. She wanted any attention from him she could get and he almost always refused because of it. But, after he died, I gave her the chance to prove herself and she did.

Our adopted brother, Hadeon, was my second-in-command but Esmeray was my third. She did everything he would have done if he were here the past five years. She was the temporary general to my army and they respected her because she's kicked all of their asses at least once. And while she is wild and strong and stubborn, she is a great confidant.

Panic courses through my veins as I realize that Hadeon is missing. My voice trembles as I admit the truth to my companion, "He's not responding to anything. He should have been here by now with the girl."

Her head snaps toward me, her eyes wide with concern. "What do you mean?"

I pause, my mind racing for an explanation. "Its just silence. I always know when he's sleeping but there's been no communication from him since we spoke an hour ago, they were close to the border. Something must have gone wrong."

I stand up abruptly, my heart pounding in my chest as I pace back and forth by the edge of the dais.

"Calm down, big brother." Her long slender fingers rest on my shoulder. "We'll go to the border, since it isn't a far ride, and we'll take some guards in case there is trouble. It's Hadeon, we're talking about." Her voice calm, cool, and collected. I otherwise would be as well if Hadeon hadn't been like a brother to us. When it came to family, I was tired of losing them.

"Gather who we need to take and inform Ruelle's guard. I don't want to wake her but in case we aren't back before she does waken then he can let her know of our whereabouts." I tell her before turning away and heading toward my suite to prepare myself for travel.

* * *

Our company consists of ten strong and determined men, all mounted on powerful horses. As we ride off toward the border, the adrenaline surging through our veins.

But in a cruel twist of fate, I can not simply cross over into the enemy territory without risking a full-blown war. Despite him being my brother, I can not risk such a dangerous move at this crucial moment. The unknown dangers that await us on the other side made me shudder with apprehension.

We ride fast, finally arriving after what feels like forever with the weight of his life looming over us.

I worry about Hadeon, but what about the princess he travels with? She could have easily changed her mind traveling here, turning her back on him. We know nothing about her true character. I know Hadeon has informed me of the young woman for five years, but people surprise you.

I jump off of the horse, handing the reigns to another guard, waiting for movement on the border. I feel my sisters presence next to me and we all go silent.

Hadeon has been a member of our family for as long as I can remember. My mother, known for her compassionate heart, took pity on the orphan boy. His parents were once part of our loyal guard, so we had already grown up alongside each other. Despite my father's initial disapproval, she took him in and raised him as one of her own. It wasn't until many years later that the king finally welcomed Hadeon into his heart- or whatever equivalent he had. He was a harsh ruler, driven by greed and a constant thirst for war.

As time passed, my father's health began to fail. His once strong heart and sharp mind were deteriorating, and he could no longer remember that we were his family. It was a difficult time for my mother and my sister Ruelle, but Esme and I were quick to move on from our grief. Our responsibilities to Khyrel and our family takes precedence over our personal feelings. My father had always been more of a king than a father to us, but we found a way to make it work.

For the past decade, I have ruled with Hadeon and Esmeray as my trusted advisors. The kingdom has prospered under our leadership, until about five years ago when a mysterious creature appeared before us with a prophecy that would change everything.

"Your Grace!" A guard calls out, riding toward us, "I tried to stop her!" The horse in front of him was familiar. I groan in irritation and march over as they ride to a halt.

"Ruelle! What are you doing here? I told your guard to make sure you stay put. It is dangerous out here." I scold her in my kingly voice.

"You may be king but you are my brother first and Hadeon is family to me too. You should've woken me." Her tone was firm and I groan again, rubbing my hand over my face.

Stubbornness might run in our family a bit.

"Everything is under control, Ruelle. It's fine." Esme tells her softly, playing the mediator.

But our baby sister will have none of it. "And if that were the case, you wouldn't be here. Something feels wrong to both of you. Do not forget I am High Fae too." She was too smart for her own good. She has always had the gift of empathy— mainly consisting of being able to tell what others are feeling but she has smaller gifts too. "What happened?" Before I can say anything, rustling noise comes from the threshold of the border trees and we all turn to watch.

A woman. "We made it, Hade."

Her voice is like a gentle whisper, floating through the stillness that surrounds us. My instincts urge me to move closer to her, but I remain rooted in place. Verena carefully eases Hadeon's limp body off her back and gently lays him on the ground, taking a moment to catch her breath. Her features are delicate and graceful, with a hint of exhaustion etched onto them. A small smile forms on her lips, accompanied by a light, airy laugh that fills the air like a sweet melody.

Her hair is as dark as midnight, a rare sight in Zorya where most have lighter locks. It is pulled back into a messy braid, revealing the elegant curve of her neck. Despite her petite frame, I can see the subtle definition of muscles beneath her tattered clothing, the black fighting leathers clinging tightly to her form.

I remind myself that this is the same woman I met only a week ago, who is now the wife of Dryston Whitewell— the same woman I sent Hadeon to find. Yet now, as I gaze at her exhausted but determined form, she seems like a completely different person. If not for Hadeon's confirmation of her identity, I would have thought this to be another fae entirely.

My time to observe her is quickly dwindling as she leans forward, placing her hands on her knees. My instincts kick in and I start to lunge forward, hoping to catch her before she falls. However, my sudden movement causes her to stand and move in front of Hadeon, as if guarding him. How close had they become over the past five years? The question lingers in my mind as I watch their interaction, trying to decipher the dynamics between them. Her protectiveness toward him speaks volumes.

I narrow my eyes at her, trying to gauge her next move and suddenly, she's unconscious and Esmeray and I start to move but my general tells me to stay back, pushing my chest away from their direction, and she rushes over with a few guards before picking the woman up off the ground and having them gather what looks to be a half-dead, Hadeon.

Chapter 12: The Betrayal

Verena

Water trickles down the side of my head, stirring me from slumber. I want to move, open my eyes, something. But, my body feels frozen and my eyes feel as if they are sealed shut. My throat feels no different.

"Shh." A voice close to me makes me flinch, but I don't think they notice. "She's still sleeping. Poor thing. I can feel the turmoil running through her heart." The voice was a young female and she spoke softly to whomever was in the space with us.

I try to orient myself, taking in the sensations around me. The bed beneath me is more comfortable than any I've ever slept on, and the fluffy comforter envelops me in warmth. Soft light filters through the room, creating a cozy yet not blinding atmosphere. A faint but soothing scent lingers in the air, and I can't help but relax into it.

"Why hasn't she woken?" A deep, velvety voice speaks from nearby, sending shivers down my spine. My subconscious recognizes it, but my conscious mind struggles to place it. I sense movement as the woman approaches him.

Come on, wake up! I mentally urge myself.

"She's been through a terrible ordeal, brother. The poison in her blood, the arduous travels, and being constantly on the run have taken their toll on her body and mind. She needs this rest." The feminine voice is gentle and comforting. An exasperated sigh escapes from him.

Impatiently, he urges her, "What? What are you not telling me?"

A heavy sigh escapes her lips. "She has a large wound on her arm... like someone tried to remove her skin." The thought of my wedded rune makes my arm throb with pain as I reflect on the agony of its removal.

Who are these people?

With great effort, I manage to pry open my eyes.

"She's awake," the female voice exclaims in surprise. She rushes over to me, placing a damp rag on my forehead. Cool water trickles down the side of my face and provides some relief. At least now I know why my head is wet.

I squint, trying to make out the unfamiliar faces in the dimly lit room. My eyes finally land on him, the Dark King, and I gasp in shock. Hastily sitting up, my body aching and groaning from the exertion, I push myself as far away from him as possible. The space between us serves as a barrier as I quickly grab the blanket to cover my not-naked body.

My attention is then drawn to the fae female standing before me, her hair tucked behind small, pointed ears. With a sense of wariness, I ask her, "Who are you?"

She raises her hands in a peaceful gesture, a sweet and soft smile gracing her features. "Hi there," she introduces herself. "My name is Ruelle. And may I know yours?"

"Princ- Verena. Just, Verena." I tell her, saddened by the reminder of my tragic fate at the Court of Dawn. I don't even want to glance at the king, last he heard or saw, I was married to Dryston and practically had become an rival to his kingdom.

"Well, Verena, I am the youngest princess of Khyrel. This is my brother, Eryx, King of Khyrel. I believe you both have met previously. He is mostly just here to make sure that I am safe and you are no danger to us. After you and Hade-"

The curiosity and concern in my voice interrupts her flow of words. "How is he?" I ask urgently, unable to contain my questions any longer. But before she can even answer, a barrage of inquiries spills out of me. "Wait, how do you know his name? Has he spoken to you yet? Is he awake?"

Her previously composed expression falters, as if she has revealed something she shouldn't have. She looks over at Eryx, her light eyes no match for his intense gaze. He pushes himself off the wall and saunters toward me, an aura of darkness radiating from him that seems to swallow up the room around us.

"He is fine, for now." He starts, sounding angry and squinting his eyes at me. "I would like to know why you carried him for over an hour to get to the border." His voice is firm and steady. His dark and deep eyes are cold and calculating as they watch me. I can feel the heat radiate from his surprisingly tan skin. He looks as if he is trying to be intimidating but for some reason, I can't find it in me to care once the initial shock has worn off. I know I should be afraid of him, especially after hearing what Hadeon said to me, but I can't. Not after the moment between us at the gala. I know the risk of coming here and honestly I'd rather die than be in the Court of Dawn.

"I'd like to know why you haven't killed me already. You know who I am so I can only assume that you want something from me." I counter, trying to dig for answers, feigning courage with the Dark King. His right eyebrow quirks up before turning away and taking a few steps back before looking at me again as he leans against the wall. I release a breath, holding it steady as my heart pounds in my chest.

If he wants something, maybe it'll help him feel more inclined to help me with my situation.

"I know who you *were*." I'm not sure why, but if it were anyone else that would feel like a slap to the face. When he said it, though, it sounds… inviting. A challenge to show who I truly am now. The only problem was, I don't know. "I haven't killed you because I know you aren't a threat." Before I can defend my capabilities, he continues. "I know you are not a threat because as far as I am concerned, nothing is more dangerous than I am on this continent and I don't exactly expect you to get the better of me." I glare at him, hoping he can feel my discontent. Even after the confusing dance— that lingers in the back of my mind— I want to fight my immediate attraction to him. I want to not like him. Even at the gala there was something pulling me toward him. Does he feel it too?

My eyes dart around his face, taking in every detail — the curve of his jawline, the dimple on his left cheek, the flecks of black in his brown eyes. Try as I might to keep my gaze locked on his face, it inevitably travels down his body. His casual attire does nothing to diminish his attractiveness; if anything, it only adds to his charm. I take a deep breath and decide to give him some information, hoping to distract myself from his alluring presence.

I thought the only place Dryston wouldn't look was Khyrel but maybe I am so predictable that this is the first place he knew I'd come. It has to be why there's a bounty on my head over there. "Hadeon has been my royal guard for five years. It started when he saved me from being attacked and the former king titled him fresh out of training. He knew I wasn't getting any training at all as the princess so he has been secretly training me for five years, building my muscles, making me earn my skill, allowing me to trust and hone in on my intuition and instincts. And he is my only friend, as pathetic as that is to hear." I humorlessly chuckle and stare at my hands as I pick at the nail beds cleaned of the dirt and blood that had been caked within. "I had a duty in the court, that is all I was good for. But, he saw me for more than the future queen. He saw me as a person, someone worth more than a crown on her head or the womb in her body." Glancing back up at them, Ruelle stares sadly at me while King Eryx just stares, almost looking bored.

"Your point?" Eryx asks, impatiently.

"*So*, I carried the giant lug of a male because he is the only family I have left." I tell them truthfully, waiting for the pity looks from him and his sister but they don't come. A look of understanding passes between the two of them. While she looks sad, it isn't pity and I'm thankful. "And to answer your burning questions about my arm; it *was* my wedded rune. I couldn't risk Dryston tracking us so I cut it off before we left." I tell them, watching Ruelle's eyes widen in shock. Eryx raises a brow as if he's genuinely surprised and I smirk to myself.

After a moment of silence, King Eryx meets my gaze, his jaw clenching profusely as his dark eyes stare. "Ruelle will help you with any questions or concerns. As of this moment, you are her guest since she has practically begged me to let you stay. She likes strays. For now. Until I decide what else to do with you. But do not believe that I trust you and I do not believe you will do us any good being here." He stands away from the wall, kissing his sister on the cheek as his right hand brushes down her hair and turns away.

She lets out a light scoff once the door is shut, pointing at her brother's long-gone figure, "He exaggerates. I did not *beg* him." Ruelle stresses to me, her cheeks become red and it warms my heart a bit. "I just said you should stay because I trust you and that goes a long way with him." She laughs shyly.

"Is he always that *friendly*?" I ask, sarcasm dripping. Her laugh is more bubbly and light like she doesn't carry any stress or worry now. That makes me smile.

"He'll warm up to you, promise. He's protective of his family and having you here could be dangerous since you were Princess—soon to be the Queen Dawn. But, like I said, I trust you and my word is the most trusted one. I've never lied to him and I have empathetic abilities." She says proudly, sitting on the edge of the bed.

Ruelle was a beautiful young fae. Her small nose suits her small frame. Her skin was paler than her brothers, which fit the Dusk vibe. Her hair was black as night, just as his was but her eyes are blue, while his are so dark they look black but when he moves his head and turns toward a light, there was a faint brown tone.

"Can you get me some food, please? I am absolutely starving." I smile and she jolts up.

"Oh, my Gods! Of course! I can't believe I didn't think of that! Be right back!" She exclaims and excitedly leaves the room.

As soon as the door shuts, my lungs release a large breath.

Now that I am alone, I can properly freak out in silence. What did I get myself into?

* * *

Once I had my stomach full and my mind calm, Ruelle told me we can see the castle. It was daylight still but the night will be arriving soon and she was very excited to show me the throne room.

"I am sure you heard through rumors that we are really only awake during the night and while this can be the case, it's mainly our city, Asterlayna. It's a mouthful, I know. We also call it Aster as a shorter name. She is the city that never sleeps. Most of the shops don't anyway. Some do close during the night..." Her tone is cheery as she rambles and I tune her out for a period of time. I am not sure if I can handle her being so joyful. I am supposed to be their enemy, why is she being so nice?

Ruelle waves and greets everybody we pass and it's nice to see someone part of their court so hospitable. No one was like that in the Dawn Court.

It makes me second-guess everything I thought I knew about Khyrel.

As we walk, court members gaze at me, curiosity in their eyes.

"Can I see Hadeon?" I ask quietly, not wanting others to hear as I cut off her babbles. She looks at me as we walk and I note something in her eyes I can't read.

"Of course!" She said in her cheery tone. The sun was fully set by the time we are finished looking at every other room she showed me, gossiping about other court members.

There was something off about this place. About her and the king. There was a secret, of that I was sure. I buried my true self down deep for decades so secrets are something I know well.

"Welcome to the most breathtaking room in all of the continent," she beams, her smile contagious. With a graceful sweep of her hand, she opens a side door that leads to a grand balcony-like space. The walls are simply made up of open arches, giving way to the northern side of the castle and offering an unobstructed view of the night sky above. The moon shone down, casting its gentle light upon the floor below. Pillars decorated with ornate sconces line the edges of the room, providing gentle illumination to the already beautifully lit space. And as if to further emphasize the enchanting ambiance, there was no roof above, allowing for an uninterrupted view of the twinkling stars above us.

"I need to see her. To explain." A familiar voice spoke out. I had thought the space was empty, but now two male voices are audible the further we walk into the room.

"She doesn't know yet. If she did, we'd hear about it. I am sure. Something tells me she isn't one to show her anger quietly." This voice was the king. The other sounds much like Hadeon.

"With all due respect, Eryx, you do not know her. I do. I have spent five years with her. She hides her emotions well, she had to." A huff from the king follows that response.

What in the Underworld are they talking about? Explain what?

Ruelle clears her throat, making Hadeon jump from surprise and he stares at Ruelle before looking at me and smiling wide. "Verena." He breathes out, rushing over. I meet him halfway before wrapping my arms around him, eyes tearing up.

"I thought I had lost you." My voice wavers, my feelings over-whelmed. I have been trying not to think about his health but it's all I could do. His arms follow my lead, wrapping around me as one of his hands brush my hair down. My eyes squeeze tight, relishing in his comfort in this foreign place, before opening them and meeting eyes with the king. A look that I am not familiar with flashes in his eyes, his fists clench on the thrones armrests as shadows billow around. He looks angry but why would he be?

"You would never lose me, I swore my loyalty to you, Verena, and I meant it." He pulls back, staring into my eyes before glancing at the royal family duo and back at me. "But, you are not the only one I have sworn my loyalty to." He takes a deep breath and I can't help but wonder why. Obviously, I know this. He took an oath to the king.

"I understand how royal guards are graduated, Hadeon." I let out a shaky laugh, wondering why we are having this conversation in front of the royal family.

He shakes his head, "When I told you that Dryston is not my king, I meant it. You were at my graduation in Zorya. I swore loyalty to *my* king, not *the* king." I step back from his grasp, shaking my head, confusion lining my features.

He glances back at King Eryx and I shake my head again, "No." All eyes are on me. "No, absolutely not. Are you trying to tell me your king is Eryx? You're from a small town in Zorya, how would Eryx be your king?" He speaks to me with his eyes; five years with someone will give you that. "No." I shake my head profusely, my hands keeping anyone from nearing and I start stepping back further and staring at the floor as tears brim my eyes.

But he says it out loud anyway. "I am not from Zorya, V. I am Khyrelian." I shake my head more and he takes a step closer but I throw my hands out further, staring at him with betrayal featuring in my teary gaze.

"No! Do not come closer to me. I do not *know* you." I speak and the hurt in his eyes makes me want to take it back.

"I know it's not easy to hear, Verena but it is the truth. There is an entire reason you do not know! I-"

"The reason is to make me look pathetic!" I yell. "You made a fool of me." My voice breaks at the end. I clear my throat, willing the tears to not gather in my eyes. "You *lied* to me. I thought you were my friend," A humorless laugh leaves me, "my *only* friend. How pathetic, the princess is so desperate for just a sliver of affection, of friendship, of someone who would accept her for who she truly is, that she completely ignored all signs pointing to a spy!" My voice stays raised, anger radiating off me in waves. King Eryx stands from his throne but betrayal burns my heavily beating chest. My hands shake and my eyes continue to water. I do not even care if it offends the king. My life had already been turned upside down and now this?

"No, of course not. You are not pathetic and I am not a spy, Verena, I was sent-" A voice clears, interrupting him and we look at the king, who is the culprit keeping him from speaking. I narrow my eyes at him before looking back at Hadeon, hurt filling his eyes.

"Loyalty to both," I laugh again, "Wow. It's all clear to me now

111

why Dryston's abuse always went unpunished. It wasn't a lack of knowledge or understanding on your part; you knew exactly what was happening and probably even found amusement in it with your little circle of friends here. As the *weak and pathetic* princess of Zorya, I realize now that I was nothing but a source of entertainment for you. How foolish I was to think there could be an escape from this fate. I should never have come here." I turn sharply and storm toward the main doors, ready to leave.

Hadeon grabs my arm, keeping me from walking out of the room. "Verena..." He says, more hurt spilling from his voice, willing me to understand his dilemma. "Please." He begs quietly. I want to believe the tears in his eyes are real but my heart will no longer be fooled.

"What hurt the most, Hadeon, is while I carried you for over an hour on my back, both of us poisoned and bleeding out, I cared more about saving you than myself. I wanted to get you through that border in hopes of giving you a better life that was far from me, my emptiness or even my lack of title. I didn't want to but I was willing to part from you to give you something more than I could ever have now. I was fully prepared to die in enemy territory as long as you'd live."

With a sharp and sudden movement, I wrench my arm free from his grasp. My heart pounds in my chest and tears prickle at the corners of my eyes before falling free. I squeeze my eyelids shut and take a deep breath, willing myself to stay strong. Without looking back, I slip through the door, the cool air hitting my face— a welcomed relief after the heated exchange. "Fuck!" His voice yells out, audible through the doors. The sound of my footsteps echo loudly in the empty hallway as I make my escape. I *almost* hope he chases after me. That our friendship means more to him, regardless of what I said. But I know him well enough and I know he will respect my wishes even if it kills him.

Chapter 13: Little Bird

Verena

A s I walk through the moonlit night, my only possessions are the tatters of clothing from Ruelle that clung to my body and the dagger I snuck out. The chill in the air was not unbearable, but it seeps into my bones nonetheless. As I made my way from the castle, the forest surrounding it seems to envelop me in its dark embrace. The moon casts eerie shadows through their branches.

I lost track of time, but I know it had been hours since the sun had set. The scent of pine and damp earth fills my senses as I trod on the soft grass, slick with evening dew. The usual cacophony of nature sounds was absent, leaving an eerie silence in its wake.

My cheeks are still sticky from the tears that had stained them earlier. But now, they were dry and stiff against my skin, a reminder of the pain and heartache that had led me to this lonely place under the stars.

I cannot believe Hadeon has been Khyrelian this entire time and lied to me about it. He could have helped me escape Dryston long ago but instead, he ignored it. Ignored me. Did he even have a plan to get out of the castle after he was beaten nearly to death? Was he going to leave me? Just that easily?

There are so many questions I needed answer to. The anger surges through me and I can't hear another word— another lie come from his mouth.

He was the only one I have trusted since my mothers death. The only fae who cared about my well-being, not just as a future queen but as a person. Five years have gone by and I just now realize I know so little about him! How could I have allowed myself to get close to him? I should have known as future queen that the only person I can count on is myself. The more I think about it, the more I feel wretched and deplorable. There's a self-destructive ember in me wanting to burst and just stop caring. How could I let myself get so desperate for another being to genuinely care about me?

I want to understand why but I also don't. I'll find another way to get my revenge on Dryston without Eryx and Hadeon's help. I'll-

My breath catches in my throat as I come to a sudden stop, gazing up in awe at the dazzling display of colored lights painting the night sky. Blues and purples swirl and dance across the black backdrop, making the stars seem like mere decorations in comparison. It's like something out of my wildest dreams, but even more vibrant and real. Tears prick at my eyes, but this time it's not from sadness or fear — it's pure wonder and joy. This is something I never knew I was missing. The same unfamiliar energy that pulsed through me during my encounters in Zorya now hums within me again, but this time it's soft and soothing instead of intense and overwhelming. I realize that this must be what Ruelle was trying to show me in the throne room — the magnificent Aurora Borealis in all its glory. Unlike back home where we could only catch glimpses of it, here it reveals itself every night without fail, unhindered by any buildings or structures. My jaw hangs open as I stand transfixed by the wondrous sight before me.

Not even the Aurora Australis is this beautiful, to me at least. It feels as if everything I have ever imagined clicks into place. I close my eyes, taking a deep breath in.

There is a reason I am here. Fate led me down this path. I can't give up now, I have to make Dryston pay. I open my eyes again and wipe the tears away, not wanting to miss any more of this.

For reasons unknown I have been dreaming of these lights my entire life and the marked hand for at least ten years. This is where I am supposed to be.

A noise breaks me from my watchful gaze, hearing sticks crunch. I was a bit further from the castle, I hadn't thought anyone had followed on foot but it's hard to hear anything over my sobs.

I look around; trying to see something, anything.

A mysterious figure appears before me, their silhouette shroud in darkness. Despite my best efforts, I can not make out any distinguishing features.

"You have quite the journey ahead of you, little bird," a voice spoke from the figure. It was close yet distant, with a feminine tone and an air of wisdom and age. The accent carries a sense of history, something rarely heard nowadays. My eyebrows furrow in confusion.

Naturally, I ask the only question that came to mind. "Who are you?" A soft laugh echoes through the empty space around us, as if we are in an expansive amphitheater.

"The questions you should be asking are: Who am I? Why am I here? What is my journey?" The figure steps forward, revealing themselves to be a woman illuminated by the moon and scattered lights. With each step she takes, her presence seems to grow stronger, pulling me in like a moth to a flame.

Her skin is a dark brown but stark white paint decorates her face with runes and markings so old, they were not in books anymore. Her smile isn't normal, its stretched across her face like something from nightmarish folklore. White runes decorate her arms, neck, chest, and one single one on her forehead in blood red. The nails on all four of her arms are longer than what is deemed normal. A snake wraps around one, looking to be as her pet with orange, black, and white scales. Where her eyes should be, are only black holes. And her hair is a dark silver, long enough to tangle around her bare feet while her gown is old, ragged, and creme colored from aging. She doesn't look as old as her accent deemed her to be. She was... pretty.

"Thank you, child." She says, hearing my thoughts and suddenly all the hairs rise on my skin and my blood runs cold.

"You- you can hear my thoughts?" I ask, my voice raw and shaky. She stalks closer, another hand petting the snake as it eyes me.

"They are loud." It was a state of fact. Her arm darts out as she grabs mine, holding my wounded forearm up as she peers down at it.

With a sudden burst of strength, I try to wrench my arm from her grasp, but she holds on with an iron grip. Her other hand tears away the bandage, exposing my raw and bleeding wound. Before I can even react, she presses her fingers into the open flesh, smearing my blood across her lips as she licks them hungrily. I wince in pain and struggle to break free, but her strength is unyielding. Desperately, I try to remain calm knowing that if she truly wants me dead, she would have killed me already.

A low hum escapes her lips as she places her now bloodied fingers back onto my wound, this time with a gentleness that sends shivers down my spine. In a voice full of ancient power, she mutters words in a language I've never heard before.

As she pulls back and releases me, I watch in awe as my wound miraculously disappears and my skin is left unblemished. "What is the purpose of my journey?" I demand, emboldened by the fact that she has just healed me. She smirks with a twisted smile that refuses to budge, still stained with my blood.

We're a couple of feet apart now and she trails a set of fingers through my black locks. "The white is prettier." She throws me off guard before continuing, "Your questions can be answered at a price." My eyes widen at her remark. How did she know of the white?

"I have nothing to my name but I can grant you-"

She cuts me off, "Your dagger." Nothing was in my name now; no money, gold, or anything worth value. But, owing a favor was something very few beings turn down. I was going to offer that. The dagger surprises me.

"Why?"

"Does it matter?" Her question makes me ponder. It was a gift from Hadeon and while I might regret gifting it to her later, I need answers now. The curiosity too much to turn down.

Her left brow picks up, surprise written on her face as I pull the blade from under my dress and hold it out to her. Something tells me she is not surprised often but she graciously takes it. Why do I feel like I made a mistake? "Your journey will not be safe. You will have to make hard choices. Trust the king. You and the Dark King will be important together in this journey. The prophecy..." The holes where her eyes should be glow golden, "together you shall bring about war, pain, misery and the utter desolation of the continent..." Her words shake me to my core. Why the fuck would I stay with him then?! "Or... you will empower this continent to flourish in a way never seen before."

"Why Eryx?" I ask her.

"The Dark King is already tied with you, such a gift happened by the fates, decades ago."

"What? What does that mean?" The deep thunderous sound of hooves break us from our conversation. It's hard to see the figure in the darkness and I go to ready my hand on my blade before realizing I gave it to the witch.

"Woah, careful now. Wouldn't want you to hurt yourself." Rumbles the familiar deep and sinfully smooth voice of King Eryx. I roll my eyes at him, even as my heart picks up pace and chills tickle my spine. I look back toward the lady but she is nowhere to be found.

"I'd much rather hurt you first." I spit back, turning away from her direction and facing him. He rides his horse closer before stopping dead in my path and jumping from the steed.

"You have no right to speak to me that way, I am King." He stares me down, more shadows billow around us and I scoff— because I clearly have a death wish— and take one step toward him, trying to make him believe I am not afraid of him.

"I care extremely little of your title or anyone else's. It gives you no automatic respect from me, not anymore." I try to go around him but he stops me by grabbing my arm and I swiftly turn around before throwing my open palm over his cheek, leaving a pink print on his tan skin. "Do *not* touch me without my permission." I leave my head high, which is easy since I have to stare up at him.

He rubs his jaw, an arrogant smirk resting on his face. "Are you done abusing me?" He asks and I scoff before trying to turn again and walk away. "You had no right to speak the way you did to Hadeon. You have no idea the sacrifices he made for you." His voice was firm now, irritation slipping through. But, it's enough for me to stop.

I can't seem to get the witch's words out of my mind. They echo around like it's an empty chamber.

I look up at the northern lights again, sighing. "I have every right. He is almost worse than Dryston ever was. Dryston never hid his true colors from me. Hadeon has been lying about who he was this entire time. I can never believe another word that comes from his mouth." I can't even force myself to look at the king, how are we going to save the continent if we can never see eye to eye. He does not respect me.

"Then believe *me*. You have no reason not to trust me." He's closer now, I can feel heat radiating from his body as he towers over me from behind. I roll my eyes.

"I do not know you," I whisper, suddenly unable to speak normally.

"Yet." He says. "I sent Hadeon to look for a high-fae woman. We knew she stayed in the court, her hair white as the moon with a dark blue streak and indigo eyes. She doesn't belong there and whichever higher power knew that, made me believe it too when a witch crossed my path to tell me." My chest rises and falls rapidly at the mention of the witch and my natural hair color. I can't breathe. "I sent him to look for her and when he found you I knew we couldn't just take you. There was no proof that you were her since *your* hair is black. He did not want to get involved with you except I became aware of a threat to your life and couldn't take the chance of us being wrong. His orders were to protect you, yes, but at some point you became more important than anything to him, even me." Did the witch tell him the same prophecy? His words make sense, my heart wants to believe him. I can't imagine being so important to someone they would blatantly disobey orders from their king with such a high standing.

"So you just sent him into enemy territory, planning to leave him there? For how long?" It doesn't sit right with me. "Why?" I was breathless and everything in me was screaming to turn around to face the king, so I did. I look up into his eyes, dark like a warm autumn night sky, vacant of clouds, stars, or even the pretty lights yet beautiful anyway. "Why?" I push when he doesn't answer the first time. He looks as if he's searching for something in me.

Moments pass, silence surrounds us and the lights reflect off our faces. His voice is deep but quiet, "I do not know. I didn't plan on leaving him there forever, not even for as long as he was. I told him if you were safe and that he could come home but he grew to care for you, Verena. He *is* your friend. He told me he had to stay but he never told me why."

Gods damn it. I knew I had no choice but to stay. From his speech and the witch? I needed answers I couldn't get on my own.

Somehow, my talk in the woods with Eryx and the witch convince me to head back to the castle. I try to walk, but the irritatingly handsome fae king threw me over the back of the horse he rode upon. Then continues to position me in front of him, pressing his very warm and frustratingly strong body against me for the duration of the ride.

I need to speak with him about my plan, but with all the information being dumped into my hands, it was hard to find the right time. Does he know about the prophecy? What will the witch want as her favor? Do I even trust her?

What do I do if he says no? I mean, he seems to have a strong dislike for Dryston anyway, getting my revenge on him should seem like fun for the Dark King.

What did she mean when she said our fates were already combined decades ago? I had never met the Dark King. It didn't make any sense.

The horse slows at the stables and he jumps down, grabbing my waist and setting me down right after. It happens so fast that I barely have any time process it.

"Goodnight, Verena. You should get some rest." He steps back to take leave but I grab his arm, making him turn around again. His glare on my hands makes me jolt away and rest them against my chest as if he burned me.

"I have a proposition for you that I would like to speak with you about," I tell him. The worst he can say is no. I need to do this.

"Tomorrow. There is an issue I must handle." He leaves then and I somehow find myself back in the luxurious room all alone.

The bed was giant with four posters hanging in dark blue sheer tulle, matching the black sheets and duvet. It had a couple of floor-to-ceiling windows, facing North.

The floor was tile, black with gold marble. All metallic decor seems to be the same; gold. It adds a beautiful contrast to the black. I would think they'd have silver to match the moon. I'd have to remember to ask Ruelle at some point about it.

My eyes narrow as I scrutinize the intricate carvings on the ancient wooden bed frame. The image of a raven, accompanied by a sinister snake, repeats itself throughout the castle. But in this room, the birds outnumber the serpents. At first glance, it appears as if the snakes are attacking or consuming the ravens. Yet upon closer examination, there is a surprising harmony between them.

Suddenly, my mind flashes back to the old witch's words — her sneering laughter ringing in my ears. "Little bird," she had called me mockingly. Could she have known about this symbol? About Eryx's family crest, bearing the same snake and raven? My heart quickens with fear and realization — was Eryx the snake in this scenario? And was I meant to be the innocent bird in his grasp?

Dread settles over me like a shroud as I realize how little I truly know about this Court of Dusk and its mysterious symbols. And for the first time, I am overwhelmed by questions without answers.

Chapter 14: Trust

Eryx

"What did you say? To make her come back?" Esmeray asks, her voice full of curiosity and concern. We— my sisters, Hadeon, and myself— all sit in the office, adjacent to the throne room. The room is furnished with opulent decorations of gold, purple and blue, reflecting the grandeur of the palace. I take a deep breath before responding to Esmeray's questions. It had been several days since we returned from the woods.

"I told her most of the truth. That's all I'm willing to share." My tone is resolute, signaling an end to the discussion. While my words may have convinced Verena to return with me, there was something else at play in those woods. A mysterious force that even my horse sensed. Something happened within those trees.

"I hope you know what you're doing." Esmeray's concern is evident in her voice as she speaks again. I roll my eyes at her but she doesn't back down. Her mismatched eyes, one brown and one bright blue, stare intently at me as if trying to read my thoughts. "You know what the prophecy says, Eryx."

"Of course I know. It's been engraved into my memory since her funeral. It doesn't matter. It's not happening anyway. The only reason she is staying, is so I can figure out *why* she's in the prophecy. Please leave me, I need to get this work done." I say, rubbing my temples to ease the creeping migraine. My sisters sigh in unison glancing to one another as if in some secret conversation, something I'm sure they practice, and Hadeon escorts them out before following them and closing the door.

I sit back in my chair, letting out a strong groan of frustration. I am so tired. I wish I never would've learned of that bloody prophecy in the first place, stupid witch.

As the sun dips below the horizon, casting long shadows across the palace grounds, I found myself drawn back to the woods where it all began. The forest looms dark with trepidation, the rustle of leaves sounding like whispers in the wind. Determined to uncover the truth that lay hidden within those ancient trees, I grab a lantern and set off into the fading light.

The path was overgrown and twisted, as if nature itself was trying to keep me away. But I push forward, my heart pounding with a mix of fear and excitement. These woods are dangerous to those with no knowledge of them. I continue wandering, hoping to find something of meaning, praying for the witch to show her face again.

* * *

Verena

Bringing up my proposition to Eryx feels like walking on thin ice. On one hand, he had been surprisingly kind to me in the woods and I can't help but feel drawn to him. On the other, he was the notorious Dark King— known for his cold demeanor and past tragedies. The thought of him with another woman, possibly the late princess who should have been queen, made my heart ache with jealousy. However, I push those feelings aside and try to focus on our mission.

Meanwhile, Hadeon seems to have all the inside information on Zorya's scandals while I was left in the dark. It frustrates me to no end as we sat in the library, attempting to learn about their culture. No matter how much I search, I can't find a reason for their crest depicting a raven and a snake. And even though Ruelle was by my side, I couldn't bring myself to ask her about it — she seems too kind to burden with such questions.

I have felt like a prisoner my entire life and after everything I have been through, I will not waste another second feeling the same.

"I need to speak with the king," I start, adding "please," for pleasantry. Ruelle, who sits with me in the library, jolts from my sudden speech.

"What of?" Ruelle asks. "I'm sure I can pass it along, he is very busy." She tries and I smile as if it's a welcoming idea.

"It is not something I can discuss with others. I will only speak to him about it and he will definitely want to hear it." She purses her lips, eyebrows furrowing, before nodding.

"I'll send a maid to see if he is available to meet with you." I nod and continue reading, trying to ignore the burning sensation from her stare. I was not going to be embarrassed in front of a whole court again, if he said no. This will be a private conversation.

I continue reading, pretending to be calm and collected but really on the inside, I was screaming.

Part of me wants to avoid men altogether after Dryston and Hadeon. I can't say I didn't love Dryston. We've been betrothed my entire life and for most of our childhood we are close friends. But, when I think back on it, he was always fond of bullying me before he stated that it was just because he loved me.

Thought I'd have to grieve my old life but being here, it's easy to slip into the way they live, to forget where I came from and what had happened to me. Was that a bad thing? Should I hate myself for it? In fact, I wasn't even sure I knew what I wanted anymore.

Ruelle's voice breaks through my thoughts, pulling me from my reverie. I stand up, letting her lead the way since I still had no clue where I was going in this massive palace. My heart pounds faster as we approach our destination — the king's office. I hadn't seen Hadeon since I came back, and to be honest, I was grateful for that. I wasn't ready to face him yet and I pray I don't run into him now.

We come to a halt in front of an ornate door but before Ruelle could knock, I step forward and do it myself. It gives me a small sense of control in this nerve-wracking situation. Ruelle gives me a supportive smile before Eryx's voice calls through the door.

"Good luck," Ruelle whispers, her hand on my shoulder. "I'll be out here waiting for you."

Her attempt at comforting words actually work, somewhat calming my racing heart.

I take a deep breath and step through the threshold into Eryx's office. The room matches the opulent style of the rest of the palace, but there's also a cozy feeling to it — perhaps due to the warm lighting and comfortable furniture.

"Verena, to what do I owe this visit? It was something to discuss in private?"

His observant gaze, filled with curiosity, fixes upon me. Despite his muscular build and imposing demeanor, there was a hint of exhaustion in his features that I can sympathize with.

Summoning my courage, I began to speak. "I have a proposition for you," I state confidently, though I can't hide the tremble in my voice.

He reclines in his chair, crossing his strong arms over his chest as they strain against the fabric of his tunic. Though he exudes an air of disinterest, I can sense a spark of interest beneath the surface.

As his intense gaze roams over me, I stand tall and try to steady my trembling hands behind my back. Taking a deep breath, I prepare myself for his response.

"Ah, yes. The proposition." He nods. "Not interested," he declares with finality, causing my stomach to drop to my feet.

"But you don't even know what it is," I protest.

"And I don't need to," he replies firmly.

"I disagree." I say louder, irritated like I have never been before. His eyebrows raise and I step closer to the desk, resting my now steady palms on the dark wood, ignoring the papers strewn about. "I have something you are very interested in. Hadeon might have been at court for five years but I have been there my entire life. I have been princess my entire life. I came here knowing Dryston would underestimate me. Hadeon might have been my guard, but he was not privy to information that I was. Getting raised and trained to be queen has it perks." I inform him. It's mostly the truth but I still can't get the picture of the war table out of my mind. When I went to drop off Dryston's wedding present, seeing where he planned to drop Zoryan scouts and army groups was something no one else saw.

My gaze remains locked with his, unyielding. A surge of determination electrifies my body, a feeling I've never experienced before but now crave. He leans forward, intertwining his long fingers and resting them on the desk. After a brief pause, he speaks. "Go on," he says, carefully considering his options. My eyes flick to the black marking on his hand, the one that appears in my dream. What did it mean? I push the thought away. Right now, my focus is on convincing him.

"I have all the information you could possibly want on Dryston and Zorya's plans to attack Khyrel. It's all stored in my brain," I tell him confidently. "But I can't do this alone. I need your help." Despite trying to make it sound simple, I'm still anxious about how he will react. "I want revenge. Against Dryston and against the court." These words are spoken with a fierce determination, fueled by a burning desire for retribution.

He smirks but I can sense the irritability from him, "I can just torture the information out of you and not help you in return."

"You can certainly *try*." This seems to make his arrogance pause. "But I personally do not believe anything you do to me can be worse than the emotional or physical torture I endured with *him*." His hands tense on his arm rests, squeezing them so tightly I was surprised it doesn't shatter. He rolls his shoulders back. Honestly he probably could do worse than Dryston did but I still wouldn't break, especially if it's the only leverage I had.

"How can I help you then?"

"Marry me."

He laughs.

He fucking *laughs*. My cheeks go red, suddenly, and I am ready to walk out but I fight against my urges. "You can't be serious," He chuckles out.

"Deadly serious. We don't have to necessarily follow through with a wedding or marriage. But when Dryston hears that you are getting married, he'll throw a hissy fit when he sees me by your side. A huge one. He'll make mistakes," I pace back and forth. " I start talking out my plan as I wave my hands around for emphasis, "You are on the brink of war with him because he is an asshole. He is already planning on attacking you first and I know how and where. You and I pretend to be engaged in a betrothal and it gives me enough power to get revenge. You get knowledge which is arguably more powerful than the strength you'd give me, and we destroy him. We can kill him." I breath heavy, out of breath from my rambling, waiting for an answer from him. He takes so long to answer that I doubt he ever will. I begin walking toward the door, "Think about it if you must. It is a seemingly big decision. I don't blame you for wanting to not risk it but I am speaking the truth."

I open it, about to start walking out of the room but his voice stops me. "Wait." I close the door.

"I care too deeply for this kingdom to endanger it with a war on our own soil. My court and people will not accept a simple marriage of convenience; they must believe that I have found true love." It surprises me to hear this from him, knowing his aversion toward women except for his family.

"They have such strong convictions?" I question, not used to a kingdoms whose people who care so much for a persons reason for marriage.

"Annoyingly enough, yes. And if we don't make them believe it, Dryston will not either and it will fool our plans. I will," He pauses, looking desperately uncomfortable s he adjusts his dress shirt, "I will have to court you, make it seem as if we are falling in love." He breathes out, pained by the thought. If I cared, it would hurt my heart but truthfully I do not. "We can not tell anyone other than Esmeray. I trust my court but not that much." I nod, agreeing even though I don't trust her but for now I will have to trust him. We will have to trust each other.

"Looks like we're getting married."

Chapter 15: Dinner with the Royal Family

Verena

As soon as I step out of his office, I breathed a sigh of relief. Finally, something was going my way. He trusts me, even if he had no choice, and he knew we could accomplish this. Ruelle's cautious smile greets me as she approaches. With her gentle demeanor and kind eyes, she was the epitome of sweetness.

"Everything go okay?" she asks in a soft voice. "I know he can be a handful."

I nod grateful for her kindness and assistance. "Everything is perfect, thank you Ruelle. For everything you've done for me here. I know it's not easy taking in an enemy, but I promise I mean no harm to your family, court, or kingdom. I am hoping to help all of you."

As if on cue, Hadeon appear from around the corner. His steps falter when he sees us standing in front of his intended destination. He looks up before his gaze settles on me and softens.

"Verena-"

I turn from him, facing the raven-haired woman next to me, "Ruelle I am ready to go back to the library." I smile at her, ignoring my former guard. "Away from liars." I almost feel bad for saying it and for acting as if I hate him. But the truth is that I hate myself more for not. I wasn't lying when I told Eryx about how hurt I was and how in my heart, Dryston never lied about who he was, just what my position in his court would be. Hadeon pretended to be my friend and lied to me for years. Sure, he couldn't exactly tell me his secrets from the start, but what about before my coronation? What about after I met Eryx? After he knew of my wavering loyalty to the Court of Dawn?

"Ladies," He bows in dismissal before slipping into the king's office and allowing us to take our leave. I want to forgive him and I will, sooner rather than later because he has been my only friend for all these years and I can't just give that all up. I won't. He is too important to me.

* * *

Ruelle and I continue reading in the library, enjoying the silence. I've tried learning more about this kingdom and the history of the continent that might have been left out in Zorya's book— a common theme I've noticed. Anything good or helpful about Khyrel isn't found in any books in the Court of Dawn.

"My mother would like you to join us for dinner." A deep voice sends chills down my spine. I jump from my spot, swiftly turning my head to look up into Eryx's eyes. Those deep gorgeous eyes that I want to hate but I can't seem to.

"I am not dressed for dinner." I inform him, running my hand over my outfit. "Are you sure it is a good idea?"

"Ruelle can help you to your room and she had the royal seamstress bring you some dresses. I'll see you in an hour." He leaves with nothing else to say. My brows furrow as he walks away. Was this apart of his courting? Inviting me to dinner with his family?

I blink my thoughts away and look at the youngest royal sibling.

"You did?" I ask, my heart clenching.

She smiles brightly, nodding before looping her arm in mine once we rise to our feet, "Of course! You are going to be here a while, at least I hope so, and I want you to be comfortable. So I had her make up some different options we'll try on and that way she knows what you like and do not." She spoke in her usual cheery tone.

We depart from the library, gliding through the corridors with ease. My admiration for the castle's layout grew with every step. It was a perfect blend of functionality and grandeur, and I found myself quickly becoming familiar with its winding paths and secret passages. The design of the entire structure surpasses even my wildest dreams, with towering spires and intricate stone carvings that seem to come alive in the glimmering torchlight. As we walk, I can't help but feel a stirring within me, as if this place held some kind of ancient power. Everywhere I look, the distinctive snake and raven crest adorn the walls and furnishings, a constant reminder to me of the witches words.

"I have one that is my absolute favorite. I think it'll fit you so well." She states, opening the closet in the room I've been staying in and pulling out a beautiful floor-length dress, it's a lovely violet color and has a long slit down the leg with delicate thin straps holding it up over my shoulders before crisscrossing the back, leaving my skin viewable until it reaches the small of my back.

"Oh wow. Are we sure I should wear that tonight? It's just dinner."

"Trust me, Verena, we all get dressed up for family dinners. Eryx is usually off doing something so we do not get a lot of dinners together anymore, since the funeral a few years back." She speaks sadly before shaking it off and thrusting the dress into my hands. "Try it on!" She sings before leading me to the divider so I get a little bit of privacy. I slip out of my current dress, staring at my body. I haven't been able to train again since I've been here, not even sure if they'll let me, but I made a mental note to ask soon.

131

The wine-colored mark on my hip bone catches my eye. The birthmark shaped like a bird. It wasn't big at all, tiny as if the size of two thumbs side by side. I almost believed it to be a raven, quite similar to the trimming around this castle.

I shake from my thoughts, removing my hand from my hip and getting into the beautiful violet dress. It fits snugly against my chest and bust before the material drapes naturally to the floor. "How does it fit?"

I let out a small laugh, "Actually, like perfection." I smooth my hands over the silky fabric. I wasn't allowed to wear many darker colors in Zorya, it was 'a bad look' since the court colors are pink and green. I love those colors too, but purple has always had my heart. It's a piece of me. It is the color that made me feel different from the hue of my irises. Children and adults alike pointed and whispered about my eyes many times when I was a young girl. It used to make me feel so out of place but once my parents died, I stopped caring so much about what they thought of my physical appearance.

A tear slips from my eye at the thought. It still doesn't feel real that I am no longer there in the court, like every time I wake up I'll be back and this would've been a dream.

"Hey now, no tears. Save that for tonight at dinner with our mother." Ruelle laughs softly, "She can be a very soft and warm woman and she can be a tough woman. She was queen after all and until she's comfortable with you, she might give you some grilling. But, you will be fine. She'll love you, I can tell." I smile at her, taking a deep breath and letting her help put on my shoes before touching up my hair and adding some rouge.

I had been here for a few days and had yet to step foot in the dining hall. I was trying to avoid everyone, avoid the questions. But, I know that with Eryx and I's plan, I'd have to be more open and amicable toward everyone else here. I don't have a problem with it, I just don't want to deal with more whisperings about my intentions.

We walk through the halls again, winding down until we reach the level that also held the throne room. Guards open the ornate double doors for us, and another woman walks up to the doors at the same time.

She appears to be youthful, perhaps only a few years younger than myself. A beautiful array of colored floral tattoos grace her arm, contrasting elegantly against her jet-black hair. Her eyes are a striking contrast, one a deep brown and the other a pale, almost ethereal blue. Her skin was fair and glows in the dim light of the room, similar in complexion to Ruelle but with a hint of Eryx's golden tan. The strapless dress she wore hugged her curves perfectly, accentuating her figure and drawing attention to her full chest and defined waist. As my gaze travels down her other arm, I can't help but notice the skull with a dagger piercing through it, and the seven tally marks on her chest. Despite my attempts not to stare, I couldn't deny the sense of power emanating from her. She was definitely someone important within the royal family, possibly even the middle sibling? But there was something about her energy that made me uneasy, like she could easily overpower me without breaking a sweat.

"Ruelle, you look beautiful. I see you dressed up in one of the gowns you ordered for Verena." She smirks. Ruelle smiles sweetly, a blush tinting her cheeks.

"It was too pretty to not."

She looks at me then, and it feels as if she were staring into my soul, "Esmeray," I assume she was announcing her name.

I try standing straighter, feigning confidence, "I'm Verena. It's nice to meet you. You are the middle sibling, yes? Ruelle's older sister?" I ask bravely, something akin to fear trickling along me, faint and confusing. There was no reason to be scared, so why did I feel it trekking up my spine?

133

Another smirk graces her face as she watches me adjust my standing and she nods. "Correct." She says nothing more as she steps in front of us and walks into the room. The fear flees from my body and I wrack my brain on what just happened. Ruelle walks side by side with me, sensing my discomfort. I was used to this, but it feels weird when you don't know anyone.

As I take in the room, my eyes fall upon the other dinner participants. Eryx sat at the head of the table, a regal and powerful presence emanating from him. On the opposite end was an older woman, her face lines with age but still bearing a striking resemblance to Eryx. Beside him sat Hadeon, his sharp features highlighted by the soft candlelight. And next to him was Esmeray, her delicate features seemingly glowing in this company.

The older woman must be their mother, I realize, noting the matching features that ran through the family. As my name was called, her gaze met mine and a flash of confusion flickers across her face. She stands and began to make her way over to me, her movements slow and deliberate as if she were lost in thought. The others at the table remained still, but I caught a glimpse of tension in Eryx's posture, as if he were ready to jump up at any moment.

"You..." She starts speaking but stops until she is standing directly in front of me. Her face softens and it seems like she snaps out of whatever thoughts were consuming her. "You are so beautiful." I can't help but throw a glance at Ruelle, who watches her mother with attentive eyes. But from her expression, I can tell that wasn't what she had intended to say. There was something more there, hidden behind those words.

"Hello, ma'am." I break the tension in the room, bowing my head. "I am Verena."

"Yes, you are." She lets out a light joyous laugh before looking at her children and back to me, "Where are my manners? My name is

Calanthe, former queen, and the mother of these four." She looks at me as if waiting for something but I'm not sure what reaction to give her.

"It's lovely to meet you." I smile, noting the way she warmly looks at me.

"You as well. Come. Sit and eat with us." She walks me to sit in front of Esmeray, next to Ruelle who takes Eryx's right but not the immediate chair next to him— that one stays empty.

I take my place at the table beside Ruelle, feeling Esmeray's intense gaze on me as I sat down. The room is full with a tense silence, interrupted only by the soft clinking of utensils against plates. I glance around at the faces of the royal family members, each one so different yet sharing a certain air of power and authority.

Calanthe, the former queen, raises her goblet and everyone follows suit. "To new beginnings," she proclaims, her voice strong yet tinged with a hint of sadness. We all drink, the wine warm as it trickles down my throat.

The meal proceeds with polite conversation, though I can sense an undercurrent of tension lingering beneath the surface. Esmeray's eyes never seemed to leave me, her gaze like a weight pressing down on my shoulders. Ruelle chats animatedly with Hadeon, their laughter filling the room, while Eryx sat stoically at the head of the table, his eyes flickering between each of us. But it's Calanthe who breaks the uneasy silence that had settled over the table.

"Verena, tell us about yourself. Where do you come from?" Her voice was soft, but her gaze was piercing, as if she were trying to unravel the mystery of my past with just a look.

I hesitate for a moment, unsure of how much to reveal. "I come from Zorya," I began cautiously, but before I can continue, Eryx cuts in.

"She was betrothed to Dryston and left because her and Hadeon's

135

lives were in danger, mother. Please do not bombard her with questions." His tone held finality and his mother drops it after their eyes spoke more than their mouths ever would.

How many secrets did this family have?

Chapter 16: Seren Fach

Verena

As we progress through the courses, Hadeon's eyes constantly dart toward me while I try my best to avoid his gaze. The royal family engages in conversation about tactics for the upcoming war with Zorya, but amidst the chatter and laughter, I find my thoughts wandering to the Dark King sitting across from me. He appears composed and at ease with his family, a stark contrast to the image I had in my mind of him before.

I can't help but be reminded of myself when defending Hadeon. And in hindsight, I understand why Hadeon did what he had, but I still struggle to fully trust him.

Suddenly, a figure enters the room and walks over to the king at his beckoning. They whisper something in his ear as I sip on my soup. Without warning, King Eryx slams his hand down on the table, causing me to jump in surprise. However, no one else seems fazed by this abrupt outburst, as if they have grown accustomed to such behavior from their ruler. My eyes remain fixed on King Eryx as he whispers a response back to the fae messenger. He then stands from the table and addresses everyone in the room with a commanding presence. "If you'll excuse me," he declares before swiftly leaving the room.

"He gets very protective of his kingdom, when something goes wrong it upsets him. He gets his anger from our father. It used to not be as bad but ever since Amaelya's funeral, it has been more than uncontrollable at times and we just have to ride it out." Ruelle informs me in a hushed reveal. I nod my head as if I understand.

We finish our meals and begin our departure to our own rooms But, as we step out of the dining area, Hadeon grips my arm softly.

"Verena, please, talk to me." Ruelle stops walking, waiting for me when she realizes I'm not following her.

"Hadeon, I understand why you did what you did. And I am sure I will forgive you since my heart would never allow me to hold a grudge against you. You had a duty and you followed it out. I appreciate everything you've done for me over the years but for right now, please just give me some time."

Hadeon's eyes drop to the floor, his grip loosening on my arm as he nods solemnly. "I understand, Verena. I will give you all the time you need." He releases me, "Just…" He pauses his leave, trying to find the right words. "I meant it. When I said you were my queen all those times. I know that title is no longer yours, but I will always view you as my queen. And I know you don't want to be friends right now so I will respect that. But, if you need anything, do not be afraid to ask." He steps back and leaves us standing in the middle of the hall.

"That was so regal of you," Ruelle speaks this time, breaking my trance from where he stands. "I know it's not easy to forgive, I've seen it firsthand with Esmeray and our father but you handled it well. I admire you, you know? You would make a great queen." I look at her, softly smiling.

"Would have," I confirm with her as we walk back to our rooms in silence. Ruelle gives my hand a reassuring squeeze before leading me down the corridor to our rooms.

As we settle in for the night, I found it difficult to shake off the events of the evening. The tension in the royal family, King Eryx's sudden outburst, Calanthe's peculiar behavior—it all weighs heavily on my mind. But amidst the chaos of emotions swirling within me, one thing remains clear: I need to uncover the secrets and mysteries that surrounds this family and myself.

The moon cast a silvery glow through the window, illuminating the room in a ghostly light. Ruelle takes to her room near mine.

As I lay awake in bed, my thoughts are a tangled web of excitement and nervousness. The castle was waiting for me to explore its secrets, but I can't do it with anyone else around. So I wait patiently until the late hours of the night, making sure that everyone had gone to bed before I finally snuck out. My attire was not quite appropriate for sneaking around a castle — a short gown that barely reaches mid-thigh and a thin robe that did little to hide my body. This was all Ruelle could provide for me, claiming it's all they had. And so I was left with bare feet, as shoes were not something I enjoy wearing and since I don't expect to run into anyone, there was no need for them.

Carefully and quietly, I made my way through the halls of the castle, taking in every detail with wide-eyed curiosity. To others, it may have just seemed like a quick dash from one place to another, but for me it's an opportunity to experience the grandeur and mystery of this ancient fortress.

Thankfully, my lack of shoes help me move with ease— something I silently thank the Gods for. As I crept along, I can't help but feel a sense of thrill and adventure coursing through my veins. This was my first taste of true freedom since arriving at the Court of Dusk, and I intend to savor every moment of it.

Enriched with intricate designs and rich colors, the artwork that graces the walls of some rooms is a striking contrast to what one would expect in a place like this. The portraits depict the royal predecessors, their faces stern and regal, along with the apparent Gods and Goddesses who held power over this kingdom. And then there were the portraits of the current royal family, both before and after their father's untimely death.

But it wasn't just portraits that don these walls— vibrant scenes of the aurora borealis, the heart of this court, were painted alongside serene beaches, bustling cities, delectable food, majestic animals, and other random inspirations. Though the court itself boasted plenty of natural light and dark walls, it was the golden trims and accents along with these colorful paintings that truly lit up the entire castle, casting a warm glow throughout its grand halls.

A muffled scuffle and hushed voices echo from around the corner, sending shivers down my spine. I push myself to move further down the hallway, not knowing how far I've gone or where I am. My heart races with fear as I realize I must be close to the dungeons, but my attention is caught by the breathtaking art that lines the walls.

Suddenly, a familiar voice cuts through the air like a sharp knife. "You think you can spy on my people?" I cautiously peek around the corner and see a cell further down, its doors flung open. The only occupants are two men - one standing tall and regal while the other kneels at his feet, sobbing.

"I-I wasn't...I swear!" The desperate plea of the kneeling man reaches my ears, but it's too far for anyone else to hear. My breath catches in my throat as I recognize the figure before me - it's Eryx, and not the same Eryx from dinner that had saved Hadeon and I, but the Dark King himself. Eryx may have shown me some kindness, but this? This is pure darkness and terror.

The king's fingers dig into the kneeling man's face, gripping his head with a vice-like force. "You swear with lies," he seethes his voice dripping with venom. The intensity in his gaze made me shudder.

"Tell me everything you know before I rip it out of your throat," Eryx demands, his grip tightening even more. The fear in the other man's eyes was palpable as he stammers out an answer.

"He... he wants her back. That's all I know, I swear!" His stuttering only seems to enrage the man further.

Could it be Ruelle or Esmeray that they're after or could it be me? But who would want his family? That question burns in my mind as I watch the man suddenly convulse in agony. The sound of his screams echo around us, causing me to gasp in shock. This was a level of violence that I had never witnessed before, and it both horrifies and fascinates me. Could I be the cause of such anger in Eryx's gaze? Shadows billow around him and I realize they aren't just here, they are apart of him. They are him. He has shadow manipulation, a fitting high fae ability for the Dark King.

My hands grip the wall so tightly that my nails dig into the stone, drawing blood. I can feel my heart pounding in my chest as I watch the king move with calculated ease, his smug smirk sending shivers down my spine.

I try to steady myself, but my legs tremble beneath me. This should be terrifying, but instead, it fills me with a strange mix of pride, contentment, and a twisted arousal.

The king leans in closer to the man writhing in agony on the ground. "You tell your *master* that if he dares to harm Verena, even by sending a weakling like you, I will tear him apart piece by agonizing piece until he is nothing more than a pile of dust." With one swift motion, the king releases the man and he scurries away, fleeing the castle in terror.

As the adrenaline rushes through me, I meet the king's intense gaze, his deep brown eyes meeting my indigo ones, feeling both drawn to —and fearful of— his powerful presence.

"Enjoy the show, Seren Fach?" He asks me. I wasn't sure what that meant, I don't speak their elder language, but for some reason it made chills sweep up my spine.

My chest heaves with each ragged breath as his words hung in the air like a threat. Anxiety coils in my stomach, tugging at me, but my body was frozen in place. I can't deny the pull I feel toward him, a primal need that I had never experienced before.

As he prowls closer to me, his eyes gleam with a dark intensity that matches his title of Dark King. It wasn't until I saw him summon shadows at the gala that I realized his true power. This place was undoubtedly crawling with other shadow summoners. My mind races with fear and suspicion, and I frantically scan the surrounding shadows for any sign of danger. But his predatory gaze told me he knew what I was thinking, and it only made me more uneasy.

"I am the only one of my kind left. Most of the royals used to have this power but now it's only me." This comforts me. Or was it the cast of darkness that ghosts down my arms like a cool wisp of air? "Why are you here, Seren Fach?"

"Why do you call me that?" My question is barely audible in it's breathy whisper. He stalks closer as the air shifts into something more… something heavy and dangerous but I have yet to be truly scared by him. He ignores my question. I try to step back but instead only end up meeting the cement wall behind me. Finally my gaze looks up at his face, into his eyes as I try to read him and what may be trampling through his mind. Is he feeling what I am? Does his mind burn with a million questions just as mine?

"Why are you here?" He asks, his eyes darkening with his perusal of me. He towers over my body, his hands resting next to my head on the wall as they trap me between them. His eyes meet mine once more.

A pull tugs from within me, begging me to answer him. "I wanted to explore and I- I am not sure why but I made my way down."

"And did you enjoy the show?" A smirk slips onto his face, and an air of arrogance radiates off him, along with heat. His eyes cast down to my lips before retreating to my eyes again and I can't help but do the same.

"No."

"Liar." He counters. I scoff, fiddling with the hem of the nightgown, why was it so short? And now I'm lightly regretting the decision of no shoes. "Are you afraid?" He asks quieter and I can't help but stare into his dark eyes, trying to read him.

Truthfully? No. I wasn't scared of him. And maybe there's something wrong with me for it. Maybe I'm deranged for not being terrified of seeing a man tortured right in front of me and dark shadows of unknown billowing around, suffocatingly close.

They feel as if they caress me but was I imagining it? Did I want them to? It doesn't match the look on his face— anger at the man and unbothered by me.

The feeling was similar to that of when I touched myself at the reminder of his hands on me after the gala, when the wind caressed my body. Could that have been him? Could Eryx have sent his shadows after me in the dead of night as I brought myself to ecstasy in thought of him?

"No, I'm not," I answer him finally. He hums, not quite believing me. He looks down, trailing my body again, and pauses, eyes narrowing before looking at me, his eyes impossibly darker than before.

"Where are your shoes?"

"Not on my feet," My response slips out before I can catch myself, sarcasm dripping from my lips. Do I have a death wish?

"Do you know how dangerous it is to be walking down in these lower levels without shoes? What if you get a cut and it gets infected?" He was angry at me now. How in the underworld is he possibly mad at *me*? His complex feelings send my heart through a loop.

"Careful, Your Majesty, or someone might think you care for me." I joke softly. He pushes himself off the wall, taking a step back. His shadows disperse into a thinner wall surrounding us, allowing the minimal light to bleed through.

"You hold secrets that can destroy my home and we have an agreement. My word is my vow and I do not want it broken because you are reckless. Wear shoes." He takes a few more steps back before turning and walking away.

I know one thing for sure; I was most definitely *not* going to start wearing shoes.

Chapter 17: Stained

Verena

I hadn't slept at all. The command he gave about shoes grinds my nerves and out of sheer petulance, I wasn't wearing shoes today at all. Ruelle looks at me weirdly as she tries to pull out shoes for me but I turn her down. I wasn't sure if he had told his trusted family of our plan, even though he said only Esmeray will know, but I keep my mouth shut just in case. She helps me dress in an elegant and simple, dark green and silky slip-dress.

"So, why are you not wearing anything on your feet?" She asks, brows furrow in confusion.

I smile at her. "Should I? I mean I see the staff of the palace constantly cleaning the floors, so they should be safe enough, right?" I ask her. "Plus, I simply hate shoes." She laughs with me as we make our way toward the dining room for breakfast. I decide to join them this time.

"Verena, you're joining us." The former queen greets me. Everyone looks up, gauging my presence. I smile brightly at them, my head held high and politely wave. Even though I hadn't slept, I still feel fresh and more awake than I had been in a long time. Something about last night made me feel more alive than I ever had before.

"Good morning, Your Majesties and Hadeon. Did everyone sleep well?" They exchange looks with one another. The king wasn't here yet. Even Ruelle was looking at me like I had grown two heads overnight with my overly joyous tone.

"I did, thank you." The king's mother says to me, smiling softly, "But, you do not have to call me that. It's so formal. Call me Calanthe, please." She smiles widely at me, something in her is different, too. She doesn't seem as tense today.

I nod before looking at everyone else, waiting for an answer, as I sit down. "My sleep was fine, thank you, Verena," Hadeon speaks, looking eager to speak with me. I know he broke my trust but did I really want to spend more time angry at the only person who has ever felt like family to me?

Now, everyone looks to Esmeray for an answer.

"I had a dream where we had a pet buffalo who spoke to me. It was very intriguing." She says, not meeting anyone's gaze as she brings her cup of juice to her lips. "How was your sleep, Verena?" She asks me, finally looking up.

"Enlightening." She hums in. I can feel Hadeon's gaze upon me but I don't meet his eyes.

As I finally settle into my seat, I can't help but wonder when the food will arrive. Just then, Eryx enters the room with a serious expression on his face, mirroring the rest of his family. He signals to the kitchen staff to start bringing in the meals. My mouth waters as I watch plates stacked with various meats, cheeses, breads, fruits, and juices placed on the table. A bottle of sparkling wine is set between Esmeray and Calanthe, who mix it with their fruit juices. The sight makes me crave some myself, but I don't dare ask for any.

Hands stack food onto plates and when I go to reach for some fruit, Esmeray speaks up. "Add meat to that plate, Ren. We're training today." Hadeon's head swipes from her to Eryx, curiosity on his face. I didn't know her and I were close enough for nicknames but a sense of friendliness overcomes me.

"Why?" Hadeon asks. She looks at him with a brow raised.

"I know you are second in command, Hadeon, but while you've been gone, I have been running things. So I'll be training her for combat. Please remember we are on the brink of war." Esmeray's tone shows no mercy or room for questions about her ability or judgment. "Eryx and I agreed that having her continue training would be best." I nod in agreement, even though I am not a part of this conversation.

"I just think it's too soon." He pushes.

"Good thing it's not your call then, isn't it?" She drops her fork onto her plate, the ricocheting ring bouncing off the walls. "Where is this coming from?" Their eyes meet and neither looks away or blinks.

"Children! Please, let's not do this. It's morning and we all have a busy day today." Calanthe tries. Neither look away from each other yet, and Eryx stares at his friend in question as I sit there quietly next to the youngest royal sibling.

Ruelle's sweet scent lingers near me as she leans over to whisper in my ear, "They've been like this since we were children— always at each other's throats and constantly questioning the other. Esmeray wanted that position so bad but Hadeon and her fought for it and he won in the end so while she missed his challenging presence, she enjoyed his position while he was gone." She lets out a light laugh.

"Verena, do you mind training with Esmeray? Do you think it will benefit you?" Hadeon questions me, breaking their eye contact, "Because you do not have to. You do not need to learn any more than I have taught you. The danger of Dryston is no more while you're here." I'm shocked at his words. He knows he cannot promise that.

I stare at him, meeting his pleading eyes, and for whatever reason, I almost want to say no to training. I should trust him, right? I've known him longer than anyone else here. We have been friends for the past five years. But, his ego could be getting in the way of his judgment. The constant battle between him and Esmeray.

I look at Esmeray, Calanthe, and Ruelle, all waiting for an answer. Ruelle is sweet, and comforting. Esmeray looks as if she wants to stab Hadeon with the butter knife in her fist and Calanthe looks as if she's trying to understand me just by watching. Anxiety wracks my nerves, the all-to-familiar feeling of being a pushover filters through me. I want to say no, not be a burden to anyone and just use what I already know. But why does it feel like it won't be enough? I've read about the past wars and what they entail to an extent but without experiencing it, it is hard to know what I'll be getting in to.

I lift my indigo gaze up to my left, meeting dark brown eyes and suddenly I pause. My breath catches in my throat as I read him as if he is open to just me. Light flickers within them. I'd assume they would be impatient, irritated eyes that would be piercing my soul to obey and say yes. And yet, somehow, I know that if I said I don't want to train, he will support my decision without judgment.

My eyes stay on his as I speak, "I want to train with Esmeray." There's a gleam of something similar to pride in his irises as he breaks our contact, looking back down at his food to continue eating. There is a pleased look on Esmeray's face as she gleams at me and while Ruelle and Calanthe have nothing to say, negative or positive, Eryx is calm as he eats. Hadeon glares at the military general next to him and suddenly I feel bad for choosing her over him.

* * *

"I want to see where you left off with Hadeon so we'll start slow today before we get into the good stuff," Esmeray warns me, the excitement on her face makes me smile back. I always enjoyed training, since it helps me release any frustrations. I know this trainer won't go easy on me and I am happy about it.

"I can't wait," I tell her, making her smile grow more. "We did the basics. Should I grab a staff? We sometimes used them but we also used fake swords."

She takes a moment to think and looks at Hadeon as he walks into the room to watch, I assume, he leans against the wall adjacent from us. "Let's start with hand-to-hand. I want to see how far you got with him babying you like he used to do with Ruelle." She smirks at his scoff but otherwise, he remains silent, crossing his arms over his chest.

I stance myself across from her on the mat, the same one I've memorized for 5 years with Hadeon. I see her eyes following each and every movement I make— assessing me. The thing I love most is that I don't feel like she's judging me in a negative way. She is simply trying to help me and a warm feeling settles over me.

With a graceful flick of her hand, she signals for me to begin. I take a step forward, my muscles tense and ready to attack. But as I move, I can sense that she is not trying to defeat me just yet. No, she wants to test my skills, to see what I am capable of. And in order to do so, she must refrain from fighting back.

I throw a punch, my training kicking in as if it were second nature. Every movement is calculated and precise, each strike with purpose and intention. After what feels like hours, she finally calls a halt to the session. My body is drenched in sweat and my heart is pounding, but I feel stronger and more confident in my abilities than ever.

"Okay, not bad. He did better than I gave him credit for. But I can easily prove that it won't get you far against our soldiers at least. Ruelle knows more, no offense, and she doesn't even like training.

But you? You will be fun to train because you want it, I can see it." She gleams excitedly.

"She can hold her own, Esmeray. You just want to prove me wrong. If you actually fight her, she will hold her own." She quirks a brow at Hadeon, who is supposed to be silent.

She comes at me in surprise and I manage to fight back in defense. But she's going harder, faster, way more than Hadeon ever gave which almost makes me mad at him. I never wanted him to baby me.

Her footwork is impeccable. I maintain her speed and strength, showcasing just how much I trained but I knew I had more to learn. Then she swipes her foot out as I block her fist again and she takes me to the floor. I gasp from the wind being knocked out of me, unharmed though, and before she can help me up amicably, Hadeon rushes over. I am out of breath and my heart beats so hard I hear it in my ear drums.

"Gods, Esmeray! What is wrong with you? She's not some skilled warrior. Are you okay, Verena?" He asks, rushed. I look at him as if he offended me and he doesn't even notice.

"I'm fine." I grit out, shoving his hands away. Off to the side of him, I watch as Eryx turns from the open doorway to walk off, obviously seeing what occurred. A sense of disappointment flares within me.

"I'm taking you to the infirmary." I go to deny it but Esmeray beats me to it.

"That, right there, Hadeon? That will get her killed quicker than her training. You baby her for what? She is a grown woman and she did fine. It was more than I thought she'd know." She looks at me, "I'll see you tomorrow for our first official day of training, Ren." She calls me by the nickname she gave me. I smile, nodding and I take in her words about Hadeon. She had a point but he was just trying to help, right?

I will admit that it feels good, training with someone who wasn't trying to baby me like he does. I've noticed throughout the years, I just hoped that he'd get over it. He acts as if I am as fragile as a flower. Maybe I am.

Maybe I am way in over my head.

* * *

Ruelle and I sit in the library, reading silently with each other when another person walks in holding a bouquet of flowers.

They walk straight over to us and I assume he's going to gift them to Ruelle but he stops right in front me of. "From the king, lady Verena." He speaks loudly and it gathers the attention of everyone else in this surprisingly busy library.

A blush covers my face and neck, making my skin warm as I reach for them. "Thank you." The words come out ever-so-quietly I'm not even sure he heard them. I look at Ruelle, who looks just as shocked.

Another fae walks in, this time a female, with another bouquet of flowers, followed by four more fae.

I am beet red by the end and Ruelle calls someone to take them to my room but before they can grab the group of flowers in my hands, I snatch one of them so I can at least have something to prove I didn't just dream this.

"Eryx must fancy you," Ruelle speaks first, smiling wide. "I haven't seen him fancy anyone since-" She stops herself and before I can ask she fixes her words, "In a long time." I leave it, still flabbergasted at the act.

I know we said he'd have to start showing interest in me to sell the engagement but this was not what I expected. Each bouquet was a different breed of flower I hadn't seen in Zorya. I love that they aren't common either, I had seen them in one of the books I've read to learn about this country. The royal garden grows them but otherwise, they grow randomly and rarely across this side of the continent.

"You have some dust in your hair," Ruelle laughs softly before trying to brush it out of my roots.

My eyes snap to hers as I move away, "Oh, that's okay. I'll wash it out later." How could I have forgotten? "Can I bring some ink to my room?" I ask her, trying to play it off.

"Of course! Just ask the librarian for some and she'll give you as much as you need." I nod, smiling before continuing to read the books.

As the day flew by, I realize that I will need to tend to my appearance after everyone retires to their rooms for the night. Leaving the library, I approach the woman at the small desk and request some ink. She hands me a decent-size bottle, perfect for my needs.

Unlike other days, Ruelle did not accompany me to my room. After days of exploring, I had memorized all the well-traveled routes. For a moment, I enjoy the solitary journey.

Once inside my room, I close the door behind me and waste no time in getting ready. My black leather gloves protect my hands from any potential stains as I handle the ink. Placing the bottle on the dresser, I focus on removing the cork top when a sudden knock on my door makes me jump in surprise.

In that split second of distraction, the bottle slips from my grip and shatters on the ground with a loud crash. My heart races as an involuntary yelp escapes my lips as black ink splatters.

Before I can even react, Eryx flung open the door and rushes inside, his expression full of concern. "Are you okay? What happened?" he asks quickly, scanning both me and the scattered glass on the floor.

"I'm fine. I-I just dropped some ink." I tell him.

"Why do you have your training gloves on?" He sends me another question.

I scoff, "What is with all the questions? I don't want to stain my fingers and I went to open it but the cork got stuck and then I dropped the glass when your knock frightened me." I rush out, trying to calm my breathing from his sudden entrance as I blame him for me dropping it. My heart is racing, but honestly, it's not from the scare, it's from getting caught.

I'm not entirely sure why I have to dye my hair. I was just told by my mother ever since I was a young girl to do it or I'd be in danger.

Thinking about that now seems redundant since I'm already in danger. Even with my dark hair, the blue streak still gave me away, making Eryx and Hadeon think I was a part of something bigger than us.

Out of reflex, now worried he'll see right through me, I start playing with the strands, trying to push back the front parts of my hair from my face, taking steps back as he bends to pick up the pieces of broken glass.

His eyes immediately zero in on the motion, scanning my hair with intense curiosity. I feel a sense of panic rise within me as I realize there's a streak of spilled ink from my gloves running through my locks. The confusion in his eyes is evident as they flicker between my hair and my face, especially as I attempt to move the hair away from my eyes, only smudging more ink onto my forehead. The wetness of the ink seeps into my skin and I can't help but feel self-conscious under his scrutiny.

Without hesitation, he rises from his position on the floor and forgets about the broken shards of glass beneath him as he slowly makes his way over to me. I try to back away, matching his pace, but he moves faster than I expect. Before I know it, my back hits the desk behind me and I'm left with no room to escape. He stands before me, towering over me with an intimidating aura.

My heart races, unsure if it's due to his close proximity or the fact that he seems to be reading right through me. Our eyes meet, his deep brown orbs like a warm autumn night trying to unravel all of my secrets. His hand reaches up at a leisurely pace, gripping a section of my hair where the new ink has been smeared into.

"What is this? Why is the root of your hair lighter than the rest?" He inquires, his eyes moving from mine to the strands. Something burns in his gaze and I can't tell why he cares so much.

Do I lie? We're supposed to trust each other. Maybe he'll have an answer as to why it's different. While black hair isn't rare, white is. White hair hasn't been seen on a native to this continent in hundreds of years. I'd know, I read it in a history book. Not to mention the color that never fades, dyes, or changes except in length.

It's as if he can see the turmoil turning in my head, going around faster than light.

His eyes trail back to mine, "Verena," It's the way he says my name, soft but firm. Like he wants the answers but as king he needs them.

I allow my eyes to move, from his eyes to his lips. They're pink and soft. My eyes move down to his chiseled jawline before continuing down to his strong chest.

"Verena." My eyes flick back up his brown eyes now black with emotion, "Tell me. I cannot risk my country, and my people, without knowing everything. We're supposed to trust each other." There's the king in him.

"I…" I take a breath, hoping he can't hear my heart. "I don't know." I take in a deep breath as he steps back, still watching and waiting. "For as long as I can remember, my mother was dying my hair. Honestly, my father and her never got along and I remember her telling me how much she hated covering up this piece of me but that it was for my safety and that if anyone found out about it, I'd be in more danger than anything or anyone. So, even after she passed away, I've stained it with ink. I haven't seen the true white color ever. But, no matter how many times I try to stain or dye the blue, it won't take." I tell him the truth, not seeing any other way. He steps closer again, running his fingers into my hair and grabbing strands to feel.

"No more." He says, throwing me off guard. His eyes darken as he looks at my hair. "You will no longer dye it, got it? As long as you're with my family and I, you're safe. You're training with Esme and you will continue to do so, especially now. We can't get our revenge if you're dead." I nod at him, watching as the strand falls from his fingers and he steps back. "No more lies. I'll see you at breakfast, Verena." He exits, just like that, leaving me breathless and confused.

Chapter 18: Fear

Verena

I t had been a week since I told Eryx about my hair after he caught me in the act of dying it. Since then, I've trained every day with Esmeray and Eryx has donned me gifts every other day. The people in the castle are whispering, talking, and staring even more.

Some of the women are glaring, obviously thinking I've taken his eye over them but they don't know it's just a bargain— a way for both of us to get what we want.

I'm in his war room now, though, showing him where Dryston wanted to set warriors up for camp.

He hasn't mentioned my hair but everyone can tell it's changing and fast.

Ruelle asked me about it yesterday, since it had grown out a couple inches since the dye incident— almost like it knows I'm not dying it any longer and it can't wait to be back to its original color.

I was nervous about seeing the white. I was so accustomed to the inky black that it will be odd seeing it any different, especially so light in such short time.

The tone was a blonde, warmer when the sun shines down on me and more ashy platinum in the shadows

The door opens and Esmeray walks in, not noticing me until after she shut the door. She freezes, staring at me before looking at Eryx and then back at me.

"What the fuck?" She asks, cautiously glancing back and forth before staring at the giant table map with all the pieces on it. "What is going on here?"

My heart stops beating, I don't know what to say and I don't have to.

"Calm down, Esme." He says, barely looking at her but studying the board. "Verena has offered to help me out." She narrows her heterochromia eyes at me, walking over and very suddenly placing a blade against my throat as she shoves me against the wall. An involuntary squeak slips from my throat. Eryx sighs heavily, almost as if he was expecting this and it was just inconvenient. I look into her mismatch eyes and suddenly feel very ill; fear unexpectedly slides down my back, chills take over and a cold sweat breaks out over my entire body. Unadulterated fear wrecks me and tears brim my eyes at the confusing fear. I've never felt this unnatural feeling before. My knees want to give out, but I try to hold strong. He was supposed to tell her.

"Esmeray, enough."

She doesn't listen, whatever she's doing continues as she speaks. "If you so much as think about betraying my family— my brother— or this kingdom, I will show you fear you have never seen or felt. I will make you so absolutely petrified that your body will go into a shock that will kill you slowly. You wouldn't wish it on your worst enemy or the biggest monster on this planet. Do you understand?" Her voice is hard and cold as ice. I think about her power and wonder if she knows how it feels? The fear, the terror. It's almost all-consuming. I try to push it off me as if it's a solid force.

"Esmeray!" He demands but she waits and I have to push through the terrifying feeling wreaking havoc on my body to answer. I try pushing the fear back, almost as if I could remove it. Her eyes flicker with surprise, looking at me, and I notice her chest rise and fall just a little harder for a moment before she hardens her face.

"I understand." It's barely audible but she hears it regardless.

Then, as if it never happened, all the fear vanished. I take a deep breath, trying to regain my senses as she releases me, still staring as if *I* was the one doing that to *her*.

Eryx is there next to me, I hadn't even noticed he had moved closer, his arms wrapping around me as my knees give out.

I had never felt anything like that but I know exactly what it was and what Esmeray Ashwood's Dark Fae ability is. Fear. And it fit her. I can't blame her for the threat. Her family is everything to her— just as it is to Ruelle and Eryx. I can tell and I've only been here a couple weeks. Eryx never told her about our deal, as he said he would. And regardless of that reason, she was caught off guard to a practical stranger in their war room, understandably so.

He helps me stand, checking over me and glaring at his sister as Esmeray looks at the board as if everything was normal. I nod to him that I'm fine, trying to continue our planning.

"I will tell you and you alone. Do not even tell Ruelle or Hadeon about this. I'm deadly serious." He tells her before briefing his second-in-command on our revenge plot.

Esmeray doesn't hate me, that much I know. I want to say she might even like me based on how she treats me during training and our meals together but I've never seen her so scary and now that I know that's her gift? I will definitely not be getting on her bad side.

* * *

We had just finished up the meeting when Esmeray leaves and Eryx looks to me, "I wanted to let you know that we are having a party. Ruelle can help you get dressed. I wish she'd assign a lady's maid to you but she refuses." He rolls his eyes at his playfully and I smile at the act. "She deeply enjoys your company."

"I enjoy her as well. I've never had friends until Hadeon. Tarius didn't think it necessary and the one time I thought I had one, she was only friends with me to sleep with Dryston." I laugh it off, remembering the sad thought. I was over it now but at the time, it made me swear off friends at all. "And she's such a good person, a true light, it's refreshing. She's been a big help with my studies of your family and kingdom. I figured if I was going to live here, I should educate myself." He gives me a small smile.

"That sounds like a sound plan. I will see you tonight, then." He gives me a small bow before taking leave.

As I make my way to my room, I can't help but think about Eryx. He had this terrible reputation but the only time I've seen him as scary would be on the dungeon floor and when he got angry at dinner. But, it didn't seem to have a negative affect on me in any way.

There was surely something wrong with me if I wanted to see more of it, right?

As word does, it spread fast. Ruelle was already waiting for me in my room giggling. "Again?" I ask her, laughing, as she showcases dresses.

"Of course!" The exclamation was bright and cheery and I can't help but be in a better mood.

Once again, I try on the new dresses for her as she does for me while we decide which gown looks best on who. It was fun, being with a girl like this.

My mother used to tell me about her best friend but never told me her name and would explain how much fun they'd have creating mischief and trouble.

I wanted that. I want this.

"Oh! Verena! This is the one. It is gorgeous. Violet is truly your color but seeing you in midnight blue is magical. It matches your hair and everything." Her voice was in awe as she watches me emerge from behind the dressing wall.

I stare at myself in the full-body mirror I have. The dress is A-line with a triangular sweetheart neckline. It's a dark midnight blue with mini golden stars made of glitter.

In a voice so small I almost miss it, Ruelle adds, "You look like our queen." And for some reason, I know she doesn't mean her mother. She meant a queen fit for this kingdom. Her eyes widen and looking up to meet mine, as if not meaning to stay it out loud but I just smile at myself, pretending I hadn't heard her.

This is a lot of pressure. I know Eryx and I are supposed to be courting but this feels real. Too real.

The dress fits perfect and not in the way of measurements fitting correctly.

I stare at myself, running my hands down the front to smooth any lines and realize this feels good. As if a piece of the puzzle is finally within reach.

Khyrel feels like I was meant to be here all along and suddenly I've never felt more in danger in my entire life. Eryx does not want me as his queen, he wants revenge on Dryston for threatening his kingdom, his family. I can't get too comfortable here. As soon as we're done here, I'll be off to start a life I'm not sure I want anymore.

It has to be this way. I need to start closing my heart off to him. He doesn't deserve the traumatic afflictions I bring with me everywhere I go.

"I don't think I'll wear this one. Let's try the black one instead." I tell her, wanting to shove this dress far in the back of the closet I have.

But, as I meet her eyes in the mirror, I can see the disappointment in them and choose to ignore it.

Chapter 19: Ladies and Gentlefae... Her

Eryx

It's my mothers birthday and yet all I can think about is *her*.

Her hair, her eyes, her smile. I know them. Why do I know them? Where could I have possibly seen her before?

Flashes of memories from when I was a child keep flashing on the back of my eyelids while I try to sleep.

There was a child born five years after me, I vaguely remember her but I know I was betrothed to her before the girl and her family went missing. I can never remember her name but my mother might, I needed to speak with her about it.

I'm just not sure if bringing up her— presumed dead— best friend is a conversation for the night of her birthday.

This plan Verena and I came up with is messy and I knew it'd end badly but I couldn't stop myself from wanting to see it play out. When she brought the idea to me, I thought she was crazy.

I couldn't risk a war I wasn't prepared for. Especially if he was playing dirty. But seeing the fire in her eyes when I told her I wasn't interested?

It stirred something inside my chest that hasn't been anything other than frozen solid in a decade.

When my last betrothal fell through, I swore off women. Not even because I was genuinely in love with her and thought she was my fated mate. I found out she had been scheming against the crown and against me. She never truly loved me as I did her and after I learned of her treason, I knew I'd never trust another female who wasn't apart of my family again.

Verena, however, was different. As soon as I laid my eyes on her I knew she was who the prophecy was about, regardless of her hair color being the complete opposite of what it's supposed to be. I have yet to tell her the other prophetic piece of information. And now that I know it was dye and that her true hair color is white? I've never been more sure of something in my life.

Verena and I will either save Khyrel...

...Or we'll destroy it.

* * *

I sit on my throne in the best room of the palace while people chat, dance, eat, and are merry. I have yet to see Verena arrive but I know Esmeray is here, as she stands off to the side of the band, speaking with a guard who is happily giving her the attention she seeks. Hadeon, looking far more pissed than usual as he glares at the male entertaining my sister or my sister herself, it gets hard to tell. I roll my eyes and continue watching the room.

My mother basks in all the attention, smiling bright and being happy. It warms my heart. She dealt with a lot of trauma from my father in their marriage but mates are mates and she couldn't leave him without leaving us. She deserves to be happy in this life and the next.

I watch as she continuously peeks around the beings in the room and watches the entry door.

Who else could she possibly be waiting on?

The Herald slams his staff on the ground, the booming sound reverberates around the room and silence falls, awaiting the next guests arrival.

"Announcing King Perseus and his daughter, Princess Lieve of Sakaris." A tall male waltzes in with a smaller fae female. They both have golden hair and their eyes are as blue as the sea. Golden crowns adorn them and while he dons a white suit, shes in a golden gown. They greet me first, per custom, before finally he walks to my mother in greeting. I know when she was ruling, she had made friends across the seas. Our history books tells us of them and we do trade often with Sakaris.

The party continues and I start getting impatient waiting for this stubborn female.

I stand and make my way to the floor for some refreshments before a hand grabs mine and pulls me in with surprising strength.

"Alyra." I state as fact as she smiles wide at me.

"King Eryx. You have not visited me in so long, I've been worried about you and your stress. The council-"

"The council does not run this country. I do." My skin grows cold where she touches before jerking back from the sensation. She huffs.

"It's because of *her*, is it not?" Fury flashes in her eyes and I roll mine.

"If you are speaking of our recent guest then I suggest you choose your words carefully or hold your tongue. She has nothing to do with me not wanting to touch you. Leave me alone and stop grabbing me before I. Cut. Your hands. Off." Tears brim her eyes but I can't force myself to actually care. I start walking to the table of beverages and food, needing to get away from her.

"That was quite possibly all the entertainment I needed here." Another female voice sounds, this one not as familiar. I glance at her, blonde hair in an elegant bun and bright sea eyes gleaming with mischief. "Princess Lieve, your majesty." She gives me a small curtsy before grabbing her own glass of fae wine and shoving some cheese into her mouth. I stare at her in amusement. "Starving." Is all she says when she notices my attention on her as she eats as much as she can.

I chuckle before turning back to what I was gathering. I down a glass of blackberry bourbon, not my usual but still delicious. One of Asterlayna's most famous bourbons. I glance back at the doors, the Harold meeting my gaze and shaking his head. My fist clenches around my newly full glass and my jaw presses harder into the upper one. I feel the muscles in it flinch.

"Waiting for someone?" She asks, still standing next to me, downing her third glass of wine. Princess Lieve, unlike all the other females, doesn't seem as if she's trying to sleep with me, thank the Gods. She notes my tense stand before eyeing the door as well.

"Not your business." I coldly respond.

She throws her hands up in defense, "Not trying to piss you off but trust me, it's either her nerves getting to her or she's making sure every hair and speck is perfect. That's how I am. It's Verena, right?" She asks and my attention snaps to her, confusion and anger rushing through me. She waves me off, "Calm down, Eryx. Can I call you that?" She asks before not waiting for an answer, "People talk and my lady's maid heard another speaking about her. I heard she's pretty and sweet to your staff. That alone is hard to find."

I go to respond but get cut off from the Herald giving me a look as he bangs the staff onto the ground and silence falls over again.

"Announcing Princess Ruelle of Khyrel." He stops and anger floods me. I told him only to signal me when it's *her*.

Ruelle walks in, greeting everyone and arriving at my side to say hello and grab some wine, too.

Another bang of the staff. "Announcing Princess Verena." She walks in, a flash of black catches my gaze at her gown.

In strips of black tulle flowing around her looking like my wisps of shadows, You can see her long toned legs through the sheer fabric as it drops from her waist. It sits snug on her torso, trailing up her bust before splitting into separate wide double layered pieces to continue over her breasts and across her shoulders to what I can assume is down her shoulder blades before connecting back together at her waist in the back, dropping elegantly down to the floor in a puff of black markih tulle— a rare stunning fabric from another continent in the court of art, Leatus. Her hair is the same black with it's blue streak but the blonde is more prominent now. Starting at her scalp it grew a few inches before fading into the black.

I've never cared for clothes before. Not until now, as I stare in uncontrollable awe and lust as she steps off the single lifted step, gathering the attention of every being in this room. I feel eyes on me and I break the stare at Verena to look at my mother who stares at me in love, pride, and understanding, whatever that means. As I look back at Verena, I find her staring back at me. Silence ensues, or so I think it does. I can't tell with my stupid cold heart pounding wildly in my chest, drowning out any other noise.

She looks calm and collected, until she is two feet from me. I unlatch my eyes from her bright indigo ones, trailing down her face, neck, her rapidly rising and falling chest that looks like mine feels. Her breasts are covered in the tulle as it sits thick enough to keep her intimate areas hidden from others. I continue my blatant perusal of her as my eyes track each inch of her skin all the way down to her feet. Those *damn* bare feet.

When I make my way back to her eyes with fire burning in mine, I see her doing the same to me, indigo blasts with amusement before her smile drops, lingering on the open section of my pitch black dress shirt that sits on my chest. The jacket to match, rests open on my shoulders and the same colored pants sit comfortably snug on my hips and legs— well, comfortable until her gaze sends warmth down my spine and blood rushes to my cock, tightening the fabric.

"Hello, I'm Princess Lieve of Sakaris. You are quite the beauty. Very...queenly." She smirks and it breaks Verena and I from our reverie. Red travels over her, dusting Verena's chest all the way up to her cheeks.

She shakes her head from her thoughts, giving us both a curtsy.

"Good evening. It's nice to meet you. Sakaris, that's over the sea right? Long travels." She responds. Irritation bleeds through me as they converse. I want her to look at me again and then I want to slap myself for thinking so.

"Ask her to dance you brute." Esmeray's voice hits the back of my head right before she shoves me and I barely stop myself from toppling into the fae who won't escape my mind.

Ruelle giggles as I glare daggers at them before holding my hand out to Verena, who now stares at me with confusion.

"Dance." I blurt out, sounding as if it is a command. I can practically feel my sisters roll their eyes at me as Esme smacks me from behind. "If you would like to." I add softer.

A small smile plays on her face and my heart can't take it. This female will certainly be the death of me. I just can't decide if I like it or not.

* * *

167

Verena

Seeing Eryx upon my entrance was… confusing. Breathtaking. Mind-boggling.

I immediately feel his gaze as I stroll over to him to greet the king—per custom. You always greet the host first, especially if they are the ruler.

But he looks so good. The open shirt revealing his skin made me want to— honest-to-Gods— lick his smooth muscular chest. I've never felt this way before. Sure, many of the males in Zorya were attractive, Dryston and Hadeon included. But, my heart never beat faster over their presence, my eyes never wandered further and further down to wonder what was underneath, and I definitely have *never* wanted to taste anyone before.

His clothing fit him perfect, too perfect. It was tight in every right was, relaxed but still so elegant.

I was devastatingly nervous about the dress I don. The sheer fabric made me feel so open and while I never minded my body before, I did tonight. Especially seeing the stunning golden fae he stands by. The bare feet was my way of taunting him, trying to pull a reaction from him even if it were anger. I want his attention, another first for me. I don't notice anyone else's reaction but when I reach Eryx and his gaze licks flames through my body, I know I got the outcome I wanted. I can't stop the amusement and while this party is a royal ball, for Calanthe's birthday, I had to do it. I don't even let Ruelle see me skip the shoes.

Eryx stumbles forward, his sisters quietly laughing behind him as he glares before holding his hand out to me. "Dance." He commands and my brows raise in some sort of defiance. Esmeray groans out a sigh, slapping a hand to her forehead. "If you would like to," He adds hastily, cheeks dusting in pink.

My heart beats so hard and fast I worry it'll jump from my chest and run off. I nod, placing my smaller hand into his large one as he leads me to the middle of the room in the midst of other dancers.

Much to my dismay, they part for us and everyone stops moving, staring.

The Dark King dancing with some random girl. I'm sure it's the talk of the kingdom.

When the Herald titled me as a princess, I was shocked but I saw Calanthe's eyes meet mine with pride and I know she was the reason why. I don't even have to tell him my name— like I was a staple here. Like it's natural and normal and as if I had been here my entire life.

Something in my heart clicks and something in me feels the deja-vu, like this has happened before.

He pulls me to him, our chests barely brushing as he raises our connected hands and trails his other hand up from my lower back when I freeze at the attention. His hand glides to my arm, down to my fingers where fire trails after him before lightly pushing my hand up to his shoulder, where it rests and he finds my lower back once more. His familiar scent of freshly baked dessert stirs feelings within me. Sending a rush of pleasure to my core.

My breath stutters and I know he feels it, feels my chest rise and fall in rapid succession.

But the closeness? It allows me to feel his too. When I realize this isn't only affecting me, but him as well, I stare into his heated, darkened gaze. The music starts and so do we. It's like my body isn't my own, following his every lead as if we'd danced together a million times before. We fit perfectly together, seemingly made for one another and my heart clenches in my chest.

Fated mates were rare, extremely, and while I've read about them, I never thought I might have one because of the fate that awaited me in the Court of Dawn. But this? I've never felt like this.

But when you meet your mate, a mark shows up on your body, matching each other in shape and position. And as far as I know, none have popped up. I'd feel it.

I can't tell if I'm disappointed or not.

Our bodies sway, the entire time no one else joins in but I feel multiple gazes. Questions hang in the air. But his eyes? Those dark brown eyes get darker the longer he stares into my indigo ones. I can't seem to look away as he leads the dance in a traditional waltz. His jaw ticks, the pulse on his throat throbs, and I feel his hand on my waist get tighter.

I get even closer to him, basking in the warmth even as my body feels on fire.

The music is beautiful and I think I'd dream of this moment for eternity.

Chapter 20: Enlighten

Verena

When the song ends, he looks as if he wants to keep going and I almost open my mouth to ask us too. But we stop, eyes still locked. Other couples join the dance floor as another song starts.

"Thank you for the dance." I speak softly, my words seemingly inaudible but I know he hears me. My heart continues beating fast and suddenly I do not feel like partying any longer.

When he finally lets me go, I step away and find his mother in the crowd as she watches her eldest child and myself.

"Verena, dear, you look stunning."

I give her a curtsy, "Thank you, Calanthe. Merry Natal Day. I've suddenly gotten an ache in my head and I fear I need rest. I am deeply sorry for cutting your celebration short. If you'll excuse me?" I ask, seeing how pale my skin looks in the mirror behind her, noting Eryx still staring at me, making his way over to us.

She nods in understanding, her eyes reading me as if she was my own mother and I take my leave.

My bare feet hastily take me from the room, not caring who watches.

The guards at the entry doors pay me no mind as I rush out of the doors. I need to get out. I feel as if I cannot breathe.

Something in me snaps, like a taut string finally breaking under pressure, and tears fill my eyes for reasons I'm unsure of. The salty liquid blurs my vision, threatening to spill over onto my cheeks. Everything tonight was overwhelming, a cacophony of sights, sounds, and emotions that left me reeling. I'm not quite sure how to feel, my heart a jumble of conflicting sensations.

I round a corner, my feet moving of their own accord, when I smack straight into another fae. The impact is jarring, and I gasp, the sound sharp in the quiet corridor. I struggle to hold back the water in my eyes, blinking rapidly. "Verena." The voice is unfamiliar to me, melodic yet cold, and I look up to see a beautiful fae. Her features are ethereal, almost painfully perfect, with high cheekbones and eyes that shimmer like precious gems.

"Do I know you?" I ask her, my voice barely above a whisper. I try to leave without being rude, my body angling away from her imposing presence.

"You don't belong here," she hisses, her words dripping with venom. "He is not yours. Do you understand me?" Her eyes narrow, flashing dangerously. "Eryx will marry me, my father will see to it or otherwise he will lose his council's approval of any future decisions. Leave Khyrel." She steps closer, the scent of jasmine and something darker, more sinister, wafting from her skin. "Or you will not live to see another week."

The threat, so blatant and cold, makes me scoff. I look into her muddy eyes, like stagnant pools of water, and feel a surge of defiance rise within me. The fear that had gripped me moments ago dissipates, replaced by a steely resolve.

"I do not even know you but I do not care. You threaten me?" I huff a laugh, the tears drying rapidly. "You have no idea who I am, what

172

I have endured in my life, or where I come from. Eryx is owned by no one and he is certainly not owned by you, a pompous *cunt* who is probably so pampered she needs daddy to even shit." I have no control over the words flowing from my mouth, but it doesn't matter.

Her hands come up around my throat with a ferocious strength, cutting off my air supply and causing me to panic for a moment. But then my instincts kick in and I quickly reach for the small blade hidden under the fabric of my clothing. With swift movements, I slice upwards on her wrist and downwards on the other, drawing deep lines that immediately began to bleed. A warm, sticky sensation spreads across my chest as her blood drips down onto me.

She lets out a scream of pain and anger, stepping back from me. "What is wrong with you?" she shouts, her eyes blazing with fury and fear, a delicious mix of both.

I grip the blade in a defensive stance, forcing her to stop in her tracks before she can try to hurt me further. "I am not afraid to kill you, you wretched shrew," I spat out, my voice laced with venom. "Come any closer and I will see to it myself, since no one else seems to have the guts."

Blood continues to pour from her wounds and I can't help but smirk at the damage. "You should hurry to the healers," The taunting words leave my lips, "But be warned, your fae healing powers won't work against the poison on this blade."

She snarls at me before turning and running in the opposite direction of where I want to go. Dark red droplets stain the ground behind her, a satisfying sight for someone who had been treated like a puppet their entire life.

I sheath the blade and make it all the way to the stairs before Eryx catches up to me.

"I will see to it she is handled." He speaks with anger.

"No need, I did it myself."

He follows me all the way to my room and when I enter, instead of being able to slam the door shut, he places his hand there to stop it and welcomes himself in. I sigh from the motion.

"Verena." He speaks again but I do not care to listen. I want to get the blood off of me. "Are you hurt?" He asks, noting the red covering my front.

"No." My throat is a little scratchy from her grasp. She had a surprisingly strong grip but otherwise I am fine.

He approaches from behind, a presence I feel before his form comes into view. When he turns me to face him, our eyes lock in an intense gaze. "Look at me." It's a command—urgent and unwavering—but I surrender to it willingly.

"I care for you," he continues, his voice low and fervent. "I do not wish to see you dead. While Alyra lacks power, her father certainly does not. I will speak to him tonight." He pauses, the weight of his words sinking in. "Alyra is jealous of you, and I'm relieved to see that she doesn't get under your skin."

His declaration sends a jolt through my body, leaving me momentarily frozen as the air becomes thick and suffocating. Our breaths come in heavy gasps from the frantic rush that brought us to my room; his eyes blaze with a mix of anger and a deep-seated longing that has been present since the night began.

Dare I take that leap?

My gaze drifts toward his lips, drawn to their softness despite my instinct compelling me to look back up into his darkened eyes. They glisten with allure, plump and inviting, igniting a fierce yearning within me. Oh gods, how desperately I want to kiss him.

This feeling is so abnormal to me. I thought I had feelings for Dryston but none compared to this, not even as young fae when our hormones are raging to balance out. Dryston wanted me, even seemed to have no problem manipulating me into it. I thought we'd marry, that he'd be my husband. We'd have babies and live our life full of love and respect.

I want to laugh at the thought.

My entire life turned upside down just a few short weeks ago and yet here I am trying to throw myself at the next King who shows me a lick of attention. I am so pathetic.

Will this ruin our deal? We are supposed to marry if it comes to it and people will expect this. We're supposed to publicly show that we are growing feelings for each other but at this moment? We are alone... in my room... with me in a dress that leaves little to the imagination yet somehow is still regal.

I can't do this. I won't allow myself to blur these lines and assume he has feelings for me like I did with Dryston. It'll hurt too much in the end when he no longer has use for me.

I take a step back but before I can get far, his hand flashes to the back of my neck, pulling me to him. My hands rest on his chest, prepared to push him away. That is, until his lips meet mine in a desperate plea.

Suddenly I am melting into his touch, my chest completely against his as our lips meld together.

His hand tightens it's hold on the back of my neck while the other grips my waist, pulling me closer. My hands are clenched in his shirt, wrinkling the expensive fabric.

Heat flares within me, the unfamiliar feeling rising. My heart beats so hard I fear it'll pulse out of my chest. His body radiates warmth and I want more.

I go to move my arms around his neck, pulling his face down closer to mine. We both pull tighter, and I can feel every inch of him.

I feel as if I've been lit on fire when he squeezes, eliciting a light moan to slip from my lips as he grazes the inside of my mouth with his tongue. *Gods*, his tongue. My knees want to give out but he holds me too him and I feel his hardened cock push against me.

When a deep, resonant groan rumbles from his throat, it takes every ounce of willpower in me not to collapse to my knees, utterly undone. A warm wave of something akin to magic unfurls within me, sending tingling sparks dancing through my veins as if a hidden energy is awakening and purring softly.

He kisses me with a delicious urgency, prompting a helpless whimper to escape my lips. In this moment, I am profoundly grateful for the delicate fabric of my dress; its thinness allows for every sensation to intensify.

His lips leave mine only momentarily, granting me a precious breath before he begins to trail soft kisses along my jawline, down to the sensitive spot just beneath my ear where his warm breath sends shivers cascading down my spine.

With a gentle yet commanding hand on my waist, he urges me forward, and I instinctively leap into his arms, wrapping my legs around him as I seek closer contact. My body writhes against him, full of longing; another moan escapes my throat as he finds that sweet spot, drawing forth sounds of pleasure that echo between us.

I crave him—every part of him—right here and right now.

A knock reverberates around the room, jolting us both apart from the sudden noise. I slip from his grasp, tumbling backwards. Pants of air leave me as I adjust my dress and lightly touch my fingers to my lips, the scene replaying over and over. I stare at the ground, unable to remember why we stopped.

"Verena? Are you awake?" Ruelle's voice cuts through the sudden chill I have now that Eryx is several feet away from me. My eyes meet his, still darkened from our moment. I take note his fingers tracing his hip, a confusing look through his eyes, while his other hand adjusts himself in his pants and now I can't stop wondering what he'd feel like between my legs.

Ruelle's footsteps retreat and I release a shaky breath.

I go to speak to him, but he cuts me off. "Good night, Verena." Then escapes the room before a second more passes. It happens fast, too fast, and now I sit here wondering what just occurred.

How could I let that happen? Does he regret it? Do I?

He feels so good pressed against me, perfect even. He tastes like blackberry bourbon and the lingering flavor in my mouth alone makes me want to do crazy things.

He is intoxicating. And I can't help but feel like I've known him my entire life. The birthmark on my side tingles and I hold my hand to it, trying to soothe the unnatural feeling.

I strip the dress off, wanting to sleep. But, even as I lay there, rest does not come to me.

I stare at the ceiling, thinking over and over about the feeling of him pressed to me, kissing me as if he was a starving man and I was the only thing in sight to devour.

My body tingles everywhere and it's only when I finally see the sun creep up do I drift to sleep.

Chapter 21: Nightcrest

Verena

"Again." Esmeray's voice cuts through the blood pounding in my ears. My heart racing like never before as I come at her with the staff, swinging it with all my force.

I can't help but continue thinking about the nightmare I had last night. This time, it wasn't my recurring dream; it was Dryston.

"How dare you call me by name in front of guests! You know they will see that as a sign of weakness. It's disrespectful!" His voice was raised as his body shook with rage. His skin glistening with sweat he built up from anger. It's dark out and we're in my room as he yells at me. "My father is looking at me like I can't control you. How do you think that makes me look to my kingdom?" His hands grip my arms so hard they're bruised. I am 16 years old, and like usual I called him by his name. But, without telling me, he's decided to only be called Dryston by his immediate family until we marry. I've never seen him so angry at me.

"You will make it up to me, now, Verena. Get on your knees."

The rest of that memory is still ingrained in my brain. The way he forcefully shoved me to the floor and bruised the inside of my mouth. He enjoyed the tears pouring down my face. It triggered something numb through me. Gave me a part of my brain where I could just shut everything off and go through those moments of punishment without even remembering half of them. A lot of my time in the Court of Dawn was spent in my own mind.

Esmeray and I spar back and forth for what feels like forever and then it happens, I swing around low, swiping her feet from under her and she falls on her back.

The air pauses, Hadeon leans away from the wall in surprise, Esmeray starts laughing, and I breathe heavily with my eyes wide.

It was a natural reflex and I am surprised at myself for being so quick. I stand, offering my hand to her. She grabs it after she stalls her laughter and I help pull her up. I see others who had been curious enough to watch the new girl spar with the eldest princess. Their small smiles and raised brows sent a surge of pride through me. My hip tingles and as I glance around the room, I see him then, Eryx, standing off to the side— almost hidden from view with his shadows billowing around him. His face was void of any emotion but I can feel the pride from him, see it in the way the light in his eyes gleam.

"Okay, Miss Verena." Esmeray's voice breaks me from my stare. "I think we're done today. You're a fast learner and you have learned so much already. Good job." She walks off after patting my back and I turn to walk away, slamming into Eryx's body that now stands right behind me.

"Sorry," He starts, steadying me with his hands on my waist before jerking his hands away. My heart jolts, hurting inside my chest at his motion. He must regret our moment from two nights ago. "Today I was thinking you'd be available to go into Asterlayna with me. I would like to show you the town, see their reactions to my courting someone. We need their trust and I would like their approval."

I refuse to look him in the eye but I nod, untying the wraps around my hands. "I would love that." I want to speak to him about last night. I want to ask if he regrets it. Does he feel the same thing I feel? This odd connection between us? My body tingles with... something... every time he is near. Could it be the prophecy the witch spoke about?

I know I told him I'd love that and I would but it was a half truth. I was also terrified. What if they judge me harshly? I can only imagine that they all know of where I came from. Will they hate me? Does it matter? Our deal was that we'd get married and then I'd disappear after my revenge and neither of us would need to see each other again. But, was that what I truly wanted? It feels nice here. It feels like home.

No. No, I shouldn't. It doesn't matter how I feel or how he feels. It would make this entire deal messy and I do not want anymore messes. I don't expect any happy ending other than my revenge on Dryston. I don't even necessarily blame the court— I blame him and Mya and if they were all I got revenge on, I'd be content. Lianna didn't deserve anything bad. She was in the dark about most things and she, too, feels as if something was wrong. She has never trusted her brother.

I will get my revenge on him and I will leave Eryx and his family alone. They don't need any of my bad luck following them around.

The witch in the woods can't possibly know anything. She's just trying to stir up dramatics between us.

"I'll go get ready for town." I say, leaving his heavy gaze and escaping to my room.

After washing up and changing into a regular dress and slippers, I leave my hair down in waves and stare at myself in the mirror. My roots were coming in faster and at this point, I wish it'd just all change at once. It was getting distasteful with the color. Of course, the blue stays the exact same shade it has always been.

Pushing my nerves to the side, I meet up with Eryx, Hadeon, Ruelle, and Esmeray at the front entrance. Two carriages remain lined up, two footmen on each front and a footman on each back.

"Verena and I will share a carriage to show the townspeople we

are courting. You three will reside in the second one as support."
Eryx's voice left no room for disagreement and we follow suit. He
motions for me to enter it before him and while I hadn't wanted to, I
did, holding his hand to keep me steady as I step into the carriage.

After we start riding, silence remains and he has yet to actually look
at me.

I can't handle the quiet.

"Why have you been avoiding me?" I ask him point blank, staring
at his profile while he watches the window. This gets him to sigh and
finally his dark eyes meet mine.

"I am sorry for any confusion but, Lady Verena, I have not been
avoiding you." A scoff leaves me before I can stop it at his diplomatic
answer and I cross my arms over my chest. His eyes flicker down
toward my breasts at the movement and something sparks within me.

No. *No.* I tamper it down. "I do not believe you." His brows draw
close together as his eyes narrow at me, all forms of stoic emotion
fleeing him. Irritation leaks through his features and pride in myself
flares, happy I can cause such a reaction. "We kissed." I say, breaking
the silence again.

"We did." He confirms and I fight to keep my eye-rolling at bay.

"It was a mistake." The words leave before I can talk myself out
of it, wanting to see how he reacts. The irritation stays on his face.
"We are business partners, not lovers and it should remain that way.
There is already so much going on, we do not need a bigger mess by
adding in... feelings or lust or whatever it is between us." He continues
staring so my mouth continues talking. "And as promised, I still plan
to leave Khyrel whenever our business concludes. I appreciate all of
your help but we should not kiss again."

There's a long pause. His calculating gaze remains on mine. It's
the way his eyes shine from the sun gleaming through the window
to reveal the hint of caramel sprinkled in them, the way his shadows

billow around him look as if they want to reach out and touch me—and I'd let them. I want to take back my words, eat them and never speak them again. My hip tingles aggressively as if upset with me. I don't move.

And as soon as the carriage stops, he speaks. "Agreed." And even after it was my words that were shared and agreed with, something in me despises his concordance. He moves to step out of the carriage as the door opens but still offers his hand to help me down even if it seems as if he'd rather be anywhere else and I can not begin to blame him.

* * *

My fear of the people of Khyrel loathing me was far fetched. They seem so much more open minded and warmer than the people in the Capitol of Zorya. But, here in Asterlayna, people care.

Eryx and I stroll with our entourage trailing behind us, our steps in sync and our strides purposeful. I catch a glimpse of our reflection in a shop's window and can't help but smile at the fact that we look like a true family. I quickly avert my gaze, not wanting to get lost in that fantasy.

As we promenade down the vendor street, my senses were overwhelmed by the vibrant sights and scents surrounding me. From the colorful displays of food and jewelry to the variety of fabrics and indigenous beverages, everything was native to this country and it made my heart swell with pride. Despite having tried all the delicacies at the Court of Dawn, nothing compared to the flavors of Khyrel's.

"Thank you," Eryx's smooth voice broke through my thoughts from behind me. I turn to face him, his body standing unnecessarily close and his scent of maple syrup and brown sugar mixing with the other fragrant aromas on the street. But his fragrance stands out above all else, as if it were the only thing my nose wanted to smell.

Eryx hands a gift box to Hadeon and Hadeon stows it away into a bag for easier carrying while he turns to me. "For you," The king holds out a necklace that matches the one I had lost on my travels with Hadeon. My eyes follow from it to his eyes. "Hadeon said you had one from your mother but lost it during the fight at the tavern. I hope it's similar. I know it's not from your mother..." His deep voice trails off but I take it before he can retreat with it.

"I love it." I rush out, "Thank you." A blush rises to my face and I turn away, ushering him to latch it around my neck. As he does, his fingers brush my skin, eliciting bumps to appear across the expanse of my fair skin.

"You look just like your mother," The shopkeeper says aloud and my face jerks in her direction.

"Excuse me?" I ask in a small voice.

"Sorry, my lady. I was just mentioning how much you look like your mother, Vaia, correct? She was so beautiful and kind. I am not surprised you are the same." Her smile is genuine and while I can feel eyes on me, I can't help but freeze in thought. She takes my hand in both of hers with the warmest smile imaginable as she introduced herself.

"Yes. Vaia was my mother. I knew she grew up here but I wasn't aware that anyone would know of her." I can feel the royal family's presence straighten, unsure on what to do. Eryx has a stoic look on his face now but I see the confusion in his eyes.

"Oh! Vaia Nightcrest was apart of the Dusk Court families. Although she didn't have your beautiful light hair. She had your eyes, though. Shame what happened to her but we're glad you're still with us. We all thought you died with her and your father." It was like my world was spinning around. She wasn't saying anything with carelessness but it's all new information to me. My heart beats fast, struggling to keep up with my exceeded breaths.

"W-when did they die?" I ask her, needing to know if they were aware of my whereabouts.

"Twenty-two years ago."

As I stare at her, black fades into my vision but I smile weakly, "Thank you for everything, excuse me." I trip backwards before catching myself and stumbling through the crowd. Eryx and Hadeon both call my name in unison but I can't stop moving.

I walk the streets, fighting myself while trying to remain a happy person on the outside as Khyrelians watch me, greeting me, judging me. I was used to this my entire life. Queenship. How would they feel knowing I have this darkness in me? My need for revenge might seem frugal to most but it fuels me without destroying me from the inside. A hard thing to have for most people.

My body aches and my breaths come in ragged gasps as I finally find an empty alleyway. I slide into its dark depths, grateful for the momentary respite. Behind a waste bin, I sink to the hard concrete ground, trying to steady my pounding heart.

These people, with their knowing gazes, knew my mother. They had seen her smile, heard her infectious laughter. She was loved here— wherever "here" was. It's been twenty-two years since she's been in her home. I was just two years old. But, unless I missed something important along the way, I am very much alive and they were too for at least another decade. My father and mother moved to Zorya together, but apparently she was part of this court? A High Fae. There are so many questions burning inside me that I wish I could ask her now. So many things left unsaid between us.

Why would they fake their deaths to leave?

Why didn't she stay if she was a member of the court here? Did Calanthe know my mother? Is that why she won't stop staring at me?

Why does she hold back from saying what she truly wants to say to me?

The answers may lie within Calanthe herself, and I promise myself that once I make it back to the castle, I will demand them from her. For now, all I can do is catch my breath and try to piece together this mysterious puzzle of my mother's past.

I feel a presence but as I look around, no one is there. I shake the thought, it's probably a straggler from town.

"Verena," A voice startles me from my crouched position on the ground. I look up, finding Eryx now staring at me with concern etched onto his features.

I abruptly stand, wiping tears from my face and moving past him, "My apologies, your majesty." His firm grip wraps itself around my arm.

"What did the lady mean? About your mother?" He asks. I look up to the end of the alley and see the other three pretend they're not listening as I turn to face him.

"I do not know."

"Your mother was Vaia Nightcrest? Of Khyrel? And you didn't think me privy to this information?" He was getting irritated, of course he was. It looks as if I deliberately hid this from him. I jerk my arm from his grasp in anger.

"I didn't know!" My voice raises before I settle it again, moving closer to him. "I knew my mother was from Khyrel and that we moved when I was two years of age. That is it. I didn't even know Nightcrest was her last name. She went by my fathers in Zorya." He sees something in my face that crumbles him as he softens his gaze.

"If your mother was Vaia Nightcrest, we have more of a history than was to be believed." He moves closer, resting his fingers on my chin and raising my eyes to his. "But we cannot speak of it here."

Chapter 22: Damsel in Distress

Verena

"What are you saying to me right now?" I ask him, my hands pulling at my hair in frustration.

"I am saying that when Vaia Nightcrest had her baby, our parents set up a betrothal. The raven and the serpent; a prophetical union since the beginning of the two Courts. And ironically it is just as the witch told me. You are the raven. I am the serpent. Our fates are bound and clearly it's been trying to get us together from the beginning. *We* were betrothed. But Vaia and Arzhel left with you and faked your family's death. Calanthe and Vaia were best friends. I don't know why she didn't say anything to me about your mother. I barely remember the woman, let alone what she looked like." He stands in front of his desk, resting against it. I pace the room in front of him.

"Why wouldn't she tell me?" I ask him.

"I can not answer that. But, my guess is that your father made a deal with Dryston's father behind her back and took you both. She was happy here, that much I know. But, your father was very influential to her. She was stubborn and from what my mother says, very independent. Until he came along. And your grandparents hated him because of it. They died shortly after your birth which is probably why he was able to take you both so quietly."

I shake my head slowly, the motion not driven by disbelief but rather by the weight of revelation pressing down on me. It feels like everything I had known was built on a foundation of deception; my entire life now unfurls before me as an intricate tapestry woven from lies. The hardships I've endured—long nights spent in quiet despair and days filled with relentless struggle—now lay bare as mere pawns in my father's insatiable greed. Each scar etched into my soul was inflicted for his selfish gain, an ambition that he ultimately failed to savor for long.

The irony swirls around me like a thick fog, saturating the air with its pungent bitterness.

I draw in a long, deep breath, filling my lungs with air that feels almost electric against the backdrop of this harrowing truth.

"I am Verena Nightcrest." He nods. "What does that even mean?" I ask him.

He pauses his thoughts before stepping closer, his hands gently cupping my arms as he peers deeply into my indigo eyes. "It means you have a title. That you possess property, family, and a rightful place here. You belong here, Verena. Whether that is by my side or not. If you do not wish to continue with this any longer, I understand."

His genuine regard ensnares me, as if time itself has folded around us in that moment. His scent envelops me, now becoming my solace amidst the storm of emotions swirling inside. I feel myself getting too comfortable in his presence, an unsettling realization washing over me. Taking a step back, I regain some distance between us. "No. I made you a deal, and I intend to honor it. Dryston has committed…" My voice trembles slightly as I take a shaky breath, "heinous acts, and he must pay for them. We will decide what to do with me when this is all over."

His gaze continues to pierce through the layers of my soul, but I summon the strength to fortify the wall I've built around it for decades. Yet this time, I sense the chinks and cracks in its facade—the fissures that threaten to betray my resolve. "I need some time to process all of this," I manage to say firmly, if not a bit breathlessly. Without waiting for his reply, I turn and swiftly retreat from the room, leaving behind the castle's stone walls that echo with unspoken words and unresolved tension.

I need a place where no one will bother me.

* * *

Leaves flurry through the trees as the wind billows. It's the only sound I hear as I walk barefoot since I ditched my shoes in the garden. The sun shines through scattered sections of limbs and greenery, reaching for the forest floor with it's rays of warm light. Khyrel's capital was gorgeous in the night but I also love it during the day. The culture, the people, they all seem content and happy with their lives.

I walk through the forest alone. Eryx had warned me back about being here alone. He had stated there were dangers lurking here and if I wasn't traveling with someone who knows it, it's easy to get lost.

But something was pulling me here and I hadn't realized I ventured in so far until I snapped back into reality. It was seemingly peaceful regardless and this wasn't my first time. When I was planning on leaving and the witch stopped me I was also here alone and at night when it's harder to see. The feel of the earth underneath my bare feet was relaxing, soothing.

The only thing creepy about these woods was that it seemed eerily quiet other than the breeze blowing through and the birds that sang in a melancholy tone.

Oddly enough, it was somewhat comforting.

I was wearing my fighting leathers now, changing out of the dress before I left. Daggers strapped to my thighs and my sides. My hair was fading faster, the blonde halfway through my hair in a change from this morning. Chills run down my spine, feeling as if someone is watching me again. I take a look around, trying to spot any movement. A raven caws from above me, making me jump in surprise before blowing out a breath of relief.

I wish I wasn't wrong about what I said to Eryx. This *was* a business arrangement and feelings don't belong in the middle of it. But if that were the truth why did it feel as if fate herself was pulling me closer to him? Why does my heart beat faster when he's near and my lungs stop taking in air when he's away?

The crowd cheered around us when we walked through town. But why did I still feel as if I wasn't enough?

I shake my head of the thoughts. It didn't matter. Soon I'd get my revenge and I will leave them to live their lives in peace. Even if the idea of leaving them... of leaving *him*... made my chest hurt.

A stick breaks and the sound reverberates through the trees. I freeze, my blood running cold. Glancing around again, this time further in the trees, my eyes catch movement.

My heart stops as I take in the figure before me. Warm, golden blond hair falls in disarray around his face, and piercing green eyes meet mine with a flash of surprise before morphing into a familiar smile. A knot forms in my gut as I realize that he's here to kill me.

Dryston was never lacking in physical appearance. He had always been devastatingly handsome, with a charm that can melt any heart. But his temper and arrogance was always present, waiting to surface and wreak havoc. His downfall was inevitable, and yet...I can't deny that I had once loved him. He was going to be my husband, part of my family. Was I overreacting to his betrayal?

As these thoughts race through my mind, Dryston rushes toward me with a mix of worry and hope in his gaze. Despite my defensive stance, he wraps his arms around me tightly, holding on as if afraid to let go. "Verena! Thank the Gods I've found you," he whispers urgently. "Where have you been? I've been worried sick!" He pulls back slightly but doesn't release me, his concern evident in his gaze as he studies my face and clothing. "Did he take you? Hadeon? We discovered his treachery too late — he murdered one of the guards and escaped from his cell. He's dangerous, Verena. I'm just glad you're safe." His embrace tightens again before he finally lets go, searching my face for confirmation that I am indeed unharmed. "We need you back at the castle, Hadeon has told the Dark King of our plans of attack, we have to prepare for war." He grabs my hand in a tight squeeze, just uncomfortable enough to break me from my frozen state.

I rip my hand from his with haste, "I'm not going anywhere with you." My voice, while I feel shaky, remains firmer than I thought it would.

He looks at me confused. "Verena, stop being a child. You're coming with me. As future queen of Zorya and my wife I expect more of you. You're being selfish. Now, let's go before they find us." He reaches to snatch my hand back into his own and I jump back, reflex kicking in while my fingers find my daggers.

"I will say this once more. I am not going with you." My voice is deadly but my heart races in fear. "And I am not your wife."

I stare into his eyes while his face remains calm. The rage swims there before he tones it back and looks at me with admiration and a hint of condescension. "Is this about your coronation?" I say nothing. He sighs in desperation. "Verena, my love... my *wife*. I didn't mean it. I had to say that so no one knew we had a real Khyrelian in our midst. It was for the good of the kingdom. You are to be queen, you know we can't have our people in a panic. Khyrelians are savages and deranged." My stomach churns. His words make me think about the way Eryx treated the man meant to spy on me in my first week here. The darkness radiating off of him, the shadows billowing around. It sends a shock to my core that I try brushing out of my head. Now was not the time. "They are dangerous. You know this." He holds his hands up in surrender as he steps closer to me, staring into my eyes with his fake desperation.

I'll give it to him, he is good. I *almost* believe him.

"Once we return home, we will hold your coronation now that he is gone and the threat is no longer there. I don't know what I would've done if you had been hurt or worse; killed."

"There are worse things than being killed." My voice lowers, my heart clenching at the thoughts of our past. Confusion flashes through him.

"Like having your consent stripped from you. Like being manipulated into believing you're loved." Now my voice is shaky. "Like living a lie your entire life. You've blatantly ignored my hair, or have you not noticed it's lightness?" I sturdy my tone as I question him, anger coursing through me.

"None of that matters. We are married-"

"Stop saying that!" I yell, "We are no longer married." I pull up my sleeve to reveal the mottled scarring from cutting the rune off. "The thought of being married to you makes me violently ill. I will no longer fall for your empty promises and your lies. You will burn and I will light the match, Dryston Whitewell." I stand straighter and watch as the feign innocence leaves his eyes. The raven above us caws again, but he pays it no mind.

The mossy color in his irises darkens now, his face setting into a stone. "That's how you want to play this?" It's rhetorical. He laughs maniacally, "I tried being nice. But you're either coming with me or I will kill you, right now. You think you can take me? You couldn't even stop me when we were betrothed." He scoffs a laugh from his lips. "Beating you won't even feel like a chore." He uses his magic and strips the daggers from my body. A gasp leaves my lips and I'm thrown back by the metal daggers still on my body.

He laughs, condescension bleeding through. "You can't even fight me!" He yells, eye blaring fury.

I feel it then, the magic under my surface bubbling up. He tries throwing me again and my instincts kick in. As his power bursts into me, it filters back out at him when I throw my hands out to protect me.

His body hits the tree behind him and he stares at me in shock as he reaches a standing position. "What the fuck?" He sounds breathless and I can't help the smirk growing on my face. It doesn't last long though and now if I make it out of this alive, how do I tell Eryx I went against his wishes and just wandered into the woods so recklessly? He's going to think I did it on purpose.

Dryston bounces back fast but for every throw of magic he gives, my own seems to mirror it by absorbing the power from him and using it to my advantage.

I keep up, *barely*, trying to hurl it all back at him. He's fast but I'm faster, something I've never noticed before. My training with Esmeray has helped tremendously with cardio. A surge of confidence burns through me and I laugh out loud but it sounds maniacal itself and it surprises me.

How *dare* he.

How dare he come into enemy territory to retrieve me like I am some damsel in distress.

"I can do this all day!" I yell at him, lying. I definitely can't. I can already feel my energy depleting. But the feminine rage inside me boils. I'm going to have to injure him and run. I haven't practiced with my newfound powers to keep this up.

I frantically scan the forest floor, my heart racing as I search for my daggers while dodging his ferocious blasts. My once sharp and deadly weapons now lay dull and used, their edges worn down from the Zoryan king when he removed them.

But then, like a gift from the heavens, the sun breaks through the thick canopy and shines a spotlight on a lone dagger lying in the dirt. Without hesitation, I lunge for it and snatch it up before launching it at my opponent with all of my might.

The blade finds its mark, sinking deep into his muscular thigh and eliciting a howl of rage from him. Blood seeps out of the wound, staining his dark cloak and causing him to falter for just a moment.

In that brief moment of distraction, I take advantage and sprint away, feeling cuts on my face and arms from both magical attacks and the sharp branches that whip at me as I flee. My once neatly braided hair has come undone, wild strands falling haphazardly around my face.

But I don't have time to fix myself or catch my breath. The chase is still on, and I must keep running if I want to live another day.

Chapter 23: Do Not Pass Out

Verena

With my heart pounding in my chest, I frantically run in a direction opposite of Dryston. My senses are on high alert as I dash through the unfamiliar trees of Khyrel. Everywhere feels dangerous right now, but anywhere has to be better than staying here with him. As one of the few people in this town with rare hair, I know that I will stand out and potentially draw unwanted attention. But at this moment, all I can think about is finding some kind of refuge.

However, after my time in the treacherous Zoryan court, where everyone was out for themselves and betrayal was common, I find it hard to trust anyone.

My legs are burning with exhaustion, but I push myself to keep going. Just when I start to question if I should have taken a different path, I feel a sharp rock pierce the bottom of my foot and stab into the most vulnerable spot. The pain shoots through me and my inner sarcastic voice wants to comment on how maybe this wouldn't have happened if I were wearing boots, something Eryx has been onto me about. But I quickly push those thoughts away and try to focus on getting away.

As my breathing becomes more laborious and pieces of dirt from my face fly into my mouth, I feel the adrenaline from the recent fight and fear of being caught by Dryston coursing through me. But I can't stop now. Even though I can no longer see him behind me, I can hear his angry shouts and it only fuels me to keep running. With determination in my stride, I continue forward in the direction I was originally heading toward.

Any thoughts I had about going back to the Court of Dawn are all gone now. Dryston can suck fate if he thinks I'll ever be in Zorya again. Not until he dies by my hands.

I turn suddenly, running in a different direction once I feel as if it's too long to go straight. Changing up my pattern will help too.

My head starts throbbing and as I reach up to grab my forehead, I feel a warm wet and sticky substance sliding down my skin. The blood makes me lightheaded, scared of what would happen if I were to pass out right now in the middle of nowhere with Dryston hot on my tail.

I see smoke ahead, the scent of food and mead overlapping with the scent of sweat and earth. A cry of relief goes through me. I didn't think I'd feel this relieved since Hadeon and I passed through the border.

The doors swing open as I burst inside, causing a stir among the crowd. All eyes turn to me, some wide with surprise and others gaping in shock. My gaze sweeps over the room, taking note of the few individuals wearing Khyrelian armor.

"Help me," I gasp, my knees giving out beneath me. A guard quickly rushes forward to catch me before I hit the ground. My vision begins to fade into darkness, blinking in and out like a faulty light bulb. I squint my eyes, willing myself not to pass out.

"What is your name?" One of the guards asks me while another stands close by, scowling at my appearance. A maid hurries over with a cup of water, assisting me in taking small sips. My chest heaves as I try to catch my breath.

As I start to calm down, I strain to hear any sounds in the building. The once silent space is now filled with voices whispering and murmurs of concern, but Dryston's angry calls and growls are no longer audible.

"My name is Verena, I'm King Eryx's betrothed. I was just attacked in the woods by the king of Zorya." Whatever whispers were surrounding the silence, stopped too. I swear everyone can hear my heart beat fast and hard. The guard helping me is young and I take the time to look at him and the other guard here.

The one bending in front of me holds an empathetic look. He's young and handsome but I can tell he was a newer guard. Definitely not older than the king. He seemed sweet and concerned for my well-being. His dirty blond hair falls to the side of his head in curls, his tanned skin, and his hazel eyes warm like the sunny forest I just ran from; brown with hints of green drizzled throughout.

The older one standing with a scowl looks as if he isn't necessarily happy with my presence but he seems to not completely hate me. Esmeray had told me some of the guards weren't happy with the union and how they don't trust me, which I knew I'd have to rectify. But seeing it in person was throwing me off. "Liam, get word to the king." He says, his voice seemingly deeper than who I am assuming is Liam. His eyes were brown too, but more caramel-colored to stand out against his skin tone. He was taller and more built, as to be expected with the older but still young fae.

The one kneeling nods his head before giving me one last concerned gaze and booking it out to his horse outside.

"Are you alright?" The older one questions me, concerned only in the name of the king, I'm sure.

"I think so." He hands me the wet rag from the maid and let's me try to clean myself up. I don't even know how the cut on my head got there but it's slowed down the bleeding. I apply pressure to try to stop it as the guard and I stare each other down. "You don't like me much, do you?" I ask him, still breathless and barely conscious, curiosity eating away at me.

He watches the room as everyone goes back to their business, stealing glances at me every so often. "I do not know you." Is all he says but it is a loaded answer.

"I do not blame you, you know? I wouldn't trust me either. I have done nothing to earn anyone's trust. The only thing you all have to go on is the word of the royal family. I came from nowhere and out of the blue. It's hard to trust a person like that." He watches me carefully as I speak. "I'd like to earn your trust— the guards and the people of Khyrel."

He nods in understanding, "I look forward to you earning it, Lady Verena." There isn't more words to be said so we sit in silence, waiting for Liam and the king to return.

* * *

"Where is she?"

The tavern was now empty, the loud voice of King Eryx booming through the once lively atmosphere. The guard and a few others had quickly cleared out the remaining patrons, leaving us alone in the dimly lit room. As Eryx bursts through the door, his face was flushed and his muscular tanned body shook with rage. In that moment, I realized just how much trouble I was in. He was furious with me for wandering into the woods and leaving the castle grounds.

I stand from my seat, my hands trembling as I tried to remain composed. He immediately takes notice of me and even as other guards stare and watch, the one who had been here the entire time stepped forward to speak with the king. But Eryx ignored him completely, storming toward me with furious purpose.

In a sudden and unexpected move, his large hands cover my cheeks as he pulls me closer, locking eyes with me. Though his rage still burns within him, it seems to diminish slightly at the sight of me. "Where else are you hurt?" His thumb brushes gently over my head wound, no longer actively bleeding but still sore to the touch. I wince at the pressure and he immediately stops, concern evident in his features.

I can't even remember now, where my other wounds are, with him here holding me like this. I thought he would be mad at me. Not worried. Not like this. Maybe for the female that holds the secrets to protecting his kingdom from war but not as if nothing else matters but my safety. My chest rises and falls rapidly, in time with my heart profusely pounding from his proximity. His shadows caress me all over as if searching for more wounds.

"Nowhere important." I guess as he pulls me further back, reluctantly, from his own body and assesses me with his dark eyes. "Just some scratches." My voice is quiet and small. "Dryston was here." It cracks as I finally want to break down from realization. "I am so sorry. I should've listened to you. I- I thought I'd be fine but I was wrong. He tried to take me back but I wouldn't let him… I wouldn't let him! A-and he started attacking me and I tried. I tried to get away. I could barely hold him off. I-" I stop speaking, my thoughts a jumbled mess wanting to tell him about my powers but not in front of other ears. He sees this as I glance around before meeting his eyes.

"I know Dryston was here. As soon as they found me and told me what happened, I rushed over to find you and yelled for them to search the woods. But he isn't my priority." His eyes read my soul as if trying to tell me something with them. "I needed to know you were okay."

He pulls me to him with gentle urgency, his strong arms enveloping my slender frame. The sudden embrace catches me off guard, but I reciprocate, inhaling his familiar scent — a mix of maple and brown sugar and something uniquely him — to soothe my frayed nerves. I can sense him doing the same, his breath warm against my hair, sending a tingling current of energy coursing through my body. "Let's get back to the castle," he murmurs, his voice a low rumble against my ear. I nod wordlessly, my cheek presses against the rough fabric of his tunic. He slowly releases me, only to tuck me closer to his side, his arm a protective barrier as we exit the dimly lit tavern. He acknowledges the guards with a curt nod as we pass.

Exhaustion weighs heavily upon me, seeping into my very bones. The magical duel with Dryston has drained me more than I realized. My limbs feel leaden, my steps sluggish. He seems to sense my fatigue, for as soon as we return and he dismounts our horse, he scoops me up into his arms without hesitation. This tender gesture is so uncharacteristic of him, of us, that it leaves me breathless with its novelty.

This new dynamic between us sends shivers of anticipation through my body. Despite my bone-deep weariness, I find myself acutely aware of every point of contact between us. The warmth of his body seeps into mine, a stark contrast to the cool night air. His breathing is measured, as if he's consciously trying to remain calm, but I can feel the rapid tattoo of his heart echoing my own.

He cradles me securely, one arm supporting my knees while the other curves around my back. I nestle against his broad chest, the steady thrum of his heartbeat a soothing lullaby. My hand, seemingly of its own volition, begins to trace delicate patterns over his heart. I feel the muscles in his chest tense beneath my fingertips, and unbidden, my mind wanders to how those same muscles might feel moving above me. The thought sends a rush of heat to my cheeks and a flutter of anticipation to my stomach.

Why am I acting like this? I was attacked in the woods not too long ago and yet all I can think of right now is him. His body. His breathing. It sparks something in me.

I trail my fingers up, brushing his neck and watching his artery throb as blood races through him. Why do I have the sudden urge to lick him?

I hold that one back, fighting myself.

We arrive in front of his room and he opens the door before closing it with his foot and setting me on the bed. He stares at me for what feels like forever before turning away and heading for the door.

"Wait!" The word rushes out without thought and immediately I get off the bed and walk over to his still body, his back facing me.

I watch as he clenches his hands. "Please," I have no idea what I am asking of him but he turns toward me, his eyes raking over my body as if memorizing every inch. My mark tingles with a need for him.

This is crazy, wild, and completely what I was originally trying to avoid.

I can almost feel his thoughts swimming through my own mind as he reaches out and places his hands firmly on my thighs, lifting me up and pressing me against the wall beside the door.

A sharp intake of breath escapes me before his mouth is on mine, consuming me in a fiery kiss that leaves me dizzy and wanting more. I can't help but moan as he explores every inch of my mouth with his tongue, a dance of passion and desire.

"I thought you were angry with me," I breathlessly gasp between kisses as he trails his lips along my neck. He lets out a dark chuckle that sends shivers down my spine.

"Oh, I am," he growls, gripping me tighter against the wall. "I am so angry at you." Each word is punctuated with a fierce kiss, leaving my skin tingling and my mind spinning. "For being reckless..." He kisses down my jawline, trailing hot kisses down my neck. "For not listening..." His lips brush against the sensitive spot below my ear before nipping at it. "For putting yourself in danger." A low groan escapes him as he nips harder, eliciting a whimper from deep within me.

"I've learned my lesson," I'm breathless.

He grinds his center against mine, a moan this time slipping out, "I don't think you have." He moves us, my legs wrapping tightly around him, fearful he'll let go.

He carries me to the desk in the luxurious suite, my body feeling weightless in his strong arms. He sets me down and without hesitation, his skillful hands tear away the fabric of my dress, leaving me exposed and vulnerable.

My breath catches in surprise as his lips find mine once again, igniting a wildfire inside me. His tongue dances expertly with mine, sending shivers down my spine. I've never felt anything like this before.

In the past, my only lover had been Dryston, and not always by choice. But this... this is something else entirely.

His rough, tanned hands glide along my thighs, causing my body to arch toward him. My ankle digs into his backside, urging him closer. Through his trousers, I can feel his growing bulge and my hand instinctively runs over it with desperate longing.

A small voice in the back of my mind tries to warn me to stop, but it's drowned out by the overwhelming desire pulsating through every inch of my being. "We shouldn't do this." I say flimsily, attempting to keep my head.

"Probably." He answers without any conviction.

When his fingers finally reach my wet center, I let out a loud moan of pleasure. "Oh gods," I manage to gasp out between ragged breaths, completely consumed by the intensity of our passion.

"Just me." This time humor laces his deep voice and his shadows slip around us once more, grazing my skin in a cooling touch. It's like a refreshing wind on a hot summer day. They trail up my thighs and over my center. I can't seem to breathe.

A low, guttural groan escapes his lips as he runs his hand over my body, tracing the wetness that slips down my thigh. "You're so wet for me," he murmurs, a mischievous smirk playing on his lips. I can feel my body responding to his touch, grinding against his hand in desperate need of friction. He suddenly removes his hand and I whimper at the loss of contact.

But then, he surprises me by bringing his fingers to his mouth and sucking on them, his eyes never leaving mine. I am consumed by the fiery hunger in his gaze as he presses his other hand gently against my chin.

"Look at me," he whispers, and I find myself nodding obediently. I am completely bare before him, and he gazes longingly at every inch of my body — my face, my neck, my breasts— but stops before going any further due to our bodies pressing tightly together.

"I want to see you," I manage to say through ragged breaths, tugging at his clothes. With a knowing smile, he strips off his garments and I follow behind him, tracing the intricate tattoos bedeck his muscular arms and chest. There is an abundance of art painted onto his skin, but it is the small distinct one on his hip that catches my attention. My blood runs hot as I slip off the desk to get closer to him, running my fingertips over the delicate bird etched into his skin. It's in the exact same spot as my birthmark, with the same shape and size.

But that can't be possible. Because that would mean...

"Your bird. Is this a tattoo?" I ask, my voice a whisper. He looks down at it before looking at my face again, a hint of concern ghosting

202

his face.

"It's a birthmark. Been there since I was a kid although my mom hadn't seen it until I was six. It just appeared one day." He says, his voice still low as he looks at me with confusion. "What's wrong?" He asks. My heart flutters at the fact that he is more concerned about me than he is turned on.

I rub my hip subconsciously, surprised he hasn't seen it yet. But his eyes follow my hand and they widen. "Is that-"

"The same one."

"But that means…" He trails off, as if not believing it. Or it's because if he says it out loud, it becomes true. He did agree with me to stop whatever this is. Our focus supposed to be on the business side of our arrangement.

Of course. What am I doing?! He doesn't want to be mates with me. Fate or not.

Chapter 24: Let Go

Verena

I move my arms to cover myself but he's there in front of me, holding my arms at the wrists. "Don't. Do not go wherever in your pretty mind you just went. Verena." He says when I refuse to meet his gaze. "*Verena.*" He tries again and this time I do. As if I can no longer stand to not be looking at him. "We are fated mates. Can't you see? It all makes sense now. The prophecy. The reason our paths continue to cross. You are *mine*. And I am yours. And if I am honest with myself, I have always known it. From the moment I saw you— in the dress that killed me— at Dryston's coronation ball. There was something between us. I wanted to take you in the middle of the dance floor in front of everyone." I let out a small choked laugh at the preposterous notion but let myself be pulled into him with no fight. "If you want this... I want this." Even now he gives me the choice. If we continue with our wishes tonight, we'll accept the bond. If we stop before we go all the way, we can continue living in delusion that we aren't meant for each other by the Gods themselves.

I grab his head, forcing our lips to move in tandem once again. A growl slips from his lips.

Mate bonding with the Dark King was definitely not something I expected. But it's as if everything clicks into place now. My dreams. With his tattooed hand grasping my shoulder to spin around as I watch the colorful lights. I wonder if he dreams of me too.

With a forceful push, he backs me against the desk once more and I barely manage to stop myself from colliding into the mirror behind me. His hands grip my waist tightly as he kneels down, his lips trailing kisses along my thigh with a feather-light touch. I struggle to maintain my balance, my arms shaking as I watch him move closer to the growing heat between my legs.

Keeping intense eye contact with me, he runs his tongue along my inner thigh before proceeding to lick my center. A shuddering breath escapes my lips as I feel his magical tongue expertly playing with my sensitive bud, like a skilled musician. The sensations of lust, hormones, and something unfamiliar intertwine between us, creating an electric tension that crackles in the air.

"I want to hear you," he whispers, pressing his lips to my inner thigh once again.

Suppressing a moan in defiance, I bite down on my lip as he drags his hand up my leg, his fingers meeting the warmth of my desire. The pleasure from his touch is enough to make me weak at the knees. He runs gentle circles around my clit with his mouth while slipping his long fingers inside me. My voice betrays me, unable to contain the overwhelming pleasure coursing through my body.

Every breathy curse that escapes my lips only seems to fuel his desire, his body looming over mine as he pumps his finger in and out of me. Each time he hits all the right spots, I can't help but let out a string of expletives. His fingers stretch me in ways I never thought possible, the foreign pleasure igniting every nerve ending in my body. My head falls back, unable to support itself as my neck muscles give out in surrender.

"Eryx, please-" I start to beg, ready for him to give me more.

I grip his messy hair with my fingers, pulling his head up to meet my gaze before I press my lips to his again. Running his tongue along my bottom lip, he slips it into my mouth, both of us fighting for dominance. In this moment, all I can think about is how much I want him to have me, to touch me until I only know his name. He groans into the kiss, our marks burning with pleasure as the invisible string connecting us grows stronger.

"Tell me what you want, Verena." He whispers between kisses, his lips brushing against mine as he guides the tip of him over my warmth, teasing and tempting me beyond belief.

"You. I want all of you," I say without thinking, his eyes wide.

With a soft whisper, "I'll be gentle," his lips graze against mine, sending sparks of desire through my body. As he slowly enters me, I feel the stretch and the mingling of pleasure and pain. A loud moan escapes my lips and I call out his name, feeling our bodies entwine in a symphony of sensations. My hands glide down his back, feeling the muscles tense and relax with each thrust. Our mating bond snaps into place, filling us with a rush of euphoria that we both share. Our eyes meet, full of passion and determination. We have made our choice and there is no going back now, even if it means risking everything for this union.

As Eryx pauses to let me adjust, his hand gently trails up my side while the other holds my leg up to deepen our connection. But I don't want him to be gentle. "Don't," I whisper, locking gazes with him. Confusion flashes across his face before understanding sets in. "Don't be gentle," I clarify, wanting to feel every raw and primal part of this moment together.

He smirks at me, pulling almost all the way out and thrusting back in, I moan into his mouth, feeling nothing but pleasure as he moves again. Starting a slow rhythm, he moves in and out of me, the force growing with each thrust.

Our kisses become hungrier.

Hitting the spot in my lower stomach, I feel the heat rise once more. He bites back his groans and I use my heel to pull him against me harder, urging him on.

I begin trying to rock my hips in gentle motions against his, feeling him grip my sides, guiding the action. With each move, the warmth only grows within my stomach, his length throbbing, his hands gripping tighter.

"You are so breathtaking." He breathes out. His strong arms grasp me, both our bodies sweating now. The power running through us is no longer individual at this moment. He presses his lips to the spot under my ear and I groan, digging my nails into his back.

The pleasure rises in my stomach, my body anticipating its release.

"Let go," He groans out, keeping his hold as he thrusts in and out, his own body tightening in pleasure.

As one of his hands meet my clit, my release coats him as a silent scream escapes me and my grip on him grows tighter as I ride out my release. I feel his own orgasm roll through him as he comes, rolling his hips as we ride out our pleasure.

Our heavy breathes mingle as we take in the scent of each other mixing with the scent of our arousal. My thoughts are jumbled and I have difficulty forming a sentence. But he pulls out of me and I almost whimper at the loss of him before he lifts me up and brings me to the bathroom. He turns on the faucet in the tub, filling it up and depositing me inside it. I realize I am still dirty from my fight in the woods and my nose scrunches up.

"I can't believe we just did that while I've got dirt all over me." I cover my face with my hands and he chuckles, moving over to me as the water stops.

"I'd ravish your body anywhere, anytime. All you have to do is ask."

His eyes meeting mine tell me he's serious. I scoff in disbelief.

When he gets in with me and washes us clean, I realize it's changed for him too. No longer is he second-guessing anything toward me.

It's hard for me to process this feeling.

"I can feel you thinking too hard." He says quietly as he rinses the creme from my hair that makes it soft and shiny.

With the bond in place, I can feel it fully. The buzzing in my body no more, the pain in my hip is gone. I feel stupid not realizing it but how was I supposed to know?

The only question now was where does this leave us? "What do we tell people?" I ask him, sliding away from him so I can turn to face him. His eyes soften at the sight of worry on my face.

"It is none of their business." He replies and I give him a look.

"You are their king. The townspeople might like me but your guards do not trust me. And now after weeks of being together, all the sudden I'm your mate? It sounds suspicious, Eryx."

"They will grow to trust you. Once we are married, it will be different. But they're naturally suspicious of people with me because I have not been with another in ten years, no matter how hard they've tried." This surprises me. I know he had been engaged before and she passed away but I wasn't exactly sure how.

"How did she die?" I ask him, I want to know everything about him. Hell, I don't want to get out of this tub because I want to continue feeling his skin against mine.

"She was murdered by my father's guard. Who had apparently ordered him to do it. He never trusted her but I was in love, I guess. I didn't want to listen. The same day she died, she also hired someone to kill him. They died on the same day, hours apart. It was a dark time for me." He goes quiet after and my heart clenches in pain, feeling his sorrow.

Not only did he lose his betrothed and father at the same time, his

208

trust was broken, and then everyone needed him to be king. He had to fight his grieving to become what his people needed. I couldn't imagine what that was like.

"I'm so sorry, Eryx," I whisper, my hand reaching out to cup his cheek. He leans into my touch, his eyes soft with gratitude.

"Thank you for listening," he says. "But don't let that define me. We live for today and tomorrow. We'll face the future together, make our own memories." He grins, and I can't help but smile back, feeling the weight of his happiness.

We slip out of the tub, wrapping ourselves in soft towels. Our hearts beat in rhythm, tangling together in a bond that feels stronger with every passing moment. We have become something new, something special, and I feel a strange sense of gratitude for the darkness that brought us here.

Chapter 25: Love Me, Always

Verena

I sleep through the night in his bed and for once, the looming and recurring dream stays behind. I'd have to ask if he ever had any dreams of me. I awaken to light beaming in and brightening the room surrounding me.

The smell of the sheets is not what I usually wake to— now they consist of freshly baked dessert wafting through my nose in a comfort. A hard chiseled body rolls next to me, wrapping it's arms around my waist and pulling me closer. The heat radiating off him is a welcome sensation. "We have to wake before someone finds me in here, Your Majesty," Fingers grip my hip, tickling me as I jerk from his grasp with a squeal. *"Eryx."* He let's out a light groan of pleasure as he pulls me back to him and I can't help but smile.

With Dryston, everything was tense and I continued waiting for the other shoe to drop when something was going right. But it always felt as if something were missing and my body always felt sick after his visits with me. I couldn't figure out why but now I know. I had already met my mate as a child before my father ripped me from his grasp. "Let them." He answers me but I roll my eyes before hastily untangling myself from him. My naked body now on display. His eyes flash open at not being able to grasp me quick enough but he freezes, his eyes taking me all in. A blush crawls all over my body as a flash of pleasure tingles in my lower stomach at his gaze.

When Dryston saw me naked, he looked at me as if I were any other woman. It's what I expected last night and even right now as Eryx watches me. But he doesn't.

The raven-haired male's chest rises and falls in quick succession, his breathing uneven as he clenches his fists and peruses each place he wants to meet with his mouth. A shiver runs through me at the thought alone.

A knock sounds at the door, breaking his gaze. I jump out of my skin from the noise and he lazily gets up from the bed, grabbing the sheets to wrap around me reluctantly. "This isn't over, Seren Fach." His voice is deep with promise as he puts on pants.

I move to hide behind the door as he cracks it open. "Have you seen Verena? I heard about yesterday and went to check on her but she wasn't in her room." Hadeon's concerned voice echoes through the room and my eyes widen at Eryx's smirk. And I want to smack him but I knew I'd be revealed at that point. "Well actually-" I smack his arm that rests on the door handle out of reflex and mentally curse myself. A gasp is held back from me when his hand trails from the door handle to my waist. He caresses my skin upwards, gliding over my breasts before he swirls around my nipple and I bite my lip to suppress any noises I cannot control. Then, his fingers slide over my throat, feeling my heavy breathing as he goes and covers my mouth with his hand. "She's around." He settles on. I can practically feel Hadeon's heavy gaze through the door as Eryx leans against it to hide his arm reaching to me.

"Are you okay, Eryx? I know Dryston getting into Khyrel unnoticed isn't ideal." He says and I mentally bang my head against the door. I want him to leave so I can finish what Eryx has just started.

He lets out a low laugh that sends another spark between my legs. "Trust me, brother, the last thing I'm worried about is Dryston Whitewell. I have to finish some... stuff here but I'll meet you and the family in the dining hall for breakfast in about," He feigns though, "ten minutes?" I pinch his arm making another smirk arise on his face, "Actually make that thirty." Before Hadeon can say anything, Eryx shuts the door in his face, making me feel lightly bad but not nearly more than pleasure at the short interaction between the two.

"He couldn't leave fast enough," I state before dropping the sheet and jumping into Eryx's arms as he catches me, grasping my thighs with his muscular hands as they wrap around him. He walks backwards before settling on the chaise lounge at the foot of the bed.

Straddling him now, I grind my naked body against his clothed bottom half, feeling his now hard erection against my warm core. A sensuous sigh escapes me at the feel of him.

We fit together like the perfect pair of puzzle pieces.

His strong hands grip my hips, pulling me in closer to him with each thrust. Our lips meet in a fiery, passionate kiss as I tug on his hair, guiding his face toward mine.

A low, guttural groan escapes him and gets lost in our intense embrace. As I find myself completely surprised by my own actions, I realize that I have never felt this way before. With Dryston, my libido was never this high, and I never craved physical intimacy like this. But with Eryx, it feels natural, like it's meant to be. I want him with every fiber of my being, now and always.

"So greedy, Seren Fach." I moan at his words.

"What does that mean?" I ask about the nickname in a gasp as he rubs me against him.

"Wouldn't you like to know?" He plays with me.

Fingers tangle in his hair, I pull him closer in a moment of frustration. He chuckles softly against my skin, sending shivers down my spine. Lost in the sensation, I can't even remember what I had asked for. All that matters now is how much I need him.

His lips find my aching nipple and he bites down gently, drawing out another moan from deep within me. My hand moves between us, urgently pulling at his pants to release his throbbing erection. In one smooth motion, I line him up with my pulsing center and slowly sink down onto him. A guttural groan escapes from his lips as he fills me completely, his hands grasping onto me tightly.

He breaks away from my nipple momentarily to capture my lips in a passionate kiss. His tongue dances with mine as our bodies move together in perfect rhythm. With every thrust, the pleasure builds within me, threatening to consume me entirely. His other hand finds its way to my clit, sending electrifying waves of pleasure through my body.

The sensation becomes almost overwhelming, causing my movements to become choppy and erratic. But he guides my hips with skilled hands, helping me ride the wave of ecstasy. The bird tattooed on my hip feels like it's come to life, tingling with intense pleasure just like the rest of my body.

I know it won't be long before I reach my peak, but I don't want this moment to end. Every touch, every sound from him drives me wild with desire. And in this moment of pure bliss, I know there's nowhere else I'd rather be than right here with him

"Oh gods," I gasp out as his cock presses against the sweet spot inside me. The pressure builds in my abdomen, bringing me closer and closer to the edge.

"Come on, Seren Fach, almost there sweetheart." His words talking me through it push me over into my climax. "Come for me, love." He grunts out. Whimpers leave my throat as I do exactly what he says, with no control over my body. My breathing is uneven, my heart beats fast.

My body is still reeling from his movements as he continues to thrust inside me, but I can't wait any longer. With a sly smile, I climb off his lap and drop down to my knees on the hard floor. I take him in my mouth, savoring the taste of him that I missed out on last night. It's a strange feeling, willingly pleasuring him like this, but it's also exhilarating.

As I bob my head along his length, I taste myself mingling with his distinct flavor. Spit escapes the corners of my mouth, but he firmly grips my hair, making my eyes water as he pushes himself deeper into my throat, cutting off my air.

But I don't mind. In fact, I relish in the intense pleasure of it all. Eyes wide open, I gaze up at his handsome face as he releases himself into my throat, unable to stop me from holding him there until he finishes.

With a satisfied smirk, he pulls out of my mouth and lifts me off the floor to meet my lips once again. "You are absolutely stunning, Verena," he whispers against my lips. He looks as if he wants to say more. I watch he hesitation in his eyes before it flickers to something more. "Ever since you arrived, I have been falling for you. You are the shining star in my dark night sky and I will cherish you always, fated mate or not." His words send a wave of warmth and adoration through my entire being.

After our moment of passion, we slowly regain our wits and hastily get dressed. I slip back into yesterday's clothes before I can change into something new, while he patiently waits for me to be ready. As we walk toward my room, I feel a warmth in my heart that has been absent since my mother died. It feels like a long-buried door has opened, revealing a part of myself that I had forgotten existed.

* * *

214

We walk into the dining hall together silently. All eyes are on us from his family and the staff. I watch as Hadeon studies Eryx closely while Ruelle and Esmeray smirk. Their mother, Calanthe, watches us with a simple motherly content smile as if she knew all along. A servant starts pulling my chair out but Eryx holds up a hand, preventing him from doing so before sliding out the seat himself. My cheeks grow hot as I sit, the remnants of our time this morning still on my mind as I am reminded by my deliciously sore center. "Thank you," I tell him quietly, watching the smirk on his face grow at my timid embarrassment. Unlike my previous relationship, though, his smirk isn't condescending. It's playful and welcoming as it eases my nerves.

"How are you doing, Verena?" Calanthe asks me, breaking the tension from the room. I jump in my seat and turn to see her and everyone else watching me with almost knowing looks. Or am I just being paranoid? Esmeray snickers at my jumpiness and I shoot her playful daggers.

"What?" I ask, unsure on what she means. She can't possibly be asking about my morning.

"After yesterday? I can not imagine the trauma from it. Dryston is a vile being. How are you, dear?" She repeats sweetly. I try to slow my beating heart down to a normal pace.

"It was definitely surprising. But, the entire ordeal was an eye opener. Thank you so much for asking, Calanthe." We start eating the breakfast silently. While chewing, my eyes continuously find Eryx right next to me at the head of the table. And when his eyes meet mine, a blush dusts my face before I look away in haste.

"Marry me." His words cause me to inhale as I swallow, causing food to trail down my throat wrong. Forks are dropped from the sudden noise.

I start choking until the piece of bacon is forced upward with the help of Ruelle patting my back like a baby trying to burp.

215

"Verena," He starts again softly, facing me. My eyes are watered from the choking but I wipe them swiftly before looking at him with wide eyes, glancing at everyone else staring in bewilderment. "Since you arrived, I haven't a clue on what to do with you. You are a gift from the Gods. You awakened something inside me. From the profusely running around barefoot to the wandering in the woods alone to finding out you are my fated mate all along..." a gasp from Ruelle surrounds us, "I want to love you forever. I want to be yours and have you be mine. I want to survive this upcoming war with you by my side and regrow this country together. Marry me, Verena, and love me always." His eyes haven't left mine a single time.

As I try to control my ragged breathing, my chest heaves in rapid succession. The weight of the moment hangs heavy in the air, a mix of anticipation and fear. His words have the power to shatter everything, but his sincerity stops me from running away. I know that if I were to say no, he will let me leave without hesitation — even if it meant breaking his own heart. With a deep breath, I finally respond. "Of course I will." My voice is barely above a whisper, but it carries a sense of joyous certainty. He rises from his chair and stands before me, placing his hands gently on my cheeks as he pulls me into a tender kiss. In that moment, all of my doubts and fears fade away, replaced by a sense of warmth and comfort in his embrace.

Chapter 26: War Plans

Verena

"So you think you have power deflection?" Esmeray asks me as we train on sparring mats.

"Not just deflection. I felt his power course through me. It was such a foreign feeling but it was as if I had no control over my body. It took over like it knew exactly what to do and blasted his powers back at him."

"After all this time? Your powers have just been sitting dormant?"

"I guess so. I hadn't really felt them until recently. It was a tingly sensation through my body when my emotions heightened during the whole coronation fiasco. Then it happened almost excruciatingly—as if it had finally been able to be released but I was holding back when Hadeon and I were attacked at the tavern on the border…" My thoughts trail off as I realize something. My hands fly to my neck, touching the pendant from Eryx. "My necklace… the necklace given to me by my mother. I lost it at the tavern."

"I know why." A new voice interrupts and we both turn to face the fae.

Calanthe stands there, her fingers fidgeting nervously in front of her as she watches me with a troubled expression. "I've been meaning to speak with you since you arrived," she begins hesitantly. "I am so sorry I haven't. I wasn't fully sure until recently."

"What is it, Mother?" Esmeray asks on my behalf, stepping closer and taking my hand in hers with a gentle, motherly touch.

"Your mother, Vaia, was my best friend," Calanthe continues, her voice full of emotion. "We grew up together, here in this very castle." My heart clenches at the confirmation, tears prickling at the corners of my eyes. "Come, sit with me." She leads us to a nearby bench for resting. Once we sit, she turns to face me and continues. "Your mother knew something was wrong right before your father kidnapped you and took her. She had a feeling he would do something like this. I'm not sure what exactly, but I did believe that you all had perished. That's why we were all shocked to discover the truth." She sighs heavily. "She had asked me to make something for you; a pendant to suppress your abilities. She intended to tell you about them when you were old enough so that you wouldn't be a target, especially with your light hair standing out." A lone tear falls down her cheek which she quickly brushes away before continuing.

"I should have trusted her instinct and posted guards by her room or something. I feel terrible that you both were taken. But he was quick. I never trusted him but she was so in love and blinded by his charm. Her parents hated him but I suppose that made her love him more."

"He took me after making a deal with the Zoryan King, Tarius." They both look at me surprised. "He set a betrothal with Dryston and I." I scoff at the idea. "I was already betrothed to Eryx. I know that now but I had no idea of my mother's Khyrelian roots. My father was manipulative and treated my mother and I as if we were an inconvenience." Tears well in my eyes, "He broke the initial betrothal with my mate to support his own selfish greed." Anger barrels through me as I run my fingers through my hair. "He made me hide myself away so no one would know. I thought it was for my safety! But he just didn't want to get caught." I refuse to let the tears drop so I quickly wipe them away.

Calanthe reaches out a hand to gently grasp mine, offering a comforting squeeze. "I can't imagine the pain and confusion you must have felt, my dear," she says softly. "But your mother, Vaia, she was determined to protect you at all costs. She knew the danger you faced with your powers, and she did what she believed was necessary to keep you safe."

Esmeray's eyes are filled with a mixture of sadness and understanding as she listens intently. "I can't imagine how different things would have been if you had known the truth all along," she murmurs, her tone empathetic.

I take a deep breath, trying to steady my tumultuous emotions. "I may have lost the pendant that suppressed my abilities, but now that I know the truth about my past and my powers, I feel like I am finally starting to understand who I truly am."

Calanthe smiles gently at me, her eyes reflecting a mix of sorrow and hope. Suddenly, she wraps her arms around me in a hug. It's warm and comforting. And I realize how much I desperately miss my own mother.

* * *

Furrowing my brow in concentration, I watch as Eryx, Esmeray, Hadeon, and I stand around the war table, our fingers carefully maneuvering the miniature pieces as if we're playing a high-stakes game of chess. Mentally picturing the battlefield, I quickly grab figures to represent different troops and move them around accordingly. "This is what he has planned," I declare with a confident nod, pointing to the positions of his army on the map before us. "Asterlayna may be too big for him to conquer outright, but he'll try to surround it and cut us off." A surge of frustration washes over me. "I can't believe that if I weren't giving him a wedding gift, I would never had found out his plans." Rolling my eyes at the absurdity of it all, I feel Eryx's hand gently cover mine on the table, bringing my attention back to him as he leans in to speak softly in my ear.

"You wanted to believe the best in him. You wanted to love him and do what was best for Zorya. There is nothing wrong with that."

"Even if your feelings were misplaced." Esmeray states and Hadeon smacks her arm.

"Will you shut up? She already knows that." I smile at them.

"You're both right. Besides, Hadeon, I like when Esmeray speaks without a filter. It's how I know she's telling the truth." I give him a pointed yet lightly playful look while a blush rises to his cheeks and Esmeray laughs. I forgive Hadeon for lying. I don't have it in my heart to be mad at him anymore. I need him as much as I need the rest of this family to get me through this war.

"I think," I look back at the board, "If it's okay with Esmeray and Hadeon, since they manage your army, we should place troops here... and here... and here. He'll be genuinely surprised. But we can evacuate these towns here... and here where they'll be hit hard since they're small but we can minimize damage, making it easier for us to attack with little to no casualties." I stand back and watch their reactions. I can see them all contemplate the decisions; Hadeon and Esmeray meeting each others eyes to gauge what they think.

"Alright." The raven-haired general claps her hands, "Let's get this bi-."

"Esmeray!" Hadeon scolds her from cursing.

"What?" She looks around at us confused, "What did I say?" He rolls his eyes before walking from the room with her following and I let out a laugh.

Once the door shuts I look at Eryx, only to find him staring at me provocatively. "Are they always like that?"

"I am surprised they haven't slept together yet, honestly. He's like mine and Ruelle's brother but I've never been able to say that about Esmeray. They've always had this rivalry that's split between hate and lust. They'll probably come to their senses after the war." He chuckles at the pair before eyeing me and licking his lips.

A bolt of electricity surges through my body, igniting every nerve and sending tingles down to my core. My mind is consumed with the thought of his lips pressed against mine.

"Verena," he purrs my name like it's a precious gem rolling off his tongue. The sound sends shivers down my spine, making me ache for his touch.

"Eryx," I breathe out, my voice laced with desire as I anticipate his next move. He moves toward me like a wolf hunts a hare, slowly until he's right in front of me. His scent engulfs me, overwhelming my senses and leaving me unable to think clearly.

His strong hands grip the back of my thighs, lifting me effortlessly and placing me on the war table. He leans in closer, taking a deep breath as he scents every inch of my skin from my chest up to my neck. A rush of pleasure courses through me at the intimate gesture, causing my hands to instinctively tighten their grip on his muscular arms. His tongue traces a wet trail up the side of my neck before capturing my lips in a hungry kiss. A moan escapes my throat as our tongues battle for dominance, and I know that he will undoubtedly win.

As if fueled by our newly formed mating bond, he thrusts the bodice of my dress down to my waist in one swift motion. Without hesitation, his tongue continues its exploration down my jawline and chest until it finds one of my already hardened nipples. With skilled movements, he alternates between sucking and squeezing them with his hand, drawing more moans from me as I grip onto his hair and pull him closer. The heat between my legs intensifies as the moisture gathers there, begging for his touch.

When he's satisfied with me, his hands grip my fabric, bunching it up over my legs, my thighs, and resting it around my waist as well before allowing himself to lower onto his knees, staring at the apex of my body. "You're so beautiful," He whispers as he bites my inner thigh, so close to where I need him. "I'm going to devour you, my Seren Fach, and when you come all over my face, I'm going to fuck you right here and fill you with all of me until you're begging me to stop." His words almost make me finish on the spot and I whimper at the promise as his mouth meets me.

My hand, still in his hair, tries pulling him closer and away at the same time— the sensation still foreign to me.

"Eryx,"

His name is a breathless whisper on my lips as his tongue explores every inch of my body, leaving a trail of fire in its wake. I soar with pleasure as his strong arms slip under my backside, lifting me off the table and pulling me closer to him. His tongue dives deeper into my body, claiming me as if he can't get enough. I moan in surprise and surrender to his desires as he devours me, his hunger insatiable.

With expert precision, he moves his mouth to my clit, teasing and tantalizing with each flick of his tongue. As he works two fingers inside me, replacing the previous place of his mouth, I cry out in pleasure and whimper for more. "Oh, gods," I gasp, feeling his groans against me like vibrations that send me to another dimension.

"You taste so delectable, Seren Fach," he murmurs against my skin, sending shivers down my spine. His fingers continue their rhythmic movements, curving against the delicate spot inside me and bringing me closer to the edge of ecstasy.

And then it happens. I come undone in his embrace, my body jerking with pleasure as my mind goes blank and stars explode behind my closed eyelids. Euphoria washes over me, drowning out all other sensations except for the overwhelming feeling of being completely consumed by him.

Before I can enjoy it too much, or return the favor, a beating comes from the door. "Your Grace!" More pounding from the door sounds and I jump from the table, looking in haste to Eryx with wide eyes.

"Is that normal?" I ask and his face grows dark.

"No, its not." He helps me adjust my clothing before we rush to the door and Eryx opens it. "What is it?" He asks, his tone commanding.

"There's been an attack on one of our border towns."

Chapter 27: As Fate Intended

Verena

"Go, lead your men. I'll remain within castle grounds. Maybe go to the garden. You deal with this." Despite my insistence, he looks at me with sorrow in his eyes. I smile softly and nod him off, pressing a gentle kiss to his lips before releasing my grip on him. He and his guard make their way out of the room and I turn to cross the hall, descending the grand staircase and exiting through the ornate double doors that lead to outside.

As soon as I step outside, I am struck by the beauty of the night garden. It is different from Zorya's, but equally breathtaking. The flowers here bloom at night and remain open all day, filling the air with their sweet, intoxicating scent.

I make my way to a bench at the edge of the flower beds, accompanied by Ruelle. She greets me with a smile, but there is a hint of sadness in her eyes that doesn't quite reach her lips.

"What is it? What's wrong?" I ask her as we sit down together.

Ruelle sighs and begins playing with her fingers in her lap, avoiding my gaze. "I don't know how to explain it. It just feels...off," she finally says.

My curiosity piques, I give her my full attention. "Off how? Is there something specific bothering you?"

She shakes her head, her expression troublesome. "It's hard to pinpoint. There are emotions I've been feeling lately...anger, resentment...almost like betrayal."

I look around us, suddenly feeling on edge. "Do you sense anything or anyone causing these feelings?"

Ruelle hesitates before nodding slowly. "Yes, I think so. But I can't be sure."

A chill runs down my spine as I try to figure out who or what could be causing this unrest among us. This was definitely not good news. Once again, the feeling of being watched surrounds me, sending chills to run down my spine.

"Should we try to find them?"

There's hesitancy in her before she shakes her head, "It's really dark, Verena. It feels dangerous." She whispers. I stand now and reach my hand toward her.

"We definitely shouldn't be out here, then. Let's go inside and we'll tell Eryx."

She stands by my side, her hand tightly gripping mine as we approach the entrance. Suddenly, Hadeon steps through, his presence causing a chill to run down my spine.

"What's wrong, ladies? You shouldn't be out here alone," he says in a strange tone.

Ruelle lets out a small gasp and clutches her stomach, her expression contorted in pain. I turn to her with concern, but before I can ask what's wrong, Hadeon's body begins to shift and change until a familiar female stands before us.

Ruelle suddenly goes rigid and her eyes widen in shock as the female injects her with an unknown substance. Before I can react, the female turns toward me with a sinister smile. "Did you miss me?" she taunts, catching me off guard. But before I can respond, someone from behind injects me with something and everything goes black. The last thing I see is the glint of malicious glee in the woman's eyes before succumbing to unconsciousness.

* * *

Eryx

I sit upon my throne, a grand and imposing seat of obsidian and gold. All whispers are silenced in my presence. Power radiates from every inch of my being, and even my shadows seem to billow thicker than usual, as if they sense the weight of my wrath.

As news reached me of the disappearance of Ruelle and Verena, anger boiled within me and hasn't stopped since. My voice is raising to a deafening volume, causing those in the throne room to take a fearful step back. Rightfully so; for they should be trembling at the mere mention of my name.

Hadeon steps forward with Ruelle's head guard to address me with a look of trepidation in his eyes.

"King Eryx, we were with Ruelle but she wanted privacy in the garden. We were guarding the perimeter but someone must have gotten past us." I raise my hand to get him to shut up. I can't hear it anymore.

"Do you believe this was an inside job?" I ask, my voice a dangerous tone as I look at Hadeon and Esmeray.

"Yes, we do." This ensues chaos around us. My mother gasps in surprise but Hadeon and Esmeray remain stoic, if not just as angry as

I am but trying to contain their emotions, even with their family.

"King Eryx, your Majesty, are we really going to believe this is an inside job? One of us? The Guards of Night have always been loyal to the crown. We wouldn't do this." I tilt my head to look at the guard speaking. Draven is his name. He would have been my brother in law had his sister not been murdered a decade ago. His loyalty stayed to the crown, though, even after he was told of her death being the late kings fault. He even protected Verena after she was attacked by Dryston in the woods and stood with her until I could reach her.

"And who do you blame, then?" I ask, sensing something odd from the man.

He glances around quickly. "There is one person who we don't really know. She grew up in the Court of Dawn. Can we really say she-"

The sound of Draven's choke echoes off the stone walls as shadows surround him, suffocating and consuming. I tower over him, my voice dropping to a deep, menacing tone, my eyes darkening to match the color of my hair.

"Choose your next words carefully, Draven," I growl, my fists clenching at my sides. How dare he insult my mate in such a manner? He knows nothing about her. Even if she were my enemy, she would never harm Ruelle or anyone in my family. I am certain of that.

The shadows release their hold on Draven as he struggles for breath, trying not to appear weak in front of me. "I mean no disrespect," he begins cautiously, his tone attempting to soothe. "But ever since my sister's death ten years ago, you have been distant and preoccupied. And now this... woman appears out of nowhere and suddenly you are infatuated with her. Some of us believe she has put a spell on you." His words only serve to ignite my anger further. My muscles tense and my grip on the armrest tightens until it hurts.

I can't even blame the guards for being weary of her, but this?

"So." The room darkens from my shadows being pissed as well. "You think I am foolish enough to be enchanted by a witch? That the king of this country cannot simply withstand a basic spell?" The dark whisps of magic whip around furiously as I slowly stand, the ropes of black wrapping around Draven's throat once more. "Let me be *very* clear to everyone here." My voice booms through the room at the staring eyes. I wish I could pull her to me right now, show her off to everyone. Show everyone just how much she means to me but she isn't here. "Verena Nightcrest is my mate. My fated mate." Everyone gasps, "If anyone shall have a problem with that, they can take it up with me," I release the guards neck and Hadeon rushes to grab him, "Or they can take it up with the Goddess of Night. Verena and I are engaged as of recently and in a few days, she will be queen just as fate intended."

There is only one throne up on this dais. I had never intended to take another wife and when the witch mentioned I had a mate, I still had no hope. But meeting her at Dryston's coronation ball changed everything. I barely stopped myself from taking her then and there in front of everyone. Hadeon had warned me when I showed up to be careful that it might not have been her. But I knew as soon as I saw her. The black hair be damned.

The blonde looks so much better on her. I was glad we could find something that helped take the rest of the ink out of her luscious locks.

I will have her a throne by time our wedding comes. It is almost finished. I was having a man from Asterlayna make it.

After the courts gasps and whispers quiet down and Hadeon returns without Draven, I continue. "Now, let's get our queen and beloved princess back."

"King!" A familiar voice cuts in, bursting into the room with haste. All heads turn to him. He bends over, breathing heavily as if he ran all the way here. "I... have news!" He takes another breath, "We got a letter from whoever took them!"

"Everyone but the needed bodies leave." I announce. The room clears fast, not surprisingly. And all that remains is the higher up guards, Esmeray, Hadeon, our mother, and myself.

"Aerin, tell me what else the letter states." I tell the male who came with a letter.

He takes a shaky breath before starting to read, "It has a meet location set for time for two days from now. And that King Eryx must come alone." He hands the letter to Hadeon when he reaches for it and Esmeray reads it over his shoulder. The letter is passed around but I stare at the letter in my hands.

A look flashes over my face and Esmeray seems to pick up on it, "What? What's wrong?" She asks. From a strangers prospective, she seemed collected but I could tell she was worried just as much as the rest of us,

"I just... feel like I've seen this handwriting before."

I'm quiet as I study the sheet of paper. "Let's go the war room. I don't trust being out in the open like this. Hadeon and Esmeray; choose two of your most trusted warriors. Then all of you, follow me."

Chapter 28: Pain

Verena

I know when I awaken because of two things. My head is throbbing as if I'm being beaten with a hammer against it and it smells like Dryston's old grandmother— musty wet dirt.

A grating voice, like metal scraping against metal, assaults my eardrums. It is a feminine voice, one that I know but not in a way that makes me comfortable.

My blood turns to ice and my back becomes slick with sweat. Something warm and thick runs down my thigh, causing me to flinch in disgust.

What the hell is happening?

"Stop your whining," the voice spits out. "It's like you want me to stab you! Just tell me about your brother. The king. Is he really going to marry that shrew?" I hear no words in response, only the sound of a sharp slap and then an eerie silence. "Ruelle, don't make me hurt you. You were always like a little sister to me, okay? I just need answers and this is the quickest way to get them." Frustration oozes from her tone and I freeze, unable to move or speak.

How does Mya have ties to the royal family? How could she possibly know them so intimately? She was just my maid!

I search through my memories of her, which are few and far between. She was always vague when speaking about her past before coming to the castle, just before Hadeon arrived. I never thought much of it — just assumed she was from a small town near the border like Hadeon.

But now it all makes sense.

"She's Khyrelian," I whisper to myself, finally understanding why she has such a strong connection to the royal family.

"I loved him," Mya's voice quivers with emotion. "I only killed your father because he was trying to keep me from Eryx, okay? I never meant to harm your family. But he wasn't even a good person!" Her tone grows louder and more desperate, bordering on deranged. And then her words strike a chord within me.

No.

It can't be.

Is Mya the ex-betrothed of Eryx? I thought she died? Didn't she have a different name? Gods, what was it?

I try to pull on my mating bond. It's faint. Could be from the blood loss? I needed to stop this bleeding. What did she even do to me?

"Ruelle!" I whisper. Her eyes widen at seeing me awake. A tear escapes her eye for a brief moment in relief.

"Look who's awake! Honestly, I thought you'd die from the little stab wound I gave you." She laughs maniacally as I look into the deranged females brown eyes. With a malevolent grin, Mya leans over me. Her brown eyes were wild and frenzied, reflecting the madness within her. The pain from her stab wound radiates through my body as I struggle to focus on her presence.

"You are such a bitch," I groan out of pain. "Who even are you?" I watch her carefully as she strolls around the place.

231

"Who am I?" Another laugh from her echoes as she revels in my helplessness. "Honey, I am the original. I am the love of Eryx's life. Has he not mentioned me? Boo, that's disappointing." She rolls her eyes dramatically.

"Verena, don't tell her anything." Ruelle says finally, letting me know she's conscious at the moment, despite the bruised face, cut lip and cut eyebrow. Mya slaps her once more with the back of her hand and suddenly my face is red from anger.

"Leave her alone, Mya!" I yell, trying to move closer to them.

"Mya?" Ruelle questions and both of the women look at me.

A laugh leaves the brunette, "Oh, right. Amaelya is my birth name. Of course, when Hadeon showed up in the Court of Dawn, I couldn't let him blow my cover. So I changed my face shape a bit and my name."

Amaelya stalks toward me, gripping my chin within her bony fingers and squeezing hard enough to bruise. She tilts my head over to the left, then the right. "What does he even see in you? You are nothing." She spits with disgust. "You couldn't even handle Dryston and he is pathetic!" She mockingly laughs. "But I will say he is handsome, even if his head is empty."

With a sudden jerk, she throws my head back and it collides with the hard cave wall, sending waves of agonizing pain through me. "You do not deserve Eryx," she whispers venomously in my ear. "He's too good for you - too strong for you."

"No," I protest, refusing to believe her cruel words.

"You are delusional if you think he'll stay with you in the long run," Mya taunts, her face inches from mine. "He's just using you, darling."

"He doesn't even know you're alive. You betrayed his country, he will never forgive that." Ruelle spits back at her.

"I *saved* this country!" She's screams in anger. "Your father was a menace to everything and everyone. I Know that together Eryx and I would rule side by side, happily. I am his first love and I will be his last." As she speaks, I try and feel for my surroundings. My hands are tied with rope and without seeing the knot, I could never undo it. But the cave wall digging into my skin might help.

"Eryx is-" I go to tell her he's my mate but Ruelle shakes her head at me in my peripheral and I know she has a good reason why. "-in love with me. He wouldn't leave me." I finish.

She laughs, not even responding to me and turning away toward the entrance. "I'll be back. Hang out, don't go anywhere." She leaves Ruelle and I alone.

"She's the anger I felt in the garden." The youngest Ashwood explains. "If you tell her Eryx is... you know what... she'll kill you immediately. I had to buy us some time." I nod in understanding, trying to help wrack my brain on how we're getting out. Eryx has to know we're missing by now.

"How did she even get past the guards?" I question and it's as if a light pops up over her head, her eyes wide as she looks over at me.

"Her brother... Draven. He's one of our royal guards. Damnit! I knew something was off with him the past couple of days." She speaks, mostly to herself.

"Who's Draven?" I ask her, trying to think of all the guards I have names to.

"The guard who waited with you after Dryston attacked you in the forest." She sounds breathless and I suddenly realize she wasn't just beat up, she was losing blood continuously.

"Ruelle, I am going to get us out of here." I tell her with conviction lacing my voice.

"I should've taken those training lessons Esmeray pushed me for." She laughs lightly, her body slumping against the cave wall.

"Hey! No. You will not die here. Ruelle, stay awake for me, okay?" I start rubbing my hands against the cave, ignoring the shooting pains in my wrists and arms from the rocky substance scraping me and the rope.

I try to assess our situation. The cave is cold and damp, with only a few weak rays of light entering through the far entrance. My heart races with the fear of the unknown as I think of the woman who betrayed my family.

I begin to form a plan in my mind, focusing on our surroundings and the tools at our disposal. The rope that binds us can become an advantage, but it will require me to remain calm and focused. I start to silently chant a calming mantra to maintain control of the situation.

Inside the cave, my mind races with ideas on how to free Ruelle and myself. My hands ache from being tied up, but I know I had to stay focused.

My eyes dart around the cave, searching for any weaknesses I can exploit.

I assume Eryx has scouts out looking for us, but if Mya is clearly smarter than I gave her credit for, she likely spelled the cave to be hidden and soundproof.

* * *

Eryx

"Where the fuck are they!" I exclaim, throwing things off the desk in the war room. My shadows shoot from me, just as irritable and angry. I growl in frustration before facing both my number twos.

Esmeray and Hadeon are quiet, letting me get my temper tantrum out of the way.

"We've looked everywhere. Wherever he has them, it's spelled. We can't find them, Eryx." Esmeray gives it to me straight. She always has.

"Yet." Hadeon gives her a look, to which she shrugs. "We are still looking profusely. We will find them." He's adamant. "There was nothing you could have done to prevent this, Eryx." He reasons but I can't convince myself to listen. Of course this was my fault. This is my castle, my country, my *family*.

Dryston got in under my watch and tried to kidnap my mate twice! Succeeding once now. He will not get away with this. With any of it. I'll make sure of that.

"They could have left Khyrel already, Hadeon. Do not give him false hope." She points out in a hushed scold.

"I know that but he doesn't need extra stress either." They argue back and forth, getting in each others faces until they get heated.

"Will you two shut it?" I yell, breaking their attention away from one another.

"We need something different. We need-" I cut myself off remembering the one being in the forest who knows everything. "We need the witch."

"No. Deals with her never go correctly, you know this." Hadeon tries to stress to me.

"I'm with Hadeon on this one, big brother. We don't need added complications to an already stressful complicated situation."

Esmeray agrees with Hadeon, "We just…we need to focus on finding them without causing any more drama than necessary."

"Enough," I say, my voice echoing through the space, my eyes blazing with determination. "We will find them, with or without her help. We will bring them back home, safe and sound."

I turn back to my shadows, they shimmer and shift to their ethereal state, disappearing into the night air as I will them to look for Verena.

I look at my trusted generals, pacing the room. The war room has always been my sanctuary and power, but now, it feels more like a prison. My heart aches for my mate, and I can't shake the feeling of helplessness. I know that I must remain strong, I must continue to fight, but the fear gnawing at me won't let me.

"Ruelle is our baby sister, Esme. Our mother will not survive her death. Verena is my fated mate and without her, the entirety of Khyrel can be destroyed yet none of it will matter if she is gone." My body collapses into my chair behind me and I slump in it, desperate to find them.

"Ruelle and Verena are strong. They're together, that makes them better off than most people. Verena carried this lug of a male for over two hours," She slaps the back of Hadeon. "They will make it out of their imprisonment or they will die trying. But, hopefully we will get to them before they have to."

"If Verena dies, Esmeray," I pause, making sure she understands my sincerity, "You will have to take over as Queen. You will have to rule this country. I got over the last time someone I loved died..." My shadows settle around me, almost sad, "I won't get over this one."

Esmeray takes a deep breath, trying to not let her emotions get the best of her. Hadeon steps forward and places his hand on her shoulder in support.

"Ruelle and Verena are strong, Eryx. They'll make it through this, we'll find them." Hadeon's voice is steady and reassuring. It does little to assure me.

"Yes, we'll find them," Esmeray echoes him, sounding as if she's trying to convince herself more than anyone else. I know we need to stay focused, so we exit the war room and continue our search for any sign of them. I try searching the Dark Woods, trying to feel the bond between us but it is faint and muddled. I know she is alive but is she injured? Is she being tortured or worse?

Chapter 29: Merciful

Verena

As the endless night drags on, Ruelle sleeps soundlessly while I fight tooth and nail against the unforgiving rocks. My fingers bleed and blister as I frantically rub the rough ropes against their sharp edges, determined to break free from our bindings. The pain was excruciating — far worse than carving out my wedding rune from Dryston's chest — but I refuse to give up.

Finally, with a gut-wrenching snap, the ropes give way and I collapse to the ground, gasping for air and relief. My skin burns and stings from the raw wounds underneath, but I ignore it as I quickly untie my feet and stumble over to Ruelle.

My heart drops as I see the blood seeping from a deep stab wound in her leg. Ignoring my own injuries, I tear strips of fabric from my dress and tightly bound them around her leg, desperate to stop the bleeding. But as I tend to her, my head throbs and my vision blurs from the hits we took during our unconsciousness.

Gritting my teeth, I shake Ruelle's shoulder and lightly tap her face, trying to wake her. She groans in response before slipping back into unconsciousness. With tears in my eyes and anger in my heart, I look up at the dark cave ceiling and curse at the Gods for putting us through this hellish ordeal.

With a sudden burst of urgency, I strike Ruelle across the face, desperate to wake her from her deep slumber. She stirs, dazed and confused, until her bleary eyes focus on me. "We have to go," I bark at her, my tone leaving no room for argument.

"Ow," she groans as she attempts to move, and I let out a sigh of relief.

"I'm sorry for hurting you, but we have no time to waste," I apologize quickly as I frantically try to untie her hands, now slick with blood. Frustration boils inside me as I struggle with the ropes, tears streaming down my face.

"Leave, Verena," Ruelle's soft voice interrupts my efforts, and I snap my head toward her in anger. But she looks at me with tired love and understanding.

"You're insane if you think I'm leaving you behind. If you die, I die," I declare fiercely. "I won't let you sacrifice yourself for a war that isn't even yours."

"Well that will make for a beautifully tragic ending," Amaelya's voice sneers from behind me, and I whirl around to see her standing unsteadily. Dryston stands beside her this time, his expression cold and calculating.

"You could've stopped this bloodshed if you had only come to me, Verena," Dryston spits as he towers over me, his dark smirk dripping with malice and superiority.

I steel myself for the inevitable confrontation, my mind racing with memories of our previous encounter — how he effortlessly overpowered me despite my training. But then a realization hits me.

My dagger. I always carry a small blade strapped to my thigh, even when wearing a dress. For a moment, I question if provoking him was a foolish move. But then I remember his actions and words toward me.

"You should be thankful," he sneers. "I could have let you go after my father died. Instead, I simply delayed your coronation and now I'm the villain?" He scoffs, his voice laced with bitter sarcasm. "Verena. You cut off our wedded rune! That was madness! I wanted to make sure you were ready for the commitment. The responsibility. Clearly, you couldn't handle it."

He thinks he has the upper hand, but I refuse to back down.

"You're right," I interrupt, surprising everyone with my sudden compliance. Dryston eyes me warily, unsure of my change in demeanor. "I don't know why I'm acting like this. I did want this marriage. But...something changed after that cursed ball. Eryx offered me a drink and I thought nothing of it at the time. But now I realize he must have cast some sort of spell on me." My voice trembles as I speak, tears welling up in my eyes. "He got into my head and twisted Hadeon's orders to take me from Zorya."

I can see the shock and suspicion on Dryston's face as my confession sinks in. But I know the truth, and I will not go down without a fight.

My body trembles as I fall to my knees in front of Dryston, begging for his forgiveness with tears streaming down my face. "Please forgive me," I cry, my words dripping with desperation as I hide my revulsion.

Dryston places a hand on my head, stroking my hair back as he speaks. "I forgive you," he says calmly, but I can see the fire burning behind his eyes. "Come home with me and we will make him pay for this. No one disrespects the Queen of Zorya and gets away with it." His condescending tone makes my blood boil, but I force myself to nod and pretend to be grateful for his mercy.

As I speak, I slowly move my hand to my thigh, fingers brushing against a small knife concealed there. "I've been thinking about our wedding night," I say with feigned innocence, my voice dripping with false lust. "You treated me so well...I missed you terribly while Eryx tried to touch me." A wave of disgust washes over me as I continue speaking, but I channel that emotion into my performance. "But I resisted him because all I wanted was you." With a sickening smile, I pull the blade out and prepare to strike. He doesn't see the movement.

"I know you do," Dryston responds sweetly, reaching for my chin to lift my gaze up to him. But as soon as our eyes meet, my expression shifts from fake desire to a chilling smirk. In one swift motion, I thrust my hand forward and slice his arm away from me, backing away quickly before he can react. The taste of revenge is both bitter and satisfying on my tongue as I prepare to fight for my freedom.

The knife is drenched in a sickening mixture of our blood, glistening red in the dim light as I hold it up triumphantly. My opponent, seething with rage and disbelief, "You bitch!" He hurls insults at me but I can't stop the manic laughter that bubbles out of my throat. He tries to use his magic to disarm me, but for once it doesn't obey his command. The spectators are frozen in shock as they watch our deadly dance.

"What's wrong with you? Just take the damn knife!" Amaelya screams at him, her voice shaking with anger.

"I'm trying!" he hisses back, frustration etches on every feature of his face.

"Having performance issues?" I taunt him through heavy breaths, fighting the exhaustion that threatens to overtake me. His response is a guttural snarl as he charges at me. I shift into the defensive stance Esmeray drilled into me and strike at his unprotected stomach as he lunges past. He lets out another growl of frustration, and for the first time I see him without his reliance on magic. He's vulnerable and desperate, and that only fuels my determination to defeat him.

My knee nearly buckles as I dodge his attack, but I manage to regain my balance. He unleashes his magic at me again, but this time I am prepared. With a deep breath, I absorb his power and redirect it back at him, sending him crashing to the ground. Amaelya gasps in shock as Dryston writhes in agony on the cave floor. I stand over him, panting heavily.

"The real problem here, Dryston," I say through gritted teeth, "is that I don't want to kill you. I want you to suffer. I want you to witness my marriage to your enemy, who happens to be my fated mate — thanks for that, by the way. And then... only then will I grant you the bittersweet release of death."

My words drip with venom, and I use the metal on his body to control his movements like a puppeteer with the remnants of his magic coursing through me. With a sickening thud, his head collides against the unforgiving rock wall, rendering the blond unconscious. But there is no time for me to relish in this small victory.

"You're... what?" Amaelya's voice is laced with seething hatred, sending shivers down my spine. Her emotions are palpable, and I can feel every ounce of rage and betrayal emanating from her.

But I refuse to cower or hide from my fate, no matter how steep the cost may be. My love for Eryx runs too deep — lying about it would cause me physical pain. "Eryx is my fated mate, Amaelya," I declare through gritted teeth. "I won't apologize for it, even if I could. You will never be with him again."

A guttural screech pierces through the air as Amaelya launches herself at me once more. Despite my exhausted state from our previous battle, I summon all of my remaining strength to defend myself. Blood seeps through my tattered bandages, a constant reminder of the injuries I have sustained in this ongoing war over love and destiny.

Ruelle's eyes snap open with a violent jolt, her consciousness returning in a surge of pain. Her face is etched with agony as I desperately try to shield her from the wrath of Amaelya, knowing that I am alone in this moment. Ruelle's energy must be conserved for the treacherous journey back home.

Dryston's power has been completely drained after my last ditch attempt to defeat him. It was pure luck that I even managed it. My trusted blade, my strongest weapon, proved useful even against his abilities. A chilling thought creeps into my mind — could it have been because of my blood, capable of absorbing the abilities of others? But that's absurd…isn't it?

Suddenly, Amaelya's weight crashes into me and we both plummet to the ground. The impact knocks the breath out of me and sends my head slamming into the unforgiving earth once again. "What is wrong with you?" I scream at her as she viciously strikes at my raw arms, raised in front of my battered face. "Fighting over a male who isn't even yours? The Gods themselves bound us together! You're insane!"

With every ounce of strength left in my battered body, I push her off of me. Her relentless hands continue to pummel me as I struggle to stand. Each blow feels like a firecracker exploding inside me, but somehow, through the searing pain, I manage to roll away just as Amaelya charges at me again.

"I don't want to fight you," I gasp, struggling to catch my breath as I finally get to my feet. My whole body is trembling with exhaustion and agony. "It's not worth it."

But she doesn't listen. Her eyes are full of a wild fury as she hisses through gritted teeth, "You don't understand. If I can't have him, no one will. And when I'm finished with you, I'll make sure he suffers the same fate because I have nothing left to lose." With a primal roar, she lunges at me once more, landing a brutal punch on my already bruised cheekbone. My head snaps to the side and before I can even react, she sweeps my legs out from under me.

With a surge of adrenaline, I use her own weight against her and drive my fist upwards, breaking her nose with a sickening crunch. Blood pours from the wound, drenching me in a warm, sticky red that fuels my rage. Groaning with the effort, I spit out her blood and shove her off of me, scrambling to my feet. My eyes fall upon the knife I dropped and I snatch it up, straddling her body and pressing the blade to her throat.

"If this is what you want," I growl through gritted teeth. Without hesitation, I plunge the knife into her soft flesh and feel satisfaction as she chokes on her own blood, gurgling in agony. But even as she struggles for air, I can't ignore the frantic pounding of my heart or the erratic rhythm of my breaths.

"This death was too kind, but I am nothing if not merciful." I sneer at her before watching the light fade from her eyes. With trembling legs, I stumble off of her body and make my way over to Ruelle. "Let's go home," I say to her, trying to keep my voice steady as I haul her up in my arms.

"Is there a horse nearby?" Ruelle asks weakly, glancing around frantically. My heart sinks as I realize we are stranded without any means of swift escape.

"No," I admit bitterly. "How far are we from the castle?"

I struggle to catch my breath, my vision swimming with exhaustion. But I push myself to keep going, determined to get us both home safely.

She grunts in pain, "I can't tell. But, based on the night sky, I'd say go that way." She motions toward a direction and I nod, throwing one of her arms over my shoulder so she can lean on me. "You'll have to carry me soon, you know?"

"I did it with Hadeon. At least you're lighter than he is." We start to laugh before pausing in pain and taking each step slowly.

I have to ask, though, as we walk. "So, was Amaelya always that crazy?"

Ruelle lets out a sigh, "No and yes. She was more narcissistic and her moods changed a lot but not like this. Although, she was always territorial about Eryx. Her father set them up when they were young teens. She thought she'd be Queen but my mother never liked her and it wasn't until closer to their wedding did father start not trusting her either. He said something the day he died about how she wasn't trustworthy and she was against the kingdom. He was right, she was toxic. When we thought she was dead, Esmeray and I were so relieved but sad for Eryx. He didn't deserve to lose her like that but if he had found out she was a traitor, he would've killed her himself." I nod in agreement.

The rest of the trip was silent so we wouldn't waste energy. I love this country, from what I've seen and who I have met. I love this family and I love Eryx.

I never could have fathomed a life like this. As the dutiful daughter, I was expected to fulfill my father's deals and maintain the Whitewell legacy in the kingdom of Zorya. But it came at a price — punishment after punishment, fight after fight. In moments of solitude, I would cry and dream of a different fate for myself. And yet, even in my wildest dreams, I never could have imagined this — a life filled with joy and contentment. But still, I can't shake off this feeling of guilt for allowing myself to be happy...

"For the record, Verena," She starts, "I would choose you for him. In every life." She tells me sweetly and tears well in my eyes before slipping faster than I can stop them. She squeezes me as tight as she can and I do the same without hurting her.

Chapter 30: Loyalty

Verena

It feels as if time stops when we reach the castle. The Aurora Borealis twinkles in the sky as if welcoming us home.

A guard yells, unsure of the two beings stumbling upon their foyer. Our throats become dry from lack of water.

More guards tumble out from the entrance halls as they surround us. I can barely focus on them. I am entirely exhausted. I want to sleep for a week. My skinned forearms burn from the dirt and grime on them, as do the rest of my cuts and scrapes.

"Move!" My bond pulls, my sight and my hearing focus in on that one voice, immediately soothing me. My knees give out, causing Ruelle and I go crashing to the floor. I can't see who grabs her but the scent of freshly baked dessert surrounds me and I know Eryx holds me close to his chest. "You insufferable female." His voice cracks from emotion, "I was about to burn this continent to the ground to find you." I choke out a sob as he tightens his hold and I whimper from pain and longing. "Medic!" Doctors come quickly, laying down cots on the floor, "No, I'll take her. Show me where." Eryx tells them and starts moving, trying to be as gentle as he can. "Call off the search parties!"

"Ruelle," I moan out from pain and exhaustion.

"She's fine. Hadeon has her." I nod to him, inhaling deeply.

"I am so tired..." I barely speak before my eyes shut. I can't understand the words coming from him as my vision goes black.

* * *

Pain is what I expect when I stir from sleep but it never greets me. All my muscles are sore but no pain from any of the wounds inflicted upon me. I move my hands, feeling the fabric beneath me. The softest sheets I have ever felt. The plush comforter covers me to keep me toasty warm. Sunlight shines from a window glowing the back of my eye lids and the scent of my mate encompasses me. A whimper escapes me from my sore arms and legs.

I go to move, barely cracking my eyes open, but a gentle hand lays me back down.

"Verena, you need to rest, love." My eyes fully open, revealing Eryx and Hadeon standing next to me.

"How is Ruelle?" Is my first question in a whisper, immediately thinking back to when we arrived. We were both barely conscious.

Hadeon smiles, "She's stubborn and strong. Just like you. She wasn't awake last time I checked on her but she was bleeding more than you."

"I don't want to push you," Eryx starts up, "But we need answers. What happened?"

Hadeon nudges his shoulder against the king's. "She just woke up, Eryx."

"It's fine." I speak again, my voice scratchy. Hadeon motions for a maid to bring me water and I sip it slowly, sighing in relief at the feeling of it against my throat. "Ruelle and I were in the garden on a bench just talking. But she had told me someone was angry. She could feel it. It was dark and dangerous. So we start heading back inside and Mya comes out of nowhere pretending to be Hadeon. I guess she has some sort of shape-shifting ability," I tell them.

"Mya? From Zorya? Your old maid?" Hadeon questions me, confusion lining his features and suddenly I am reminded about her true self.

"Well, she told me her real name isn't Mya at all…" I trail off. They both look at me, waiting for me to finish. This will hurt him. Finding out his ex-betrothed was in fact alive and obsessed with the crown enough to kill his mate, who in turn killed her instead. "Her name is Amaelya." I state, watching his face carefully.

His expression changes from patience… to surprise. "What? No," He says in denial. Now he looks angry, hurt. My bond aches, wanting to soothe him but unsure as to how. "There is no way. She was burnt to a crisp."

"Eryx," Hadeon places his hand on his best friends shoulder in support .

He shrugs him off, "No. We saw her body, Hadeon!"

"Eryx." I say his name with a soft voice, forcing him to look at me. " It was her. Ruelle was there. She knows her, knows what she looked like. They spoke as if they had known each other for decades. She wanted the crown. She wanted you and she was about to kill me for it. Even knowing I am your mate. Who do you think gave Ruelle and I all these wounds?"

His expression turns dark, his eyes as black as his hair. He turns to Hadeon, "Go prepare Draven for me." His voice is full of hatred until he turns back to me, grasping my hand in his own and bringing it to his lips. "I am so sorry," He tells me. "This is all my fault."

My hand reaches up to his cheek, "No it is not, Eryx. This is on Amaelya. She was so angry at your father. She almost killed Ruelle! This is between her and the late king of Khyrel. I..." I was unsure on how to tell him about me murdering his ex-love but deciding to just come out with it. "I killed her, Eryx. I didn't have a choice."

"I am not angry at you, Verena. Not one bit." He removes his hand from my other one and places both of them on my cheeks, "Amaelya's alleged death had done something to me I can't even explain. But I think I was more angry at myself because everything my father had said was right in front of my eyes. We were to be wed because our fathers made a deal but that is it. Did I love her? Maybe at some point I did but it's friendly. She is nothing and was always nothing. You are the love of my life. My fated mate. A gift to me from the Gods that I in no way, shape, or form deserve but I will thank them everyday because of it." Tears brim my eyes at his words. "I was terrified at the thought of losing you." He pulls me to him, wrapping his arms around my body and I shove my face into his chest in comfort.

"I killed her..." My voice breaks. I *killed* her. Whether it's self defense or not. I took someone's sister from them. "I slit her throat and watched as the light left her eyes and felt nothing but hatred for her."

"I know," He says, not bothering to coat his words with sugar. He understands. He has done it. And he knows it isn't easy even if it is their life against yours. Except, it wasn't just my life on the line. It was all of Khyrel, if not the continent. It was Eryx, Ruelle, Esmeray, Hadeon, and the people I care about. It was everyone or it was her. I know I made the right decision. I know I would make it over and over again.

He holds me for a while until I get sleepy again.

"You need rest, Seren Fach. Go to sleep, I'll be here when you wake."

* * *

Eryx

As soon as I hear her breathing slow as she falls into a deep sleep, I stand from my place beside her and walk out the door, seeing Esmeray in the hall with one of her trusted soldiers. "Watch them, I'll be back soon." I tell her as she nods. Ruelle's room is practically next to hers so it's easy for her to guard them both.

I walk through the hall and down the steps, all the way to the lowest level— the dungeon.

Hadeon is by one of the cells, staring in wait at the male in there. Once he hears my footfalls against the dirty floor, he looks at me and moves over, unlocking the cell door.

Before I go in, my realization sets in. Draven was involved in the harm of her and it will be his undoing. My shadows unfurl around me, angry just as much as myself. I can feel my eyes swim with darkness, blackening with emotion and hatred.

"Draven." I greet him as I stroll in. The male was already stripped of his palace uniform and groaning in pain from the infliction Hadeon's caused in my lack of presence. I take a glance at the cart of metallic items gracing it, some bloodied and some rusted. I look at Hadeon over my shoulder with a brow raised in question to which he shrugs. A smirk dawns my face and I turn my attention back to the man hanging from chains in the air.

"Why?" Is all I ask.

He can barely speak. "I... you know how she is, Eryx. She's my s-sister. I had to help her..." He trails off, body weak already; likely from the lack of food. His voice hoarse.

I slice a blade across his chest. "You performed a high act of treason because she is your sister?" I question him. The darkness inside me cannot be tamed much longer. It is hungry for pain. "When you took an oath as a royal guard, which your father begged me to have you as, you took an oath to the crown swearing unwavering loyalty regardless of family, friends, or personal beliefs. That has been our rule from the beginning. I have always let you have personal opinions without punishment. I've allowed you to slack off and this is the thanks you give your king? You slander my fated mate, my betrothed, because your sister asked you to? You harm her because of a coward who was against this crown and what it stands for?" I question, my voice as dark as it can be with malice dripping thick from every syllable.

"I'm sorry..." He breathes. "I thought she was a distraction." My hands go to his throat, squeezing tightly.

"That's the problem now, isn't it? You were thinking. And now, I am going to cut out your tongue," I say, getting closer to his face, "And then we'll see what else I am in the mood for. You will be the wedding gift for my wife." I grab another blade and get to work removing the muscle from his mouth.

By the time I finish with him, A couple hours pass and I am covered in blood. I sent Hadeon to check on Verena and when he came back, it was with some of my staff to help clean up this mess. I can't help but revel in the blood coating my skin, nothing feeling as satisfying as getting some revenge for Verena. I make my way to our room, seeing her still resting before walking to the bathing room and stripping off my bloody clothes, stepping into a hot bath that Hadeon had gotten a maid to start for me, and sinking down in it to relax. Most of the blood was on my clothing so there wasn't much to wash off.

My eyes grow heavy once I finish using soap to wash off my skin and I'm almost unconscious when I feel it. There's a presence in the room with me, however quiet. But once the scent of sugared red berries wafts through my nose, I know that it's Verena. My eyes snap open wide, taking her in as she strips off the night gown, most of her superficial wounds healed now and the more serious ones were scarring. Thanks to her Fae healing and the herbs we have for wounds like that, she was almost back to normal. But it didn't stop the worry etching its way onto my face.

My brows pull tight as she steps into the bath, sinking down onto my lap as we remain silent.

"Verena," I start, trying to get her to go back to bed so I don't accidentally injure her.

She shushes me, placing her delicate finger over my lips and grasping my suddenly hardening cock in her other hand. I suck in a breath of air at the feel of her wrapped around me, my head falls back and my eyes close briefly at the contact.

"Verena," This time it's a deep warning.

"I need you," Her voice is needy, wanting and I'll be damned if I can even attempt to stop her. She takes this as her cue and moves her hand up and down until my cock aches from being so stiff.

I let her take control, sensing she needs it right now and loving the sight of her taking me however she wants.

Her arms move to my chest, running up and to my shoulders where she holds on before grazing my chest with her perfect breasts and sinking her hot, wet cunt down my shaft.

Groans leave us in unison and my hands fly to her hips, gripping with desperation for her to move. She adjusts to me, fitting perfectly in place like we were made for each other.

"You are mine," Her voice is deeper than usual, full of lust and... jealousy? My brows furrow this time in confusion and she answers my silent question as she slides up and back down my cock, another moan leaving me. "She believed no one else could have you but her. She was wrong and I made sure to tell her that." Anger wants to brew up in me at the mention of Amaelya. "My only regret was not keeping her alive to fuck you in front of her." Her words make me choke on a light laugh of surprise.

A smirk rests of her face now as she moves, grinding herself on my lap as she uses my body to pleasure herself. I could get off at the thought of it alone

I use my hands to help her grind harder, soft moans leaving her lips as I lean forward to suck a hardened nipple in my mouth, nibbling on it. Even with the water surrounding our bodies, I can feel her getting wetter. The nipple in my mouth pops out as I move to the next one, giving it just as much attention and care as her movements get faster, sloppier, and I know she's close.

"Come for me, pretty girl," I tell her, slipping my hand between us to help her as she grinds her clit against it. Her gasp catches in her throat, her nails digging into my shoulders as her body tenses, unable to move on her own now from the pleasure. I use my hands at her waist to help her ride through her climax as she shudders against me. Her cunt squeezes me tightly, enough to spur on my own release. My hands dig into her waist, surely adding to the bruises but she seems to enjoy it more than anything as I groan out my release inside her and she collapses onto my chest, her head nuzzled into my neck. I brush my hand down her hair, pulling it off her shoulders to gather at her back.

Chapter 31: Mama Zen

Verena

"So, why are you training me and not Esmeray?" I question Hadeon as he wipes sweat off his brow and I raise mine back at him, remembering when making him sweat during training was such a feat.

"She's helping Eryx with some wedding plans." He tells me, dodging another hit to his face. The bruise delivered from my fist an hour ago shines bright now. "Excited about your wedding tomorrow?" He asks me, lunging forward and grasping me to throw me down but I use his weight against him and angle our bodies so I'm on top before I start pummeling his arms.

A vision from the cave flashes over my eyes and suddenly it feels as if it is Amaelya again trying to kill me. A sob wrecks through me and I punch harder.

"Verena." I don't register his voice. I keep hitting, slamming my hands down again and again.

"Verena!"

I see him now, Hadeon— not Amaelya— and I scramble off of him backwards until I hit the cool gray wall behind me and tuck my legs under my arms.

"I'm sorry. I'm so sorry..." I swipe tears from my eyes and hide my face in my arms. He rushes over, sliding on his knees from what I can hear.

Hands lightly touch my arms, "Verena. It's fine. I am fine. See?" He tries, pulling my hands from under my head and I look up at him to see concern etched over his entire face. "You went through a trauma, V. If you don't have any side effects, I'd be concerned. Do not apologize."

"I could've hurt you." I tell him, my voice as quiet as a mouse.

He deadpans me a look, "I doubt that. I can take a lot. 'Practically un-killable', remember?" He let's out a soft laugh at the memory we share from my first training session when I had called him that after not being able to land a single hit on him the entire time . "I am fine. Come on," He helps me ease into a standing position. "Let's call it a day. We've been at it for hours." I nod at him, thankful for his friendship.

"Thank you," I tell him and he looks at me with confusion. "For everything you've done for me, Hadeon. I do not know what I'd do with out you. You've been my only friend for half a decade. You started training me and without you I'd likely still be there stuck in a loveless marriage, trapped as a kings whore." His face drops into something sadder.

"I lied to you-"

"For good reason." I point out.

"But I still lied. I can never fully make that up to you. But my loyalty is to you and Eryx, always. Lies will never be uttered from my mouth toward you or him ever again." I nod in agreement. "I am still your friend."

I hold back the tears from spilling over my eyes as we make our separate ways. I needed food after all that.

255

* * *

Barefoot in a day-to-day gown, I made my way down to the kitchen. I hadn't really been here at all since arriving. Ruelle has taken such great care of my time here— including what I ate.

I almost trip on the last step of the stairs for the service quarters, catching myself on the railing next to it. "Careful, deary. That step gets us all." An elderly feminine voice sounds from the busy kitchen. It's gargantuan in size but cozy in looks and feel. All cabinets are open— no doors or hinges in sight— the counter space is broad and spanning almost the entire wall before curving into an L. On the complete other side of the counters, there's a good size table that can fit eight beings easily.

The colorful walls were a lilac tone. Pots and pans hung from the ceiling near the stove, canisters full of, what I can only assume, flour, spices, sugar, and more. The smells were heavenly; a roast in a giant slow-cooker with carrots, celery, potatoes, and herbs being thrown in as I watch.

"Can I help you?" The lady asked me. I found her in the bustling noise, a shorter dark-skinned female with a full-bodied frame, grayed dark hair in long dreadlocks decorated with rings. She wears an apron over her clothing.

"Hello," I put on a bright smile. "My name is Verena-" The entire kitchen stops for a brief pause, watching me before glancing their eyes at her and continuing on.

"I should've known. I would know those cheekbones anywhere. You're the daughter of Vaia Nightcrest." Her words were finite and a blush rose to my cheeks.

"Yes ma'am." I answer, unsure of what to say as I stand there, rubbing my arm awkwardly.

"Well," She starts, waving her arms in a closer motion. "Come on over. Let's get a look at ya." She talks as if she has no care of my title and I do enjoy it immensely. She had a very warm motherly energy about her but I know she wouldn't let someone get away with anything. I slowly step over to her.

"I don't mean to interrupt…" I trail off as she circles me like a lion assessing prey.

"You look just like her. Vaia was one of my best students. Loved it in here. You like to cook, girl?" She asks, waving a wooden spoon around before checking her sauce.

"I wasn't allowed to even try in Zorya." I say, honestly. "But I'd love to learn." I nod at her.

"Don't you have a wedding to plan?" She asks, a brow raised.

"Contrary to popular belief, but I care more about the people staffing this castle than a ceremony meant to be a public presentation of my love for King Eryx. We're mates and we love each other. That is all that matters." I speak earnestly.

"Well then. This pasta isn't going to make itself." I give her a small smile before letting her tie an apron around me. She stays behind me before twisting my hair around with a clean thin wooden stick I recognize as a form of utensil. "Chopsticks are a great form of eating utensil but sometimes we need a little help holding our hair together, too." Somehow, my hair stays put with the stick holding it up. "We don't need your hair getting in the food, no matter how pretty it is." I let out a laugh before she instructs me on what to do.

For the next two hours, I help create dinner and dessert from scratch, and plan our wedding food for the reception. She shows me how to make the perfect citrus-y sweet beverage.

I was genuinely laughing—something I don't get to do often enough. Flour dusting my apron and my cheeks from rubbing my hands over my face. It was delightfully warm in the kitchen and I know I'd have to leave soon but this was a great way to de-stress and soothe myself.

"I want you to know, Miss Zenaida, that while I'm going to be queen, I know you run this kitchen and have spectacularly for a while. I am not picky with food either so if you make something I haven't tried, you will hear no fuss from me. I appreciate you teaching me and doing such a wonderful job with your food." She brushes the compliments off before grasping my hands in both of hers.

"Call me Mama Zen, baby. That's what I have the other kids call me. And worry not, if you didn't like something before, you'll like Mama Zens way of it." She was sure of herself, rightfully so, but I giggle anyway at her confidence and smile brightly.

"What did I tell you about wearing shoes, Seren Fach?" His deep masculine voice carries through the kitchen and once again, it's bustling noise pauses to assess the scene.

My eyes grow wide, looking down at me feet before glancing back up at him. I go to answer him sheepishly but Mama Zen cuts in.

"Whose kitchen is this?" My attention snaps to her, eyes wide in surprise. She holds a hand on her hip, wooden spoon in the other aimed at the king. Her brows are raised, awaiting an answer.

I look at the grown male, large in muscle as he narrows his eyes at her. They stare off for a moment before he relents with a sigh and a roll of his eyes, "Yours."

"That's what I thought. If Miss Verena wants to walk around barefoot like a heathen in here, then she will." Her accent reminds me of the witch from the woods just not as thick but there was a twang to it not heard in Zorya.

"Yes, ma'am." He says and immediately I'm ready to do whatever he tells me. His muscles fit his black button down, a common choice in his wardrobe that is well-deserving of its praises by me. The top few buttons are undone, tattoos peaking out on his chest. His raven hair messy and his dark brown eyes shining as he peruses me from the stairway.

I watch his eyes darken as he trails his gaze over my dusted apron and face, noting the stick in my hair and the way the dress I wore was scrunched up with a rope to keep myself from tripping over it.

"I see you're having fun. I was coming to finalize the menu for the wedding." He looks at his head chef who smiles at him.

"No need. Verena did it." This time he looks at me with surprise. I know he took over all wedding planning since Hadeon told him how stressful it was for me when I was marrying Dryston.

"You didn't have to do that." He walks over to me, eyes never leaving mine as he wraps an arm around my waist to pull me closer to him.

"I wanted to help and Mama Zen was already teaching me things. I might as well have helped her take this off her and your plates. I don't want you to think I don't want to plan this day with you. If you need me for anything, let me know."

"I can't wait to marry you." He says, kissing me softly.

Chapter 32: Little Star

Verena

Chaos surrounds me. Cries of anger, screams of pain, clashing of metal upon metal reverberates throughout my head. Where are familiar faces? Everyone around me is covered in dirt, sweat, and blood. Bodies litter the ground. My chest rises and falls in quick succession, panic swelling within me. A cry of war sounds from my left and as I jerk my head to look, I note Hadeon fighting off a soldier of Zorya. Further back is Esmeray and I can't move my legs to help as a Zoryan stabs his sword through her torso. I try to scream, but no sound comes out.

Where is Eryx?

I glance around me, tears filling my eyes. I hear his pained groan from behind me and when I twist around in haste, I have no choice but to watch as his life is stripped away.

A scream leaves my throat as I jolt upwards in bed, my breathing erratic as blood pounds in my ears and I hold my chest with my hand. Gaining my bearings, I look around to pull me back to reality. The sweet smell of brown sugar floods my nose as Eryx jerks awake with me, holding me close to him as I press my face into his chest.

"Shh." He soothes, running a hand over my hair while he holds me tightly with the other. Tears brim my eyes and I blink them away, letting them fall down my cheeks and onto the sheets covering us. "It's a nightmare. You're safe."

"It felt so real," I choke out softly, allowing him to keep me close. "I watched you die." My heart clenches at the thought. I feel him tense at my words but he continues rubbing my hair and back.

"I am safe. Nothing is going to happen to me, love." I nod, trying to force the thoughts away. "Let's try to go back to sleep." He lays down while pulling my body on top of him. The thrum of his heart fills my ear as it presses against his chest, the warmth from his body heats mine, and suddenly I am falling back asleep while his hand traces circles around my bare back.

Waking up hours later, the sun shines through the windows, casting the room in a warm glow. A knock sounds at the door before Mama Zen waltzes in with a cart full of food.

"Good morning, you two." She smiles before stopping the cart by the bed. I cover myself with the comforter but she doesn't seem to mind or note our naked bodies. "Happy Wedding day! Eat up so you don't feel weak." Then she leaves and Eryx slips out a light laugh at my red tinted cheeks and chest.

"Is she always like that?" I question, smiling.

"Zenaida is an actual mother and helped mine raise me and my sisters. She's seen it all so she doesn't mind. That's why she knocks, to give you a warning that she is coming in." He starts pouring tea for me, knowing it's my preferred drink for mornings before buttering a biscuit and adding a berry jam to it.

How does he know what I prefer for food?

"I pay attention." He says as if reading my mind. We spend the rest of the morning eating and talking, simply enjoying each others company.

Until Ruelle, Calanthe, and Esmeray burst into the room. "You're still in bed?" Ruelle exclaims. "Come on! We have to get you ready! You're gonna spend the rest of your lives together, you can go a couple hours apart." The women laugh excitedly and I can't help but join in, moving to slip from the bed.

Eryx reaches out, stopping me by my arm before pulling me in for a long sensual kiss, slipping his tongue in to brush mine that made me not want to leave.

Esmeray made a playful gagging sound as if she were disgusted by the act but when I look at them, Calanthe is smiling and Ruelle slaps her sister.

They finally are able to pull me away and out of the room, leading me down the hall to Ruelle's room.

We laugh as we rush in but I stop short in my tracks once they close the door and I look around. There is a rack to the side holding four clothing bags, her vanity is littered with makeup and hair accessories, and there stands a couple maids waiting for us.

"What is this?" I ask, turning to the females of my soon-to-be family.

Ruelle steps forward, grasping my hands in hers. People have been doing that a lot lately. "You are family. And this is your wedding day. This is for you. Our dresses are there and my mother has offered to help you with putting yours on since your mother can't be here today. And we have a sparkling wine mixed with juice, it sounds weird but its delicious!" She thrusts a glass of the fruity and bubbly concoction toward me and I take a drink. She definitely wasn't wrong. It was divine.

She squeals in excitement, clapping her hands together and leads me to sit with her mother and sister as maids walk over and start on our hair and faces once we were sat.

It is a weird thing, being doted on like this. I did everything by myself on my wedding day.

"I didn't even pick my dress out." I tell them after two hours of sitting still, laughing with them and just talking. "Should I be worried?" They look at each other with knowing smiles.

"Are we done?" Esmeray asks the maids, who nods in return, and she stands, pulling my dress to the front and unzipping the garment bag.

I stand in shock as she brings it into view.

There before me was the prettiest dress I had ever seen. It is more of a golden nude tone over all. The boning and bust cups in the torso firm and form fitting from the looks of it. Then, the puffy skirt drops to the floor in a puddle of soft tulle. Throughout the tulle sprinkled iridescent stars and sparkling gems that were so tiny you couldn't see anything other than the gleam and shine when the light cast upon them. The sleeves were off shoulder, drooping in puffed detachable forms from where my biceps would sit, flitting to my wrists.

"Eryx had it designed for you. Our seamstress wanted to add color but he said you were enough color and he didn't want to pull away from your natural beauty." Ruelle spoke softly, as if in awe of it all.

Tears well in my eyes at the thought of him doing this for me. It is better than I could've had made for myself. I can't wait to marry him.

Esmeray, Calanthe, and Ruelle dress in their stunning midnight blue silky dresses and then the princesses of Khyrel left the room.

Calanthe pulls my dress down from the hanger with delicacy before motion me over to step into it.

We stand in front of a full bodied mirror and I look in awe of myself. My hair was wavy, as it was when we met at the coronation ball for Dryston. It flows down my back like water. The blue standing out now more than ever from the pale blonde my hair fully embodied. My indigo eyes popping brightly with the smoky colors they dusted onto my eyelids before lining them with black coal. She helps slip the dress up, zipping it into place. It's a perfect fit. Snug in every right place on the bodice before flowing down to the ground.

"It's fitting, is it not?" She asks in such a sweet motherly voice.

"The dress is very fitting for the court. It's so beautiful."

I see her brows furrow and I look at her with a questioning gaze, "I meant your nickname. Seren Fach?" When I gave her the same look, she continues. "It means 'Little Star'."

Realization sets in but I don't know what to say. I just gave her a smile.

"Shoes?" I ask Calanthe, excited for what her son might've chosen.

Her all-knowing smile gets brighter, "He said no shoes." My heart clenches in love. Gods this male will be the death of me.

I nod and she rests a supportive palm on my shoulder. "She'd be so proud of you. I know I say it a lot but she wanted your happiness above all else. You are so beautiful, Verena, and having you become part of my family is such a blessing from the Gods." She tears up too, both of us wiping away the drops of salty solution from our eyes before we ruin our faces. "Are you ready?"

I nod to her and she walks to the door, opening it and allowing Hadeon to see me in full view.

An audible gasp flows from his lips, "Wow." Is all he says and I can't help the small smile gracing my lips. Calanthe leaves us, I am assuming to join her daughters in the throne room. "May I?" He asks, holding his arm out for me to grab. "Maybe let's keep this marriage, yeah? Two is a good number." He jokes and I gasp in surprise at it before laughing.

"You are an ass." I state between fits of giggles as we make our way to the throne room. As we walk, I can't help myself from getting emotional again. "Thank you, again, for walking with me." He only responds by tapping his hand on mine that's resting in his arm and nodding as if speaking will choke him up.

We make it to the doors and they open when I nod to the guards who are usually stoic but today smile at me in an endearing way. Esmeray had told me that saving Ruelle and bringing her home bought me a lot of respect from everyone, especially the royal guard and soldiers. Any who might've second-guessed my intentions with Eryx or as queen were dissipated now.

I just hate that the price was both of us almost dying for it— for if I were a male, it would've been automatic respect.

Once the doors fully open, all eyes are on us— or *me*, for that matter.

I take a quick glance around, noting all the faces in attendance before my eyes meet his.

Dark as usual but the sun beams through the window, shining a bright light upon them to make them lighter. I almost think I see a sheen from tears but he blinks them away in haste as soon as I start moving. Light music plays from the back corner, reverberating around the space as we walk down the aisle separating both sides of chairs in rows. They're filled with people I haven't seen before. I keep my eyes on him, though, not wanting to trip. And being unable to tear them away.

Again, as usual, he wears a black suit. His shirt holding a few undone buttons from the top and he stands there with his hands together in front of him. It looks like a normal suit but the closer we get, the more I notice the shining glimmer of iridescent color on his shirt, barely visual. He sees where my gaze is transfixed and the corner of his mouth twitches up before he flattens it back out.

We arrive to the front of our guests and as I look around the building, it's magical. Drapes in hues of purples and blues are strung on the beams, golden stars dropped from invisible string as if they're floating through the air. The entire place is so beautiful.

Eryx steps down a step, reaching his hand out for me to take. I place my small hand in his much larger one and he helps me step up to stand in front of him.

In his way, this entire wedding is showing me how he loves me as if I was his kingdom. I mean more to him than it does. The stars, the nickname, the sacrifices he's been through with me here, the trust he's put in me? It's all one big sign from the Gods to me. He is mine and nothing will change that.

Chapter 33: Bow

Verena

"Repeat after me," The high priestess says after a lengthy monologue of the meanings marriage. "I, King Eryx Ashwood," She speaks and Eryx copies. "Vow to be yours. I vow that the love I have for you knows no bounds. My love for you does not falter to sickness, health, joy, or sadness. I vow to have you as my equal. When you speak, I will listen. When you fall, I will catch you. When you rise to fulfill your dreams, I will be there to help you reach your greatest heights. I vow to treat you as if you are apart of me, because you are in my eyes and in the eyes of the Gods. May they bless this union and ride with us through our journey." I hold my emotions together even as I copy the same vows.

The high priestess reveals the marcam used to carve rune into ourselves. But this one is different. Eryx smirks as he hands it to me, "Queens first." I look at him with confusion before taking it from him. He opens the chest of his shirt further, revealing an open spot over his heart. "I'd go lower but I don't think anyone wants to see that." He whispers and I laugh loudly, unable to prevent the sound from slipping out. Confusion slips over the crowds faces at my laughter but only the high priestess and my self heard him. She clears her throat, clearly not amused, and I sober up, smiling at him still as I move closer to Mark him.

The design is the same wedded rune. But I pause when I see that the color isn't the usual one. It's an exact replica of the hue of my irises. A perfect indigo. My heart beats hard in my chest at the love I have for him. This answers the question on why he was smirking at me.

When it's his turn, his isn't silver like Zorya's. It is as black as his hair, as the night sky, as the look in his eyes when he peruses me in an act of coitus.

He motions for me to choose where to have him mark, so I match him with my heart, thanking the fact that the dress doesn't need to be moved.

Unlike my wedding with Dryston, I wasn't full of existential dread. It was love, hope, and joy. And the look of promise in his darkening eyes has sparks shooting through me, tightening in my lower stomach.

"Love is not a path we determine ourselves. It's determined by the gods, by the marcam itself. Our fates entwine into their twisting patterns, binding us together beyond our own desires." She says and as the high priestess chants the ancient incantations, a shiver runs down my spine, a sense of unease creeping into my heart. The marks glow with an ethereal light, pulsing with an unseen power that seals our vows in ways we cannot comprehend.

As the ritual concludes, I feel a weight settle upon my shoulders, a burden of responsibility and destiny that comes with this union. King Eryx's eyes meet mine, and I see in them a mixture of determination and uncertainty, reflecting my own emotions back at me. We are bound now, not just by words or love, but by forces older than time itself.

The high priestess steps back, her gaze inscrutable as she pronounces us husband and wife in the eyes of the gods.

Without another word, Eryx's hand grabs my hip roughly and pulls me toward him, dipping me into a fierce kiss that ignites a wildfire of passion in my body. Every inch of me is consumed by his touch as he hungrily devours my lips, leaving nothing but a trail of burning desire in his wake.

"If this room were empty, I'd take you right now." A blush colors my face.

"Why wait?" His eyes flash to mine, surprised, but debating almost.

He sighs, "No one else will see you so natural. You are mine. I am yours. And I do not share." He kisses me again, more this time as if he doesn't kiss me with the same ferocity as always.

He faces the crowd now, his face dropping solemnly, "Bow." Were his only instructions and my face reddens as if it couldn't get worse. Embarrassment floods me at the sight of everyone doing just as he demanded. The guards don't even hesitate and I take note of some of them holding back smiles. But, while the Court held uneasy glances, Calanthe, Hadeon, Esmeray, and Ruelle bow their heads with smirks and smiles. Eryx takes my hand and starts walking down the aisle once more while everyone continues to bow.

He faces them, "Now, we celebrate before we go to war. Enjoy your evenings." I feel a mix of emotions swirling inside me as Eryx's words hang in the air, heavy with unspoken truths and hidden promises. The weight of his gaze on me is both thrilling and daunting, a reminder of the tangled web of fate that now binds us together.

* * *

Once everyone arrives in the ball room, Eryx makes his way up to the dais, sitting on his throne. But I stand, announcing loud, "I graciously thank you all for your patience, and for showing your love and support. My vows are not just for King Eryx but for this kingdom. I will do everything in my power, in my queendom to help Khyrel flourish and thrive." I am greeted with applause as the entire ballroom burst into a lively celebration.

The sound of music fills the air, mingling with the laughter and chatter of the guests. I can't help but feel overwhelmed by the grandeur of it all, the extravagance of the decorations, the opulence of the feast spread before us.

I sat down temporarily and caught glimpses of familiar faces – friends and allies who had come to witness our union. Calanthe's eyes sparkle with mischief as she raises her glass in a silent toast, while Hadeon grins like a Cheshire cat, clearly enjoying himself.

But amidst the revelry, a sense of unease crept over me once more. I glance around discreetly, trying to shake off the feeling of being watched. It was ominous but I brush it off. I still haven't adjusted to having so many people wanting to meet me.

I dance through the night after we eat, spinning around in the traditional dances with Ruelle. With a wild abandon, I raise my hands above my head and spin in the open-air ballroom as rain cascades down. A lot of the rooms for big crowds were designed with this very purpose in mind— to let nature's elements join in on our revelry. Above us, the stunning Aurora Borealis dances across the sky in vibrant shades of green and pink, its magic amplified by the reflections on the falling raindrops. Unable to contain my joy, I throw my head back and laugh, taking in the breathtaking sight before me. It is a moment of pure wonder and delight.

The music seems to fade into the background, leaving only the sound of our footsteps and the racing of my heart. Eryx places his hand on my waist. It's firm and possessive, guiding me with a familiarity that speaks of countless dances shared between us in another lifetime. I look up into his eyes, dark pools that reflect the shimmering lights above like distant stars.

The metallic stars hanging from the ceiling cast a dreamlike glow over us, creating an illusion of floating through a midnight sky filled with wonder and magic. And suddenly I am not worried about the haunting war on the horizon. Nothing else matters in this moment except us. I want to make him feel how happen he makes me. I want to cherish him and worship his body. He seems to take note of the change in my eyes before leading me out of the celebratory dancing and toward our own room, calls and whistles sound from behind us and again, another blush reddens my chest, my face, everywhere at the fact that everyone in attendance will know what we were about to be doing. Eryx laughs fully, more than I had heard from him in the time of knowing him and It is more heavenly than the music playing. I want to hear it all the time.

The anticipation of what was to come mingled with nerves and excitement, creating a heady concoction that made my pulse quicken.

As we enter our room, the air was heavy with the scent of lavender and sandalwood, a soothing aroma that wraps around us like a warm embrace specifically for our wedding night. Eryx closes the door behind us with a soft click, enveloping us in a cocoon of privacy. The candlelight dances across his features, casting shadows that accentuate the sharp angles of his face.

Wordlessly, he turns to face me, his eyes dark with desire and something deeper, a raw intensity that sent shivers down my spine. The distance between us seems to shrink until there was nothing but the crackling tension that hung in the air like a tangible thing. The heavy grandeur of the castle falls away, leaving only the intimate space that now contains just Eryx and I. The air is thick with anticipation, our breaths mingling as we stand facing each other in silence. Eryx's eyes hold a tender warmth that melts away any chill from the rain or lingering fears, and I feel a rush of desire coursing through me.

Without a word, he closes the distance between us, his touch sending shivers down my spine. His lips brush against mine in a soft, gentle kiss that ignites a fire within me. I respond eagerly, my hands finding their way to his hair as I deepen the kiss, losing myself in the taste and feel of him.

Soaked clothes are shed with an urgency born of longing and love, until we stand before each other completely bare, exposed in body and soul. Eryx's gaze roams over me with a hunger.

* * *

Eryx

Verena's hands roam across my sculpted chest, tracing the lines of my muscles with reverence and desire. The heat from her indigo irises is palpable, a living thing that pulses in time with my racing heart. She sinks to her knees before me, her eyes never leaving my gaze as the blonde slowly trails kisses down my torso, tasting salty skin in a heady mix. I groan with need and impatience.

Her tongue lashes out, gliding down my skin and over the raven shaped mark of our bond. A shiver wracks my body. Her hand takes my cock, smoothly drifting over it in a back and forth motion. My eyes close in ecstasy but she squeezes my length and they flash open. "Eyes on me, handsome." Her voice is deeper than usual, heady and full of lust.

She licks up my shaft, sending my body into another shiver and my right hand finds it's way into her hair, gripping like my sanity depended on it.

She takes me into her mouth, and I gasp at the exquisite sensation that threatens to unravel me completely. Verena's mouth is warm and wet, her movements expertly driving me wild with need.

I've never felt anything like this before. I can barely contain myself. Just before I can reach the edge of ecstasy completely, I gently pull her up to stand before me by her hair.

With a hunger that—no doubt— matches her own, I guide Verena to the bed, laying her down like a precious offering to the Gods. Her wet skin glows in the soft candlelight, ethereal and luminescent against the dark sheets beneath her. I kneel before her, trailing kisses along her inner thighs and giving a small bite to her own bond mark. I needed to taste her.

My hands trace a path of fire along her skin, leaving a trail of goosebumps in their wake. I feel like I am burning from the inside out from the need to touch her, to taste her, to fill her with me until she remembers nothing but my name and who I am. Consumed by the intensity of my touch, she garbles out gibberish in a breathy moan and I smirk.

With a reverence that borders on worship, I trail my tongue across her, mapping every curve and dip with an intimacy that forces her breath to catch in her throat. When my lips meet the sensitive skin of her cunt, a gasp escapes her pink luscious lips, and she arches toward me, craving more.

The world narrows down to the sensation of my tongue on her skin, sending waves of pleasure cascading through the both of us. I lose myself in her, lapping her up like a pet with a bowl of water. Tasting her is a need, one I'll cherish for my entire life. I can't get enough of her scent, the way her body writhes underneath me, her eyes rolling back as I watch her pleasure.

She comes undone then, trying to push my head away in a whimper. I chuckle deeply, moving up after wiping my face and kissing her once more, unable to get my fill of her.

My tongue meets hers, lazily playing with one another and I trace a trail of kisses down her neck, my lips leaving a searing heat in their wake. She gasps at the intensity of the sensation, my hands clutching her hips while hers grip my shoulders as if to anchor myself amidst the whirlwind of emotions that threaten to consume me.

I feel a surge of desire pooling between her thighs again as my cock rubs her hot, wet heat. I lower myself then, my gaze locks with hers, a silent promise of pleasures yet to come.

Chapter 34: You Fight Well

Verena

After a long and arduous day of war preparations, Eryx, Esmeray, and I gather in the outside training courtyard as the sun dips low on the horizon, casting a warm golden glow around us. The air was full of the scent of sweat and leather as we gear up for the sparring session to unwind. My eyes sparkle with determination as I face off against Eryx, my new husband, something I'd never tire of saying.

Once we were ready to go, we circle each other like wolves, our movements fluid and graceful. He seems almost surprised I can keep the same pace as he, but Esmeray trained me right.

He grins, the dark brown eyes never leaving mine as we exchange playful taunts. "You've been getting better." He starts.

"I can't wait to show you the moves I've learned," I flash him flirty eyes. It had only been a couple of days after our wedding and the townspeople have been loving the celebrations. It truly was an event of the century. The love and support from everyone was surprising to me and I almost didn't want to believe it.

"Look alive." The clashing of steel rang through the air as he comes at me with the staff he uses.

"Oh, so authoritative." I say to him, breathy as I watch him remove his tunic, my gaze traveling along the tattoos and markings painting his body.

"Do not flirt with me, Seren Fach." His tone held warning as he smacks my stick with his and we suddenly spar with a passion that only fuels our connection. I move with the precision of a seasoned warrior, thanks to Esmeray. My every strike calculated and deadly. Eryx matches me, though, move for move, his eyes alight with admiration for his fierce and beautiful wife.

"Oh, tell me you're not just a little impressed." I press, knowing that he is, based on the gleam in his eyes.

As we spar across the grass in the courtyard, our movements became a dance of power and skill, each strike landing with precision but never intending harm. The rhythm of our combat echoes off the open air around us, a melody of strength and unity. Esmeray watches from the sidelines, her expressions a mix of pride and amusement as she saw the bond between Eryx and I grows stronger with each passing moment.

Suddenly, Eryx swept my legs out from under me, sending me tumbling to the ground with a laugh. I land with a thud, the breath knocks out of me for a moment as I gaze up at him, his face hovering above mine with a playful smirk.

"You fight well, my love," he said, offering me his hand to help me up.

I take it, feeling the warmth of his touch as he pulls me to my feet. "And you were going easy on me, my dear husband," I reply, brushing off my training attire and meeting his gaze with a smile.

"Not by much." He answers, taking the sparring stick from me and handing them to the weapon handler present.

My words die in my throat as Hadeon barges in, his voice booming with accusation. "You let Dryston live and didn't bother to tell us?" His tone is filled with disbelief and betrayal.

A shiver runs down my spine, the sweat on my skin turning icy as fear grips me. My heart races as I struggle to find a response, knowing the consequences of my actions will not be taken lightly by Hadeon and the others.

"What?" Eryx's voice is laced with concern as he questions his best friend, casting a quick glance at me before scanning the room for any eavesdroppers. "Leave us," he commands the staff, who quickly scurry away, leaving us alone in the quiet hallway. Eryx pulls me closer to where Hadeon and Esmeray now stand together, their faces serious and unreadable. I can't help but wonder if Ruelle had already told them what she had just told me.

"When Ruelle and Verena were kidnapped, Amaelya wasn't alone." The memory of that terrifying night floods back, sending shivers down my spine. The words echo in my mind, causing my heart to race and my palms to sweat.

Suddenly, as if on cue, Ruelle comes running out from a side door. Her hair is wild and tangled, her cheeks flushed with exertion. "I'm sorry, Verena," she gasps for breath as she joins our small group. Her eyes are wide with worry and guilt, and I can sense the tension radiating off of her.

Eryx turns to face me, his eyes cloud with a mix of emotions — hurt, confusion, anger. I can see the questions swirling in his mind, and I know he wants answers. "I didn't get a chance to tell you," I begin, my voice strained. "It wasn't meant to be a secret. After I told you about Amaelya, you made me go back to sleep. I forgot about it until shortly after I woke up, and by that point there was so much going on with the wedding."

"What happened in the cave with Dryston?" he presses.

I take a deep breath, memories flooding back as I recount the events

277

that took place. As I finish telling him, I see the hurt in Eryx's eyes deepen into a hardened gaze. "It wasn't meant to be a secret," I try to explain.

"You just kept the fact that you could've prevented this war, Verena," Eryx says, his tone accusatory. "I thought Khyrel meant something to you." His walls are coming up now, and it breaks my heart.

"It does! I never meant for it to turn out this way," I plead with him, hoping that he can understand my feelings. But his gaze remains cold and distant, and I know he is shutting me out.

"No, it doesn't matter to you like we all thought. Your revenge apparently outweighs the safety of *my* people. And you didn't even tell me. I am your husband but more than that, I am your mate. We are supposed to be one soul." My heart aches now, pained by the declaration as if I hadn't already known. Of course I did.

"Leaving him alive wasn't an easy choice. Of course I thought about the people. *Our* people." I try, my voice full of desperation. "You do not understand the gravity of the situation. Yes, I could've killed him. But we know nothing of what the cost would've been. There was no concrete evidence that he had taken us captive. However, both Princess Lianna and Queen Consort Rya could have perceived it as an act of aggression toward their kingdom. Having spent time with them, I am aware of their perspectives. Rya has blind faith in her son and cannot fathom him causing any harm. She is overly attached to him, almost disgustingly so. On the other hand, she holds a strong dislike for me. If given the chance, she wouldn't hesitate to declare war on us, likely with more strategic planning than her son. They would change his entire plans, Eryx. Then I would know nothing of their plans of attack and where we can keep our people safe. I didn't do this out of a haste." I plead with him but I know he is genuinely upset with me.

"But you never told me. That's what hurts the most." He starts to walk away, leaving me in stunned silence. Hadeon follows him, for reasons unknown to me. Esmeray comes over and puts a gentle hand on my shoulder.

"Even if you didn't consider the consequences, I wouldn't blame you. As someone who knows the lasting pains of trauma all too well, I can understand the desire for revenge instead of just a quick death. I'll talk to him."

Chapter 35: Leaving

Eryx

"I can't believe you're leaving." She speaks softly as I pack a small bag of fighting leathers.

I pause, my hands momentarily still as I feel Verena's sorrowful gaze upon my body. My heart aches at the sight of her, her eyes glistening with unshed tears. I want nothing more than to gather her in my arms, to soothe away her fears and uncertainties. But duty calls, a heavy burden that even I can not ignore.

"I must go, Verena," I explain, my voice tinges with regret. "The people of Elmswood need my help. I cannot turn a blind eye to their plight. Dryston is moving fast but thanks to your knowledge, we have an advantage. I need to start evacuations of the towns he plans on attacking."

Verena bites her lower lip, a gesture of frustration and hurt. She had always understood my sense of responsibility, my unwavering dedication to this kingdom and its subjects. But this time feels different, the weight of my departure pressing down on us like a suffocating blanket.

"Please, Eryx," Verena's plea echoes in my head as I held her tightly.

"I'm sorry." Every fiber of my being wants to stay, to be by her side and protect her. But duty called, and I know that I couldn't deny my responsibilities as king. The weight of the crown feels heavy on my head, but I can't let my emotions cloud my judgment. The border towns needed me, and It is my duty to show them that their king will not abandon them. And yet, the thought of leaving Verena behind tore at my heart, knowing she would face danger in my place. Our love was a constant battle between duty and desire, and in this moment, they seemed impossible to reconcile.

"I know, Seren Fach," I whisper to my wife, trying to comfort her. But her expression remains troubled, her eyes full of worry and fear. A sudden knock at the door interrupts us. "Just a minute!" I call out, knowing it must be Esmeray.

Turning back to my wife, I gently cup her face in my hands. "I love you," I tell her earnestly, hoping she can feel the depth of my emotion through my touch. She nods, her response a quiet echo of my own words.

In that moment, as we stand together in our large but cozy room, I am struck by the overwhelming beauty of this person before me. Her hair is like spun gold cascading over her shoulders, her skin glowing with warmth and love. The way she looks at me makes my heart swell with adoration.

But even as I revel in her presence, the world outside waits for us. War looms on the horizon and we must prepare for battle. Yet in this brief pause, I am reminded that no matter what happens, I am blessed to have her by my side. And for that, I will forever be grateful.

With a firm grip, I heft the heavy luggage and push open the creaky door to hand it off to a sharp-eyed staff member of the palace. "To the stables, please," I request, my voice carrying a hint of urgency. Glancing at my sister, I catch her giving Verena a subtle nod full of unspoken meaning that I can't begin to decipher. "Are you ready?" I inquire, searching her face for any sign of hesitation.

My sisters narrowed eyes meet mine before she finally nods and begins making her way toward the stables as well, her steps purposeful and determined. I take one final look back at Verena, seeing her clutch her chest before looking away, knowing I have to leave now or I won't at all. I know we need to talk this through but right now, this kingdom needs us. I will not fail the prophecy.

We will be fine, we are fated to be together and now we are wed. Nothing will change that. As we walk, the sound of our footsteps echo against the stone walls and the distant chatter of other palace workers fills the air. Anticipation and tension mingle in the atmosphere, making me wonder what lies ahead at the stables.

I know why Verena did what she did. But it was her not telling me that was the issue. We needed no secrets between us, no boundaries.

* * *

Verena

I decide to spend time in the kitchens after I gather myself after Eryx's departure. I know why he had to leave. I don't blame him. I just wish we had a chance to be on better terms before he did.

I had hoped Eryx forgave me. I still hadn't regretted it. Dryston deserves to suffer. Should I have told him immediately? Sure, maybe. But it didn't change any outcome. Everyone here seems to forget I endured a decade and a half of manipulation and assault from Dryston. They couldn't assume I'd be perfectly happy giving up my need for revenge. I refuse to give him the satisfaction of just dying. He will learn what it felt like to have your entire world ripped from your grasp, just as I did.

If Eryx doesn't understand that— or if he doesn't want it for me— than he isn't the mate I thought he'd be. He should want the same.

"Eryx loves this country," Mama Zen starts. It breaks me from my reverie and I face her, dusting my floured hands on the apron she had made for me. "But, I know he loves you more, mia cara. Trust in him. Trust in your marriage." Her words are wise, sage advice. And I know she is right. I shouldn't assume he doesn't feel the same as I do. I am just surprised at his reaction. "All done." She announces to me about the goodies. "Why don't you go get some training in. I can wash up here."

"Are you sure?" I ask, wanting to help but she just nods me off, untying my apron for me and practically pushing me out the doorway. I roll my eyes at her, smiling form her antics before looking for Hadeon. Hopefully he hadn't left with Eryx and Esmeray.

Luckily I find him already in the courtyard's sparring area.

My heart leaps with joy as I notice Hadeon amidst the group of guards circling around, his sword glinting in the sunlight as he moves with practiced grace. I watch in admiration as he parries a blow from one of his opponents and swiftly counters with a calculated strike of his own. The clash of steel rings through the air, the sound echoing off the stone walls that surround us.

Taking a deep breath to steady my nerves, I step forward, determination shining in my eyes. This is exactly what I need. Without saying a word, I approach the sparring match, my footsteps light on the grassy ground. I know exactly when Hadeon catches sight of me, even without turning his attention away from his current opponent. A smile tugs at the corners of his lips, his eyes alight with excitement at the prospect of facing off against his best friend and former student.

One of the guards in front of me turns to see who's lurking behind him, but he steps back at the sight of me, making room for his queen to join the circle surrounding Hadeon. He nods at me, "Your Grace, we were not expecting you." He announces me to the others. Everyone takes a notable step away from me, as to give me room. I hadn't minded the cramped space, although I understand why they did it.

Hadeon finishes his fight against one of the other guards and I take my stance opposite him, my grip firm on the sword I pick up from the ground, readying myself for the challenge ahead. The air was cooler than usual, picking up on the autumn days coming. The crisp breeze sends a burst of energy my way. I meet Hadeon's gaze, a silent understanding passing between us — this is not just a friendly spar, but a test of skill and trust between two warriors who have stood side by side through countless training exercises over five years.

I hear the guards whisper to themselves, unsure on how this will work.

"Are you sure you want to do this, Your Majesty?" He asks me.

A mischievous glint twinkles in my eyes as I meet Hadeon's gaze, the familiar banter between us sparking to life. "Oh, I'm more than sure, Hadeon. Let's see if you can still keep up with me, old man." I retort playfully, a smirk dancing on my lips.

"I'm like three years older than you," He exclaims in laughter but before he can say anymore, I lunge forward. The clash of our swords ring out like a battle hymn. Hadeon meets my strike with ease, his movements fluid and precise as he defends against my every move. The onlookers gasp in amazement at the sight of their queen holding her own against the renowned royal guard.

As our swords continue to dance in a flurry of strikes and parries, I feel a surge of exhilaration coursing through my veins, pushing harder and faster than I ever have against him. This was where I belong, in the heat of battle alongside my dearest friend, pushing each other to new heights of skill and strength.

But then, in a swift and unexpected turn of events, my sword catches his and I twist my wrist around, sliding against his sword so hard, his grip releases. Our eyes meet, both impressed and stunned for a brief moment. We begin to circle each other, knowing this isn't over. The courtyard falls into hushed anticipation. The sound of our footsteps on the soft grass is the only noise that fills the air, the tension palpable among the watching guards.

With a sudden burst of speed, I launch myself at Hadeon, a fierce determination burning within me. Our bodies clash once again, our groans of tiresome fighting reverberating through the courtyard as we each push ourselves to the limit. I wrap my legs around his head, twisting my body with speed and agility to throw myself to the ground in a calculated move. He falls flat on his back as I let go and land just as I trained with Esmeray to do.

"I see someone's training with Esmeray has gone well." He groans out with a cough, the air knocks from his lungs when he lands. I stand, forgetting I am near his feet and he swiftly kicks mine from under me, a groan leaving my lips from the impact. I go to laugh, the sound a bit breathy as I cough in a lungful of air. We both rise to our feet simultaneously, standing our ground and positioning in organized stances.

This time, I do not have the moment to strike first. Hadeon comes forward, attempting to punch me. I side-swipe the muscular fist. Every move is met with a thought-out response, every strike countered with precision. We move in perfect synchronization, our years of training together evident in the seamless flow of our movements.

Hadeon's eyes glint with respect and pride as he recognizes the fierce warrior standing before him. The playful banter is replaced by an unspoken agreement between us — this is no longer a friendly spar, but a battle of wills and strength. I feel a surge of adrenaline coursing through me as I push myself harder, faster, refusing to back down.

As we continue to exchange blows, I see an opening, a split second where his defenses waver. With lightning speed, I seize the opportunity and drop to the ground, turning hastily while sweeping my legs outward, taking his legs in a swift strike that catches him off guard. He drops to the ground and before he can move further, I'm on top of him with a dagger at his throat.

"I win." I barely manage to get out in a smirk, my chest rapidly falling as it heaves air in and out. Sweat from my face drips onto his training leathers but he is unbothered.

I see the flash of emotion in his eyes. He's never looked at me so proudly.

Finally I note the whoops and hollers form the surrounding crowd of guards and soldiers. The excitement from their queen defeating their head guard.

From what I learned, Hadeon trained most of these men and women, Esmeray the one to train the newer additions since Hadeon was gone for years.

But I had not beat Hadeon in a sparring match before. This was momentous. And the first person I wanted to share my excitement with wasn't here.

I feel my smile drop during the cheers and claps on my back. My eyes flit to the ground. It is such an unfamiliar feeling to want to share an occasion with someone and yet that someone was risking their life in another town to save their kingdom.

A hand rests on my shoulder and I look up into the forest green eyes of my only friend for the past five years. "Come on. Let's see if there is news." He seems to know exactly where my thoughts were. I nod and follow him from the courtyard, allowing other warriors and guards to spar among themselves.

Chapter 36: Aradon

Verena

L ast night I was sent a message from one of our scouts. A border town we hadn't anticipated being attacked was close to being ravaged through by Dryston's soldiers. Hadeon and I left then and there with a handful of our own ready to fight back.

Our journey to the border town of Aradon was fraught with tension and fear. The once lush forests had given way to barren rolling hills, a stark reminder of the destruction that loomed near. The air was heavy with the stench of death and burning wood, a constant reminder of the imminent danger.

As we ride closer, I can see the panic in the townspeople's eyes. They frantically pack their belongings, desperate to flee before the enemy arrives. In the distance, a small pack of Zoryan soldiers ride as a foreboding threat.

My heart pounds with worry for Eryx, who was facing a similar fate in another town. Every step I take feels like another strong pull to him, my mind consumed with thoughts of his safety. Desperately, I look up to the heavens and pray to the Gods for his swift and safe return home.

Hadeon and I look to each other, already reading one another's mind. Once we get closer to the town buildings, I dismount the horse, handing my reins to one of the guards.

Hadeon gets the attention of the locals and I jump on to the fountain in the center of town as all eyes look toward me.

"You don't know me personally. I am the new Queen of Khyrel, Verena. I am here to lead you all to safety. Zorya has sent soldiers to weaken our country and we will do everything in our power to stop them!"

The townspeople stare at me in disbelief, whispering amongst themselves as they try to process my proclamation. Hadeon stands by my side, his presence reassuring and commanding respect from the crowd. I can see the flicker of hope ignite in their eyes, a glimmer of belief that maybe, just maybe, they stand a chance against the impending threat.

Without hesitation, we began organizing the villagers, assigning tasks and formulating a plan to defend their homes while they rendezvous with a few of our trusted soldiers, who lead the townspeople toward a nearby town. Hadeon's military expertise paired with my strategic mind prove to be a formidable combination as we prepare for the inevitable clash with the Zoryan soldiers.

We eventually clear out the small village of people and as night falls, all that is left is burnt out candles, previously used for lighting the buildings and the flames of Zorya rearing closer from the south.

The tension in the air thickens, each passing moment bringing us closer to the inevitable confrontation. The sound of approaching footsteps echo through the deserted streets, sending a shiver down my spine. With a deep breath, I steady myself, ready to face whatever challenges lie ahead.

The clash was imminent, but I refuse to let fear cloud my judgment. With Hadeon by my side, I knew I'd make it out alive. Hopefully.

We stand off behind one of the run down buildings, some soldiers placed sporadically around the village in beneficial positions.

Hadeon meets my gaze, our eyes speaking in a language only we know. I nod at him, understanding to stay put and stay quiet— for now.

Apprehension fills the area as we wait in silence, every nerve on edge as the sound of approaching boots grew louder. I can feel my heart racing, adrenaline coursing through my veins as I prepare myself for the battle ahead.

Shadows flicker in the darkness, a prelude to the impending clash that will determine the fate of Aradon.

Suddenly, the group of Zoryan soldiers came into view, their menacing figures illuminated by the ominous fully lit moon that engulfs the village. Hadeon's grip on his sword tightens, his jaw clenches in determination as we watch the enemy draw closer.

As they enter the town square, a moment of stillness hangs in the air before chaos erupts. Our soldiers sprung into action, launching a surprise attack on the unsuspecting Zoryan forces. Swords clash, arrows flew, and the night was filled with the sounds of battle.

With silent footsteps, I draw my sword and charge into the thick of it. My feet pound against the ground as I move with deadly precision, fueled by the adrenaline coursing through my veins. My blade slices through flesh and bone as I fight ferociously to defend our land from Dryston's invading forces, determined to protect the innocent villagers and uphold our honor.

Blood splatters across my face and body in a vicious red spray as I slash through the enemy soldiers with ruthless efficiency. My biceps scream in agony as I swing and strike, each impact sending jolts of pain up my arm. The ground is littered with bodies — most of them down for the count — but I refuse to let my guard down.

In a swift motion, I drive my sword deep into the chest of a Zoryan soldier on the ground, watching as the light fades from his eyes. As I wipe the blood from my face, I notice Hadeon's horrified expression as he watches me take down our foes. Confusion furrows my brow as he looks like he's seen a ghost. But before I can question him, an arrow whizzes past me, grazing my blonde locks with its deadly tip.

My heart races and I spin around, ready to face another attacker. But all I see is a fallen Zoryan soldier behind me, impaled by the mysterious archer's shot. Cold fear grips me as I realize someone was sneaking up on me, and Hadeon's earlier reaction suddenly makes sense.

But where did that arrow come from? There's no one in sight and none of our own soldiers have a bow and quiver. Could there be another unseen force at play here? One that may or may not be on our side? The hairs on the back of my neck stand on end as I steel myself for whatever hidden danger may still be lurking nearby.

A groan leaves a body and I search for them.

A guttural cry escapes from his trembling lips as I close in on him, my sword held tightly in hand. His feeble attempts to crawl away are halted by the cold metal pressing against his back, forcing him to turn and face me. "Verena?" He stammers, recognition dawning in his eyes. But there is no mercy in my heart for him, only a burning rage that fuels my every move. "Why are you doing this?" He begs, his voice shaking with fear.

I feel a surge of anger at the mere mention of my name. "I am merely protecting what your corrupt ruler has taken advantage of. Khyrel and Zorya had a truce for centuries until your king broke it with his unquenchable thirst for power. Do not be fooled, he is not on your side nor has he ever been. I will leave you alive to deliver this message to your commander and king — I am fighting for the innocent people caught in this war of envy that Dryston has ignited. And I will see it through to the end, putting an end to Zorya's tyrannical reign once and for all." He stares at me in disbelief, unsure if he can trust my words. But he knows better than to stay in my presence any longer, scrambling away toward a Zoryan steed, desperate to escape the wrath of an avenging warrior on a mission for justice.

"I would've killed him." Hadeon growls, his voice dripping with venom as he stands by my side.

"I know." My eyes scan the carnage around us, the ground slick and sticky with blood from our fallen enemies. I can feel the weight of their deaths on my shoulders, but I push it aside to focus on what needs to be done. I turn to face the ten male warriors who had bravely followed me into battle, who now stand before me with heavy hearts and bloodied weapons. "Clean this mess up," I command, my tone firm and unyielding. "Our civilians should not have to bear witness to the atrocities that these invaders almost unleashed upon them and their homes." They nod in agreement, determination etched on their faces as they kneel down and begin the gruesome task of disposing of the enemy corpses. As they work, I can't help but feel a sense of pride and gratitude toward these men who were willing to risk their lives for our people.

I help as we pull the dozen soldiers into a pile before Hadeon sets a fire to it. They burn as we watch, the stench of burning flesh traumatizing my nose. "May their souls be accepted by the Gods." I speak the funeral chant aloud, hoping I am not the only one. But I allow the single tear to flee from my eye as they repeat it. The sounds of their voices carrying it in a wave of noise echoing into the night.

Once we were done, we set up camp and get ready to sleep. I hadn't wanted a large tent, but they insisted so Hadeon was placed right next to mine and the others surround me. It is nice, having people care for you in this way. Regardless of my status, I was comfortable with their presence.

I recall the sensation of being surrounded by trees, the sound of leaves rustling and twigs snapping under my boots. The heat of battle. Someone saved my life, their accurate arrow whizzing by me to demand the life of it's target. I wonder if it was a local villager we didn't account for in our mission briefing. Eryx will have made sure to search for them, but in the chaos, I had completely forgotten about that possibility. My thoughts are interrupted by the sound of a zipper— another soldier probably relieving themselves. It hits me then; my disregard for potential danger could have cost us our lives. Despite my exhaustion and injuries, sleep eludes me as I lie awake, replaying the events in my mind and berating myself for my recklessness.

I huff and turn in my makeshift cot, trying to find a comfortable spot to bring me some peace.

Chapter 37: Reunited

Verena

A s Hadeon and I approach the towering stone walls of the castle, the setting sun casts a golden hue over the land, bathing everything in a warm glow. The air is filled with the sound of birds returning to their nests and the distant rustle of leaves in the gentle breeze. The castle stands proud and strong, its turrets reaching up toward the darkening sky.

As we pass through the towering gates, my gaze falls upon familiar guards that I know had accompanied Eryx on his journey. My heart begins to race with anticipation as we enter the courtyard, my eyes eagerly scanning for any sign of him. And then I saw him, standing by the ornate fountain in the center of the grounds, his black as night hair catching the last rays of sun and giving him an dark angelic aura. His perceptive brown eyes gazing off into the distance, lost in thought as he spoke with Esmeray, the sunlight illuminating their faces like a spotlight on a stage.

Without a second thought, I dismount my horse, the leather reins slipping from my grip as I kick up clouds of dust with each step. My cloak flutters in the wind like a banner, marking my determination to reach him. Hadeon follows close behind, his keen eyes observing our reunion with a small smile playing on his lips. But my focus is solely on my husband as I run toward him, feeling the pounding of my heart and the burn in my lungs. Finally, I throw myself into his arms, feeling the warmth of his embrace and the solidness of his body against mine. He lifts me off the ground, twirling us around in pure joy and relief at being reunited. In that moment, nothing else exists but the two of us wrapped in each other's arm.

As he sets me down gently on the soft grass, I can feel the blades tickling the backs of my calves. His touch is like a warm embrace, comforting and soothing. "I am sorry," he starts, but I don't want to hear apologies. Not right now, not when his lips are so close to mine.

"None of that matters," I whisper, my hands cupping his cheeks as I lean in to meet his tender kiss. The feeling of his lips against mine is like a spark of electricity, sending shivers down my spine. The grass beneath us seems to come alive with the sweet scent of spring flowers, perfuming the air with their delicate fragrance. In this moment, nothing else matters except for the warmth of his touch and the taste of his lips on mine.

It's only been a week, but I missed him so much. I never thought I'd miss another human like this.

A loud, harsh squawk pierces through the air and my eyes instinctively search for the source. They lock onto a majestic raven, its sleek black feathers glinting in the sunlight as it takes flight. It lands gracefully on a high windowsill, its beady eyes scanning the scene below. I can't help but wonder if this is the same raven I've seen before, or if it's just one of the many wild birds that roam these lands. But something about its discerning gaze makes me feel like it's watching me specifically. A shiver runs down my spine at the thought, and I can see Eryx glancing in the direction of the bird with a furrowed brow and confusion dancing across his dark brown irises. As if sensing our unease, the raven lets out another squawk before flying off into the distance, leaving us with a sense of anxiety that lingers in the air. "That is odd. That looks just like the raven I saw in Elmswood." My gaze turns to his frantically.

"What?" I ask him.

"I was fending off Zoryan soldiers and a raven flew past me, almost signaling that someone was in trouble behind me. But I can't see any one aside from our own soldiers fighting as well and the bird whips around again, somehow convincing me to follow it before it lead me around the corner where I saw a child being cornered by a Zoryan. I saved his life. The bird saved his life." He explains to me and I gape while Esmeray adds to it.

"Ravens are very intellectual. It probably followed us."

I can't believe my eyes. The raven was the same one I had seen earlier this morning in Aradon. How can this be possible? Was it just a mere coincidence or did this bird hold some deeper meaning? My mind races with thoughts and questions, but one stands out above the rest: was this raven an ally or a foe? The idea of being able to shape-shift as a High Fae feels like a distant legend, something that hadn't been seen in centuries. Yet here I was, faced with the possibility of encountering one.

Amaelya shape-shifted but she couldn't form into animals or items. It was strictly fae or human beings and even then, Eryx had told me it was only for short limited spurts of time.

There was only one person that I knew who could possess such power. But the chances of them being here, now, seemed impossible. I can't wrap my head around it all — it feels as if chaos and order were battling within me. Was I overthinking things or was there truly more to this than meets the eye?

* * *

Exhausted, we made our way to our room, longing for some much-needed rest. But duty calls for other obligations. We had to prepare ourselves for the grand dinner being held tonight. However, before that, there were important matters we needed to discuss. As Eryx closes the door behind him, I walk over to the end of the bed and turn to face him.

"I should've made it a point to tell you. I know that. I guess in my brain, I didn't see it as important but the real reason is because I didn't want you to look at me differently." I speak first. He steps closer, taking my hands in his.

"I can never look at you differently. You are my little star, Verena. The light that leads me home every night. The moral compass that brings me back from my own dark thoughts. My northern light. I love you. You are my queen. My wife. My mate. You matter to me more than anything else on this Gods-forsaken Dimencreas."

"I should give up the need for revenge. It's childish. This country is more important. You are more important." I breathe out a sigh as I speak, the words heavy.

"No." He surprises me. "You are right. Dryston might've died but his mother would never had allowed you to continue. Dryston was planning a war before you even left him. He deserves everything you want to give him."

I feel my heart swell with love at Eryx's words, his sincerity washing away any doubts that linger in my mind. I look into his eyes, seeing the depth of his feelings reflect back at me. In that moment, I know that we were truly meant to be together, no matter the challenges we have faced.

"I love you, Eryx," I tell him softly, my voice full of emotion. "You are my rock, my strength. I am grateful every day that our paths finally crossed again."

Eryx pulls me into a warm embrace, holding me close as if he never wants to let me go. We stand there, wrapped in each other's arms, finding solace in the presence of our love.

As we prepare for the grand dinner ahead, I can't shake off the feeling of unease that the raven had stirred within me. I wonder if it was a mere coincidence or a sign of something more sinister lurking in the shadows.

But as we enter the grand hall filled with nobles and dignitaries, all thoughts of the raven are pushed to the back of my mind. I want to enjoy the few good moments left before this war. The room was a spectacle of opulence, with chandeliers casting a warm glow over the guests and tables swathe with lavish decorations. I feel a sense of pride as I stand by Eryx's side, my hand resting in the crook of his arm as we greet our esteemed guests.

My dress was a stunning masterpiece, its deep blue shade perfectly matching the hue of my hair. Within the soft tulle fabric, flickers of golden sparkles caught and shimmered in the light. A regal crown, adorned with purple jewels, graces my golden locks as a symbol of royalty. The material was so delicate and intricate, it feels as if I was wearing a piece of art. As I twirl and move, the dress sways and flows around me like an enchanted spell. Each step I take feels like I am walking on clouds, as if transported to another world where beauty and elegance were magnified tenfold. It is definitely a Queen's gown and I wore it with pride.

The evening progresses with music and laughter filling the air, but I still can't shake off the feeling that something was amiss. I glance around, catching sight of a hooded figure watching us from a dark corner of the room, their eyes hidden in the shadows. A chill runs down my spine as I try to catch a glimpse of their face, but they remain elusive.

As the music swells and the guests chatter around us, Eryx notices the tension in my posture and follows my gaze to the dark corner but no one is there now. His fingers tighten around mine, a silent gesture of reassurance as he scans the room for any signs of trouble. But the figure had disappeared now into thin air, leaving behind a trail of unease that lingers in the grand hall. For all I know, it was apart of my imagination.

After exchanging a few polite words with a nearby noble, Eryx leans in close to whisper in my ear. "Did you see something, my dear?" His voice is laced with concern, his eyes searching mine for answers.

I hesitate for a moment, unsure if I should voice my suspicions amidst the festivities. But the memory of the raven's keen stare and the mystery savior from Aradon spurs me to speak. "There was someone watching us from the shadows," I confess quietly, glancing around discreetly to ensure no prying ears overhear our conversation.

Eryx takes another glance around the room, speaking with a guard close by before looking at me. "It was probably a staff member. But I'll have Hadeon check it out for us. Okay?" I nod, content with his answer, shaking it off to enjoy his company.

His hand around my waist rubs against the dress and I think of how handsome he looks in fighting leathers.

I squeeze my hand against him, trying to gain his attention but he continues the conversation with another noble.

The rubbing on my waist sends shivers down my spine and a buzz of energy to my core.

"Eryx," I mumble and he catches my gaze. "My king. I am... exhausted." I try to tell him with my eyes, wanting him to understand my meaning.

Recognition flickers within his own eyes and suddenly, he's bidding goodnight to anyone who needs to know before he whisks me to our room. I giggle, giddy with excitement for what awaits me as he leads me through the halls.

Chapter 38: Impatience

Verena

With a burst of anticipation, he flings the door open with unrelenting impatience, his hands grasping at any surface they can find as he pulls me into the room. Our lips collide in a fiery kiss, his hand firmly holding my head against his as we melt into each other. My own hands feverishly work to undo his shirt, peeling it off him with eager haste before moving on to the buttons of his trousers.

My lips fall open in surprise as he gently brushes his tongue against mine. Our mouths move in a dance, each one trying to gain control over the other. My arousal intensifies and I feel the heat between my legs growing more intense. With a swift movement, he tears the dress from my body, exposing me completely to his hungry gaze. I respond by quickly unfastening his pants and watching them fall to the floor with a soft thud, revealing his own desire for me. The anticipation and heat between us is electric, like two forces colliding in a passionate clash.

My breath catches as I immediately fall to my knees in front of him. My hand wraps around his length, tracing the veins and contours with my fingers. As I run my tongue along the underside, I can feel his pulse quicken beneath me. Slowly, sensually, I flatten my tongue against the tip before taking him into my mouth and pushing all the way to the back of my throat. The taste of him is like an intoxicating elixir, driving me wild with desire. His fingers weave through my blonde hair, tugging tightly from my skull as exhilaration runs through him. A delicious moan falls from his lips and I smirk.

He guides me back and forth and I allow him to take control of my mouth, pounding in and out of me in quick succession as he hits the back of my throat with a light force.

I hold back the gag that hits, feeling my tonsils tighten around him and another groan leaves him.

He uses me, his rough movements causing tears to slip from my eyes as wetness seeps from deep within me. I can feel it trickling down my thigh, a physical manifestation of the desire he ignites in me. Desperate for some kind of release, I press my thighs together in a futile attempt to ease the tension coursing through my body. But nothing can satisfy me except him. As he reaches his peak, his ragged breaths matching the frantic pace of our bodies, I eagerly take him into my mouth further, pushing my boundaries, and swallow every last drop with insatiable greed. The taste of him only fuels my need for more, and I am left trembling and wanting as he comes down from his high.

He pulls me from him, out of breath but I can see the need in his eyes and know we are not finished.

He picks me up with ease before falling back onto the bed as I land in a straddle over him before he pushes my body up toward his face.

"Grab the headboard, Verena." I know his tone means business and I can't help but let out a whimper at it. "I want you to ride my face."

"What if I suffocate you?" I ask, my breath raspy from the rawness of him taking me.

"Then I will gladly welcome the Gods in the afterworld. Now get up here." His eyes convince me, full of dark greed and I position myself, hovering over him.

His strong arms wrap around my thighs, pulling me downward toward him. I am ensnared in his embrace, unable to resist the pull of his passionate desire. Suddenly, his warm mouth is upon me, sending shivers down my spine. I gasp in pleasure, my body instinctively grinding down against him in search of more. The intense need to climax overwhelms me, building with every movement he makes. As my hands find purchase on the smooth wooden headboard, I steady myself and surrender to his touch. His skillful movements guide me back and forth, while his tongue teases and explores my center. Waves of pleasure wash over me as his nose nuzzles against my sensitive clit and his tongue plunges deeper inside me. I can't help but moan in pure ecstasy as he expertly brings me closer and closer to the edge of bliss.

I never can have imagined that anything could feel better than his touch, but as his hands wrap firmly around my legs, a sudden coolness envelops us, swirling around my vulnerable and exposed body. It creeps up my skin, causing goosebumps to rise and linger on my already taut nipples. The sensation is almost too much to bear and I can't help but let out a gasp as I drop my head back in ecstasy, my fingers releasing their grip on the headboard. The air is alive with anticipation, electricity crackling between us like an invisible force pulling us closer together.

The sharp sting of his hand on my skin sends me jolting forward, my hips grinding against him with newfound urgency. A low growl rumbles from his chest as I respond eagerly to his touch, my body trembling with anticipation. He increases the pressure and I am consumed by a wave of pleasure, my entire being engulfed in ecstasy as I reach climax. My juices flow freely from within me, coating his face and slicking our bodies together as I shake with the aftershock.

Again, he moves my pliable body. I'm thankful for it considering I feel like gelatin. "You are a goddess, Verena." His voice is a seductive mixture of honey and smoke, sending shivers down my spine as he speaks. His lips move languidly up my body, tracing a path from my lower stomach to my navel with feathery kisses. When he reaches my tender breasts, he lavishes them with his mouth, teasing and tantalizing until they are wet with desire. Finally, his lips continue their journey up to my neck, planting soft and leisurely kisses as he positions himself over me. My body writhes with anticipation, craving more of his touch.

As if we have all the time in the world, his plush lips meet mine in a slow, unhurried movement. Each kiss is filled with passion and longing, drawing us closer together with each breathless moment. I feel him harden back up, pressing into my sensitive nub, forcing shivers to run through my body once more.

Impatiently, I reach between us to take him in my hand before lining him up to my entrance, our eyes meeting in the intimate moment as he pushes against me, meeting initial resistance before his tip slips fully into me. A soft gasp leaves my throat. "You're so perfect," He professes. Another gasp falls from my lips as he continues, "I want you to take me all the way, Verena. Relax your body." I try as he commands, relaxing. But as soon as he moves again, my body tenses up, wrapping around him tightly. He groans, "If you keep doing that, I'm not going to last long." Another gasp as he continues moving in and out, sliding his cock all the way out as his tip rubs the entrance of me before pushing back in to the hilt.

Once my body adjusts, he moves quicker as if he can't get enough.

I wrap my legs around him, pulling him closer, matching his rhythm, our bodies moving in perfect synchronization. The sensation is intense, overwhelming, a full-body experience that leaves me breathless and weak in the knees. His thrusts become more fervent, his pace unrelenting. Sweat glistens on our bodies, mingling with the salty taste of our passion.

He leans down, crushing his lips to mine in a fervent kiss, his hands exploring my body as he thrusts, deep and hard against me. My own desires build, growing more and more urgent, the need for release becoming almost unbearable.

"Fuck me harder," I gasp, my voice barely audible over the sound of our heavy breathing and the slap of our bodies meeting.

His eyes blaze with heat, and he obliges, increasing his pace, his hips pounding against me with intense ferocity. I cry out in pleasure, my fingernails digging into his back as a white-hot sensation takes over, coursing through me. My body convulses, shaking violently, and I feel my climax rising up from within me, threatening to overwhelm me.

With a roar, he thrusts deeper into me, his hips moving with wild abandon. The pleasure is too much to bear, and my body shivers and twists as an indescribable release washes over me. I feel my muscles clench, gripping him tightly, and I scream his name, the sound drowned out by the pounding of my heart and the ragged breaths that escape my lips.

My body goes limp, my muscles resigning to the pleasure that has overflowed them. He pulls out, and I can feel his warmth slipping away from me. He collapses beside me, spent, and huffing out ragged breathes.

"You are amazing," he whispers, his voice thick with emotion. I can feel his satisfaction in every single breath he takes. A slow, grateful smile spreads across my face as I lay my head on his chest, feeling the rhythm of his beating heart next to mine.

This...this is what love feels like. This is what it is to be truly desired, and I am grateful for every moment, every touch, every caress.

As we lie spent on the bed, our bodies glistening with sweat, our breaths slowing down to a more manageable pace, I can't help but wonder how we got to this point. How did we find each other in this vast, indifferent world? Was it fate or chance that brought us together?

It doesn't even matter. Nothing can change my feelings for him. But now, the only thing that scares me is losing him.

Chapter 39: Prepare Our Defenses

Eryx

I stare out from the balcony of the throne room; the sun setting behind the distant mountains casting a golden hue over the sprawling kingdom of Khyrel. The air was filled with the sweet scent of blooming florals and the distant hum of the bustling city close by, a stark contrast to the looming threat that now hung over us. Verena was close by, going over details of our home with Mama Zen.

As I watch the last rays of sunlight fade away, a hushed voice breaks through my reverie. I turn to see Hadeon walking with a loyal scout, Garret, a look of urgency in their eyes. Without a word, I motion them over to the throne where Verena is standing, also watching the duo. Garret rushes forward with Hadeon hot on his heels.

"Your majesties," He greets my wife and I, bowing kindly in front of us. "I come bearing terrible news. The Zoryan army, led by King Dryston Whitewell, advances toward our dear castle. I fear war looks upon the horizon."

My heart sinks as I listen to him speak. The time for peace talks had long passed. I glance at Verena, who stands with steely determination. She meets my gaze with a nod, her indigo eyes flashing with a fierce resolve. I know then that she is prepared to defend our kingdom at any cost.

I turn back to the scout, "Thank you, Garret. How much time do we have?" I say, my voice steady despite the turmoil in my heart.

"I estimate him being just past the border in a day." He informs me.

I nod, "Prepare our defenses. Send word to our soldiers. We will not go down without a fight. Hadeon, find Esmeray and meet us in the war room."

As the castle springs into action, the once tranquil atmosphere is now charging with adrenaline and tension.

Verena and I barricade ourselves in the war room once Hadeon and Esmeray arrive too, walls lined with maps, charts and battle plans. We pour over every detail, strategizing our next move with a sense of urgency and desperation. The weight of lives hang heavy on our shoulders as we consider our options, calculating the risks and sacrifices that must be made. Each decision is met with tense silence and furrowed brows, our minds consumed by the gravity of the situation at hand.

In the midst of our planning, a soft knock interrupts us. Mama Zen enters, her wise face etched with concern. She approaches us slowly, as she pushes a cart of refreshments and light snacks before leaving it here and making her way back to the kitchen after Verena voices her thanks.

We huddle together in the darkness, our faces illuminated by the flickering oil lamps as we pour over every possible outcome. Esmeray's knowledge of the terrain proves invaluable as she traces potential paths for attack and retreat with her sharp eyes. Hadeon, his body tense with memories from his time serving alongside the Zoryan army, offers valuable insights into their tactics, honed over years of bloody battles. We strategize until the early hours of the morning, with each passing moment bringing us closer to a final plan that will determine our fate on the battlefield.

As the first light of dawn creeps over the horizon, casting a pale glow over the war room, we finalize our strategy. Verena's leadership shines as she assigns roles and responsibilities to each member of our small council.

Hadeon, his expression grim and determined, clasps my shoulder in silent solidarity before heading out to rally our troops. Esmeray nods in silent agreement with our plan, her eyes ablaze with a fierce loyalty to our kingdom.

I take a moment to gaze out the window, watching as the kingdom stirs awake under the morning sky. The air is crisp with the promise of battle, and I draw in a deep breath, steeling myself for what is to come.

Verena stands by my side, her hand finding mine in a reassuring grip. "We will get through this together," she whispers, her voice unwavering.

We head toward our room, in an attempt to sleep.

But sleep eludes me, the weight of impending battle pressing down on my chest like a heavy stone. I lie there in the darkness, the faint sounds of the kingdom outside my window a stark reminder of what we stand to lose. Verena's breathing is steady beside me, a calming presence in the midst of chaos.

As I turn to gaze at her sleeping form, a wave of protectiveness washes over me. She is not just my queen, but my partner in every sense of the word. The thought of anything happening to her sends a shiver down my spine, and I vow silently to myself that I will do everything in my power to keep her safe.

I slip out of bed quietly, careful not to wake Verena. The floorboards creak softly under my weight as I make my way to the balcony overlooking the kingdom. The moon hangs low in the sky, casting a silvery glow over the landscape below.

In the distance, I see the faint glimmer of light in the woods and immediately I know who it is.

The witch of the woods has come, her presence an omen that sends shivers down my spine. I leave Verena, blissfully unaware and sleeping soundly, as I descend from the balcony. The forest calls to me, its gnarled trees whispering ancient secrets that only I can interpret. As I step into the darkness of the woods, a sense of eerie familiarity washes over me. In a clearing illuminated by a haunting moon, the witch awaits me with her wild silver locs glinting like shards of starlight, her piercing gaze burning straight through me.

"Witch," I address her with reverence, "What message do you bring in this time of turmoil"

The witch's piercing gaze bores into me, her smirk revealing centuries of cunning and unfathomable power. She raises a hand and the very air around us seems to tremble with unseen magic. My mind is bombarded with strobing images of epic battles fought, lives lost, and destinies entwined.

"The threads of fate are in chaos, Eryx," she intones gravely. "But there is still a glimmer of hope, if you have the courage to listen." Her words send shivers down my spine. "Verena will perish in this war, but only you have the power to save her life."

A frigid shiver races down my spine as the witch's words linger in the air like a cursed enchantment. The prophecy of Verena, my cherished queen, destined to meet her end in battle unless I take action. The realization of her potential demise crushes me under an avalanche of fear and anguish, my heart pounding erratically as I struggle to comprehend the enormity of this foretelling.

"What must I do?" I ask, my voice barely above a whisper, fear and determination warring within me.

Chapter 40: We Will Not Falter

Eryx

As the first rays of dawn creep over the horizon, the castle awakens with a sense of impending doom. I hadn't slept after the witches words to me but I know what I had to do and I would try not to worry about it until then.

The clang of metal, rustling of leather, and the stamping of hooves fill the courtyard as soldiers hastily arm themselves, their weapons glinting in the early light. With grim determination etched on their faces, our forces gather, prepared to fight to the death to protect our home from the looming danger that hovers over us like a vulture waiting to strike.

Verena and I get ready in our room, donning the same black as night fighting leathers as our soldiers.

With Dryston's ability to manipulate metal, we couldn't chance wearing it. However, after learning that he can't manipulate metal once Verena's blood coated the steel, we had our blacksmiths lace each new sword and dagger with some drops of her blood she had donated while I was at Elmswood.

She is so ravishing in whatever she wears and I have to constantly adjust myself in my leather pants at the thought of her being the Queen this country needs.

Ruelle watches everyone getting ready, helping soldiers when they need it, as does my mother. Barely anyone speaks as we ready ourselves.

I face Verena when we make it from our rooms to the courtyard. Civilians watch as we ready to leave.

"No matter what happens, we leave the battlefield together." I say.

Her bright eyes shining at the sight of me, "Always, my love."

Verena clasps my hand tightly, her grip a reassuring anchor in the midst of turmoil.

Beneath the crushing weight of our insurmountable responsibilities, we trudge through the corridors toward the courtyard. The air is thick with the stench of fear and the anticipation of battle, a palpable tension that threatens to suffocate us. As the sun rises higher in the sky, it casts a crimson glow over the fortified castle and its inhabitants, standing strong and resolute in the face of inevitable peril.

Silence descends upon the courtyard like a heavy blanket as we make our way through the crowd of soldiers and civilians. Their eyes are alight with a dangerous mix of apprehension and courage, mirroring the tumultuous emotions raging within each of us. Verena's mere presence demands respect, her unyielding gaze observant through the bravado of our troops. With a voice like steel, she addresses us, instilling a fierce determination in our hearts that echoes off the stone walls around us. I nod to her, allowing her to speak instead of me.

"My fellow Khyrelians," her voice carries with authority, cutting through the tense silence. "Today, we stand on the brink of battle. Our enemy approaches, seeking to claim our land and our freedom. But we will not yield. We will not falter. We will not cower in the face of adversity." The crowd of soldiers raise their swords in the air, cheering for her, for each other. "And most importantly, we will not die cowards." More cheering sounds.

We all mount our horses, waving goodbyes to our loved ones and riding off toward the border.

The pounding of hooves echoes in my ears, each beat a reminder of the impending clash that awaits us. The wind whips through my hair as we gallop out of the castle grounds and around Asterlayna, the sun casting long shadows behind us. Verena rides beside me, her eyes fix on the horizon with unwavering determination. The weight of our kingdom's future rests heavy on our shoulders, but in this moment, all that matters is the thundering rhythm of our horses' strides and the unity of our army riding as one toward destiny.

As we ride, I hear constant chatter. Some are quiet, silent in their turmoil. A raven seems to follow us and I note Verena's gaze upon it every time it flies by her. The landscape stretches out before us, a vast expanse of rolling hills and dense forests that hide both friend and foe alike. We don't slow our pace, knowing that every step brings us closer to the enemy that lurks just beyond sight but the faster we are, the less likely Dryston will make it far past the border.

We hadn't planned on stopping for rest until we arrive in a border town for the night. We have scouts still tracking their movements.

The sun begins its descent toward the horizon after hours of riding, casting long shadows across the land as we ride on through the rugged terrain. The urgency of our mission propels us forward, each passing mile bringing us closer to the inevitable clash that awaits. Verena's presence beside me is a source of strength, her unwavering resolve a beacon in the gathering darkness.

As the sun dips below the horizon and a blanket of stars starts to twinkle in the darkening sky, we eagerly reach our destination — a small border town where we plan to rest for the night. The townsfolk, weary from their daily tasks, cast wary glances our way as we ride into their midst. The clatter of hooves on cobblestones echoes through the narrow streets, punctuated by the occasional neigh of our horses. With practiced ease, we dismount from our steeds, feeling the familiar ache in our muscles from hours spent in the saddle. Yet our minds are still sharp and alert, ready for any challenges that may arise in the coming night. As we settle into our campsite surrounded by towering trees and chirping crickets, the sense of adventure and camaraderie among us only grows stronger.

Verena stands in the center of the bustling town square, her strong voice ringing out with an air of authority that demands immediate attention. The tension in the air is palpable as she addresses our group, her words holding with the weight of responsibility. "Secure the perimeter," she commands, her sharp gaze scanning the faces of her soldiers. "Set up watchtowers and keep a vigilant eye out for any sign of movement from the enemy. We cannot afford to be caught off guard." The urgency in her tone is mirrored by the swift movements of our troops as they spring into action, their well-honed training kicking in with precision and efficiency. Each one knows their role and executes it flawlessly, a testament to their dedication and discipline. As we work together to fortify our defenses, a sense of determination fills the air — we will not let our guard down, our survival depends on it.

With our defenses firmly in place, we huddle together around a roaring campfire the townspeople help create that crackles and spits sparks into the night sky. The flames dance and illuminate our faces as we settle down at the edge of the center of town. The scent of woodsmoke fills our noses, mingling with the fresh pine and earthy scents of the surrounding forest.

Verena convinces the civilians to not worry about our presence, easing the fears in their minds.

We share stories and jokes, passing around warm mugs of hot cocoa or steaming bowls of stew. The twinkling light from the fire casts shadows on the nearby buildings, creating an atmosphere of comfort. For a brief moment, we forget about the dangers lurking outside our safe haven and simply enjoy each other's company in this peaceful moment.

Their are multiple camp spots for the army, separate fires to warm each set of them. We hadn't brought tents, not needing them since we were only going to be here for a day or two hopefully. We knew we'd only need a blanket per person and we all carried our own.

As the night wears on, the town settles into an uneasy calm, the only sounds are the crackling of the fire and the soft murmurs of conversation among our comrades. Verena sits beside me, her profile illuminated by the warm glow of the flames, her gaze fixed on the horizon where unseen dangers lurk. I reach out and grasp her hand, seeking solace in the touch of her skin against mine. We share a silent moment of understanding, a wordless exchange that speaks volumes of our shared burdens and unspoken fears. In that fleeting instant, I find strength in her presence, a resolve to face whatever challenges lie ahead with unwavering courage.

As the night deepens and a blanket of stars unfurls overhead, casting a shimmering tapestry across the sky, we prepare to take our rest. Verena's eyes meet mine in a silent promise, a reassurance that no matter what may come, we will face it together. With heavy hearts and weary bodies, we retire for the night, finding privacy in the towns bed and breakfast. Hadeon and Esmeray insisted we sleep in a building, so we are more protected since we are the reigning queen and king of Khyrel. I don't argue.

We lay down in the bed together and her lips find mine.

"Can't get enough of me?" I tease her.

Verena's eyes sparkle with mirth as she leans in closer, her breath warm against my lips. "Never," she whispers, her voice husky with desire. The weight of our responsibilities fades into the background as we lose ourselves in each other, seeking solace and connection in the intimacy of the moment. Our bodies entwine, the world outside forgotten as we succumb to the passion and love that binds us together. In this fleeting respite from the chaos of war, there is only us — two souls intertwined in a dance as old as time itself. And as we lay together in the embrace of the night, I know that no matter what challenges may come our way, as long as we face them side by side, we will emerge stronger than before.

But before we can get far, I stop us. "I don't want to treat tonight as if it is our last. I want to wait. I want to ravish you in celebration of slaying our enemy." I watch as her eyes water, brightening the indigo in them. "I would love to have you scream my name so loud everyone in the town knows you're mine and how much I love you and after this war maybe I will." The promise shines in my own dark eyes, making her smile softly up at me. "But, I'll give you your very own 'first war' gift." Now I look at her with dark deep desire.

With each kiss, Verena's breath catches in her throat, a physical manifestation of the desire that courses through her veins. The trail of kisses I leave along her neck is like a flame, leaving a searing path in its wake. She grips my hair tightly, pulling me closer as I explore every inch of her skin with my lips and tongue. The intense heat between us only intensifies as I take my time to savor every touch and taste. Her body responds eagerly, a symphony of soft gasps and whispers of my name filling the air. In this moment, there is nothing else but the two of us — consumed by an all-encompassing world of passion and longing that knows no bounds.

With each slow movement, I peel off her pants and expose her bare skin to the flickering candlelight. Her body trembles with a mixture of excitement and fear, aching for the raw and primal connection we are about to share. The charged air crackles with electricity as we teeter on the edge of carnal desire, our hearts beating in unison like a war drum. In this quiet room, our bodies speak a language of passion that words could never capture.

I lean down to capture her lips in a hungry kiss, relishing the taste of her on my tongue. The heat between us rises with each passing second before I move my body down further this time, kissing up her thighs before reaching her warm, wet center. I kiss her body again, around where she needs me most as she writhes under me. My hands trail up tantalizingly soft before gripping her hips and holding her down. A whimper falls from her soft pliable lips and it takes all my self control to not fill her mouth with my hard cock that stands at attention for her.

I fight against my primal urges, my focus solely on pleasuring her with my tongue and lips. I delve deep into her core, savoring the sweet nectar that drips from her, relishing in the symphony of her gasps and moans. Her hips thrash wildly beneath me, matching the frenzied rhythm of my tongue as she reaches new heights of arousal. My exploration intensifies, flicking relentlessly over her most sensitive spots and teasing her entrance until she is consumed by a maddening desire.

My gaze meets Verena's, and her eyes are a molten pool of desire, burning with intense pleasure. Her breath catches in her throat as I skillfully explore her body, driving her to the edge of ecstasy. Plunging two fingers deep inside her, I expertly curl them up to hit her sweet spot, feeling her muscles clench around me. Each slow thrust brings her closer to the brink, her moans growing louder and more urgent. As she nears her climax, Verena's grip on my hair tightens almost painfully, and her body shudders uncontrollably, completely consumed by the intensity of her pleasure. I remove my face from between her legs, her thighs no longer holding onto me in a vice grip.

I wipe my face on the sheet we lay on before I lay next to her, tucking her into my side and refusing to let her go as we rest.

The night passes in a haze of dreams and whispered promises, the warmth of Verena's body pressing against mine a comfort in the darkness. With the first light of dawn creeping over the horizon, we rise from our slumber, renewed and ready to face the challenges that await us. As we step out into the cool morning air, the town begins to stir with life once more, the townspeople going about their daily routines with a newfound sense of hope in their hearts. Verena and I share a quiet moment of reflection, our hands clasped together in silent solidarity as we prepare for the battle ahead.

Chapter 41: Forces

Verena

T he time has come to resume our journey toward destiny, to meet our fate head-on and emerge victorious. With a final glance back at the town that offered us refuge in our time of need, we mount our horses once more and ride out into the wilderness, our army trailing behind us in a determined march toward the enemy stronghold.

The tension among us was palpable, but we carry on undeterred, our determination unshaken.

And then, on the distant horizon, we saw them — Dryston's army approaching from the other side. The Zoryan soldiers ride with a menacing energy, their banners snapping in the wind like claws ready to strike.

The sky above was a canvas of swirling purples and oranges, a stark contrast to the imminent clash of swords that looms before us. My eyes gleam with fierce determination, my every movement radiating strength and resolve. Eryx rides beside me, his gaze fixed ahead with unwavering focus.

As we approach the border, we can see Dryston's army arrayed in formation, their armor glinting in the dying light of day. Banners flutter in the wind, embezzled with the crest of the Zoryan kingdom. The ground trembles beneath the hooves of our horses as we came to a halt, facing our adversaries with steely determination.

A hush befalls over the land as they spot us too.

The tension in the air was thick, each side waiting for the other to make a move. I can see the muscles tensing in Eryx's jaw as he grips the hilt of his sword, his eyes locked on Dryston's looming figure at the front of their army. The wind carries whispers of war, stirring the banners of both armies like restless spirits urging us toward conflict.

A lone raven caws overhead, its dark silhouette a foreboding omen that seems to hang over us all. My heart pounds in my chest, adrenaline coursing through my veins as I prepare myself for the inevitable clash.

Then, without warning, a shout rang out from Dryston's ranks, and the ground beneath our feet quivers as their army surges forward with a thunderous roar. Eryx and I exchange a silent nod, our shared determination fortifying our resolve as we raise our swords, spurring our horses into a gallop to lead our own army into treacherous war.

The clash of swords and shields reverberate through the valley, a cacophony of violence and desperation. My horse trots with purpose, my heart pounding in time with the galloping hooves beneath me.

As we collide with Dryston's army, the chaos of battle engulfs us in a frenzy of steel and blood. My sword met the enemy's with a resounding clang, the impact vibrating up my arm as I fought with all the skill and ferocity I possess. Nearby, Eryx was a whirlwind of lethal precision, cutting through the enemy ranks like a force of nature.

Hadeon and Esmeray showing just exactly why they were his army's generals. I can't tell who was more lethal.

318

Hadeon moved like a tyrant, his every motion dripping with the blood of his victims. With the same deadly precision as Eryx, he struck down anyone who dared to oppose him. Esmeray, on the other hand, used her powers to manipulate her enemies' emotions, instilling such paralyzing fear that they were frozen in place or draining them of their fear until they were overconfident and fell into fatal errors. Together, they were an unstoppable force, wielding terror and death as their weapons of choice.

The battlefield was a swirling vortex of death and destruction, the deafening sounds of clashing swords and screams of agony filling the air. I fought like a possessed demon, channeling every ounce of strength and cunning I had to survive amidst the blood-soaking chaos. My mind blazed with an all-consuming determination, like a laser cutting through the darkness around me.

But even as we clash with Dryston's forces, I caught sight of something on the periphery of the battlefield — a group of Zoryan soldiers attempting to flank us from the side. With a surge of adrenaline, I spur my horse toward them, determined to thwart their deadly maneuver.

As I ride toward the flanking force, a sudden explosion rocks the battlefield, sending shockwaves through the earth and momentarily blinding me with smoke and debris. I struggle to maintain control of my mount, my senses reeling from the impact. But as the smoke clears, I saw that the explosion had hit the Zoryan flanking unit, scattering them and shattering their formation.

With a fierce determination, I surge forward, my sword catching the sunlight as it glints and slices through the remaining soldiers. The metallic tang of blood mingles with the acrid stench of sweat, filling the air as I plow through their ranks. My heart races in my chest, pounding like a war drum as adrenaline flowing through my veins. All around me, chaos reigns as swords clash and bodies fall, but for now, our rear was secure. The cries of victory echoes in my ears as I continue, determined to claim our ultimate triumph.

I glance back to see Eryx and our army pressing forward, their relentless advance gradually pushing back the enemy lines. Dryston, his face contorting with rage and desperation, fought at the front of his army with unmatched ferocity, but our forces were too overwhelming. The tide of battle slowly began to shift in our favor, and the once-confident Zoryan soldiers start to show signs of doubt and anxiety.

Esmeray's influence over the enemy's emotions grew stronger, causing many to falter and hesitate, while Hadeon continues to rack up a bloody toll amongst their ranks. Our warriors fought with renewed vigor, their spirits buoyed by the sense of victory within their grasp.

The once-formidable Zoryan army began to fall apart, its once-sturdy defenses crumbling like sandcastles in the face of our relentless onslaught.

In the distance, I can see the gates of Dryston's stronghold, now within striking distance. A faint glimmer of hope sparks within me as I realize that we were so very close to achieving our goal. The end of this war was within our grasp, and I can already taste the sweet flavor of victory.

I make my way toward the stronghold, a sense of angst washes over me. A nagging feeling told me that this was not the end, that there was still more to come. The battle fought so fiercely was not yet over, and I knew that we needed to push harder, faster, if we were to secure our victory.

With renewed determination, we charge forward, our soldiers screaming their battle cries as they breach the gates of Dryston's stronghold. The air becomes thick with the stench of blood, sweat, and fear as we engage in hand-to-hand combat with the Zoryan soldiers inside.

The battle was fierce, and it seems as though the enemy could never be overcome. I had lost sight of my friends and my husband but I continue. I can't worry about others when I was trying to stay alive on my own.

From the dark sky above, a shadow descends. Black feathers glimmer with an otherworldly blue sheen as the figure comes into view. It's a raven, but its form twists and contorts until it transforms into a woman — one that is painfully familiar to me. Her penetrative gaze locks onto mine, sending a shiver down my spine. In a flash of black wings, she lands before me, her presence radiating with inexplicable power.

Her blonde hair shines bright in the sun, her indigo eyes matching mine. Whatever magic she has, gives her clothes when she transforms back into a fae. I can't take my eyes off of her, no matter the destruction happening around me.

The sun glints off her golden tresses, making them seem like liquid fire. Her inquisitive indigo eyes lock onto mine, mirroring my own intensity. As she transforms back into her fae form, her clothes are imbued with a mystical glow that radiates power. Despite the chaos raging around us, I can't tear my gaze away from her, drawn in by her familiar ethereal beauty and otherworldly energy.

Without warning, my horse is yanked out from under me, sending us both tumbling to the hard ground. I desperately try to roll away from its massive frame before it crushes my leg like a fragile twig.

As I regain my bearings, I see my mother standing over me, her eyes full of concern. Her hand extends toward me, and I hesitantly grasp it, allowing her to pull me to my feet. Her touch is cold, yet it leaves me feeling unexpectedly warm and safe.

"You should not be here," she says, her voice as familiar as her appearance. "The battle is too dangerous for one such as you."

I am about to protest when I see Eryx fighting his way through the enemy ranks, his face grim with determination. His eyes search the chaos for me, and when they finally find mine, they lock onto me with a fierce intensity that fills me with both relief and a strange sense of longing.

"I need to be here," I tell her, more forcefully than I intended. "My friends and my husband are fighting, and I will not abandon them like you apparently had no problem doing to me. You were dead!" My voice raises before breaking on the last word among the surrounding bodies clashing.

"I am so sorry, Verena. I had to fake my death to protect you. I don't expect you to understand" She cut off as she takes a blade from the ground and stabs it into someone behind me. "I was going to be killed but I made a better deal with the assassin sent to kill me."

My eyes widen in shock and anger. "I was alone! I had no one for a decade. Do you even know what I endured for the sake of the crown?" The thoughts that cross my mind race through me like wildfire. can I trust my mother? The woman who had walked out on me when I was just a child, leaving me to fend for myself in this unforgiving and dangerous world

But now, here she was, in the thick of a battle she had never asked for, her heart heavy with the burden of the choices that had led her to this point. As I stare at my mother, I see a flicker of something in her eyes — regret, perhaps, or perhaps the ghost of a different life.

"I had hoped," my mother says softly, "that you would have been taken care of. I do not know what happened when I left but you and Dryston got along so well. I thought my fears of him turning into his mother were dramatic paranoia." She fought more beings away from us. "Can we talk this out after we survive this?" She asks and it breaks me from my thoughts— my shock.

A chill runs down my spine as I come face to face with the truth. The raven, that ominous creature that has haunted me since her death, was actually her all along. My heart races as I realize she never truly left me. Every time I saw a black bird, it was her watching over me. How could I have been so blind? My grief turns into a mixture of fear and wonder at this realization. She's alive, in some form, and she's been with me all this time.

Chapter 42: Blood, Smoke, and Ash

Verena

I pick up my sword from the ground and charge into the fray, my heart heavy with the knowledge that every clash of metal could bring me closer to losing Eryx forever. The ground trembles beneath the weight of armored soldiers, the sky darkens with the smoke of war, and I feel the weight of destiny pressing down upon me. My mother fights along side me as I make my way to Eryx. If we kill Dryston, all these lives can remain whole. We don't have to lose every body here, fighting for their home.

The deafening brush of swords and shields reverberates through the air as I cleave my way toward Dryston, driven by a fierce determination to reach him before it's too late. My mother stands at my side, her formidable presence lending me a surge of strength. Our blades move in perfect unison, twirling and thrusting with precision amidst the chaotic frenzy of battle. Together, we were an unstoppable force, blazing a path through the enemy ranks toward our ultimate goal.

The closer we approach Dryston, the weight of his malevolent stare bore down upon us like a heavy shadow. His twisted grin curls with sadistic glee as he anticipated our arrival, reveling in the challenge that lay ahead. But we were not going to let him emerge victorious in this war. The fate of our world rests on our shoulders and we were determined to crush him into oblivion, no matter the cost.

With a final burst of unwavering determination, we tore through the wall of Dryston's soldiers, our blades flashing in the sunlight as we close the distance between us and our ultimate enemy. His sneer contorts into a maniacal grin as he meets our gaze with wild, bloodlust-filled eyes. But we refuse to be intimidated, fueled by an unbreakable resolve to put an end to his reign of terror once and for all. My mother goes to step forward, but she pauses when I push my hand out to stop her. "I've got this." I tell her and she nods, fighting soldiers away from me.

With a fierce determination burning in my chest, I heft my sword high above my head. The weight of the world seems to rest on my shoulders as I prepare to strike down my opponent. As my blade descends, it lets out a resounding clang that reverberates across the battlefield, signaling my unwavering resolve. But Dryston is a skilled warrior, and he swiftly counters my attack with a swift flick of his wrist. Our blades meet with a deafening crash, sending sparks flying and shaking the very ground beneath us. Each contact feels like a jolt of lightning coursing through the air, as we fought with all our might for victory in this epic battle.

The acrid stench of blood and charred flesh hung heavy in the air, suffocating our senses. Each step we take sends tremors through the ground, as if it could no longer bear witness to the violence unfolding. Above us, the sky blazes a fiery red, as if it too had been smeared with the blood of our enemies. Our unyielding pursuit of victory paints the world in shades of crimson and death.

Undeterred by the relentless rays of the sun bearing down upon us, our determination only intensifies as we battle for our rightful place in the world. Our movements mirrored those of ancient warriors, as if we are being guided by powerful deities from a distant time. The sound of our blades meeting echoes through the air, a fierce symphony of steel clashing and ringing out. Sweat drips down my face, stinging my eyes, but I push through with every ounce of strength within me, refusing to back down in this deadly dance of survival. Victory was within reach, and I will not let anything stand in my way.

But nothing lasts forever, even as my body grows tiresome.

I feel the impact of every blow, the sting of every wound, as they weaken my mother and I with each passing moment. The weight of our adversary is formidable, and with each passing exchange, doubts begin to creep into my mind. Yet, I refuse to succumb to them, knowing that the fate of our world is at stake.

Our battle grows increasingly intense, a blur of flashing blades and grunts of exertion. The air around us crackles with the electric charge of our relentless pursuit, building an energy that seems to feed us and our opponents alike.

Despite the mounting fatigue, my heart races with an unwavering resolve, propelling me forward in the face of our adversaries. Each strike, each parry, each dodge feels fraught with the potential to change the tide of the battle.

My feet slide on a slick pool of crimson, sending me careening to the ground where my skull collides with the grimy earth. Pain sears through my head like fire as I struggle to regain my senses. "Verena!" Eryx's voice rings out, drawing closer to Dryston and I. His golden locks glimmer in the sunlight, his chartreuse eyes glinting with malice.

"You thought you could defeat me? You dare to challenge my power and believe you could triumph?" His laughter echoes through the chamber, sending shivers down my spine as my heart pounds against my ribcage, threatening to burst free.

With a sinister smile, he raises his sword high above his head, ready to deliver the final, fatal blow. My own weapon lies just out of reach, and I steel myself for the inevitable end, knowing that Eryx will seek vengeance for my death. Our eyes lock in a final moment of defiance as Dryston ends my life, but I refuse to look away, channeling all of my fury and determination into one last gaze before the darkness claims me.

Eryx charges toward Dryston, his body a blur as he plows into him with incredible force. The impact sends Dryston flying across the ground, crashing into the dirt with a bone-jarring force. Before he can even recover, Eryx is on top of him, raining down powerful blows to his face. Desperately, Dryston writhes and wriggles, trying to escape the relentless assault from above. But Eryx's grip is like iron, and it takes all of Dryston's strength just to push him off for a moment before the relentless attack resumes.

They both stand up, panting heavily, their eyes locking in a battle of defiance and determination. A sense of dread hangs heavy in the air, as if the outcome of this fight will decide the fate of the world.

In the distance, the sounds of battle still rage, but the focus now is solely on Dryston and Eryx.

Eryx's rage is palpable, every blow landing with the force of a thunderbolt. Blood drips from his sword, staining the ground beneath him, as he plows through Dryston's defenses with unrelenting determination.

Dryston, however, is not one to give up easily. He manages to dodge another of Eryx's strikes, but the force of the blow sends him tumbling into the dirt. With a cry of rage, Dryston surges to his feet, his eyes blazing with fury. His sword flashes in his hand, matching Eryx's fury with a determination to match.

The battle between these two titans of destruction intensifies, each strike carrying the force of a thousand suns. The air crackles with electricity, as if the very fabric of the world is being torn apart by their battle.

In the midst of this chaos, the world begins to change. The hues of the battlefield shift, the colors bleeding and smear together in a blur of emotion. The mountains and valleys around them warp and twist, as if they too are being consumed by the intensity of the battle.

As the ground shakes beneath their feet, Dryston and Eryx continue their unrelenting assaults on each other. My breath catches in my throat as I see Dryston's cruel smile, a glint of malice in his eyes as he sought to strike a fatal blow. Someone shoves me over, making a yelp slip from my lips at a distracting volume. Eryx's eyes meet mine and just as they do, he realizes his mistake.

And then it happens — a swift, brutal thrust from Dryston's blade pierces through Eryx's defenses, sinking deep into his stomach. My world shatters in that instant, an uncontrollable scream tearing from my throat as I feel our mate bond weaken a fraction.

Blind rage consumes me, overtaking every thought and emotion. I can feel the raw power coursing through my veins, a volatile energy waiting to be unleashed. My vision turns violet as my body trembles with an otherworldly force, building until it reaches its boiling point. With a primal scream, I direct all of my fury, my anguish, my agony at Dryston, unleashing a devastating explosion that sends his body hurtling backwards. A deafening silence falls as I collapse to my knees, drained of every ounce of strength as I crawl toward my broken husband's bleeding form. I am angry he doesn't get to watch his country turn their backs on him, but none of that matters now.

I collapse next to Eryx, my heart shattering into a million pieces as I touch his cold cheek. The tears that fall from my eyes scorch like acid, burning a trail down my face. A tsunami of emotions crashes over me, drowning me in sorrow and rage. My gaze locks with his and I can sense the faintest hint of regret in his glassy stare.

I gasp, my voice barely audible as I struggle to form words. My heart splinters into shards of pain, aching with the realization of what he has done. "How could you?" I rasp, my voice raw from both the battle and my emotions. Blood drips from his lips as he grunts out an explanation, his body shaking with the weight of his actions. "You don't have to," I cry out, feeling betrayed and shattered in that moment. "We were supposed to leave this battlefield together," I remind him, my voice trembling with anger and hurt. "Together, Eryx. You promised." A sob wracks through me and I want to strike him, to unleash all the fury and pain coursing through my veins at this ultimate betrayal.

"I had to. You were going to die and I would rather perish before I allow you to leave this world, Little Star." His voice breaks, spitting blood from his lips.

My voice trembles as I plead with him, "No. You are not allowed to die. Not today. If you die, I will follow." My anger boils over at his reckless decision.

A hand grips my shoulder and I spin around, ready for a fight. But it's my mother, her eyes burning with determination. "Allow me, my dear," she whispers, stepping in front of her king. With a flick of her wrist, she places her hand on his chest.

My heart races as I try to pull her away, but she holds steadfast. "What are you doing?" I demand, panic creeping into my voice.

"I am saving his life," she declares, her voice full of power and purpose. "By giving him the gift that gives me my shape-shifting abilities." My jaw drops as I realize what she is sacrificing for him – and for us all. "I won't die but I will no longer be able to change into the raven, or any form and it will heal him."

A sudden burst of magic swirls around his wound, knitting together flesh and skin with a blinding blue light. I am mesmerized by the sight as he gasps, sitting up with newfound strength. Without hesitation, I throw myself into his arms, overcome with relief and love for this powerful being before me.

My own heart feels a different type of shattering – the weight of the knowledge that my mother has given up her powers in order to save him. Her decision is one that is both unimaginable and selfless, but I can't deny the bittersweet emotion that pours through me.

As the dust settles on the battlefield, I find myself holding onto Eryx with one arm while the other rests on my mother's shoulder. The world around us stills, as if every ounce of magic has been drained from existence, leaving only the heavy silence that follows unimaginable betrayal and sacrifice.

Everyone is unsure of where to go from here. I can't believe it's over.

In the wake of the battle, we find ourselves standing in the aftermath of a war that has left us both physically and emotionally shattered. The air around us is thick with the scent of blood and magic, a bitter reminder of the violence that has just unfolded.

The horse's hooves pound against the ground, carrying the wounded Eryx on its back. His eyes are clenched shut in agony as he struggles to stay upright, his body still sore from the brink of death. The horse's steady gallop threatens to jostle him off at any moment, but Eryx holds on with all his remaining strength, determined to survive and reach our home.

The wound on his chest, once a deep and gaping gash, is now just a faint scar, a testament to the power of my mother's sacrifice. I trace my fingers over the delicate line as I stand next to him, feeling a sense of gratitude and sadness wash over me.

Hadeon helps an injured Esmeray onto her own horse before starting toward us. "We'll need to leave this place soon," he says softly, his voice cheery and bubbly in this time of sorrow. I nod in agreeance, about to mount the horse with Eryx since mine disappeared.

A sharp gasp pierces through the air, jerking my head toward its source. My heart races as I brace myself for what I might see. To my horror, Hadeon stands before me, his hands clutching at his chest with a look of confusion and pain etched on his face. The sight is seared into my mind, a haunting image that will never leave me.

My eyebrows knit together in confusion as I open my mouth to speak, but before I can utter a single word, blood erupts from his mouth in a violent gush. His body slumps off the dagger that impaled his heart, and I realize with horror he's been stabbed.

Dryston, barely clinging to life, stands behind him with a wicked smirk on his face. Esmeray's scream echoes through the air before I can even process what has happened, her sword drawn and slicing through the air at lightning speed. She decapitates Dryston in one swift motion, his head rolling across the ground as she lets out a primal roar of vengeance.

I sprint to my friend's side, my hands desperately trying to cover the gaping wound in his chest. But it's futile, blood gushes out between my fingers like a relentless waterfall. I stare into his lifeless eyes, the shock and surprise still etched on his pale face. "No... no no no!" I scream at him, as if begging for him to come back to me. My voice breaks into a hoarse whisper, tears streaming down my cheeks like a torrential downpour. Eryx stands frozen beside me, his eyes wide with disbelief and tears threatening to spill over. Even Esmeray, who always seemed emotionless, is weeping next to me. "It's okay guys, he's going to be okay," I lie through gritted teeth, trying to convince myself more than anyone else. "Hadeon! Come one, you are not dying! What about your dream? Mom, you have to do something, use your powers to fix him like you did before!" My words are desperate and pleading as I turn to our mother, but even she looks defeated and hopeless. The realization hits me like a punch to the gut — there is no coming back from this. And it shatters my heart into a million tiny pieces.

Her eyes hold a haunting sorrow as she shakes her head. "I can't, sweet girl. It was all I had to save Eryx. I have nothing left."

"No!" I scream, my voice cracking with desperation before coming to a devastating realization. "It's fine. I'll sacrifice myself instead. How do I do it?" My hands tremble as I try to summon any trace of magic, but there is nothing left within me. "What's wrong with me? Why won't it work?" I roar in frustration, clutching onto his lifeless body with fierce determination. A guttural growl escapes my lips as I attempt again, only to be met with the same result. "No! Mom, show me how!"

But it isn't my mother who grips my shoulders, it's Eryx.

His once bright eyes now sad and apologetic as they bore into my soul. "He's gone, Little Star." Tears stream down my face at his words, my heart shattering into a million pieces with raw grief and agony.

"No, he can't be!" I scream, struggling against the hands that try to hold me back. I reach desperately for my best friend, my only friend, as tears blur my vision. "Let me go! I can save him! Tell me how to save him!"

But no one moves, no one helps. Instead, Eryx turns to a solemn looking Khyrelian soldier and gives a grave order. "Make sure his body is brought back with us. He deserves a proper burial."

The reality crashes down on me like an avalanche, and I am consumed by agonizing sobs.

Hadeon cannot be dead. It's impossible, the Gods wouldn't be so cruel.

Yet the truth is staring me in the face and there's nothing I can do about it.

Epilogue: Dreams of Ash and Smoke

Verena

1 year post-war

I jolt awake, drenched in sweat and gasping for air. The nightmare has become a routine, haunting every night since the war ended. It always starts with Eryx's lifeless body, before shifting to Hadeon's confused eyes as he chokes on his own blood and then Dryston with his hard unrelenting gaze, practically blaming me for the entire war.

Leaving Zorya was the hardest decision I ever made. Every day, I am haunted by the thought that if I had stayed, Hadeon and all the other lives lost in the war would still be alive. But at the same time, I know that staying meant being a part of that endless cycle of violence and loss. It's a constant battle between guilt and regret, with no clear answer in sight. Not to mention, I'd have never found Eryx again and that thought sends jolts of pain through my heart like no other.

A relentless grief consumes me, a blazing inferno that never dies down. It lies dormant beneath the surface, waiting for any moment of distraction or solace to creep up and steal away any sense of peace I might find. Eryx's attempts at comfort only serve to intensify my guilt for not being able to save Hadeon. I am torn between desperately wanting to move on and clinging tightly to the memories that continue to haunt me, like ghosts refusing to leave my side. This sorrow weighs heavily on my heart, a constant ache that I cannot escape no matter how hard I try.

He is— no, was my best friend, and now he's gone without me getting to say goodbye. That is the hardest part. It's surreal how death can either give you time to prepare or take everything away without warning.

As I lay there, trying to calm my racing heart, I feel a presence next to me in the darkness. Eryx, always the silent pillar of strength, reaches out and gently touches my shoulder. His touch is warm, grounding me in reality.

"Verena," he whispers softly, his voice a soothing balm to my frayed nerves. "You're not alone in this. We're in this together."

I turn to look at him, his face illuminated faintly by the moonlight filtering through the curtains. His eyes are filled with understanding and compassion, a silent promise of unwavering support.

"I miss him too," Eryx continues, his voice barely above a whisper. "But we have to stay strong for each other. For him."

His words resonate within me, breaking through the walls of grief and guilt that I have built around myself. In that moment, I realize that I am not alone in my pain. He lost a childhood best friend, a brother in his heart. Together, Eryx and I can carry on Hadeon's legacy, honoring his memory with our actions and choices. The weight of responsibility settles on my shoulders, but this time it feels different, lighter somehow with Eryx by my side.

As dawn breaks, casting a golden hue across the room, I make a silent vow to myself and to Hadeon. I will no longer be consumed by the past; instead, I will forge ahead with Eryx, looking toward the future we can build together. The nightmares may still visit me in the dead of night, but now I know that Eryx will be there to chase them away with his unwavering presence.

Standing up from the bed, I reach out and take Eryx's hand in mine. A flicker of a smile crosses his lips as he squeezes my hand gently, a silent affirmation of our unspoken promise to each other.

In this new chapter of our lives, we will carry the memories of those we have lost with us, but we will not let them weigh us down. Instead, we will use their memories as fuel to drive us forward, to make a difference in the world that they no longer inhabit. Eryx and I share a solemn nod, a silent agreement passing between us as we prepare to face whatever challenges lie ahead.

He helps me dress for the day, brushing my hair out behind me as I sit in the vanity chair in comfortable silence.

Leaving the room behind, we step out into the morning light, a fresh sense of purpose guiding our steps. The war may have scarred us deeply, but it has also forged a indestructible bond between Eryx and me.

As we walk side by side, the weight on my shoulders feels bearable with Eryx. Together, we will navigate this new reality, honoring the past while striving toward a brighter future.

And as we venture forth into the unknown, I know that no matter what obstacles may come our way, as long as Eryx is with me, we can face them with courage and resilience.

He has work to attend in his office with Esmeray so I make my way to the kitchen, needing some love from Mama Zen.

She greets me with a large smile and wraps my apron around me in haste. "We have a lot to do today, Miss Verena. Your esteemed guests get very hungry." I laugh, knowing the three guards have been stressing her out with how much they eat.

"They sure can put it away," I laugh boisterously with her as we start on the meats and vegetables. I help season them.

The savory aroma of seasoned meats and vegetables fills the kitchen as Mama Zen and I work side by side, a comfortable rhythm flowing between us. The simple act of cooking alongside her brings a sense of normalcy to my otherwise tumultuous world. As we chat and laugh, the weight on my shoulders lightens, just for a moment.

Mama Zen places a hand on my shoulder, her gaze warm and understanding. "You're a strong one, Miss Verena. Stronger than you think," she says softly, her eyes twinkling with wisdom earned through years of experience.

I smile gratefully at her words, feeling a surge of gratitude for her presence in my life. Mama Zen is more than just a cook; she is a confidante, a source of comfort in times of need.

Together, we prepare a feast fit for royalty, knowing that our esteemed guests will appreciate the effort and care we put into each dish. The clinking of pots and pans, the sizzle of meats on the stove, and the aroma of spices fill the air, creating a symphony of warmth and familiarity that helps to drown out the lingering memories of the war.

As I turn to slice some ripe, juicy tomatoes for the crisp summer salad, my eyes catch a glimpse of Eryx and Esmeray entering the outer courtyard. They move with grace and confidence, their footsteps light as they exchange small talk with the guards stationed at the entrance. The sound of their laughter and easy camaraderie reaches my ears, filling me with a sense of warmth and familiarity. A gentle breeze carries the scent of blooming flowers and fresh herbs from the nearby gardens, adding to the tranquil atmosphere around us. Despite the looming danger outside the castle walls, this moment feels peaceful and idyllic.

As my eyes fall upon them, a warm smile tugs at the corners of my lips. Eryx stands tall and strong, his presence a steady force amidst the turbulent currents of grief and guilt that threaten to overwhelm me. Esmeray's sharp wit cuts through the darkness, her unwavering loyalty a beacon of light in the midst of chaos. And Ruelle, with her gentle kindness, sweet smile, and lighthearted jokes, completes our quartet with a touch of warmth and joy. Together, we weather the storms of life, anchored by our unbreakable bond.

They have each other, and they have me. And we will face whatever challenges come our way. We will honor the memory of Hadeon, and we will forge a new future, one full of hope and purpose.

* * *

He finds me shortly after that and we make our way to the grand throne room, knowing we are receiving a highly admirable visitor from a distant land. As we enter, the majestic hall comes into view, its high walls decorated with intricate tapestries and its floor covered in plush carpets. We take our seats on the thrones side by side, sitting tall and regal. The throne room has always been my favorite place in the castle, with its open ceiling revealing the beautiful sky above. Even in moments of rain, I find solace in its beauty.

The visitors enter the room, their movements graceful and polite as they bow deeply before us. Their voice is filled with gratitude and respect as they address us, their eyes shining with admiration.

Eryx, being the more familiar of the two, takes the lead in greeting our guest. His voice is warm and welcoming as he speaks. "Lieve, you know there's no need for such formalities. We've known each other practically our entire lives." He playfully rolls his eyes at her. A genuine smile spreads across Lieve's face as she looks between us, her bright blue eyes and expression radiating friendship and fondness.

"What can I say? I love the theatrics."

"Our hospitality was not intended to extend to your three...guards." His words are hesitant, mirroring my own uncertainty over how to refer to the three different males constantly by her side.

Though they were all known to be skilled in charming women, rumors abounded about their true natures. One was said to have a dangerous and unpredictable thirst for blood, lurking behind his suave facade. Another exuded a bright charm and playfully flirted with any woman within reach. The third had a mysterious aura, often keeping to the shadows and giving off an air of reserved intensity. Some whisper that he was the queen's spy master, but in this place of secrets and whispers, it was hard to know what was the truth and what was just speculation.

"I am grateful for it nonetheless." Her smile is bright and contagious, reminding me of Hadeon's. Sunlight catches in her warm blonde hair, giving it a golden glow that matches her vibrant personality. She is dressed elegantly in a flowing gold gown, befitting of her royal status. I have only met Lieve once before, at Calanthe's grand party last year, but she had been accompanied by her father then.

"As you may know, my father has passed away." She does not mince words. We nod, understanding the gravity of her loss. "I am now the rightful heir to the throne, but there are sinister forces at play and I am in need of your assistance." Her gaze is earnest and pleading. Eryx motions to our guards and they leave the six of us alone before shutting the doors as she reveals the true reason for her visit.

* * *

I swipe the staff at the feet of my husband, forcing him to jump to avoid it. He chuckles deeply at me, coming toward me with his own move to throw me off balance on the beams we currently spar on.

Esmeray attacks from behind him, making a curse flee his lips as we laugh. I'll give it to him, he sure knows how to fight us both off at the same time. But, I guess with him being king it is almost expected. Ruelle and Calanthe sit on a large blanket that rests over the grass in the courtyard. They munch on fruit and crackers, sipping fruity wine and enjoying the sun just as we all are.

The chilled breeze of seasons changing cools my hot skin as I use every muscle I have to throw another blow at Eryx just as his staff smacks into his sister and she falls to the ground with a grunt.

"Now it's just you and I, Seren Fach."

I narrow my eyes at his attempts to smirk at me with his darker charm and intimate thoughts that I can only guess are running through his brain.

"For now." The wooden stick I hold lets out a loud *thwack* as it meets its mark on his side. He hisses and almost topples over. I don't give up, moving forward to aim again for him, hoping he blocks me so I don't hurt him but wanting him to lose this game.

His weapon deflects me, but I swiftly duck and spin, delivering a quick strike to his knees that sends him stumbling backward. Eryx regains his balance with a grin, admiration shining in his eyes as he faces me once more.

"Well played, my love," he concedes, his voice laced with both challenge and affection. The familiar thrill of competition pulses between us, igniting the air with tension and exhilaration.

As we continue our sparring match, the courtyard fills with the sounds of laughter and playful banter. Ruelle and Calanthe cheer us on from the sidelines, their infectious mirth blending harmoniously with the sunlight dancing around us, Esmeray counting on me to avenge her in this playful battle.

I lock eyes with Eryx, a silent promise passing between us—a promise of unspoken vows and shared battles yet to come. In this moment, surrounded by loved ones and bathed in the golden glow of the setting sun, I know that no matter what challenges lie ahead, we will face them together.

With a dramatic sweep of our staffs, I manage to deftly knock his feet out from under him. Like a marionette with their strings cut, he tumbles to the ground with a satisfying thud. The earth trembles beneath him as he hits the dirt, sending dust and debris flying in all directions.

My victory leaves a lingering sense of triumph in the air as I stand over him, my staff held confidently at my side. Our duel comes to an end, both of us breathing heavily but grinning like fools.

Eryx extends a hand toward me, and I take it gladly, feeling the warmth of his touch seeping into my skin as he helps me down.

"You never cease to amaze me," he murmurs, his eyes filled with pride and adoration. I feel a rush of emotion welling up inside me, grateful for this man who stands by my side through every trial and triumph.

As the sky above us transitions into a canvas of dusky hues, we gather our belongings and make our way over to join Ruelle and Calanthe on the blanket. The sweet scent of ripe fruits and the gentle hum of laughter envelop us, creating a sense of contentment that settles deep within my soul.

We bask in each other's company, sharing stories and dreams beneath the tapestry of stars that begin to twinkle overhead. In this moment of perfect serenity, I am reminded once again of what family feels like.

Hopefully, my *dreams of ash and smoke* will cease and then maybe I will be truly healed.

Thank You + Book 2

Firstly I want to say thank you to everyone who read this book! It took a lot of work that hopefully pays off. This book is my debut novel and only the first in a 5+ book series where each romantasy will be a standalone and can be read in any order but have some connection.

You're all a piece of my heart and I can not tell you how many hours went into this book so I hope you all enjoyed it!

Keep in touch with my social media to stay updated on new books! Book 2 of the Fates Aligned standalone series title and cover will be revealed there! Follow to learn more about the other genres I will touch base in— including but not limited to: sports romance, dark mafia romance, and contemporary romance!

Tiktok: brooke__mariee
Instagram: brookeofficial
Facebook: Brooke Marie
You can find all profiles with this picture!

Acknowledgments

I first want to thank my mother for giving birth to me and supporting me in literally all my dreams and being my biggest fan. I want to thank my husband for the support and giving me time and space to write and not judging anything that comes from this brain too hard lmao. A big big thank you to my girls; Tracy, you've been my friend the longest and we've been writing books together since 2012. I absolutely love you and thank you for all your help and advice. Haley, I love you so much and you are literally a dream, the constant love and support from you has been so heartwarming and the fact that you said yes to being my illustrator is chefs kiss. I'm in love with you. Abby and KayLee: the best sister in laws literally ever in the world. Both of you are me in different forms and I love that we love the same books and that you are also such a helpful support system. I love yall and I appreciate yall and I couldn't have done this without you both. You've been so much help with choosing a direction for the scenes I've needed help with and so patient with me changing things and rewriting and all my ideas.

And a big thanks to my beautiful niece, Khaleesi JoAnn, for being my reason for breaks during stressful times and for being the silliest and funniest person alive. May you grow into a gorgeous gorgeous book girl.

My appreciation for all of you cannot be put into words. I love every single one of you and I can't imagine doing this without yall. Thank you for responding to every mass text, every double text, every second-guess and plot change and the continuation of ideas. None of you ever made me feel like 'too much' or annoying or boring with my book(s). And with this as my debut novel, I couldn't have asked for a better support system.

And lastly, a big big thank you to Anna, Erika, and Kat: my proofreaders in the order of how they read it. You ladies saved me so much embarrassment. Editing myself during sleep deprivation was not ideal and you girls fixed my dumb dumb misspellings, errors, and sentences that made no sense when read naturally. The appreciation I have for you three goes beyond words and I hope the new updated version tickles your fancy in a more professional way!

xoxo

About the Author

She lives in a small town on the outskirts of Memphis, Tennessee with her husband, and their pittie Jace. She's been writing— starting with *One Direction* fan-fiction on *Wattpad*— since 2012. She enjoys singing, recreational dancing, reading, and writing. She has amazing best friends that have helped her with her books and have been her biggest supporters aside from her mom and her husband. She also enjoys spending time gardening. She's a sucker for the color pink, *Pepsi*, potatoes in every form, and crunchy dill pickles. Brooke is also a '97 baby with the bubbly extroverted personality and a total girls girl.

Milton Keynes UK
Ingram Content Group UK Ltd.
UKHW040900301024
450479UK00005B/187